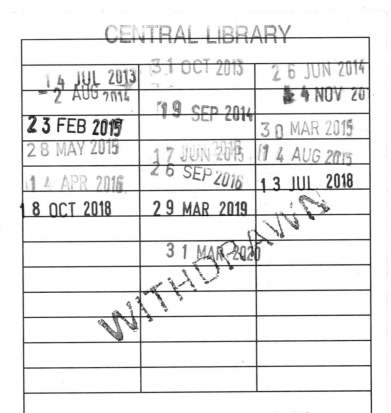

The Magpies: A Psychological Thriller

Cover photograph: Sarah Ann Loreth
http://sarahannloreth.tumblr.com/

Cover design: Jennifer Vince www.jennifervince.com

Prologue

She crossed out 'Paradise' and wrote 'Hell' in its place. The caption didn't fit the photograph any more. She felt like tearing up the whole album, ripping each picture to shreds, or throwing it on a fire, watching her memories burn. But even that would not erase the images from her mind: they were locked inside her, and she could only hope that time would erode them. More than anything else, she wanted to forget.

It was hard to believe they had once been so happy here. No, that wasn't right. Looking around at the bare walls, the carpet that bore the imprints of their furniture – which was now waiting in the van outside, ready to be transported to their new home far away from here – it was easy to believe how happy they'd been.

At this moment, the flat looked almost exactly as it had the day they'd moved in: untainted, full of promise, like a blank sheet of paper. Just as it did in the photograph she'd relabelled. Her dad – who had helped them move in – had taken the snap: her and David in the empty room, his arm around her waist, watery sunlight flooding the room. When the photo was developed she stuck it on the first page of the album, writing 'Paradise' beside it because that was what it represented. Her and David, looking at the future, full of excitement and hope.

She closed the album and threw it into a packing crate.

She heard voices outside and shivered. For months she had been hearing them, all night, every night, babbling men and women's voices, sometimes whispering, or shouting, or just talking, talking, never shutting up. She had to sleep with headphones on. She had tried earplugs but somehow the voices got through. The only way she could drown them out was by playing slow, orchestral music that flowed into her dreams and created a soundtrack to her nocturnal life.

In her dreams she would often be carrying a gun. She would be walking down a hallway, determined, white-knuckled as she gripped the handle of the weapon, finger twitching on the trigger. Sometimes the gun would be replaced by a knife: a large knife with a long, fat blade. It didn't matter. As the music played she would see herself walking down the hall to meet her enemies, the architects of her living hell. She was going to harm them, do to them what they had done to her, but in a more visceral way. As she had explained to her new therapist, she didn't have time for games or psychology. She needed to deal with her problem more directly. In the dreams, she was filled with the urge to kill.

But she was always frustrated. Just as the people she wanted to hurt stepped out in front of her, the gun or knife would melt, liquid metal dripping to the floor, and the people before her would laugh, and in the worst dreams they would pull out a gun or knife themselves. Whatever: at this point she always woke up.

No more bad dreams, she told herself now. When we're in our new place – our little house, in the middle of nowhere – there'll be no more nightmares.

At night it will be silent. It will be dark. There might be animals or birds outside, rustling, hooting, scratching around. That wasn't a problem. As long as there were no people.

She reached into her bag and took out her cigarettes. God, she hadn't even smoked until a few months ago. Maybe in their new home she would be able to give up. Her lungs would be clean again. All of her would be clean again. She put the cigarettes away. Maybe she would quit right now.

She ran through a list in her mind. Had they done everything? Was everything packed? She opened the airing cupboard, checked inside. She went into the bathroom, made sure she hadn't left anything in there. She didn't want any trace of her and David left in this place. She didn't want any connection with it at all. At that moment she decided she would get rid of her photographs after all. But she wouldn't leave them here – she didn't want anyone getting their hands on them. She would throw them away en route – park and find a bin beside a motorway, far from anyone who had ever known her or would ever be likely to meet her.

Yes, she had to erase all traces of herself from here. She had to wipe out this chapter of her life. The therapist had said that, although it was hardly a great insight, was it? So she vacuumed the place until the bag was full; she had scrubbed the walls until every muscle in her arms and shoulders screamed out for her to stop. She had disinfected the cupboards and the bath and the toilet. She had thrown open the windows and left them like that for days, so all traces of her and David would fly away, out the window, going, going, gone.

'Are you almost ready?'

David came into the room, looked around at the empty spaces, at the final crates. He had been outside talking to the removal men, telling them to be careful, asking them to be quiet. 'My girlfriend's very sensitive to loud voices,' he said, greeted only by a look of incomprehension.

Now he spoke to her in a hushed tone, pointing to the crates. 'Are these the last two?'

She nodded.

'And everything's packed? Good. Come on, let's go.'

'Give me a moment,' she said.

He sighed, as he so often sighed these days, then bent down and lifted one of the crates, which was just light enough for him to carry on his own. She waited for him to return, looking around for the last time. That was where they used to watch TV. That was where David cooked her birthday meal. There was the spot where they christened the flat, making love on the bare floorboards the day they moved in. There was the spot where...

She squeezed her eyes shut and shook her head, shaking away the memory. She sat down on the edge of the crate, feeling the room lurch around her.

She went outside, walked to the car without looking around her, staring at the concrete in front of her feet. She knew the removal men were looking at her, laughing at her inside the cab of their van, the weird chick who can't bear the sound of people's voices and walks with her head bent like an old woman. They thought she was mad. Well, maybe I am fucking mad, she thought. So would they be if they'd been through what she had. She wanted to tell them. Wanted to scream it at them.

She got into the car and tried to calm down. David went back into the flat and brought out the last crate. He put it down and turned round to close the door. She saw him weigh the keys in his hand for a second, and she wondered what he was thinking.

He opened the car door and for one awful moment she thought he was going to tell her that he had changed his mind, that he wanted to stay, that she would have to go back inside. But he started the engine and pulled into the road, the removal van following them.

He didn't look back. She looked in the rear-view mirror and watched the flat retreat into the distance, into the past, into memory.

'It's over,' David said.

It's over.

One

'It's going to be the hottest flatwarming party of all time,' Jamie enthused. 'I think we should make it a fancy dress party.'

'Excellent idea,' said Kirsty. 'With a theme?'

'No. No theme. Freestyle fancy dress – come as whoever or whatever you like.'

He fell with her onto the bed in the soon-to-be-vacated bedroom in the house she shared with three other nurses and buried his face in her soft hair. He kissed her neck and breathed in her scent – a cocktail of skin and apricot shampoo and the perfume she applied every morning. Walking into her bedroom, where her fragrance hung constantly in the air, always made him feel happy and loved and sexy. And soon they would be living together. They would be sharing a bedroom and he would live with her fragrance – as part of the background of his life – every day. Breath and hair and skin and sweat and all the atoms and particles shed by their bodies day after day – these things would merge to create an atmosphere that was not solely of Jamie or Kirsty, but of them.

'What will you dress up as?' she asked as he unbuttoned his shirt and tossed it behind him so it landed among the stacks of cardboard boxes and packing crates that covered the floor: books and clothes and handed-down kitchen utensils crammed together in a haphazard jumble that Kirsty described as her 'system'. Old CDs and framed prints and her childhood collection of wooden elephants. Her whole life, packed up and ready to go.

Jamie adopted what he thought was a wicked grin, snaking his hand around her back and pulling her against his bare torso. She kissed his chest and looked up at him with her big brown eyes.

'What will I go as?' he asked. 'How about the devil?'

The flat was perfect. From the moment they stepped into the living room and saw the way the light flooded in through the bay windows, they both knew it. Kirsty put her arm around Jamie's waist and as the estate agent took a call on his mobile, facing into the kitchen behind them, they exchanged a look, excited but fearful. They didn't even really need to see the main bedroom – although that too was exactly what they'd hoped for – or the spare room or the small, functional kitchen or bathroom. The walls of this place had spoken to them. They both believed they had heard it say their names. Jamie pictured himself collapsed on a comfortable sofa with the TV flickering in the corner, Kirsty in paint-splattered jeans, decorating these walls with a thick brush. Recently, he'd started to picture her with a baby bump. It was like watching an advert of their future life.

The slightly-warped floorboards. The pipes that shuddered when you turned the taps on. The cracks in the window frames. Even the blossom of damp in the bathroom. All of these things contained a kind of charm that was absent in the new-build properties they had seen – places that were sterile and lacking in history. The flat felt warm, a place with a past, with rooms that had housed generations, breathed with life. As they had crossed the threshold, the estate agent had said, 'Mind the step', but Jamie had already negotiated it. His feet knew instinctively where to tread.

'This flat is the best bargain I've ever seen,' the estate agent said, rubbing his bald spot. 'You're lucky – you're the first people to view it. The owner needs a quick sale so they're asking way under the market value.' He shook his head.

When they got back to Jamie's flat, he and Kirsty tried to play it cool. They would wait a while, pretend to be thinking about it. If they didn't come across too keen they might be able to knock the price down even further. Even at a bargain price, the flat was at the very top of their price range anyway. They would only be able to afford it by sacrificing a few other things. They would have to stick with Jamie's battered car, for a start.

'Let's wait till tomorrow,' said Jamie.

'Yes.'

'But what if somebody else makes an offer in the meantime?'

'They won't.'

'No...'

'But they might.'

They both looked at the phone. Jamie snatched it up and called the estate agent. They made an offer: £3,000 less than the asking price. They chewed their nails while they waited for the agent to call back.

Later that night they were celebrating. They ended up reducing the price by just £1,000 – and they spent a small chunk of that on a bottle of expensive champagne which they drank together in the bath at Jamie's. They weren't even going to be stuck in a chain. They were first-time buyers and the flat was empty. 'Tomorrow,' Jamie said, as he popped the cork on the bottle of champagne and Kirsty held her glass out, 'I'll phone Richard and give him my notice on this flat.'

They clinked glasses.

'To our new home.'

The day of the party arrived, and during the afternoon Paul turned up with a white van full of bottled lager and four crates of white wine. 'I know a bloke who does runs to Calais,' he said. 'Fills up a van and sells the contents to his mates. He can get you anything: booze, cigarettes, perfume. A nice wife from Latvia. Whatever you want. Not that you need a mail order bride, you lucky bastard.'

Jamie and Paul sat on the front step in the sunshine and sipped from small green bottles of continental beer while Kirsty and her best friend, Heather, blew up balloons indoors. It was a gorgeous day, gossamer clouds strung out like dinosaur bones across the blue sky. The city was warming up and London was coming back to life after a winter that had felt like a new Ice Age.

Kirsty came outside and crept up behind Jamie. She put a finger to her lips to quieten Paul, held a fully-inflated balloon behind Jamie's head and jabbed a sharp fingernail into the balloon's rubbery flesh.

'Jesus!'

Jamie dropped his drink and clamped his hand to his heart. Kirsty and Paul rocked with laughter.

'That's for leaving Heather and me to do all the hard work. Now, give us a beer.'

She stooped and kissed him and he handed her a lukewarm bottle.

Six hours later, Jamie was standing among a crowd of party-goers feeling queasy but still very happy. He'd long since lost count of how many bottles he'd drunk. He'd also lost the plastic trident that went with his devil's costume, which consisted of a red T-shirt, red velvet trousers and a matching cloak, plus a pair of plastic horns strapped to his head. People kept asking him if he was feeling horny. He roamed the party, chatting and drinking and laughing and feeling…wonderful. He still couldn't believe the flat was theirs. All evening, people had told him and Kirsty how lucky they were to find it. This guy called Jason, who 'dabbled' in property, told Jamie he'd made a very wise investment. He shook Jamie's hand. 'If you ever want to sell,' he said, 'I might know a few people.'

But Jamie didn't care about investments, or property booms, or making a quick profit. He simply loved this flat. It had spirit. It had soul.

'Soul!' he shouted, holding his bottle aloft and squeezing between a sailor and James Bond. 'That's what we need.' He bent over the iPod in its dock and found the track he wanted.

The first bars of 'Get Up' blared out, and Jamie danced off across the floorboards, ignoring the ground-out fag butts and puddles of spilt beer, looking for Kirsty. He banged into the doorframe on his way out of the room and grinned to himself.

Before finding his girlfriend, he came across Heather, standing outside the bathroom, talking to this guy in trendy glasses who Kirsty knew from somewhere or other. What was his name? Matthew? Or Luke? Something New Testament. Heather was dressed as a St Trinian schoolgirl and her friend was a vampire.

'Have you seen Kirsty?' Jamie asked.

Heather shook her head. 'Last time I saw her she was talking to your neighbour, out the front.'

Jamie thanked her and went out through the front door of the flat and down the hall, which was crammed full of people he'd never seen before. He didn't know if they were friends of Kirsty's or gatecrashers. He didn't really care. He caught sight of Kirsty, standing just inside the front door talking to an older man. He stopped for a second and looked at her in her Catwoman outfit. He wanted to drag her to the bedroom and do delicious things to her.

Pushing his way past a girl dressed as Morticia Addams, Jamie crept up behind Kirsty and blew gently on the back of her neck.

'I know it's you,' she said, turning to give him a hug.

'This is Brian,' she said, introducing the man she was talking to. He was in his fifties, with a neatly-trimmed beard and black-framed designer glasses. He was one of the only people at the party who wasn't in fancy dress. 'He lives in the top flat.'

'Hi. Pleased to meet you.' The two men shook hands. 'Do you live on your own?'

Brian shook his head. 'Oh no. My wife, Linda, is here somewhere. Probably chatting up some young bloke, knowing her. This is a great party. I was really pleased to see another young couple move in. We need some more young blood round here. The prices put a lot of young people off.'

'We were lucky,' said Jamie.

Brian nodded. 'I think you were. And I hope I'm not being presumptuous when I say I think we're lucky to have you. It's so important when you live in a small block of flats like this to get the right type of people, by which I mean people who are easy to get along with, who are easy-going and who believe you should live and let live. You both seem like you fit the bill, and I hope you won't prove me wrong.' Brian raised his bottle. 'Welcome to Mount Pleasant Street.'

12

They stood in silence for a moment and looked out at the street. This could almost be a suburban town thirty or forty years ago, the roads were so quiet, the gardens so well-kept, the cars so shiny. But central London was only a ten-minute Tube journey away. They were close to the hub of things, which was where Jamie had always wanted to be. When he moved to London after finishing university he had always imagined himself living in a place like this. For five years he had been stuck in a poky little flat in Camden Town, dreaming of a better place. And now he was here. He had found that better place.

He turned back to Brian. One of their big worries about throwing this party was that they might upset the neighbours. To avoid this, they had invited them all. Brian and Linda had accepted, and judging by Brian's welcome speech, they had won him over with very little effort . Mary – the woman who lived in the first floor flat – had scribbled them a quick note saying she'd love to come but she'd made other plans and would be out all night. The couple downstairs in the garden flat hadn't replied. Jamie could see the lights on in their front room and the colourful glow of a TV. Maybe they weren't party people.

'What are the other neighbours like?' he asked Brian.

'Well, Mary's lovely. She lives on her own with her cat. Doesn't seem to get many visitors, but I think that's because she always goes to them. If you ever want to borrow a cup of sugar, and you can catch her at home, she's the kind of person who'll always be happy to help you out.'

'What about the couple in the basement?' said Kirsty.

Brian laughed. 'Oh, you mustn't call it the basement. I did that once and they got very upset. It's the garden flat. That's what I was told. But they're nice people, very quiet, keep themselves to themselves. Linda and I haven't had very much to do with them at all.'

'What are their names?'

'Lucy and Chris. The Newtons.'

Jamie peered down the steps at the illuminated window. 'We'll have to introduce ourselves to them. Soon.'

He noticed Brian studying his beer bottle. It was empty. 'Do you want another?'

'Hmm. Please. I'll come in with you, see if I can find Linda.'

'And I want to see what Heather's up to,' said Kirsty.

They went inside. Kirsty found Heather chatting up the vampire. Jamie led Brian over to the fridge and pulled out two bottles of beer. In the living room, people were dancing badly to James Brown.

'So is this all your furniture?' Brian asked. 'A fridge and a stereo?'

'No. We're moving the rest of it in tomorrow. I thought it was best to have the party while the flat was empty. Didn't want anything to get wrecked. Plus there's more room for everyone.'

'Very true.' He paused and sipped his beer. 'Where did you and Kirsty meet?'

'In hospital. Kirsty's a nurse.'

'And you were her patient?'

14

'No. That's what everyone assumes, and it would be nice to say that our eyes met above a hypodermic needle or that she helped me recover from some terrible illness...'

'Sitting by the bedside, keeping watch, mopping your brow.'

'Or she told me to bend over for my injection and fell madly in love. The truth is rather more mundane. I was installing software on the hospital computer system. I saw her and fancied her immediately, so I found out her name and left a message on the terminal for her: NURSE PHILLIPS. I REQUIRE URGENT MEDICAL ATTENTION. PLEASE CALL ME. Tacky, I admit, but it worked. She phoned me the next day.'

'You're a very lucky man. She's very attractive.'

'I know. Actually, it would have been hard for me to meet her as a patient because she works on the children's ward.' He smiled. 'She told the kids about my message and they teased her about it for months afterwards. Going to give Jamie his medicine, nurse Phillips? Cheeky little sods.'

'And you're in computers?'

'That's right. I work for a firm that installs and maintains computer systems for organisations like hospitals, schools, local councils, etcetera. It's not glamorous but it's alright, you know.'

They spent the next ten minutes talking about computers and the internet. Brian was about to buy a new PC and Jamie said he'd help him set it up if he wanted. He asked Brian what he did for a living.

'I'm a writer.'

'Really? Anything I might have come across?'

'Probably not – unless the kids in Kirsty's ward are fans. I write young adult horror. The Scarlet Moon series – have you heard of it?'

Jamie was about to respond when they heard the wail of a siren outside, drowning out the music for a moment. The siren ceased and a woman dressed as Cleopatra – who was looking out the front window – turned to her friend, Julius Caesar, and said, 'It's the fire brigade.'

Kirsty, Heather and the vampire came into the room, along with Brian's wife, Linda, and they and everyone else crowded round the front window, looking out as two fire engines pulled up to the kerb. Half-a-dozen fire fighters jumped out and Jamie noticed the looks of puzzlement on their faces. They looked up and down the road. Where was the fire?

Someone said, 'Maybe there's a cat stuck up a tree,' causing a ripple of laughter.

Then Cleopatra said, 'They're heading this way.'

Jamie and Kirsty looked at each other, and backed out of the crowd. Paul, who had been out the front, smoking a spliff, hurried into the room and staggered up to Jamie.

'They want to see you,' he said.

'Me?'

Jamie made his way outside, followed by Kirsty, Paul, Heather, Brian, Linda and anyone else who could cram into the hallway. A pair of disgruntled-looking firemen stood on the doorstep. Looking around at the mock policemen and fake doctors, Jamie could have believed the firemen were also party-goers: a couple of unfortunates who had turned up in the same outfit.

'Are you Jamie Knight?' said the older fireman, who was clearly in charge.

'Yes. That's me.'

'You phoned to report a fire. Where is it?'

'What?'

The fireman sighed. 'We don't have all day, Mr Knight. Is there a fire? Is it out?'

'I don't know what you're talking about...'

'You phoned 999.'

'I didn't. I haven't phoned anyone all evening. I–'

'It's an offence to make a hoax phone call to the emergency services, Mr Knight. Maybe you thought it would be funny. You're certainly wearing the right outfit for it.'

Jamie looked down at his devil's outfit and felt his mouth go dry. 'But I didn't do it.'

The fireman stared at him. It was a long, hard stare that made Jamie feel like a schoolboy who'd been brought up in front of the headmaster. When the scrutiny was over, the fireman said, 'Maybe it was one of your guests.'

Kirsty stepped forward. 'Nobody here would have done that. Can't you trace the call?'

The fireman treated her to the same hard stare. 'Maybe we will.' He turned to his colleagues. 'Come on, we've wasted enough time here.' They marched off down the path.

The party wasn't quite the same after that, even though it carried on for a couple more hours. Brian and Linda said goodnight and went up to their flat on the top floor. Heather got off with the vampire (and later complained to Kirsty that he had blood-curdling halitosis). Paul got very drunk and threw up in the toilet. Jamie and Kirsty sat and worried about who had called the fire brigade.

'It's such a stupid, irresponsible thing to do,' Kirsty said. 'Somebody could have died in a real fire while they were here. I can't believe any of our friends would have done it.'

'It must have been someone at the party, though. One of the gatecrashers.'

'But why?'

'I don't know. For a laugh?'

'Some laugh.'

They were quiet for a moment.

'So who do you think could have done it?'

'God, Jamie, I really don't know. I'm too drunk to even think about it.'

Jamie looked at the floor, deep in thought.

'I'm going to bed,' said Kirsty, crawling under the quilt. They hadn't moved their new double bed in yet: just the mattress. She looked up at the high ceiling. Her eyes rolled up into their sockets and she closed them tightly.

'What about the guests?'

She buried her head under the pillow. 'I'll let you chuck them out.'

'Kirsty...'

But she was already asleep.

Two

The city opened up before them. From the top of the hill Jamie could see for miles: clusters of tower blocks standing up like chipped stalagmites; patches of parkland and the curve of the Thames; flyovers and bridges and dirt-streaked trains.

A song came on the radio that reminded Jamie of his first summer in London, after leaving uni. During those heady days – days when the sun's heat seemed to last all night – Jamie had thought the possibilities that lay before him were infinite. It was almost too overwhelming. He could do anything, be anyone. He was going to make loads of money and become famous, just as soon as he put that brilliant idea for a website into action. In the meantime, life was good. Too good to worry about actually going out and trying to achieve his admittedly-vague ambitions.

That summer had ended and Jamie had taken a job as a trainee computer technician with ETN. Systems. It would pay the rent on his little flat until he found out what he really wanted to do. He wanted to start his own business or maybe write a screenplay that would transform the British film industry. Now, five years later, he was still working for ETN, but he had been promoted and was earning okay money. The job was boring sometimes, but hey, things could be a lot worse.

He was twenty-nine years old and he felt like, at last, he was entering the adult world. He was a property owner. There was rumour of a further promotion at work. He and Kirsty had talked about getting married and starting a family, and he could see that happening in the not-too-distant future, when the time was right. The thought of it made him feel light-headed, but it was a welcome sensation. Kirsty wanted the same. She loved children – why else would she work in the children's ward of a hospital? Some days she would come home in fits of giggles over something one of the children had done or said; sometimes there would be tears. Jamie would hold her while she recounted whatever story she had to tell. Some of the tales were so terribly sad. Jamie, who had never met the children involved or their families, would get upset too. Sometimes, now, Jamie would find himself looking at Kirsty and thinking to himself: she'll make a great mum. She thought that when he looked at her all he thought about was sex. But half the time he was actually thinking about getting her pregnant.

Now, he put his arm out of the open window of Paul's van and tapped along to the music on the radio. His hangover had gone, blown away by the fresh breeze that blew in through the window. The sky was Bondi-blue. The people they passed wore T-shirts and shorts or little summer dresses. There was something about England in the summer – the way its inhabitants seemed to wake up, cast off their frowns and complaints. He couldn't imagine wanting to be anywhere else. And when he thought about Kirsty, he couldn't imagine wanting to be with anyone else.

'What are you thinking about?' Paul asked. 'You've got the stupidest grin on your face.'

'Oh, I was just thinking about…stuff.'

Paul smiled and shook his head. 'Soppy bloody git.'

After picking up the furniture from Jamie's they drove back across the city and parked outside the new flat.

Paul, who had been Jamie's best mate since he'd moved to London, opened up the back of the van and began stacking boxes on the pavement while Jamie jogged up to the front door and unlocked it. He wedged a piece of cardboard beneath it to hold it open.

'God, look at all this junk!' Paul held a battered tennis racquet with broken strings in one hand and a moth-munched giant stuffed rabbit in the other. 'Why don't you chuck all this stuff out?'

Jamie took the rabbit from his friend. 'This is Kirsty's.'

'Then what's it doing in your stuff?'

He shrugged.

Paul reached out and tweaked the rabbit's ear. 'I bet it's not really Kirsty's. I bet you've had it since you were four and it's called something like Mr Bun-Bun, and apart from Kirsty it's the love of your life.'

'No Paul – you're the other love of my life.'

Paul lifted a red plastic crate out of the van. It was full of seven-inch singles. He took out a handful and studied them. 'Fuck, how old are these? Madness, The Specials. Did you inherit these off your grandad?'

'Those are classics.'

Paul rolled his eyes. 'You're a hoarder, mate. You'll probably end up like one of those old blokes who can't bear to throw anything away, living in a flat surrounded by yellow newspapers and empty baked bean tins. Kirsty will have got fed up with you and run off with a bloke who's into Japanese minimalism. '

'Has today suddenly turned into Slag Off Jamie day?'

'I'm only teasing. Come on, we'd better get the rest of this stuff into the flat.'

Paul went to pick up the box containing the tennis racquet and some folders full of training notes from when Jamie joined ETN, but Jamie stopped him.

'Leave it.'

'Eh?'

'I saw a skip on the way here. When we've unloaded the rest of the gear we'll take this junk there and dump it.'

Paul raised his eyebrows.

'And before you ask, yes I am sure.'

They picked up a crate of records each and began the process of transferring the favoured boxes and binbags into the flat. The sun beat down on them and they sweated their T-shirts a darker shade.

'Almost finished,' Jamie said, a while later. 'Just the chest of drawers.'

It was an old chest of drawers that Jamie had bought at an antiques auction. It was made of dark, heavy oak, and Jamie grunted a little as he and Paul lifted it. Paul, who was marginally stronger, went backwards up the path, holding his end up firmly but not being able to see where he was going. Just before Paul reached the front door, Jamie started to say, 'Look out,' but it was too late. A woman had come up the concrete steps from the basement flat, and as she reached the path – not really looking where she was going – Paul bumped into her, dropping the chest of drawers and swearing loudly.

The woman stared at him for a second, her expression grim – and then she smiled. Jamie would never forget that sudden change in expression. He had never seen anything like it – not in real life anyway. It was more suited to a cartoon. She smiled, her face relaxed, her brow uncreased. Jamie stared at her for a second, wondering how she had transformed her features from Gorgon to Angel so quickly, then he remembered how to speak.

'I'm sorry,' he said, then, rather obviously, 'We're moving in.'

She looked at Jamie then at Paul.

'Not me,' Paul said.

'No, my girlfriend and me. I'm Jamie. You must be Lucy?'

She was in her early- to mid-thirties and had blonde hair scraped back and fastened by a grip. Her skin was very pale and smooth; she had no laughter lines around her eyes, even when she smiled like she was smiling now. She was as tall as Jamie – five foot eleven – and broad-shouldered. If Jamie had had to pick one word to describe her it would have been 'Amazonian'.

'Lucy Newton. I live in the garden flat with my husband, Chris.'

'Yes, I know.'

'You know?' For a fraction of a second her beatific expression flickered.

'Brian upstairs told me.'

'Of course.' The smile returned. 'Well, this is a very nice collection of flats we have here. I'm sure you and your girlfriend will like it here.'

'Yes, I hope so. Actually, I'm certain we will.' The sun was in his eyes and he found himself squinting at her. 'I hope you weren't disturbed too much by our party last night. We did put an invite through your door.'

'Yes. We would have liked to come but Chris wasn't feeling too well. He had an early night.'

'Oh, I'm sorry. All the noise...'

She waved his anxiety away. 'No, don't worry. When Chris is asleep nothing can wake him. There could be an earthquake or a herd of dinosaurs thundering down the road and he wouldn't stir. Shame he wasn't well though. It sounded like a good party. Maybe we'll come to your next one…if you have one.'

She smiled.

Paul looked at his watch. 'We'd better get on, Jamie.'

'Hmm.' He addressed Lucy: 'We've got to go and pick up Kirsty's belongings now.'

Lucy looked at the front window of the flat. 'Where is she?'

'At work. She's a nurse.'

'Really? Which hospital?'

'St Thomas's. In the children's ward.'

'How lovely. I'm a nurse too. But I work at the other end of the scale. I work in a nursing home. Orchard House.'

'Jamie…'

He looked at Paul, who was keen to get on. He had a date later in the day – a girl he had met at the party, who had been dressed as Wonderwoman – and he didn't want to be late.

'I'd better get on myself,' Lucy said. 'Shopping, you know.'

'It was nice to meet you.'

'Likewise.'

She walked off and they watched her go down the road.

'Look at it all,' said Kirsty, when she arrived home from work. Paul had gone off to meet Wonderwoman, leaving Jamie surrounded by his and Kirsty's belongings.

'I met the woman downstairs earlier,' Jamie said now, bringing Kirsty a cup of Earl Grey tea as she changed out of her uniform.

She ripped open a couple of binbags in her search for the outfit she wanted. 'Really? What was she like?'

'She seemed nice. She wasn't at all pissed off with us about the party, which was a relief. I was quite worried about it.'

'The considerate neighbour, that's you. Did you meet her husband?'

'No. He's not very well, apparently.'

Kirsty sipped her tea. She always left the teabag in the cup while she drank it, a habit Jamie couldn't understand but nevertheless found endearing. He didn't drink tea himself – he was a coffee man – but he liked the taste of it on Kirsty's lips. He sat beside her and kissed her now.

She broke away gently. 'We've got to get on with the unpacking, Jamie.'

'I guess so.'

'What do you want to do about dinner? We've got no food in. Let's get a pizza delivered.'

'Good idea. And there's some wine left from last night.'

Kirsty pulled on the black, sloppy jumper she had been searching for and stood up. She prowled around the flat, just looking at it, marvelling at every empty cupboard, at the Victorian fireplace, the intricate ceiling rose, the taps in the bath, the grain in the floorboards.

'I still can't believe that it's ours,' she said. 'I was convinced that something would go wrong before we moved in. I thought we would get gazumped, or the owners would decide they didn't want to sell after all. Even today, at work, I was stressed out, thinking that the phone was going to ring any minute and it would be you, telling me that the flat had burned down taking all our possessions with it.'

She came to a halt before the bedroom window and Jamie came up behind her and put his arms around her, resting his chin on her shoulder. They looked down at the garden. It was very neatly kept, with a large square of lawn surrounded by flower beds, the flora in full bloom. There was a little shed at the back of the garden. Only the occupants of the basement flat had access to the garden, although as this block of flats had once been a single house (only converted into flats earlier in the century) it was physically possible for the occupants of the ground floor flat to get down there. A set of concrete steps led from the bathroom balcony down into the garden. Kirsty planned to set a washing line up on this balcony. It was tiny and not at all private so it would have little other use.

'You smell really sweaty,' she said as Jamie kissed her cheek, wrinkling her nose.

'That's because I've been labouring hard all day – sweating under the hot sun.'

Their first task was to put up the curtains in the bedroom. That morning, they had been woken up at five a.m. by the blazing sunlight that filled the room. With last night's alcohol still circulating through their veins, they had both winced and groaned and tried to hide under the quilt. It was no good, though. They couldn't sleep, and Jamie had pulled on his jockey shorts and padded into the kitchen to make coffee. There was a strange man asleep on the floor, dressed as a cowboy with his stetson over his face. He opened one eye, said, 'Morning,' then got up and let himself out. Then, while most of their new neighbours slept, Jamie and Kirsty cleared up the mess from the night before.

'I'll put the hooks up and then you can hang them,' said Kirsty. 'You order the pizza while I make a start.'

Jamie phoned the pizza place, then fetched the iPod dock, finding an acoustic playlist.

As he was attaching the curtains to the rail, standing on a wobbly chair with Kirsty holding onto his leg, there was a knock on the door.

Kirsty raised her eyebrows. 'That was quick.'

Jamie clambered down from the chair. 'That was the inner door, so unless someone left the front door open it can't be the pizza guy.'

He opened the door to the flat and found himself looking at a large man with a crew cut. As Jamie had expected, the man wasn't holding a pizza.

'Hello. Can I help you?'

The man looked him up and down, then said in a quiet voice that clashed with his bulky physique, 'I'm Chris Newton. I live…'

'Downstairs! Hi.' Jamie stuck out his hand. 'I met your wife earlier. Are you feeling better now?'

'Oh, yes. I'm fine. I thought it would be a good idea to come up and introduce myself.'

Kirsty came up behind Jamie and looked over his shoulder.

Chris smiled at her. 'You must be…'

'Kirsty. Pleased to meet you.'

'And you.'

There was an awkward silence, during which Jamie quickly appraised Chris in his mind. He was very fit and muscular. He looked a little like a nightclub bouncer or a security guard. But there was a gleam in his eyes that spoke of a sharp intelligence. Jamie also noticed that Chris was carrying a bunch of keys in his left hand; he clearly had a key to the front door. Jamie wasn't worried by this. The four sets of neighbours paid service charges for the upkeep of the whole building, and therefore they all had every right to access the halls and stairways that they shared. They were equally responsible for keeping the building clean and in good condition.

'I noticed the front door was sticking a bit and squeaking nastily,' Chris said, as if reading Jamie's mind. 'I might have a look at it over the weekend.'

'OK.'

Chris nodded and ran the palm of his hand over the soft bristles on his scalp. 'Well, I hope you both settle in alright. I'm sure we'll see each other around.' He turned to go. 'Oh, by the way, would you mind turning the music down a bit? Only, Lucy's in bed. It would help if you could move your dock into the living room as well.'

'Oh…sure.'

At that moment the front doorbell rang. It was the pizza courier, standing there with the visor of his crash helmet pushed up, revealing a look of impatience, and a twelve-inch pizza held out before him.

'Smells good,' said Chris, winking at Kirsty, then walking off, brushing past the pizza courier.

Jamie paid for the pizza and carried it inside.

He knelt by the dock and turned the volume down a notch. He couldn't believe anyone could be disturbed by the music. It was at a very low volume, and it was hardly heavy metal. 'What time is it?'

'It's only eight o'clock. He did say Lucy was in bed, didn't he, or was I hearing things?'

Jamie pulled a face. 'Maybe she's ill.'

'I thought you said he was the one who was ill.'

'That's what she said.'

Kirsty shrugged. 'Maybe she's caught it now.'

They went into the kitchen and Kirsty uncorked the wine.

'She seemed fine this afternoon,' Jamie said, thinking about Lucy. 'And the music was so soft. How could it have disturbed her?'

'Like I said, she must have caught whatever Chris had. And I suppose sound must carry down through the floorboards where there's no carpet. We'll have to be careful whenever we play music. We don't want to antagonise anyone.'

They perched on the edge of a wooden crate and bit into their pizza. By the time they'd finished their food and drunk their wine, their conversation had moved on to other things. But when the playlist ran out, they didn't put another one on.

Three

Moving into the flat invigorated and reawakened them. It was like it had been when they'd first started going out, unable to keep their hands off each other. They soon christened each room: making love in the bath, on the sofa, on the worktop in the kitchen, Jamie banging his head on the kitchen cupboard, both of them collapsing with the giggles. They held hands all the time; phoned each other at work twice a day, texted constantly; wrote each other silly notes that would have made other people puke and exchanged cards and gifts. They had never felt so close. Some of their friends had warned them that moving in together would diminish the magic between them, that the close proximity to each other's dirty underwear and annoying habits would spoil things. In fact, the opposite had happened.

Sometimes, when he allowed himself to think about his good fortune, Jamie felt sick. This wasn't because he was a masochist who craved misfortune and pain, but because he was so scared something might go wrong. He had never done anything particularly wonderful – he didn't think he had too many credits in the karma bank. He had never saved anyone's life, and he only gave money to charity occasionally: usually when someone rattled a tin in his face. He had never made any great contribution to world peace, unless you counted that time he broke up a fight between Paul and some moron who had given them grief in the pub. Then again, he had never done anything very bad, either. He had never broken the law, other than speeding a few times and smoking the odd spliff. He had never been unfaithful to any of his girlfriends and he had never stabbed anyone in the back, literally or metaphorically. He wasn't bitchy or two-faced or deceitful.

Because of this neutral position – a position he was sure most people held – he was convinced that sooner or later his good luck would have to be balanced out by a spate of bad luck. Kirsty told him he was crazy. 'So if you won a million in the Lottery you'd then be convinced that it would be stolen from you?'

'Either that or something worse would happen. Like I'd get cancer. Or have a horrible accident.'

She shook her head. 'God, you're so morbid.'

'I think the word is paranoid.'

'Oh, look, it's Lucy.'

Jamie turned to look. They had just back from the supermarket.

Their neighbour was coming up the road in her care assistant's uniform, her head down, the sun beating on the back of her neck. She reached Jamie and Kirsty's car and stopped, clearly waiting for them to get out.

'Do you think we should apologise for disturbing her the night we moved in, when Chris asked us to turn the music down?' Kirsty whispered. She had yet to meet Lucy. She worked odd shifts, and she assumed Lucy did too, so their paths hadn't crossed.

'I don't know. I didn't get the impression they were too upset about it. And we turned it down straight away.'

They got out of the car and Kirsty came around to the pavement, offering a smile to her neighbour.

'Hello, I'm Kirsty. You must be Lucy.'

Lucy nodded. The transforming smile she had shown Jamie materialised, lighting up her face. 'I've been looking forward to meeting you. It's nice to have somebody my own age move in.'

Kirsty was seven or eight years younger than Lucy, but she didn't point that out. She didn't really know what to say.

Lucy elaborated. 'I was worried we might have some really young people move in, with all the problems they bring, if you know what I mean.'

Kirsty said, 'Well, yes.'

Jamie could tell she was perturbed by Lucy's assumption that they were the same age, and he tried not to smile.

'Or a deaf old couple, with their TV turned up to full volume day and night.'

'Yes. You wouldn't want that, I guess.'

Lucy smiled and touched Kirsty's forearm. 'Maybe we could get together some time. Go shopping, or go for coffee. What do you think?'

Kirsty was taken aback. She opened her mouth to speak, but Lucy got in first, saying, 'And the men could get together too, talk about cars and football, or whatever it is men talk about.'

Jamie said, 'Yes. We must.'

Lucy looked at Jamie and Kirsty's car, and a troubled look replaced her smile. 'Oh. I don't suppose you'd mind backing up a bit, would you? It's just that Chris always parks in that spot and he'll be home soon.'

Jamie wanted to ask why Chris couldn't park behind him, but he didn't want to be the cause of any tension between them and their new neighbours. 'Sure,' he said instead.

He climbed back into the car and reversed into the space behind. Lucy said to Kirsty, 'So, we'll meet up soon for a chat and a coffee, yes?,' then she headed up the path and down the steps to her flat.

Jamie got out the car.

Kirsty's eyes were wide. 'That was a bit off, wasn't it? Asking you to move the car.'

Jamie shrugged. 'I guess they're just used to always parking in the same spot. Their car is always parked right there, and you know what some people are like about routine.'

They carried their shopping up to the front door and Jamie noticed a piece of white card on the doormat. It was from Parcel Force, addressed to Mr J Knight.

'Somebody's tried to deliver a parcel,' he said, coming back inside.

She looked up. 'Been on eBay again?'

'No! Hey, maybe someone's sent us a housewarming present. It's been left with the neighbour in the first floor flat.'

'Mary.' Kirsty stood up. 'Well, now's your chance to meet her. Today is obviously the day for meeting neighbours.'

'What did you think of Lucy, then, apart from the car-parking thing?'

'Hmm. I don't really know if she's my kind of person, but, yeah, I thought she was alright. It's nice to have neighbours who seem keen to get to know you – as long as they don't want to interfere with your life.'

'It's better than having neighbours who ignore you completely. My mum's lived next to her neighbour for fifteen years and they've barely even said hello.'

'Yes, but that's your mother.'

'Don't start.'

'Hadn't you better go and see what the postman left you?'

Jamie went up the stairs to the first floor. Halfway up the stairs was a frosted window with an air freshener on the sill. The window was open a couple of inches and Jamie peeked through the gap. He could see the Newtons' garden and the backs of all the houses in the next street. He continued upwards and found himself standing in front of a plain brown door. He knocked and immediately heard footsteps.

Mary opened the door. She was in her forties, but her soft features and long brown hair made her look younger. She had large, alert eyes, and as soon as she saw Jamie those eyes lit up.

'Hi. You must be the fellow from downstairs? I've got a parcel for you. Come in.'

He stepped into her flat and straight away noticed the strong smell of patchouli oil. Ah, a hippy, he thought. Mary disappeared into the living room, gesturing for him to follow.

He stood in the doorway, looking in at the room. There was an oil burner on the mantelpiece: the source of the patchouli smell. He felt something brush against his leg. It was a fat snow-white cat. He crouched down and scratched it behind its ears, eliciting a purr.

'Lennon likes you,' Mary said. 'That's nice.'

She came over and handed him the parcel. It was a package from Amazon. Must be a present.

'Are you a big reader?'

'Pardon?'

'That. I assume it books?'

He studied it. 'I haven't ordered any books. How weird. Maybe Kirsty ordered them in my name.'

'A present? How lovely.' She bent down and scooped up the cat, cradling it like a baby. 'You must bring your girlfriend up to say hi.

I've seen you both coming and going but I haven't had a chance to introduce myself yet.'

'You're Mary.'

'Ah, you've done your homework.'

'Brian upstairs told me.'

'At your party? How did it go? I was sorry to miss it. Brian's a lovely man, and extremely talented. Have you read any of his books?'

'They're kids' books, aren't they?'

'Yes, but please don't let that put you off. They're wonderful. And Linda's lovely too.'

He nodded. 'Yes. I liked them.'

'So what do you do, James?'

'Call me Jamie.'

'Sorry – Jamie.'

He told her. 'What about you? What do you do?'

'I'm a herbalist.'

'Really? Wow, that's really unusual.' He couldn't think what else to say.

'It's not that unusual.'

'No. I suppose I'm just a bit ignorant when it comes to such things. What does it involve?'

'Well, people come to me with their problems – physical, emotional, mental, whatever – and I advise them about different herbs and alternative treatments for their ills. I get a lot of people who've got nowhere with their doctors so they try me. People are sceptical at first – I'm a kind of last resort. That's until they try it. I've got books that are hundreds of years old, detailing medicines that have been passed down from the beginnings of history.' She smiled broadly. 'I prescribe tinctures and infusions and decoctions. Lotions and potions that can help practically any ailment. For example, basil is great for curing stomach cramps, and sage is good for anxiety or depression.'

'It seems like all the women in this building work in the health industry.'

'You're right. Even Linda upstairs does. She works in Boots the Chemist.'

They laughed, then Jamie said, 'I'd better get back downstairs. Kirsty will wonder where I've gone, and we've got loads of decorating to get on with. But thanks for taking in our parcel.'

'Any time.'

She showed him out and he went back down the stairs to his own flat. Kirsty was spreading newspaper out across the floor, and she had pulled the sofa into the centre of the room.

'What was she like?'

'Really nice. She's a herbalist. She was telling me about all the lotions and potions she makes.'

Kirsty rolled her eyes. 'Alternative medicine. It's all bullshit, Jamie. They're all frauds and charlatans, the lot of them.'

They had had this conversation before, so Jamie kept quiet. He wished he hadn't mentioned it. It was one of Kirsty's personal bugbears.

'We get all these kids coming in who've been dragged by their parents from herbalist to homoeopath to acupuncturist to hypnotist. It's all a waste of time. These people just offer false hope. They sell false hope. When none of these miracle cures work they end up in hospital. They put their faith in science again – but I've seen cases where it's too late. This poor little boy who had leukaemia. His mother thought the NHS was a last resort – if you can believe that – and by the time he came in for treatment he was too far gone. He died..'

Jamie sighed.

'Well, she may be a fraud and a charlatan but she seemed really nice. I liked her.'

'Hmm.' She lay down the last sheet of newspaper. 'So what was in your parcel?'

'Oh, some books. Did you order them?'

'No, I would have told you. What are the books?'

'Let's see.'

He opened the box and lifted out half-a-dozen books, reading out the titles: '*Making Love Last – how to keep the sexual magic in your marriage. Burning Fat – a 20- minute workout. A History of Satanism. Australia – a guide to emigration. The British Beef Cookbook.*' Kirsty was vegetarian. '*The Book of Embarrassing Illnesses.*'

'Oh my God.'

They both laughed. Jamie held up *A History of Satanism*, which featured a goat's head and a pentagram on the cover.

'Paul. It must be.'

He took out his phone and sent Paul a text: *Thanks for the reading material. Haha!*

A minute later Paul texted back. *Eh??*

Jamie smiled. 'I'll get him back.' He flicked through the sex manual. 'Now, actually, this has got some good tips in it.'

Heather came round at eight-thirty. She worked with Kirsty at St Thomas's, and as they wielded their brushes – inch-by-inch turning the walls of the flat a pale, even blue – they chatted about people from work. Dr Singh was having an affair with an anaesthetist called Claire. Pat and Michael had had a blazing row about the allocation of beds in Ward F. Jamie enjoyed listening to their conversation. He had met most of the characters discussed, and listening to Kirsty and Heather gossip about their colleagues was like tuning in to a particularly interesting soap opera.

'How's Dracula?' he asked Heather teasingly.

'What? Oh God, him. He keeps hounding me, ringing me up, telling me he thinks he's fallen in love with me.'

'How sweet.'

'He makes me feel sick. He really smells.' She grimaced.

'How's Paul's wild love affair with Wonderwoman coming along?' Kirsty asked.

'She dumped him,' Jamie said.

'Oh, poor Paul,' said Heather.

'I know. I think he really liked her. But he got an email from her saying they should call it a day. That she didn't want to get serious.'

'She dumped him by email? Nice.'

'So now he's young, free and single again,' said Heather.

Kirsty glanced up at her. 'Why, are you interested?'

'No, of course not.'

Jamie and Kirsty exchanged a knowing look.

'I'm not interested in Paul, OK?'

Jamie laughed. 'So why are you blushing?'

'I'm not!'

Before Heather could get any more embarrassed, the doorbell rang. Jamie looked at his watch. It was ten o'clock. 'Are we expecting anyone? Hey, maybe it's Paul. Maybe he telepathically tuned in to your lustful thoughts about him, Heather, and came running.'

Heather flicked paint in Jamie's direction. 'You're such a wanker.'

Chuckling to himself, Jamie went out to the front door.

It was a pizza courier, holding out two boxes and a litre bottle of Coke. 'That'll be £21.'

'But I haven't ordered a pizza.'

The courier checked the name and address on the order slip. 'Jamie Knight. Ground floor flat, 143 Mount Pleasant Street.'

'Yes, that's me, but I haven't ordered…' He sighed. 'Hold on a minute.'

He went into the flat. 'You didn't order a pizza, did you Kirsty?'

'No, you know I haven't.'

'Oh God.' He ran his hands through his hair. 'It's looks like we've has another hoax. Still, at least this one's not as bad as the fire brigade turning up.'

Heather said, 'This is really creepy. Have you made an enemy recently?'

Kirsty's face creased with anxiety. 'I don't believe this. Who can be doing it?'

Jamie said, 'I'd better go and tell the pizza guy to take it away.'

He went back into the hall, leaving Kirsty cursing behind him. He felt sick.

'Sorry mate, but I think you've been hoaxed. You'd better take it back.' He pulled an apologetic face.

The pizza courier turned round and stomped back to his moped. As he rode off down the road, Jamie stepped onto the front path and looked left and right, up and down the street. For a city street, there were hardly any signs of life. It was almost unnaturally quiet and still. He turned to go in and the oddest feeling came over him – the feeling that he was being watched. Despite the balmy summer air, he suddenly felt cold. Goosepimples ran up his arm and he shivered a little. He looked around again. No, there was no-one about, although there were lights on in most of the flats in the street; windows thrown open to let in whatever breeze there was.

He looked down at the Newtons' flat. The lights were out. There were no signs of life. But their car was there, parked in the spot Jamie and Kirsty had had to vacate earlier. He looked up towards Mary's window. The light in the room flickered strangely, and at first he thought it was the flicker of a television. It took him a second to realise she must be sitting in candlelight.

He hugged himself. He still felt cold. The hoaxes had really unnerved him. Nothing like that had ever happened to him before. He had never been targeted for mischief by anyone.

He thought about what Heather had asked. Had they made any enemies recently? He honestly couldn't think of anyone. With the flat-buying and everything, they had hardly seen anyone lately, apart from at their party. He didn't think they'd upset anyone at all. It was a mystery.

He turned round and went back inside, rubbing the skin on his arms, not warming up until he was safely indoors.

Four

Jamie woke up and looked at the bedside clock, the LED numbers phosphorescent in the dark. It was half-past-midnight – or half-past-nothing, as the digits 00:30 seemed to indicate. He groaned and pushed the covers down to his waist. It was unbearably hot, even with the sash windows open as far as they would go. During the day, the temperature had hit the high Eighties, and it didn't feel any cooler now, with the heat of their bodies adding to the humidity. The sheets were damp with sweat. His skin was slick and his hair was stuck to his scalp. He had a sudden, wonderful image of a tub of Häagen-Dazs. He would press its frosted exterior against his brow before devouring the cold, delicious ice cream inside. He groaned again.

Kirsty turned over and said, 'Are you alright?'

'I can't sleep. It's too hot.'

'I know. And I've got to get up in a few hours.' She reached out and touched Jamie's side. 'God, you're burning up.'

'I need a cold shower.'

'Oh yeah?' She put her hands on his chest and kissed him.

'I thought you were worried about getting up.'

'Mmmm.'

They kissed, Jamie running his hands up Kirsty's back, over her bottom and hips, from the small of her back to her shoulder blades. Her skin was warm but dry, and so soft. He had spent the last two years marvelling over the softness of her skin. If somebody asked him to draw up a list of what he liked best about Kirsty's body, the softness of her skin would be right up there competing for pole position – although, really, he loved everything about her body: the way she was slim but still endowed with curves that felt so good beneath the palm of his hand; the ever-clean scent of her; the constellations of pale freckles on her shoulders and breasts; the crescent-shaped scar on her hip, obtained during a childhood cycling mishap. He loved it all.

'What was that?' Kirsty opened her eyes and broke away from the kiss.

'What?'

'I heard a noise outside.'

Jamie sat up, reluctantly breaking contact with her flesh. He hadn't heard anything. He had been lost in that kiss, the rest of the world fading away in a haze of arousal. He rubbed his face with the palms of his hands, trying to remove the blur from his vision. 'Are you sure?'

'Yes!' she whispered harshly. 'I heard someone moving around. It sounded like it came from the garden.'

Jamie got up from the bed and crept over to the back window. He peeked out through a gap in the curtains, and a cool breeze caressed his face. He was still half-asleep, and he stood there for a second with his eyes closed, enjoying the sensation but wishing it was Kirsty cooling him with her kisses.

'Jamie? Can you see anything?'

He remembered where he was and opened his eyes. He peered out at the garden, and straight away saw a shadowy figure move beneath him, a few feet from the Newtons' back door. He ducked down beneath the windowsill and looked back at Kirsty.

'There's somebody down there,' he whispered.

Kirsty's mouth formed an O and she climbed out of bed and came over to the window, walking in a curious half-crouch, her arms folded over her breasts. They knelt together on the carpet, both of them naked, as if they were offering up a prayer to some nocturnal god.

Jamie stuck his head under the curtain and looked out again. He could see the person moving around. He didn't think they would be able to see him, but then the moon came out from behind a cloud and the garden was illuminated. He ducked down again.

'It's Chris,' he said.

'Chris? What's he doing?'

A second later, they had their answer. There came the sound of rushing water: the hiss and splash of water coming out of a hosepipe.

'He's watering the bloody garden!'

They collapsed together on the floor, trying not to laugh aloud. Jamie covered Kirsty's mouth with his own to stop her laughter ringing out.

A week ago, the local council had announced a strict hosepipe ban because of the hot weather. It hadn't rained for weeks, and reservoir supplies were running alarmingly low.

'Should we grass him up?' whispered Kirsty, after they had clambered back into bed. She was still trying not to laugh, not just because she found the situation funny but also because she was relieved that they weren't about to be burgled or murdered in their bed. She couldn't believe how silly she'd been.

'Kirsty!'

She tutted. 'I wasn't being serious. It's a bit sneaky though, isn't it? Watering the garden under cover of darkness.'

'Loads of people do it.'

'Yeah. I guess you're right. Anyway,' she said, inching closer, giving him that look he loved so much. 'Where were we?'

Jamie pulled her towards him. 'Right about here.'

They didn't get another full day together until Sunday. Jamie didn't work at weekends, and Kirsty – who did – had the day off. It was another glorious, hot day and they had decided to take the train down to the coast for the day. In an hour and a half they could be in Brighton, eating greasy chips and sticky candy floss, or enjoying a drink in a seafront pub. As Kirsty got dressed, Jamie – who had been ready for almost an hour – looked out of the back window. There were Lucy and Chris, up early, working in the garden. Actually, it was just

Chris doing the work. While he knelt beside the borders, pulling up weeds, Lucy stood over him, hands on hips, pointing at bits he'd missed or had yet to do. Jamie noticed they were wearing matching T-shirts which bore the logo of a large computer software company, Scion.

As he stood there looking at them, Lucy turned around and spotted him. She waved, the gold of her wedding ring glinting in the sun. She said something but he couldn't make it out. He cupped his hand to his ear and she pointed at the balcony, gesturing for him to come out.

'Lucy wants me to go out and see her,' he said so Kirsty would know what was going on.

He went into the bathroom, opened the back door and stepped out onto the balcony. Sunlight hit him in the face and he shaded his eyes with his hand. Lucy walked up to the edge of the garden and stood at the bottom of the steps that led up to the balcony. Chris carried on working, only stopping briefly to nod hello.

'Hi. Beautiful day, isn't it?' Jamie said. 'You're so lucky having a garden. It must be very therapeutic.' He hoped his insincerity wasn't evident. He didn't want a garden. He had the exact opposite of green fingers, although he wasn't sure what that was. Grey fingers? Concrete fingers? When he saw a garden he only thought what a hassle it must be to have to mow the lawn and pull up the endlessly-proliferating weeds.

Lucy nodded. 'Yes. It is. We were just saying that, weren't we, Chris?'

'That's right.'

Jamie smiled. He imagined it was therapeutic for Lucy, watching someone else do all the work while she supervised.

'The reason I beckoned you outside was to ask you and Kirsty if you wanted to come round for dinner.'

'Oh.' His mind raced. 'That's really nice of you to ask. But why don't you come round to us?'

Kirsty was, at this point, standing behind Jamie in the bathroom – unseen by the Newtons – with a look of horror on her face, making throat-cutting gestures with her finger.

'Kirsty's a great cook. We could come round to you next time.'

Lucy's face lit up with a smile that stretched from ear to ear. She nodded.

'That would be lovely. What do you think, Chris?'

He peeled off his gardening gloves and stood up. His T-shirt showed off the bulge of his muscles: his thick arms and broad chest. He nodded up at Jamie, one side of his mouth twitching in what Jamie interpreted as an attempt to show enthusiasm. 'Sure. Sounds good.'

'Great. Well, let's make a date. Say, seven-thirty, this Friday? Fantastic. We'll see you then.'

He went back inside, shutting the bathroom door behind him. Kirsty punched him lightly on the arm. 'What the hell have you done?'

'I thought you'd prefer to meet them on your own home territory.'

'Oh God, I don't believe this. That's my week ruined.'

'What? Why?'

'Because I'm going to be worrying about this bloody dinner party now. What to cook. What to wear. Does the flat look a state? Why couldn't you have accepted their invitation? Or if you didn't want to go down there, why didn't you make up an excuse?'

'I thought I was doing the right thing.'

'Huh! I should make you cook the meal. That would teach you.'

'OK, I will.'

'Don't be stupid. You're the worst cook in London.' She marched back into the bedroom and sat down on the bed. 'I think I'll invite Heather and Paul too. Paul can entertain them.'

Jamie tutted. 'Look, Kirsty, it will be fine. I genuinely thought it would be easier to invite them up here. We don't want a repeat of that time we went to Sally and Jason's and they served lamb because I'd forgotten to tell them you were a veggie.'

Kirsty shook her head. 'I know, I know. I realise you were doing what you thought was best. I just wished you'd stalled them and asked me first.' She looked at her watch. 'We'd better get going now, before the tide goes out and I miss my chance to drown you.'

Paul turned up first, bearing a bottle of cheap Chardonnay.

'So what are we having?' he asked after he had handed Jamie the wine and kissed Kirsty on the cheek.

'Jamie's having beans on toast.'

'Yum. And the rest of us?'

She tapped the side of a saucepan with a wooden spoon. Onions and garlic cloves lay on the worktop, along with a bowl of shelled pecan nuts, a plate of mushrooms and artichokes, bottles of olive oil and vinegar, a can of tomatoes and a tube of tomato puree. Fresh tagliatelle already waited in the saucepan. 'The rest of us are having pasta.'

'Veggie stuff.'

'That's right, and if you don't like it' – she waved the wooden spoon at him – 'you can have beans on toast too.'

'But beans on toast are veggie as well! No, actually, it sounds great, Kirsty. And it smells delicious.'

'My beautiful, talented girlfriend.' Jamie put his arm around her.

'Don't start creeping. Remember, if it all goes wrong tonight, it's your fault.'

He sighed. 'Yes, I know. But nothing's going to go wrong, is it? We're going to have a pleasant, civilised evening. Which we might even finish with a couple of new friends.'

'What time are you expecting them?' asked Paul.

'In about half-an-hour,' Kirsty replied. 'Now, pour me some wine then bugger off while I get this meal cooked.'

Jamie and Paul took their drinks into the living room, where Jamie had set up the dining table. The TV was on, and the newsreader was talking about an eight-year-old girl who had been found strangled and raped and dumped behind some dustbins in Colindale. Jamie turned the TV off.

'The world is full of sick bastards,' he said.

Heather turned up five minutes later. She was wearing a tiny dress that ended four inches above the knee and was sleeveless, revealing the small cat tattoo on her shoulder. She went into the kitchen to help Kirsty.

Paul said, 'My God, what's happened to Heather?'

'What do you mean?'

'She's suddenly gone all sexy. When did that happen?'

'She's always been attractive.'

'Yeah, I guess so. Shame she hates me.'

'What the hell makes you think that?'

'She's an intelligent, attractive woman. Ergo she hates me.'

Jamie rolled his eyes. He knew Paul was desperate for a girlfriend but couldn't work out why he found it so difficult to get and hang on to one. He was quite good-looking, witty and clever. To Jamie – and Paul even more so – it didn't make sense. The only explanation they could come up with was that fate was saving Paul, preserving him in a state of singleness until the right woman came along.

The doorbell rang and Jamie hurried out to open the door.

'Lucy, Chris, hi, come in.'

They were both dressed up to the nines, Chris in an expensive Italian suit, Lucy in a scoop-neck maroon dress. Jamie was struck again by how tall she was. Chris handed Jamie a bottle of red wine which he took into the kitchen, leaving them with Paul.

'They're here,' he whispered to Kirsty.

She took a big gulp of wine and went out to greet them.

They had already sat down on the sofa, both sitting stiffly upright, looking uncomfortable, like somebody visiting their parents-in-law for the first time. Chris stood up when Kirsty entered the room. She went to kiss him on the cheek but he shuffled away awkwardly and stuck out his hand. Bemused, she shook it.

'I like what you've done to this room,' he said.

'Thank you.'

'Still, you couldn't go far wrong with a place like this. Nice straight walls. Very solid.'

'…Yes.'

Half-an-hour later the six of them were seated around the table. They made smalltalk and everyone complimented Kirsty on the food; there was a brief discussion about vegetarianism, Kirsty fending off the usual questions about whether she ate fish or chicken; the wine and conversation might not have flowed easily, but it was steady and there were no awkward silences. Kirsty started to relax, and, seeing her do so, Jamie winked at her across the table. He touched her foot gently with his.

Lucy told them about her job – about the old people and their peculiar habits, including the old lady who wrote phrases like 'Piss off' on pieces of card and flashed them at the other residents if they annoyed her (a kind of non-verbal Tourette's Syndrome) – and Paul asked Chris what he did for a living.

'I work for Scion Systems, the computer company.'

'Oh right,' said Jamie. 'I saw the Scion logo on your T-shirt when you were gardening.'

'Jamie's in computing too,' said Kirsty.

'I work for ETN,' he confirmed.

Lucy beamed. 'That's amazing. We girls are both in healthcare–'

'And me,' said Heather.

'–and the boys work with computers. We're such kindred spirits. Amazing.' She had already drunk a couple of large glasses of red wine and Jamie noticed with amusement that there was a slight slur to her words.

'I'm the odd one out,' said Paul, 'being a mere banker.' Paul worked for one of the High Street banks, a job he hated.

Heather leaned across the table and lightly pinched his cheek. 'You're always the odd one.'

Paul blushed.

'Even the woman upstairs is in health,' Jamie said.

56

'What, Mary?' said Lucy, putting down her wine glass. 'I'd hardly call what she does health.'

'What does she do?' asked Heather, who hadn't come across Mary before.

Jamie said, 'She's a herbalist.'

'Is that what she calls it?' said Lucy. 'I'd describe her as a witch.'

Chris nudged her. 'Lucy…'

But all eyes were fixed on Lucy now. Jamie laughed and said, 'A witch? But her cat isn't even black.'

Lucy wasn't laughing. 'It's not funny, Jamie. There's something about her I don't like. She gives me the creeps. I'd hate to know what kind of things she gets up to all alone in their flat. She gets some very strange-looking mail, from people like the Pagan Society, and the Society of Wiccans.'

'How do you know?'

'Because I've seen it. Our post often gets delivered through the communal front door, even though we have our own letter box, so I have to come up and check. I've seen Mary's letters. And I've also seen the way she looks at me. It wouldn't surprise me if she's up there right now, carrying out some sort of black magic ritual. Pulling the legs off spiders as she chants a spell.'

'Oh God, don't,' said Kirsty. 'Just the mention of spiders makes me shiver.'

'I'm sorry.'

Everyone looked at the ceiling, then Paul spluttered with laughter. 'The Blair Witch comes to Mount Pleasant Street. Maybe this building is haunted by dead children.'

'Paul!' Kirsty protested. 'That's not in very good taste.'

'Oh God, I'm sorry.' Both Kirsty and Heather were giving him filthy looks; it wasn't the best comment to make in front of two nurses who worked in a children's ward. Lucy, too, was perturbed by his comment. She stared into the remains of her meal, a tense expression on her face.

'How long has Mary lived here?' Jamie asked.

Chris answered: 'She was here before we moved in.'

Jamie thought that Lucy was tense because no-one had taken her comments seriously. Feeling the need to humour her and make her feel better, he said, 'And have you ever seen any evidence that she's into witchcraft? Because I went up there and she seemed like a bit of a hippy, but definitely nothing worse.'

Heather said, 'This is getting surreal. Can we change the subject?'

'Yes!' said Kirsty, standing up quickly. 'Who wants dessert?'

'Yes please,' said Paul.

'I'll give you a hand,' said Jamie.

In the kitchen, Jamie whispered, 'How do you think it's going?'

'Quite well, I think. Apart from that stuff about Mary. What was all that about?'

Jamie shook his head. 'I think Lucy's a bit drunk. Chris seems like an OK bloke, though. It's spooky, isn't it, that we all have such similar jobs.'

'Hmm. It's good though – we all have something in common. Just promise me you won't turn the conversation around to computers. I don't want to hear about e-commerce and gigabytes and HTMS.'

'It's HTML.'

'I said I don't want to hear about it.'

As Kirsty picked up the bowls, Jamie grabbed her round the waist and kissed her. 'You know what HTML really stands for? How to meet ladies.'

She batted him away. 'Do you think Paul fancies Heather? I've seen him looking at her all evening.'

'In that dress, anyone would look at her. Except me, of course. As I only have eyes for you, my darling.'

She ignored him. 'He blushed when she pinched his cheek.'

'But then he blew it with his dead children comment.'

'Oh, she'll have forgotten about that by now. I reckon something might happen between them.' Kirsty loved matchmaking. She was always trying to get mutual friends to get off with each other. She had this image of herself as some kind of urban Cupid, firing arrows of love into the hearts of her friends.

'Promise me you won't interfere,' Jamie said.

'As if I would.'

They carried the dessert into the living room. Paul, Heather, Lucy and Chris had resumed their conversation. They were talking about their favourite pastimes.

'Chris is into go-karting,' Lucy said.

'Really?' said Paul. 'I've always thought that looked like great fun. Where do you go?'

'This place in Kent. They've got fantastic karts there, and a really good track. You should come along. And you, Jamie.'

'Is it just for boys, then?' said Heather.

'Oh no. Anyone can do it.'

'What, even women?' said Kirsty.

Chris looked at her blankly. 'You should all come.'

Jamie nodded. 'Yes, we'll have to sort something out.'

'Definitely,' enthused Paul.

Lucy seemed to have sobered up a bit. As Kirsty set down the large bowl of strawberries, Lucy said, 'Oh goodness – my favourite. How did you know?'

Kirsty had opted for a very simple dessert of fresh strawberries and cream. She had instructed Jamie to go through all the punnets in the greengrocers to ensure he got the plumpest, reddest fruits.

'God, I'm stuffed,' said Paul after they'd all finished and sat back.

'That was gorgeous,' said Heather.

Paul produced a pack of cigarettes from his pocket. 'Anyone mind if I smoke?'

'Go ahead,' said Kirsty.

Lucy coughed and looked at Chris.

'Lucy's asthmatic,' Chris said.

'Why don't you go out onto the balcony?' Kirsty said to Paul.

'I'll come with you,' said Heather. 'I could do with some fresh air.'

Jamie and Kirsty were left alone with their downstairs neighbours. There was an awkward silence between them for a few moments. Jamie thought he might have to start talking about computers. Then Lucy said, 'I'm sorry if I was a bit weird earlier, with what I said about Mary. I don't normally go around accusing people of being witches. And I don't want you to think we have problems with our neighbours. We get on very well with Brian and Linda upstairs.'

'Although we were glad to see the back of the couple who lived here before you,' said Chris.

'Oh God, yes,' said Lucy. 'They were awful.'

'In what way?' asked Kirsty.

'Don't get me started. They were noisy – unbelievably noisy. Sometimes it sounded like they were playing drums in here. And they had visitors at all hours. And they smoked out of the window and threw the butts into our garden. We're sure they dealing drugs, too. There was definitely something dodgy going on.'

'They made our lives a misery from the moment we moved in.'

'You poor things,' said Kirsty.

Lucy touched Kirsty's arm. 'Oh, we're fine now. And anyway, we can look after ourselves.'

Kirsty wasn't sure what she meant by that, but before she could say anything, Jamie said, 'We never met the previous owners. The sale was done through their solicitor and Andersons, the estate agent.'

'Well, you're lucky.' Lucy touched her ears. 'They were so noisy.'

Kirsty and Jamie looked at each other. 'So you don't think we're too noisy?' said Kirsty.

'Oh no. I'd soon tell you if you were.'

Paul and Heather came back into the room, smelling of smoke. Jamie looked at them both and wondered if they'd been up to anything out there. He decided that Paul would have been smiling more broadly if they had. He got up and made coffee.

All in all, he was pleased with the way the evening had gone. He couldn't imagine that they would ever be best friends with the Newtons, but they seemed like a nice enough couple, and they did share common interests. Plus it was in everyone's best interests to maintain peace in the building. It was a shame Lucy was so antagonistic about Mary – but he was intrigued by the idea of her being called a witch. It was an attitude that didn't seem to belong to this century.

After drinking their coffee they said goodnight and Lucy and Chris went down to their flat. Paul and Heather remained behind for a while. Jamie got the PS3 out and he and Paul played FIFA soccer. Kirsty and

Heather chatted and finished up the wine. Jamie noticed that Heather kept glancing over at Paul, who was oblivious, too involved in the game. He smiled. It had been a good evening.

But that night, Kirsty woke up with her heart beating fast and a cold sweat on her brow. She grabbed hold of Jamie and shook him awake.

'What is it? What's wrong?'

She pressed her hand to her chest and waited for her breathing to return to normal. 'I had an awful dream. I was being chased through the woods by a witch, and she was trying to put a spell on me. I came to this house – and it was like the house in Hansel and Gretel, made of delicious-looking gingerbread. I ran inside and I felt safe and happy, and I was thinking about all the gingerbread I could eat. Until I realised it was actually the witch's house, and I was trapped. She put me in a cage, just like in the story. God, it was horrible.'

She lay back down and Jamie held her. After while her breathing pattern changed so he knew she was asleep. All that talk about witches over dinner. He didn't realise Kirsty was so sensitive to things like that.

The next morning, when Jamie went out to get the mail, he found a dead rat on the carpet outside their door.

Five

Jamie hurried back inside.

'What is it?'

'You don't want to know.'

She pushed past him. 'Oh, it's horrible! Jamie, get rid of it. Now. Please.'

'OK, OK. I'm going to.'

The rat was dark brown and eight inches long, with a tail that stretched on for a number of inches more. It was the tail that Kirsty really hated. The thought of a rat's tail touching her, or even coming anywhere near her, made her flesh go cold. This rat was never going to trouble anyone, though. It was stone dead, its eyes closed and its mouth open, frozen in a final squeal, exposing its long yellow teeth. There was a patch of blood on its chest.

'Poor thing,' Jamie said.

'It's gross,' said Kirsty, shuddering. The only creatures she hated more than rats were spiders. 'You've got to get rid of it.'

Jamie went into the kitchen, found a carrier bag and went back out into the hallway. He knelt down beside the dead rodent and put his hand inside the bag, grasping the rat through the plastic and pulling the bag inside out. He tied a knot in the top of the bag and carried it out to the dustbins. He was amazed at how heavy it was; how solid its body felt as he gripped it through the makeshift plastic glove. He wished he could have buried it, but they had no garden to call their own. The whole thing made him feel sad. As a teenager he had kept a pet rat called Roland. When, near the beginning of their relationship, he had told Kirsty this – extolling the virtues of pet rats, hinting that one day he might like to get another one – she told him that if he ever brought a rat near her she would never ever talk to him again.

She sat on the sofa with her hands covering her face. 'Is it gone?'

'I put it in the dustbin.' He tutted. 'I don't understand what it was doing outside our door.'

Kirsty grimaced. 'Ugh. It was probably trying to get in. It probably smelled the meal last night and wanted some.'

'You're mad. Rats don't try and get in through closed doors!

'Got a better explanation? I just hope it was the only one. What if there's a nest? We'll have to call the council, get the pest control sent out.'

'Come on, Kirsty, let's not over-react. It probably got into the building, got trapped and either died of fright or hunger. Although it didn't look very hungry. It was pretty fat.'

'Don't. I don't want to talk about it. After that dream I had last night, I want to think about pleasant things. Like shopping. Are we still going to go into town this afternoon?'

'If you want to. But I've got to nip down the shop first to get some milk. Do you want anything?'

There was a convenience store just down the road. Jamie went out to buy a paper and a pint of milk. As he walked back up the hill he felt out of breath. He was going to have to get that gym equipment he had promised himself. Get fit. He would be thirty soon, after all. He was already starting to develop a small paunch. When he was twenty-one he had promised himself that if his stomach ever started to curve he would go on a starvation diet to make it flat again: he would give up beer, do two hundred sit-ups a day. Anything to avoid the dreaded spread. But now his metabolism was slowing down, and his willpower was weakening. If he didn't do something soon he would be well on the way towards looking like all the forty- and fifty-year-old men in his office, their belts holding up their guts, their ties not hanging straight down but curving over like inverted question marks. God, it was a horrifying thought. Far scarier than a dead rat.

As he walked back up the front path, Brian opened the front door and came out.

'Ah, Jamie, good morning.'

'Morning.'

Brian stopped. 'Actually, I was hoping to bump into you. I bought that computer I've been promising myself and I'm having a few teething problems with it. I can't seem to get the internet connection to work properly.'

'Really? I'll come and have a look at it if you like.'

He nodded enthusiastically. 'That would be marvellous. I'm just popping out for a minute. Shall I knock on your door on the way back up. Would that be alright?'

'Of course.'

The postman had called while Jamie was at the shop. He and Kirsty just had a couple of pieces of junk mail, forwarded on from their previous addresses. Kirsty took the Culture section out of the paper and started to leaf through it.

'I don't feel that great,' she said. 'I feel a bit sick and dizzy.'

'You're not hungover, are you? I didn't think you drank that much last night.'

'No. It's not that. I think I might be coming down with that horrible virus that's been going round. Either that, or it's the after-effect of seeing that rat.'

Jamie was concerned. Kirsty was very rarely ill. Working in the hospital, where she was always surrounded by germs and viruses, her immune system had built walls that were six feet thick and bulletproof. He put his hand on her forehead.

'You feel quite hot. Maybe we'd better stay in this afternoon.'

'Oh, I'll probably be better by then. But I'd love a cup of tea. That might help.'

He prepared her tea, and there was a knock at the door.

'That'll be Brian. I promised I'd have a look at his PC for him.'

'Sure. I'm just going to lie here and read the paper.'

He kissed her clammy forehead then opened the door. Chris was standing there, holding a bright green envelope.

'Oh. I was expecting Brian.'

'Sorry to disappoint you.'

'No, I didn't mean it like that.'

Chris pulled a face to demonstrate that he didn't really care if Jamie had meant it like that or not. He held out the envelope. 'This is from Lucy and me. It's just a card to say thanks.'

'Oh.' He felt embarrassed. 'You needn't have, really. It was our pleasure.'

'Yes, well, we believe in being polite. By the way, do you still want me to take a look at that door for you? It's still sticking.'

'Yes, sure. If you don't mind.'

'Leave it with me.'

Chris went back down the hall and began to examine the door. Jamie felt puzzled. Chris didn't seem very happy. In fact, he seemed downright miserable. Jamie's first paranoid thought was that he had done something wrong – that he had said something to offend Chris at the dinner party. Or maybe Chris had the same virus as Kirsty. If so, he must be pretty unlucky, and unhealthy. He had been ill when they had first moved in, or so Lucy had said. It didn't fit. Chris looked like an ox, ruddy with health. In the end, Jamie decided he must simply be in a bad mood, and put it from his mind.

Brian came in through the door, saying hello to Chris as he passed him, his face lighting up when he saw Jamie. 'There was no need to wait in the hallway for me.'

'I wasn't. I, oh, never mind.' He realised he was still holding the card. He slid it under his door and then followed Brian up the stairs.

As they reached the top of the first flight, there was a thump at the window, and a shape appeared behind the frosted glass. Jamie jumped, his heartbeat skipping. It was Lennon, Mary's cat. He poked his head through the gap where the window was open, mewing as he did so, then jumped down onto the stairs and ran up to Mary's front door.

'How the hell did he get up there?' Jamie asked.

'There's a fire escape just to the right of the window there. He climbs up it from the garden then jumps across to the windowsill. It's a death-defying leap, actually. I've watched him do it. It's terrifying. Every time I see it I'm convinced he's going to miss the windowsill and plummet to his death.'

As they walked up the stairs past the cat, Jamie looked down at him. Lennon rubbed against his ankle. Jamie had a thought, but didn't say anything.

They went up another flight to Brian's front door. Brian unlocked the door and they went inside. There was a strong smell of fresh coffee, which was one of Jamie's favourite smells in the world. As if he had seen Jamie's nostrils twitching with pleasure, Brian said, 'Coffee?'

'That would be great.'

'The computer's in there, if you want to take a look.'

'OK. Is Linda not in?'

'No, she works Saturdays.'

'In Boots.'

'That's right.'

Jamie went into the room Brian had pointed out. Brian and Linda's flat was slightly bigger than Jamie's. It had a larger second bedroom, which Brian had converted into a study. As he stepped into the room, Jamie caught his breath. 'Bloody hell.'

It was like stepping in to a vampire's crypt – or a gothic teenager's bedroom. The walls were painted black, and a black blind was pulled down over the window, blocking out all light. Dyed-black fisherman's netting was strung across the ceiling. Statuettes of gargoyles sat on dark wood cabinets. Packets of tarot cards lay among piles of books; fat candles protruded from elaborate candleholders, their bases encrusted with dried rivulets of wax. There were pictures of ghosts and witches and demons all over the walls. Jamie quickly realised these were the reproductions of the covers of Brian's books. One showed a child being held over a cauldron by a green-faced witch. Another showed a vampire bending over a sleeping girl.

'Boo!' said Brian, coming into the room behind Jamie. For the second time in five minutes, Jamie jumped.

'I was just admiring the decor,' he said nervously waiting for his heartbeat to slow down.

Brian laughed. 'Atmospheric, isn't it? I have to keep it this way to make sure I'm in the right mood when I'm writing.' He picked up a book off a pile on his desk. It was called *The Creature in the Cradle*. The cover showed a pair of red eyes peering out of a cot, and a clawed hand reaching out towards the reader.

'That was one of my early books, before the latest craze for vampires started.'

'Wow. I'd have loved this stuff when I was a kid. I was really into monsters and make-believe. I remember watching Doctor Who with a cushion over my face.'

'At least you weren't behind the sofa. You can have that if you like.'

'Are you sure? Thanks. Now, let's have a look at this problem of yours.'

He booted up the PC and sat down in front of the monitor. 'It's a nice system. Must have set you back a fair whack. But you're having problems with the internet? Is it the router, I wonder?' He mumbled to himself.

He checked the phone line then pressed a few keys. Within a few minutes he had solved the problem. The router was working fine.

'What was wrong?'

Jamie sipped his coffee. It tasted as good as it smelled. 'It was something to do with your WEP key. That was all. Dead easy to sort out. But you're ready to go online now.'

'Thank you so much.'

Jamie left him to it. He went back down the stairs carrying his copy of Brian's book. Lennon had gone, either into Mary's flat or back out the window. At the bottom of the stairs, Chris was working on the door, planing its edges. Jamie waved at him then went back into his own flat. The thank you card was still lying on the carpet. He carried it in to Kirsty, who was where he had left her, lying on the sofa. She had managed to put the TV on and was watching a makeover show.

'How are you feeling?'

She coughed and said, 'Not too good. It's come on really quickly. I felt fine when I got up. Why were you so long?'

'I had to help him get on the internet. Look, he gave me a book.'

'Oh. For readers aged ten to fourteen. Your kind of book.'

'And we got a card from Lucy and Chris.'

'What for?'

'It's to say thanks for last night, apparently.'

She took the card from Jamie and opened it. 'Oh God, there are rats on it.' She closed her eyes and thrust it back at Jamie.

'They're mice, Kirsty. You must be ill. Look, they're cute little mice. Squeak squeak.'

She grimaced. 'Take it away.'

'Shush. Chris is just out there. He'll hear you. And you're certainly not well enough to go into town. In fact, you ought to be in bed.'

After he had led Kirsty into the bedroom and watched her curl up beneath the quilt, Jamie went back into the living room. He picked up the card and read the message inside. It simply said To Jamie and Kirsty. Thanks. From Lucy and Chris.

He put the card on the mantelpiece. The funny thing was, Kirsty was right: the creatures on the front did look a bit like rats.

The next morning, Kirsty's condition had worsened. She had lain awake half the night, coughing and keeping Jamie awake as well, and now she had a sore throat and a headache, and she said her bones felt like lead-lined pipes and her skin was sore. 'I need drugs,' she said. 'Paracetamol, Lemsip, Anadin, cough mixture, Tunes...'

'Then I'd better go down the shop.'

He got dressed and opened the front door.

'I don't believe it.'

From the bedroom, Kirsty called hoarsely, 'What is it?'

'Oh, nothing – my shoelace came undone. I was just over-reacting.' He had decided to lie because he didn't want to upset her when she was ill. There was another dead rat lying in the same spot as yesterday. In fact, it looked like the same rat. Jamie felt as if he had entered some weird time-loop, like in Groundhog Day. He crept back inside, grabbed a carrier bag and picked up the animal's body the same way he had the day before. Then he went out to the dustbin. He had a horrible feeling that it was the same rat – but there was yesterday's carrier bag, in the same place. He wondered how hygienic this was, putting dead rats in the dustbin. But he didn't know what else to do with them. He dropped the second rat on top of the first and replaced the dustbin lid.

When he got back from the chemists, he noticed the front door had stopped sticking. Chris had done a good job. He would have to thank him when he next saw him.

He went into the bedroom and watched as she took a couple of spoonfuls of cough medicine. Then he went back into the kitchen to prepare a Lemsip for her. While waiting for the kettle to boil he looked out of the front window. He saw Chris come up the steps from his flat and head towards his car. Jamie hurried back outside.

'Hi, I just wanted to say thanks for fixing the door.'

Chris nodded. 'No problem.'

Jamie hesitated. 'I wanted to ask you – have you ever had any problems with Mary's cat?'

'How do you mean?'

'Well, we've had a couple of dead rats left on our doormat, and the only thing I can think of is that it's the cat. I know it goes up and down the fire escape, and I thought it might be catching rats somewhere and bringing them in, leaving them as little presents for us.'

Chris shrugged. 'It's never left anything outside our door. Probably knows it would get a shovel over its head if it did. Best have a word with her upstairs, mate.'

'Yes.'

Chris opened his car door. 'How's Kirsty? We could hear her coughing all night.'

'She's not well at all. I thought maybe she had the same cold you and Lucy had.'

'Yeah, that was a bad one. Talk about a thumping headache. Christ. Anyway, I must shoot off. There's an emergency at work.'

'On a Sunday?'

'Yeah. No peace for the wicked.' He got into the car and wound the window down. 'And don't worry – you don't owe me anything for the door.' He drove off.

Jamie went back inside and took Kirsty her Lemsip. She was asleep. This was going to be a crappy Sunday, what with Kirsty sick in bed. He looked around the flat. The housework needed doing, but he didn't want to disturb Kirsty with the vacuum cleaner. That was his excuse, anyway. He decided to go up and see Mary, ask her about the rats. Maybe Lennon had a history of it.

He went up and knocked on the door. No answer. Shit. Maybe he should write her a note, or try again later. He sighed, pissed off that he was stuck indoors on a day like this, when it was so glorious outside and the sky was so blue. Still, if he had to be stuck indoors, he couldn't think of a better place to be.

He turned to go down the stairs and then heard a noise out in the garden. He looked through the gap. Lucy was standing in the middle of the lawn, facing the house. She was holding Lennon, stroking his head and jiggling him a little, like a mother holding a baby. As Jamie watched, she walked inside with him and closed the door behind her.

Six

Kirsty's flu dragged on for the rest of the week. She was too ill to go to work so she carried the duvet into the living room and spent four days in front of the TV. Jamie went to work, phoning her a couple of times every day to check how she was feeling. She told him she felt like death, but, truth be told, she was quite enjoying her spell at home. Apart from the throat-shredding cough and the constant nose-blowing, she rather liked being the patient for once, groaning hoarse requests for cups of tea and medicine. During the days, she gorged herself on daytime TV and staggered around in her dressing gown, feeling wonderfully decadent and sluttish.

On Thursday afternoon, there was a knock at the door.

Kirsty, who had been flicking through the channels, trying to decide between a Jeremy Kyle repeat and an ancient episode of Morse, dragged herself to the door and opened it. The woman standing there had an anxious expression on her face.

'Hello, I'm Mary.' She offered her hand. 'You must be Kirsty.'

Kirsty's first concern was how awful she must look. She always hoped to look her best when meeting someone for the first time. She was a firm believer in the importance of initial impressions, and here she was with a red-raw nose, flaky skin, greasy hair and most probably the sour smell of someone who hasn't left the house for days. Her second thought was, It's the witch. Then she thought, She doesn't look much like a witch – just a hippy, like Jamie said. All this flashed through her head in the second it took her to shake Mary's hand.

'Are you ill?' Mary asked, looking concerned.

'Oh, just a touch of flu, that's all.'

Mary nodded. 'That awful virus that's going around. Everybody I know has had it. You should try drinking ginger – it kills flu in its tracks, stops it dead. Ginger with a drop of honey in it.'

'I'm quite happy with paracetamol and codeine, thank you.'

Mary looked appalled. 'They won't help. Trust me, ginger's what you need. I've got some upstairs. I'll fetch it for you in a minute.'

'But...'

'And I won't take no for an answer.'

Kirsty smiled politely. Now she was thinking, What a pushy cow. She sniffed. Suddenly, she felt cold, and she wanted to get back to her quilt on the sofa.

'The reason I came down was to ask if you've seen Lennon, my cat. I haven't seen him since Sunday and I'm really worried. He does sometimes wander off for a couple of days, but he's never been gone this long before.'

Kirsty shook her head. 'No, I've been stuck indoors since Sunday morning. I've hardly even had the curtains open.'

Mary sighed. 'Oh well. Just thought I'd ask. Brian and Linda haven't seen him either.'

'I'm sure he'll turn up.'

Mary looked at the front door, listening to the traffic beyond it. She had a sad, worried look in her eye, and Kirsty felt an twinge of sympathy. She understood the agonies of anxiety: she dealt with the worries of parents every day. This was a cat, not a child, but at its root lay the same emotion. Mary lived alone with the cat; she probably treated it like a child.

Mary forced a smile. 'I'll get you that ginger.'

Kirsty waited while Mary went up the stairs, her long skirt rippling around her ankles, forcing her to go slowly. She returned a minute later with a pale-brown lump of vegetation in her hand. She held it out to Kirsty who took it tentatively.

'This is root ginger. All you need to do is cut off about an inch, grate it into a mug then pour boiling water onto it. Leave it for about ten minutes then strain it. Add a spoonful of honey. It will take away your flu. I guarantee it.'

'Thanks. I'll give it a go.' She felt her nose start to run and sniffed. 'I hope your cat turns up.'

'I'll be heartbroken if he doesn't.'

Jamie came through the front door struggling under the weight of a large cardboard box and perspiring heavily. He wiped his forehead with the sleeve of his T-shirt before making his way back out to the car and bringing in another box. Kirsty had fallen asleep on the sofa, and he woke her with a kiss. She sat up, rubbing her sleep-gummed eyes.

'What have you bought now?'

He tore open the boxes to reveal a barbell and set of weights. Kneeling on the carpet, he screwed a weight to each end of the barbell, then lifted it above his head.

Kirsty applauded. 'It's Mr Universe!'

'That's right. Bullies will no longer kick sand in my face!' He paused. 'Actually this is hurting my arms.'

Kirsty laughed.

He put the weights down and knelt beside her. 'How are you feeling? Any better?'

'Not really. I still feel really tired, as if I've sprung a leak and all my energy has ebbed away.'

'Poor Kirsty.' He stroked her hair, then turned back to his weights. 'So what do you think? There are a couple of smaller, single-handed ones which I thought you could use. And I've ordered a rowing machine as well. I thought I might start swimming again as well. I haven't been for ages.'

Kirsty coughed. 'I'm not really in the mood to talk about physical exercise right now.'

'So you don't want to go to bed then?' He winked at her and she groaned and covered her face with a cushion. Whenever she was ill,

Jamie became even more libidinous. His theory was that it was because she seemed so vulnerable, lying there sniffling: his primeval instincts came out and he wanted to carry her off to his cave.

'Lemsip?' he asked, putting thoughts of passion aside.

'Yes please.'

He went into the kitchen and saw the chunk of ginger sitting on the worktop, untouched. 'What's this?' he asked, going back out to Kirsty.

'That's root ginger. Mary came down earlier and gave it to me. She said it would cure my flu.'

'And have you taken any?'

'No, of course not. How's that going to help me? I'll stick with my Lemsips, thanks.'

Jamie tutted. 'You should try it, Kirsty. What do we have to do with it?' She explained the process. 'Right, I'll make you a cup.'

After Jamie had strained the ginger, he carried it out to Kirsty. She sniffed it and pulled a face, but then took a sip. 'It's foul.'

'Come on, drink it.'

He knelt beside her and stroked her hair as she sipped it, screwing up her face in with distaste. 'So what was Mary doing down here? Did she hear you coughing and blowing your nose and come down to offer you her miracle cure?'

'No, she came down to ask if I've seen her cat. It's gone missing.'

'Lennon? Oh no. When did she last see him?'

'Sunday, I think she said.'

Jamie scratched his head. 'Oh. Because I saw him on Sunday. Lucy had him. I saw her carry him into her flat.'

'Lucy?'

He stood up. 'I'd better go and tell Mary.'

'What was Lucy doing with him?'

He shrugged. 'I'll see you in a minute.'

At the top of the stairs, he knocked on Mary's door. He felt uncomfortable. He had this strange, irrational fear that Lucy had done something to Lennon. She had made it clear that she didn't think much of Mary (calling her a witch was hardly a display of neighbourly good feeling), but surely – surely – she wouldn't do anything to harm her cat.

Mary opened the door. She was smiling, and Jamie noticed that her pupils were dilated. He guessed she had been smoking weed – in fact, there was the distinct smell of cannabis in the air as he stepped into the hallway.

'Kirsty told me Lennon has gone missing. It's just that, well, I'm not sure how to say this…'

Mary cut him off, a wide grin on her face. 'He's come back. Come and see.'

She led him into the living room and there, sitting on the sofa with his legs tucked under his body, was her cat.

'I was so relieved,' Mary said. 'I thought he'd been run over, or, well, I don't know what. You hear of awful things happening to people's cats. In the paper last week there was a report of these children shooting a cat with an air rifle and killing it. Horrible. But Lennon's safe and sound. As you can see.'

Jamie crossed the room and bent to stroke the cat, who rolled over onto his back, inviting Jamie to scratch his belly.

He remembered what he had meant to ask her. 'Does Lennon ever bring rats in?'

Mary shook her head. 'God, no. He never brings anything in apart from the odd earthworm. I remember he caught a butterfly once, and that was a major achievement. He was really proud of himself. But rats – well, he'd run a mile if he saw a rat. Especially the big ones you get round here. Linda upstairs told me she saw a rat that was as big as a puppy – a monstrous thing.' He wasn't really convinced by what she said about her cat. It reminded him of the parents of a school bully who think the little brat is in fact an angel. It probably was Lennon who had left the rats on their doorstep.

Mary walked over to the fireplace and took a silver cigarette case off of the mantelpiece. She produced a ready-rolled spliff, confirming Jamie's suspicions. She held it up. 'Care to join me?'

Jamie wondered if this was the reason why Lucy disliked Mary so much, accusing her of being a practitioner of the black arts. Maybe Mary had offered her a smoke on a previous occasion. He smiled. He could imagine Lucy being the type who would freak out at the mere mention of illegal substances.

'I'd better get back to Kirsty,' he said. 'She needs nursing.'

83

'Yes, of course.' She lay the unlit joint on the edge of an ashtray. 'What did you come up here for, by the way?'

'Pardon?'

She smiled. 'You haven't told me the purpose of your visit.'

'Oh. I just wanted to check if Lennon had come back.' He felt foolish now for suspecting that Lucy had harmed the cat, so he decided not to mention it.

'How sweet of you.'

As she saw him out, she said, 'Did Kirsty drink that ginger I gave her?'

'She just drank it ten minutes ago.'

'Good. She'll feel much better in the morning.' She spoke with certainty. 'But if she needs any more, you know where I am.'

Downstairs, Kirsty was sitting on the sofa, staring into the middle distance, not moving or reacting when Jamie came in.

'Are you alright?'

'Sorry? Oh, listen, I was just reading that book Brian gave you. *The Creature In The Cradle.*' She picked up the book and Jamie took it from her.

'What's it like? Isn't it a bit childish?'

'Huh. I'll tell you what – if I'd read that when I was a kid, I would have had to sleep in my mum and dad's bed for a month. It's really creepy. But listen to this bit.' She took the book back and flicked through it. 'Here. Listen.' She read aloud: '*The next morning, Barbara went downstairs to get the milk in. She was tired and crabby where Suzy had cried all night* – that's the baby, the one that's being terrified by these creatures that run amok in her bedroom every night. *Barbara opened the front door and let out a shrill scream. There, lying beside the milk bottles, was a dead rat, one eye open and seemingly staring at her. It was the biggest rat she had ever seen. It was as big as a puppy.'*

Jamie and Kirsty stared at each other.

'That's bizarre,' he breathed.

'Spooky, isn't it?

'A spooky coincidence.'

'Of course.'

'Do kids really enjoy this stuff?' Kirsty said. 'I suppose they must do, or they wouldn't publish it. Hey, are you OK? You've got goosepimples all up your arms.'

He nodded. 'I'm fine. Maybe I'm catching your cold.'

'I hope not. For your sake.'

He picked the book up and reread the passage Kirsty had just read aloud. 'A coincidence,' he said, 'but damn spooky.'

The alarm clock beeped and Jamie stuck out an arm and quelled it. It was his least favourite sound in the universe. He imagined his ancestors must have developed a severe loathing for cockerels. The first thing he would do if he won the Lottery would be to throw away his alarm clock. If he was rich he would never get up early again. That was his idea of heaven – waking up and knowing that if you wanted to you could stay in bed all day. Bliss.

He got out of bed and wandered into the kitchen where he made a coffee for himself and an Earl Grey for Kirsty. Standing in the kitchen, waiting for the kettle to boil, he had one of those moments where he realised how much he loved the flat. As he opened the curtains and looked out at the waking street, the photograph of him and Kirsty that sat on the mantelpiece was rendered opaque by the light. He picked the photograph up. They were standing in front of the Colosseum in Rome. It had been their first holiday, and an American tourist had taken the picture for them. Kirsty had a tan and a big smile on her face. He thought she looked like a model.

He was about to carry the drinks into the bedroom when Kirsty came into the room. 'Oh, the curtains are open.'

She was naked, and she instinctively covered her breasts. Jamie caught his breath. They had been sleeping together for years; he had seen her naked countless times; he had touched and kissed every inch of her – but still, every time he saw her body he wanted to touch and kiss it again. He put down the mugs and went over to her, putting his arms around her and stroking her naked back, then tracing the chain of freckles that ran along her upper thigh with a fingertip.

'How are you feeling?' he asked.

'Much better. I think I'll be OK to go into work.'

'So the ginger worked.' He kissed her forehead, then her eyelids, then her lips.

'I think the cold was about to...expire anyway,' she said between kisses.

'So you're feeling a lot better?'

'Yes.'

'Oh good. Because–'

They sank to the carpet and Jamie kissed her neck, ran his hands over her breasts, her nipples stiffening under his fingers.

'Do you want me to close the curtains?' he said.

She shook her head. 'I don't want you to move. Except...like this.'

'Oh.'

They made love on the floor, Jamie on top, burning his knees on the carpet but not caring. Kirsty grabbed his buttocks and pulled him in deeper, pushing her pelvis hard against his. The bookcase rattled and shook in time with Jamie's thrusts. She bit into the muscle where his neck met his shoulder and he shivered with pleasure.

He pushed himself up on his arms so he could look down at her, at her flushed face, her nipples that stood erect, a bead of sweat running between her breasts. He slowed down, pausing with the head of his cock just inside her, then moved into her slowly, the feeling of intense pleasure spreading from his penis through his entire body.

'Fuck me from behind,' Kirsty said, and he withdrew, letting her turn over onto all fours, positioning himself behind her and teasing her for a moment before pushing back inside her and making her gasp.

The full-length mirror was just in front of them and Jamie looked up, watching himself fuck this woman he loved, the whole world outside this act of desire disappearing. Kirsty looked at him over her shoulder with an expression of pure lust and he held her by her hips as she tilted her body so his cock struck the sweet spot inside her. He pushed harder, deeper, and looked into the mirror at Kirsty with her eyes squeezed tight, hardly aware of how noisy they were being and not caring anyway. Right now, in this moment, life was the best it had ever been, would ever be.

'Ah, fucking hell.' Kirsty shouted as she came, and a moment later, Jamie cried out too. Then they collapsed together in a damp heap, short of breath.

Kirsty ran a finger down Jamie's chest to his belly button. 'I love you,' she said.

'And I love you.' He kissed her again. She tasted of ginger. 'I'll have to write Mary a thank you note.'

Kirsty tutted. 'Like I said, I would have felt better anyway.'

Jamie opened the front door cautiously, worried that there might be another rat lying there. Thankfully, the hall was free of dead rodents.

He checked the post (junk mail and bills, as per usual) then went out to his car. Chris was just about to get into his car, and Jamie said, 'Good morning' cheerfully. He was aware that he had a big grin on his face. Chris looked him up and down and raised an eyebrow.

'I was going to come up and see you later,' he said.

'Really?'

'Yes. Do you remember I told you I was into go-karting? I was going to go down to the track this Sunday and have a go. I wondered if you and Kirsty and your friends fancied coming along.'

'I don't know.'

'It's a great laugh. You'd really enjoy it. And I think your mate Paul would like it too.'

'OK. I'll ask him.'

'And his girlfriend.'

'What, Heather? She's not his girlfriend.'

'Whatever. Ask them all. The track's near Orpington. In fact, there are a couple of tracks – one for beginners, one for more experienced karters. I guarantee you'll have a good time.'

Jamie nodded. 'OK, it sounds good. I'll ring Paul and Heather and let you know tonight.'

Chris opened his car door. 'Nice one.'

Jamie watched him drive off up the road. He was happy – truly happy. And what better way of spending a summer Sunday than going out with a group of friends and doing something you'd never done before? He was sure Paul and Heather would be interested. And Kirsty too.

He got into his car and wound down the window. As he drove to work he forgot all about rats and hoaxes. He turned up the radio and sang along.

Seven

The city exits were clogged with traffic, thousands of people leaving the fume-filled greenhouse that London had become as the summer went on, heading for the countryside and the coast. It took almost an hour to get out of London into the spaces of Kent. Jamie drummed his fingers on the steering wheel impatiently. Kirsty rummaged through the glove compartment, trying to decide what CD to put on. Paul and Heather were in the back seat. They sat with their legs touching, and they were holding hands, their fingers tightly entwined.

Jamie spotted this in the rearview mirror when they were stuck in gridlock on the outskirts of the city. He turned around, smiling. Kirsty turned to see what Jamie was staring at.

'Bloody hell! You two! When did this happen?'

Paul and Heather exchanged a look. 'We weren't going to tell you the details,' Paul said. 'It's quite embarrassing.'

'Oh come on. You've got to tell us.' Kirsty turned round as much as her seatbelt would allow. She was thrilled – but also a little disappointed. She'd always hoped that if and when Paul and Heather got together it would because of her matchmaking efforts. Now, it seemed, they had gone and done it without her help.

'I went to that big Waterstones in Oxford Street on Wednesday night.' Paul squeezed Heather's hand. 'I was just browsing, looking around, you know, trying to find a good book...'

'Come off it,' laughed Jamie.

'Oh, OK. I hold my hands up. I'd read in the Sunday Times that it was a good place to meet women. Intelligent, cultured women. A couple of years ago Tesco was supposed to be the cool place to hang out and meet other single people, but now, apparently, it's bookshops. So I thought, why not give it a go? What have you got to lose? Besides, I really did need something to read.'

'So there you were, lurking around the shelves,' prompted Kirsty.

'Yes. Actually, I felt pretty stupid. I didn't know which section to go to. Was there some sort of code I needed to know? I wandered from cookery to economics to modern fiction to crime. I saw a couple of nice-looking women looking at travel books. I was about to go and talk to one of them – she had a book about China and I was going to ask her something inane about whether she'd ever been there – when her boyfriend appeared. So I went for a coffee, and I thought, I'll have one more go – one more look around – and then I'll go home.

'I finished my coffee and went back to the fiction section. I grabbed a book and took up a position on one of the sofas. Then this woman appeared from behind the bookshelves. A vision. It was Heather. It turned out she was there doing exactly the same as me.'

'Heather!' Kirsty spluttered.

'Yes, and I was having about as much luck as him,' she said.

'Ah yes,' said Paul. 'But your luck was about to change.'

She smiled, leant forward and kissed his cheek. 'It certainly was. To cut a long story short, we went home together.'

'And we're going to hold our wedding at Waterstones,' said Paul.

Heather slapped his arm lightly. 'Fool.'

'For your love.'

Jamie made a retching sound. 'Please, don't. I'll be sick.'

Kirsty nodded at them as they smiled at each other. 'Well, you certainly look happy together. And, Heather, you can tell me all about it later. In detail. Graphic detail.'

The traffic began to thin out and soon they reached the go-kart track. Chris and Lucy had been driving ahead of them all the way. At one point, shortly after Paul and Kirsty's revelation, they had almost lost them. But now, here they were, about to reach the venue. Jamie felt the butterflies in his stomach stir. Although he hadn't admitted as much to any of the others, he felt nervous. He had never been in a go-kart before. He'd played Super Mario Kart on a friend's Nintendo, but that was as far as it went. Paul had never been karting either, but he was really excited, as he kept telling everyone. But then, Paul had always had a penchant for speedy, adrenalin-generating activities. He had been snowboarding and rock climbing, water-skiing and even bungee-jumping, things that made Jamie – who couldn't even roller-skate – break out in a cold sweat.

A parking attendant showed them towards a couple of good spots, then the six of them walked towards the entrance. At the pay-booth, Chris produced his membership card and they paid their entrance fees. The woman behind the counter handed over their crash helmets.

'Where's yours?' Jamie said to Lucy.

'I'm not taking part. It doesn't really appeal to me. To be honest, I find it too frightening. The karts go so fast.'

Jamie turned his crash helmet over in his hands. He could imagine himself skidding on a patch of oil, crashing into a wall, his go-kart exploding, a fireball consuming him. He imagined himself as one of those horribly-disfigured burn victims, having to undergo reconstructive surgery and being called 'brave' by everyone. He could just see it: this would be the point where he cashed his good luck chips in. At times like this he wished he was a woman: it would be much easier to say no; he wouldn't have this ridiculous masculine front to keep up, whereby if he said he didn't want to do it, he would be accused of wimping out. He could just imagine Paul ribbing him about it. And Kirsty too. She seemed perfectly relaxed, although a little impatient to get Heather on her own so she could find out the salacious details of her and Paul's tryst.

'Are you alright?' he said to Kirsty.

She nodded. 'Yes. I can't wait to get started.'

He smiled weakly. 'Me neither.'

'So what are we waiting for?' said Chris, and he led them outside, Paul and Heather holding hands, Kirsty beside them, Lucy and Jamie following behind.

They found themselves standing in a large, noisy area, the smell of petrol and burnt rubber smoking in the air around them. The track was directly in front of them: a figure of eight, its shape marked out by hundreds of tyres, stacked up to chest height. The go-karts zipped around this track, the racers gripping the steering wheels tightly, moving at great speed, overtaking and being overtaken. The karts buzzed like wasps trapped in bottles, brakes and tyres squealing intermittently as they took sharp turns around corners. The karts came in all colours, patterned with checks and stripes, and each kart had its own number and name on its side. Jamie noticed that all of the drivers were adults: there were a few children hanging around, but they were spectators only. This was an adult sport. He felt sick.

An attendant in dark-blue overalls came over and said hello to Chris. 'Brought some friends with you, I see. Any of you karted before?'

They all shook their heads.

'No?' He chuckled. 'You're going to love it. It's tremendous fun. And these karts are top-of-the-range, with very powerful five horsepower engines. We import them from the States.'

To Jamie's horror, the man looked at him and said, 'Hey, mate, you look a bit pasty. Don't be nervous. You'll love it.'

Chris clapped Jamie on the shoulder. 'He's right, Jamie. It's really good fun. I was a bit nervous before my first time, but once I was out there, I was fine.'

Jamie nodded, but he didn't feel very reassured.

'Where are our karts?' said Paul. 'I can't wait to get started.'

The attendant held up his hands. 'All in good time. First I have to explain a few rules. First of all, no bumping...'

Jamie tuned out the man's words and stared at the track. He watched the karts, tearing round and round. He felt awful. He kept having visions of a crash, a wrenching of metal and bone. He looked at the sky, hoping storm clouds might suddenly appear in the clear blue sky and make it too dangerous for them to go onto the track. No such luck.

'...the right pedal is your accelerator, the left pedal is your brake. Don't stamp on the brake too hard or you'll stop with a real jolt. And I wouldn't recommend putting your foot down too far on the accelerator either. OK. Are we all set?'

They followed the man over to the start-point of the track, where half-a-dozen go-karts sat waiting for them.

'Right, take your pick. They're all the same.'

Paul chose a bright red kart, Heather picked a dark green and yellow one, Kirsty chose a blue one and Jamie sat down in a black kart marked with silver stripes. Chris remained where he was.

'What's up?' said Paul, looking up at Chris. 'Aren't you joining us?'

Chris gestured beyond the track. 'This is the beginner's track, so it's a bit too tame for me. I'm going to head over to the other track. But I'll meet up with you later.' He smiled and said, 'Have fun,' then walked off, Lucy following him.

'Right,' said the attendant, clapping his hands. 'Seatbelts and crash helmets on.. Remember, right for speed, left to brake. If you have any problems, give us a shout. Now, away you go.'

Paul put his foot on the accelerator, made a thumbs-up gesture and sped away, joining the other karters, belting around the first corner. Kirsty headed off next, a little more cautiously, then Heather. Jamie sat and stared through his visor, sweat rolling down his forehead. The attendant was looking at him, making a sweeping gesture with his hands, encouraging Jamie to put his foot down. He gripped the steering wheel, his knuckles white,and then his body took over. His legs stretched forward, his feet found the pedals, and his right ankle applied pressure to the accelerator.

He was away.

He shot over the starting line far too fast, overtaking a blue go-kart on its second or third lap. Panicking – thinking he was going to crash – he took his left foot off the pedal and his go-kart almost stopped. He heard a screech of brakes behind him as a kart nearly crashed into his tail, and the driver of that kart shook her head at him as she went by. Jamie knew he had to get moving, so he gently applied pressure to the pedal. His kart sped up, and once he was moving at a reasonable speed he kept his foot steady. He rounded the first corner, then the second. Paul sped past him, as did Kirsty, who waved. He couldn't wave back as he wasn't confident enough to take either hand off the wheel. But then, as he began his second lap, he realised to his surprise that he was enjoying himself.

He started to go faster, taking corners more confidently, even overtaking a few people, including Heather and then Kirsty. He waved at her. Paul was still bombing around the track in his bright-red kart at almost twice the speed as some of the others. Jamie couldn't believe he hadn't done it before, but he had no reason to lie. He was clearly a natural. Or maybe now he had found a girlfriend he felt capable of anything, and that added confidence had turned him into a superstar karter. Jamie was pleased about Paul and Heather. Not just because he was tired of listening to Paul bemoaning his lack of luck with women and saying how dearly he needed a shag, but also because he wanted Paul to be happy. Paul was a good bloke, and a good friend. He deserved to be happy. It was an added bonus that he was going out with Heather. They didn't have to worry about Paul introducing a new girl into their circle, a girl that they might not get on with. In fact, it was good news all round. They could go out as a foursome – maybe even go on holiday together. That might be a laugh.

He kept on karting for another hour, although the time seemed to go much quicker. Jamie saw Kirsty slow down and head off the track, then Heather did the same, and he followed. Paul kept going.

Jamie got out of his kart and pulled off his helmet, then went over to Kirsty and kissed her. 'That was fantastic,' he said.

She nodded. 'I know. But I need a drink.'

'Me too,' said Heather. She looked back at the track, following Paul's go-kart with her eyes.

The attendant that had spoken to them earlier came over. 'Your friend's very good,' he said. 'Very few people pick it up as quickly as him.'

'That's my boyfriend,' said Heather.

'And she's so proud,' laughed Jamie.

They headed off towards the cafe, where Lucy was already ensconced, nursing a cup of tea. When she saw them come in, her face did that thing that Jamie had noticed before, flicking from a frown to a smile in a peculiar instant. Jamie, Kirsty and Heather went over to join her.

'Having fun?' Lucy asked.

They chorused their enthusiastic assent. Jamie went over to the counter to buy lunch and the women sat down. Lucy had a novel lying in front of her, but it looked untouched, with no bookmark protruding from the virgin-white pages.

'Aren't you bored, sitting in here on your own?' Kirsty asked.

'Not at all. It's nice to get some peace and quiet. It's so important to me – silence is something I treasure, but I experience it so rarely.' She looked right into Kirsty's eyes. 'Anyway, I've been watching Chris most of the morning – but it got a bit noisy out there so I came in here. Is Paul still out there?'

'Oh yes,' Heather grinned. 'He's having a fabulous time.'

Kirsty nudged her. 'He's a real speed freak, isn't he. Is he speedy at everything?'

'No way. The Paul I'm coming to know is slow and gentle.'

Jamie returned with a tray of teas and chips. 'Stop it, please, or I'll throw up.' He sat down. 'Actually, I'm really pleased you two got together.'

Heather's smile widened. 'So am I.'

'Why didn't you admit that you fancied him?' said Kirsty. 'We could have fixed you up long ago.'

'Well, I did try dropping hints. Quite explicit ones, if I remember correctly. But we're together now, that's the important thing.'

Kirsty touched her friend's hand. 'You seem really happy.'

'I am. It's all happened so fast – this great rush of emotion. A thunderclap, almost. Now I feel like we've wasted years and we've got so much to catch up on. Paul's so funny and sweet and...'

'Behind you,' said Jamie.

They looked up. Paul had come into the cafe, his fringe stuck to his brow where he had been sweating beneath his crash helmet. He came over, bent down to kiss Heather on the lips, then said, 'This is so excellent. I love it. It's brilliant.'

'We thought you were having a good time,' said Jamie.

'Too right. But now I want a go on the other track.'

Lucy said, 'Well, here's Chris. He'll take you over to that track if you want.' She looked up at Chris as he came over, swinging his crash helmet in his right hand. 'Paul wants a go on the advanced track.'

'Does he? The big boys' track. Do you think you're ready then, mate?'

Paul nodded. 'Ready, willing and able.'

Chris looked at his watch. 'Come on then. No time like the present.'

'Aren't you going to stop for a drink?' asked Heather.

Paul kissed her quickly. 'I won't be long. I'll just give Chris a quick thrashing, then I'll be back.'

'A quick thrashing? You're hoping, mate. You might just catch a glimpse of me in the distance.'

They walked out together.

'Boys,' said Kirsty, sipping her tea.

'He won't beat Chris though,' said Lucy, seriously. 'Nobody ever does.'

Heather looked at her. 'We'll see.'

They stayed in the café for another half-hour, finishing their drinks and eating their chips. They stayed there until they heard the bang.

The bang was audible across the whole park, reverberating from the advanced track, above the heads of the spectators, over to the beginner's track and the cashier's booth. In the cafeteria, it made everyone turn their heads towards the door. A communal look of concern spread from face to face, and Jamie felt all the blood drain from his. He knew it in an instant: something terrible had happened to Paul.

He jumped to his feet. 'I've got to go and see,' he said in a tremulous voice.

Kirsty stood up and grabbed his arm. Around them, other people were standing up, drifting over to the windows and door to see if they could catch a glimpse of what was going on. 'We'll come with you.'

They headed towards the door. Jamie broke into a run as soon as they got outside, Kirsty, Heather and Lucy following close behind. He pushed through the maddening crowd, headed towards the advanced track. Further ahead, he could see half-a-dozen blue-overalled attendants running in the same direction. Two of them were carrying a stretcher.

The crowd thickened nearer the track, and as they got closer Jamie could smell smoke. He ran to the front of the crowd, stopping where the go-karts were lined up, ready to take people on the ride of their lives.

Somebody was lying on the track near the starting line, surrounded by medics and attendants. Two medics laid the stretcher on the ground and the process began of shifting the person onto the stretcher. As they lifted the person Kirsty, Heather and Lucy arrived by Jamie's side and the person's face became visible.

Jamie saw Chris standing there, looking down at Paul on the stretcher.

Heather cried out.

She ran towards the wall of tyres and tried to throw herself over it, panicking so much she didn't realise that a few feet to the right was a gap which would have allowed her onto the track without this athletic display. She shouted, 'Paul!' and as she hurtled over the top of the tyres, she was caught by two of the attendants, who stopped her from throwing herself on her prone boyfriend.

Jamie, Kirsty and Lucy moved around the wall of tyres onto the track. Chris was standing over the other side. Jamie saw him look at Lucy, then look away.

Jamie caught hold of an attendant's arm. 'What happened? Is he dead? Tell me!"

It was the same man who had advised them earlier. He wiped his face with his sleeve. 'No, he's not dead.'

Jamie exhaled with relief. He could see Heather, just a few feet away, kneeling beside Paul, tears rolling down her cheeks.

'What happened?'

The man looked over at Chris – whose face was downcast, staring at the track – then back at Jamie.

'Your friend and Chris had been bombing round the track, racing. Paul won by quite a big gap. He crossed the finishing line and came into the pits here. He took off his helmet, unfastened his seatbelt and stood up, ready to get out of his kart. I could see his face from here. He looked dead proud of himself.'

He shook his head. 'Then it happened. Chris came up to the finishing line with another kart right on his tail. As Chris hit the finishing line he slowed right down, not realising, I guess, that the other guy was so close behind him. The other driver didn't have a chance to brake – he swerved right into the pits and into the back of Paul's go-kart. As he hit the kart the fuel tank exploded – Paul was thrown out. There was an explosion – a great ball of flame, I'm sure you must have heard the bang – and it was like he flew out of the flames. Landed right there, where you see him now. God, he hit his head hard.' The attendant swallowed. He looked green.

'What happened to the other driver?' Kirsty asked. 'Is he alright?'

The attendant pointed towards a man sitting beside the track with a blanket around his shoulders and a smoke-blackened face. 'He'll be OK. I think he's just in shock.'

An ambulance arrived, its siren wailing. It stopped next to Jamie and the others and the paramedics lifted the stretcher and carried Paul inside. Heather climbed in with him. The other driver was helped in by one of the attendants.

Kirsty spoke to the paramedics who told her they were taking Paul to the hospital in Bromley.

'We'll follow them in the car,' said Jamie. 'Come on, Kirsty. Oh, hang on.' He'd remembered Chris and Lucy.

Lucy had crossed the track and was standing talking to her husband. Jamie was about to ask them if they were going to come to the hospital, then he felt a surge of anger and thought, *Fuck them*. If it wasn't for Chris they wouldn't be here. And Paul wouldn't be in the back of an ambulance with his head all smashed up. He would talk to them later – but for now, he was only interested in his best friend.

'Never mind. He followed Kirsty towards the car park, holding tightly onto her hand as they squeezed between rows of stationary cars to get to their own. 'I *knew* something was going to happen,' he said. 'But I thought it was going to be me.'

Kirsty just looked at him, her expression unreadable. 'Let's get to the hospital.'

Eight

Jamie sat beside Paul's bed and stared at his friend's motionless face. Behind him he could hear the *bip bip bip* of the heart monitor. He had seen enough films and television dramas to know that if the line on the screen were to run flat – to flatline – he should shout for a doctor, and then panic would render him frantic and helpless as doctors and nurses would come running, their footfall heavy in the long corridors. They would bring out the defibrillator and Jamie would stand there and watch as they fired electricity into Paul's chest, making his body buck, rising up and falling back onto the bed, the bed where he had lain since the accident, six weeks ago.

But nothing like that did happen.

Six weeks, and nothing had happened at all. Paul did nothing except lie motionless beneath NHS sheets, his eyes closed, his body continuing to function at the most fundamental of levels (his heart beating on, his chest continuing to rise and fall, his hair and fingernails growing, skin being shed) but his mind locked away in that body, doing nothing. Nothing but dreaming. If he did dream at all.

Paul was never alone. His family and friends took it in turn to sit beside his bed: his parents, his sister, his grandmother, Heather, Kirsty,

Jamie. Most of them would sit and talk to him, chatting about life as it went on outside the hospital, pleading with him to wake up, expressing regret for things said or unsaid in the past. Sometimes Paul's parents played recordings of his favourite football matches. Paul and his dad were both Arsenal fans – it was pretty much the only thing they had ever talked about – and Mr Garner would record matches off Radio 5 and play them back to his son, hoping a dramatic moment might reach into Paul's sleeping brain and draw him back to the surface.

That's what it seemed like to Jamie: that his friend had slipped deep beneath the surface of the world, into a deep lake of dreams or darkness, and although he was still there – still with them – he couldn't communicate with them. He was too deep. He had been swallowed up, and all they could do was wait and see if the subterranean place in which he now dwelt would spit him back out. Or if he might float upwards, blinking with sleep-clogged eyes as he emerged into the light.

It was what he prayed for.

Jamie barely spoke to Paul when it was his turn to sit beside him. He didn't tell stories or jokes or play music. He merely sat and watched. He didn't believe that his friend needed chatter and prompts; no-one could pull him back to the surface with songs or football commentary. He believed that Paul needed to rest – he was sleeping off the results of the accident like a bad hangover. Jamie and Paul used to joke that after a night on the beer, Paul would slip into a coma, and that nothing could wake him but time. Of course, Jamie knew that this coma had nothing to do with alcohol or over-indulgence, but something told him that the same principle applied. All they had to do was wait.

'He's suffered a serious head injury,' said the doctor at Bromley Hospital, where the ambulance had taken Paul after the accident. 'It's very difficult to say at this point what the long-term outcome will be.'

After a day, Paul fell into a coma. The doctor told them that he might never come out of that coma, and if he did he might be brain damaged. He might not be able to talk. He might have lost the use of his limbs. On the other hand, he could make a full recovery, although it would not be quick. He could spend months or years in therapy.

'All we can do,' said the doctor, 'is wait and hope. And pray, if you're that way inclined.'

'So there's a possibility that he might never wake up?' said Heather. She was trying to maintain her professional nurse's stoicism, but was not succeeding. Her voice cracked as she spoke. Jamie's parents had shuffled off to get coffee from the machine down the corridor.

The doctor spoke softly. 'There is that chance, yes. He might slip into a vegetative state, in which case the family would have to make a decision. Or the coma could continue for a long time. If at any point his brain stopped functioning completely – if it died, in effect – we could keep him alive with machines, but as you know…well, is that really living?'

Heather, Kirsty and Jamie looked at each other. Heather started to cry, and Kirsty put her arms around her. Jamie stood there, wishing he was somewhere else, wishing life was like TiVo: that he could press rewind to change history, or even fast forward to find out what would happen.

He could still see the look of joy and cocky assuredness on Paul's face when he first climbed into the go-kart. And then he saw Chris, standing on the other side of the track, not catching anyone's eye.

After the accident, Chris and Lucy had driven straight home. They hadn't visited the hospital, or even phoned to see how Paul was. Jamie hadn't noticed at the time – he had been too preoccupied to worry about the actions of his neighbours – but afterwards, when he began to process what had happened, dwelling on it on sleepless nights, he began to feel outraged that the people who were responsible for Paul being at the track in the first place hadn't bothered to find out how he was. They hadn't even sent a card, or expressed any sort of regret. Chris, for God's sake, had even been involved in the accident! And now he was hiding.

No, that wasn't right. He was acting as if nothing had happened.

Three days after the accident, Chris came up to Jamie and Kirsty's and asked them if they wanted their windows cleaned: he knew a window cleaner who could do it cheap.

'I've noticed your back windows are looking a bit grubby.'

Jamie was speechless. He had only come home to take a bath and change his clothes. In ten minutes he would be heading back to Bromley to sit in a room with his comatose best mate.

'I don't give a toss about the windows,' he said after a long pause, and Chris looked surprised.

'There's no need to be rude,' he said, and he turned around and walked off, leaving Jamie, once again, speechless.

Jamie and Kirsty hadn't spoken to their downstairs neighbours since. They saw them coming and going, but they didn't even attempt smalltalk. Jamie was waiting for Chris to say something about the accident, or ask after Paul's health. But it never happened. Most of the time he didn't think about it. His annoyance and anger were there in the background, but that was all. He felt too weakened by what had happened to Paul to care much about anything else – work, his other friends, his family. Lucy and Chris were the least of his concerns.

Three weeks after the accident, Heather and Kirsty pulled some strings – calling in a few favours from consultants they knew – and got Paul transferred to St Thomas's, which meant that they could see him every day. Heather usually spent her lunchbreak sitting with him. Now, when Jamie spent his shift beside Paul, he did so knowing that Kirsty was close by, working, dealing with her own patients. It made him feel comforted – and also gave him some perspective. Theirs was not the only unfortunate situation in the world. There were many people in the same boat. When Kirsty told him about the sick children she had to deal with, he remembered that there were a lot of people worse off. It didn't make what had happened to Paul any less painful or easier to accept, but it made him feel less alone.

Paul's condition continued. He was stable. There was no sign of a recovery, but nor did his condition worsen. As Paul slept on, Jamie and Kirsty's life returned to a normal routine – normal but for the shadow of Paul hanging in the background. They started to cope. Jamie realised he was grieving, even though that grief was for somebody who wasn't actually dead. Grief was another thing that only time could aid. By the time summer ended, he and Kirsty felt like they had re-entered the real world. Now all they wanted was for Paul to join them.

Nine

Making love felt like an affirmation of life. They hadn't had sex for weeks, but suddenly, one evening, they looked at each other and a moment later they were pulling off their clothes and falling onto the bed, Kirsty pushing herself backwards with her heels as Jamie trailed kisses from her ankles, up her thighs, tasting her arousal, moving up to her breasts, his hands grasping her shoulder blades as their mouths met in a hard kiss. He had to be inside her, right now, and she raised herself up to meet him as he pushed into her, as deep as he could go, the headboard banging against the wall, Kirsty scratching his back, pulling him in, grinding her hips in a circular motion. He bit her neck. She pulled his hair. They turned over in a blur of limbs and she rode him, rocking back and forth with her hands gripping her own hair, his hands holding her breasts, pushing upwards with his pelvis, wanting to disappear inside her, wanting to get all of her inside him, so they could devour one another completely. Kirsty bucked and trembled and shouted his name. He rolled her off him and they fell off the bed, landing on the floor with a thump. Kirsty turned over onto her hands and knees and Jamie entered her from behind, both of them collapsing as he came. Kirsty twisted around to face him, kissing him as they lay in a tangle on the floor.

She had stopped taking the pill.

From that moment on, they made love whenever they could. They didn't sit down together and talk about it in hushed, serious tones. They didn't say, Is this the right time? or Can we afford it? – they just knew it was the right thing to do. It was what they both wanted.

Then, two weeks later, they received the first letter.

Kirsty was having her early morning bath. Jamie was still in bed, just waking up, dreams receding from his mind in which go-karts collided. He got out of bed, going over to the mirror to look at himself, out of damage-assessment habit rather than vanity. His body was in pretty good shape, caused by a combination of loads of athletic sex and all the working out he had been doing, putting his weights to good use. His face, though, was a different matter. He had bags like coal sacks beneath his eyes; he looked pasty and tired, his skin like the underbelly of a fish. He looked the way he did at the end of a long winter. It didn't seem real that just a few weeks ago summer had blazed.

He wandered out of the bedroom, naked and needing to pee. Passing the front door, he looked down and saw that an envelope that had been pushed under it. He crouched down and picked it up, taking it with him into the bathroom.

Kirsty was washing her hair, leaning back in the water, her eyes closed against the shampoo, her ears submerged in water so she didn't hear him come in. He leant over and kissed her wet face, causing her to open her eyes.

'Oh shit, Jamie, now I've got shampoo in my eyes. Pass me a towel, quick.'

'Sorry.'

She dried her face. 'What's that?'

He ripped the envelope open and began to read. He read the letter twice, turning it over in his hand as if he couldn't believe it was real. Then he read it aloud.

To the Ground Floor Flat

We have become increasingly disturbed recently by the level of noise coming from your flat. The music you play at high volumes is bad enough, but recently the sound of you having sexual intercourse has become quite intolerable. We both have to get up early, and are finding it difficult to get sufficient sleep because of the noises that emerge from your flat night after night. It is quite disgusting to listen to.

We do not want to cause too much of a fuss over this. We understand that you have urges to fulfil, but we do not all want to share in your exertions. We hope that you will act to ensure that we do not need to write to you like this again.

Kirsty grabbed the letter and read it, just to make sure that Jamie wasn't making it up. She held it at the corner so as not to get it wet.

'It's unsigned.' She looked up at Jamie. 'Do you think it's meant to be a joke?'

'No. I mean, I don't know. I hope it's meant to be a joke.'

'Do you think it's from Lucy and Chris?'

'Who else could it be? There's no-one else who could possibly hear us making love, apart from maybe Mary, and this from a we, not an I.'

'But look at the way it's addressed: to the Ground Floor Flat. Not even our names. It's so cold and impersonal. It doesn't make sense.'

'Well, we haven't spoken to them since Chris offered to find us a window cleaner. Maybe they think we're no longer on first name terms. Or even second name terms.'

'It's ridiculous.'

Jamie took the letter back from Kirsty and read it again. 'The noises that emerge from your flat night after night.' He laughed. 'It's quite flattering, really.'

'It has to be a joke.'

'If not, it's very sad. It makes me feel sorry for the person who wrote it. They're obviously not getting any.'

Kirsty rolled her eyes. 'Don't you feel angry, or insulted?'

'A bit. But, to be honest, it's so stupid I can't really take it seriously. I mean, what's the point of writing something like this? If it's meant to be a joke, it's not funny. And if not…well, it's just stupid.'

'It's horrible, though, Jamie. It makes me feel like I'm being watched. Or listened to, at least.'

She climbed out of the bath, her skin warm and pink, and Jamie took a towel from the rack and wrapped it around her shoulders.

'We'll have to talk about this later,' he said. 'I'm going to be late for work.'

While she dried herself, he cleaned his teeth and washed himself at the basin. He thought about the letter: did Lucy and Chris really have cause for complaint? It wasn't the most pleasant situation in the world, having to listen to someone else having noisy sex. When he was a student his room in the halls of residence was next to this guy called Terry, who had a girlfriend called...Jamie couldn't remember her name. But he could certainly remember Terry's name, because of the number of times he had heard it called out: *Oh Terry, Ter-ry, Oh God Terriiiieeeee.* Jamie hadn't had a girlfriend at the time, and the nightly orgasm-fest going on next door had driven him half-mad. But that had been different. Lucy and Chris were married, they were in their thirties. The best way to drown out the sound of someone else having sex would be to do it yourselves. That's if the letter really was from them. But then, like he'd said to Kirsty, who else could it be from? It had come through the inner door, so it had to be from either Lucy and Chris, Mary, or Brian and Linda.

It had to be the Newtons. And if they were trying to be funny, well, he wasn't in the mood for jokes, especially not from them.

116

Driving to work, he put the letter from his mind. His thoughts turned to the coming evening. Heather was coming over for dinner, and the conversation would undoubtedly centre on Paul. Jamie sighed. Heather and Kirsty were able to talk about the situation endlessly, but some days Jamie just wanted to try to forget about it. It made him feel weary and weak; helpless and afraid. He couldn't admit this to the others, or they might accuse him of not caring as much as them, of being an emotionally-stilted male, unable to cope with feelings. Well, that was bullshit: he cared as much as – if not more than – anyone. It was just that some days – days like today – he felt too tired to deal with it. He wanted to get on with his life.

Kirsty wasn't home yet when Jamie arrived back that afternoon. He took off his tie, threw it on the bed, then went to the fridge and tried to decide between beer and orange juice. The beer won out. He'd had a shitty day at work. His computer kept crashing, and then there were all the whispered rumours that something was 'going on'. The managers and supervisors were called away to an important meeting and, when Jamie's supervisor returned, he appeared worried and distracted, but would not be drawn on what the meeting had been about.

Cold beer. That was exactly what Jamie needed. He cracked open a can and took a deep swallow. He found a half-empty tube of Pringles in the cupboard and carried them over to his desk. A game of *Mass*

Effect was in order, he decided. Blasting a few aliens would help to relieve the stresses of the day.

He was happily shooting 'em up when Kirsty arrived home with Heather in tow. Jamie turned the Playstation off, kissed Kirsty on the lips, Heather on the cheek, and asked them if they wanted wine. Immediately, Heather started to cry.

'Oh Jamie, you should have seen him today. I sat beside him and held his hand and it hit me: he didn't even know I was there. I was telling him all these things – telling him about our future together – and I might as well have been talking to a plant. He looked like an empty shell. Oh God, it makes me feel so horrible saying that.'

Jamie put his arms around her. 'He is in there, Heather, I promise you. And he will come back to us.'

She blinked at him, shedding tears that rolled down her cheeks. 'But what if he doesn't?'

'I don't know. I...' He ran out of words. He had known this was going to happen, and suddenly he felt angry. He didn't need Heather to remind him that he might have lost the person who, behind Kirsty and his close family, meant the most to him in the world. He couldn't cope with this, not right now. He wanted to shout and scream at the injustice. But he didn't. Instead, he let Heather cry on his shoulder, and then he opened the wine. It was going to be a long evening.

At eleven, after several hours spent trying to mop up Heather's tears – a task much better handled by Kirsty, who held her friend while

Jamie stared at the TV, feeling numb and exhausted – they called her a taxi.

'Why don't you take a few days off work?' Kirsty suggested. 'Call in sick.'

'I might.'

They watched the taxi sail away, then went back inside. Kirsty stared at the empty wine bottles and beer cans, the crumpled, soggy tissues that lay on the floor by the sofa. 'I'm shattered.'

'Me too.'

'I don't think we'll be giving the neighbours cause for complaint tonight.' She smiled wryly.

'No. I don't think so.'

But when they had both got into bed, they somehow found themselves rolling together, clinging to one another. In the darkness beneath the quilt, they made love slowly, their hot bellies pressed together, slick with sweat, and when Jamie came he saw a flash of light behind his eyes.. Afterwards, they realised they had made love in silence. But it felt to Jamie that something had happened – something they felt no need to talk about, although he knew Kirsty knew it too.

The next morning, Jamie opened the front door and found a small Jiffy bag lying on the carpet in the hall, addressed to him and Kirsty. He picked it up and tore it open. Inside, there was a CD. He turned it over in his hand. How peculiar.

'What is it?' Kirsty asked. Jamie was going to give her a lift into work, as she didn't feel like taking the Tube this morning. She wanted to keep her contact with people to a minimum.

'We'll soon find out.'

After they left Mount Pleasant Street and joined the traffic on the main road, Jamie inserted the CD into the car stereo and pressed PLAY. For the first ten seconds there was nothing but the hiss of silence.

'It's blank,' Jamie said.

'No, listen.'

'I still can't hear anything.'

Kirsty turned the volume up. 'Now, can't you hear it?'

Jamie could. It was a soft, rhythmic banging, plus a creaking sound further in the background. Then he heard a human sound: a gasp. The banging increased in pace and volume, and the gasping sounds got louder. At first it was just woman's voice, and then a man joined in with a deeper grunt.

'Kirsty.'

Hearing his voice on the CD made him stamp on the brake. The car behind stopped just in time, the driver sounding her horn angrily. Jamie pulled over to the side of the road, out of the traffic. On the stereo, the gasping and groaning grew steadily louder. It was them. Making love.

They looked at each other in horror. Kirsty had gone pale.

'Jesus Christ.'

He pressed stop and ejected the CD. He was going to throw it out of the window but Kirsty stopped him. She said, 'We might need it. And I don't want anyone else to pick it up and listen to it.'

'They recorded us having sex. I can't believe it.'

'Jamie, it makes me feel violated.'

'I know. When the hell was this made? It can't have been last night. We were quiet last night, weren't we?'

She nodded. 'They must have already recorded this when they sent us the letter. Maybe we did make noise last night without realising it and they sent this as, what? A warning?' She shivered. 'I feel like I need a bath. It's horrible. Horrible.'

'What are we going to do?'

Jamie looked at the CD in his hand. He felt that awful sense of weariness weighing down on him. 'I really don't know. I guess we'll have to talk to them. Fucking Lucy and Chris. Christ, I thought we were meant to be friends.'

'There was no note with it?'

'No.'

'So we don't know for certain it's from them.'

'Kirsty, it has to be. There's nobody else, apart from maybe Mary, who could hear us having sex. Unless somebody stood outside our front door recording it on their phone or something. Which also brings Brian and Linda into the equation.'

'That's ridiculous.'

'Exactly. So it has to be the Newtons. It has to be.'

Kirsty imagined them in the flat below, holding a microphone up to the ceiling.

'So tonight, we'll go and talk to them, yes?'

The thought made Jamie feel nervous. He thought about Chris's physical strength, those muscles. But he couldn't allow himself to be a wimp or a coward. The Newtons had invaded their privacy. They had made Kirsty feel violated, as she put it. Something had to be done. So he said, 'Yes.'

'Hopefully we'll be able to sort something out sensibly, like adults.' She sighed. 'God, we really don't need this at the moment, do we?'

'No.' He put the CD in his pocket. He knew she wasn't only talking about Paul. She was talking about the thing that had happened last night – the knowledge that had come to them in that flash of light as he came inside her. 'We don't.'

Ten

It was still light when they returned home from work. The Newtons' car was parked in its usual spot. There were streaks of bird shit on the window on the passenger's side. Jamie knew Chris would be annoyed by this, as he always kept the car immaculately clean, soaping and waxing it every Sunday as if he was adhering to an age-old custom, passed down through the generations, father to son.

'We ought to get it over with now,' Kirsty said.

Jamie really didn't want to do this. He hated any sort of confrontation. Nothing in his experiences had prepared him or taught him to deal with a situation like this. Of course, he'd had run-ins with people before – at school, at work, in many different situations – but this situation had an edge to it: a weird edge. It made him feel nervous.

'Come on then,' he said.

They descended the concrete steps to the basement flat. Garden flat, Jamie reminded himself. He went down first, Kirsty a step behind him, holding onto the back of his shirt, pinching the cloth between her fingers. The space outside the Newtons' front door was very well kept, with small potted trees in the corners, and window boxes alive with pink and yellow flowers. There was a doormat with WELCOME spelled out on it and a ceramic plate displaying the house number, with the words Garden Flat added beneath.

Jamie rang the doorbell. He rubbed his palms – which had started to sweat – on the thighs of his trousers and held Kirsty's hand.

There was no answer.

'Maybe the bell doesn't work,' said Kirsty. 'Try knocking.'

Jamie lifted the letter box and banged several times, quite loudly. He stood upright, stretching to his full height. He had been practising what he was going to say all day, running through several variations, from angry ('How dare you record us.') to reasonable ('Let's talk this through, shall we?'), but now he felt thoroughly confused. He wasn't sure what he was going to say.

'The best thing,' Kirsty had said in the car on the way home, 'is to appeal to them as friends. After all, that's what we're meant to be. I mean, we were never going to be blood brothers and sisters, but we got on with them OK. I think once we've spoken to them – made contact – we'll be able to sort this out, nip it in the bud. The worst thing to do would be to go down there and start shouting at them.'

'You're right,' Jamie agreed. 'We'll simply explain to them that it isn't polite to record your neighbours having sex.'

Kirsty smiled, despite herself.

'They're definitely in,' she said, after Jamie had knocked on the door and they had waited ten seconds without a response. 'I can hear the TV. Knock again.'

Jamie did, rapping on the wood three times. There was still no answer.

'They don't want to talk to us,' he said. 'They must have seen it was us, but they're hiding.'

'Why would they do that?'

'I suppose they think we're going to have a go at them. No, actually, I've no idea what they think – I don't understand them at all any more.' He walked away and started to go up the steps. 'Come on. I don't want to waste any more of my time.'

Kirsty followed him. He walked purposefully into the living room and picked up the phone. 'I'm going to call the police. Tell them we're being harassed. It's got to be illegal, recording your neighbours having sex. Actually, it must be illegal recording your neighbours full stop.'

Kirsty stepped in and took the receiver from him. 'Jamie, if you get the police involved it will only make things worse. We've still got a chance to sort this out.'

'But they won't even answer the door to us.'

'So let's write them a letter. That's obviously how they want to communicate.'

She opened a desk drawer and took out a writing pad and a pen. Then she sat on the sofa and chewed the end of the pen thoughtfully.

'What are you going to put?'

'I don't know. You'll have to help me. I haven't written a letter on paper for years.'

Jamie sat beside her and, over the next hour, they composed a letter, Kirsty holding the pen because she had the neatest handwriting (Jamie had been using a keyboard to write everything for so long he had almost forgotten how to do joined-up writing), with Jamie looking over her shoulder, making suggestions.

Dear Lucy and Chris

We have to confess that we were surprised by your letter. We class ourselves as your friends, as well as your neighbours, and we would have thought that if you have a problem with the levels of noise (of whatever sort) coming from our flat you would have felt able to approach us in person. We could then discuss the situation as friends – and as adults.

As it is, the tone of your letter is very unpleasant, and we also find it difficult to express how unhappy we are that you recorded us. We insist that you delete the recording and destroy any physical copies you've made.

'Should we state that if they don't we're going to go to a solicitor?' said Jamie.

'Jamie, you know what I think. I don't think we should get too heavy – not yet anyway. I'm hoping we can sort this out among ourselves.'

'Yes. You're right.'

We will make sure that we don't play music loudly, and will try to ensure that we don't make any unnecessary, excessive noise. However, when you live in a flat you have to accept that you will experience a certain amount of noise from your neighbours, and you need to learn to tolerate this. For example, when you had your barbecue a fortnight ago we did not complain about the raucous laughter coming from your garden until late at night (or the smoke that came in through our back window).

We do hope that we can rebuild our relationship as neighbours, and live in harmony. We would like to discuss this, so feel free to visit us at any time.

Yours sincerely

Kirsty and Jamie

P.S. You may be interested to know that Paul is still in a coma following the accident. The doctors are unsure when – or even if – he will recover.

'Are you sure we should include the bit about the barbecue?' said Jamie.

Two weeks ago, Lucy and Chris and two other couples had stood in the Newtons' back garden, eating burnt sausages and telling bad jokes loudly. Jamie and Kirsty hadn't been at all disturbed by the event, although they both thought privately that it wasn't right that Lucy and Chris were out there having what they clearly saw as fun, while Paul lay in a hospital bed, especially when Lucy and Chris hadn't even asked how Paul was. Jamie was still outraged by this – almost as much as he was outraged by the letter and CD. He had insisted that Kirsty add the P.S. about Paul's condition. He wanted the Newtons to be reminded that Paul existed.

Kirsty considered Jamie's question about the barbecue. 'I don't see why not. We're making a valid point about neighbourly tolerance. Maybe it will make them see things from our point of view.'

They both signed the letter and sealed it in an envelope. Then they went outside to post it, Kirsty waiting at the top of the steps while Jamie ran down to put it through their neighbours' front door. The letter box closed with a loud thud and Jamie hurried back up the steps. Earlier, he would have been just about able to handle a confrontation. Now, though, he was tired, and he wanted to get indoors, to the safety of the flat, his haven.

They went back into the communal hallway and Kirsty closed the front door, the hinges squeaking noisily. They heard a door close above them and Mary came into view, heaving a large suitcase down the stairs. She smiled when she saw Jamie and Kirsty, and they waited for her to reach the bottom of the stairs. As she descended, the smell of some herb or flower that neither Jamie nor Kirsty recognised, drifted ahead of her.

'How are you both?' Mary asked in a concerned tone. Jamie had told her about Paul – who she said she had seen coming and going – when he had bumped into her a couple of weeks before.

'Oh, not bad. Just waiting to see what happens.' He shrugged sadly.

(Kirsty told Jamie later that she was convinced Mary was going to suggest some kind of herbal remedy to rouse Paul from his coma. 'If she had,' Kirsty said, 'I would have really lost my temper.')

'That's the worst part, isn't it? Waiting. Hoping time will heal.'

Jamie nodded. 'That's exactly right.'

Mary touched him at the top of his arm, then did the same to Kirsty. She opened her mouth to say something, then changed her mind.

'Are you going on holiday?' Jamie asked, gesturing towards the suitcase.

'I wish. But I'm going to a convention in Birmingham. It's a kind of trade fair for practitioners of alternative medicine. I go every year. Actually, I was going to come and knock on your door because I need to ask you a small favour. Would you mind feeding Lennon for me while I'm away? I'll only be gone three nights.'

'Sure. No problem at all.'

Mary fished her keys out of her bag and handed them to Jamie. 'I've left the tins of food on the worktop in the kitchen. He won't need feeding now until tomorrow morning. Half a tin morning and night.'

'I'll pop in before I go to work.'

'That's marvellous. Thank you so much.'

When Mary had gone and Jamie and Kirsty were in their flat, Kirsty said, 'I think she fancies you.'

'Don't be silly.'

'Haven't you noticed the way she looks at you?'

'What way?'

'Like she wants to eat you for breakfast.'

'You're loopy. Although, of course, one couldn't blame her if she had developed an overwhelming lust for someone as gorgeous as me. It would only be natural, after all.'

'That's right. I've had such a terrible life since we got together, fighting other women off you, never a moment's peace.'

Their laughter filled the flat, and as they laughed the tension in the air dissipated. Jamie put Mary's keys down on his desk, where the writing pad lay open, displaying the rough first draft of their letter.

'Do you want a drink?' he said, going to the fridge and taking out a bottle of wine.

'Hmm, yes please. I need one.'

That night, in bed, Jamie moved close to Kirsty and began to kiss her face and neck, stroking the silk-soft skin of her inner thigh. He moved down beneath the quilt and kissed her breasts and tummy, gradually moving lower until his head was between her legs. He kissed her and moved his tongue in slow circles around her clitoris, an action that usually made her groan and push herself against his face. Tonight, though, she didn't react. Something was wrong.

He tried again, pushing his tongue inside her, stroking her thighs with his palms, moving his tongue in motions that normally made her gasp. But still, she gave no reaction.

He shifted up the bed so he was lying beside her. 'What's wrong?'

'I'm not in the mood, Jamie.'

'Oh. OK.'

She kissed him, grimacing slightly at the taste of herself on his lips. 'I'd like to, but I can't really relax. Listening to that CD really freaked me out. Do you know what I mean?'

'I do.' He sighed. 'I still can't believe they did it.'

'When you started to go down on me just then I imagined that they were down there, listening, maybe even taping us. And I couldn't let go. I couldn't get into it.'

'Do you think they get some kind of perverted thrill out of it?'

'I don't know, Jamie. But do you remember all the things they said about the couple who lived here before us? Lucy even said something about noise that day at the go-kart track. They're obviously very sensitive to noise – more than we ever suspected. It seems crazy, though – to buy a flat when you're obsessed with peace and quiet: obsessed enough to make recordings of your neighbours to prove your point.' She sighed. 'Let's wait and see what reaction we get to our letter. Maybe we can sort this thing out.'

'Because otherwise we're going to have to soundproof the bedroom.'

They kissed goodnight and turned over to face their separate ways. Jamie kept his eyes open for a few minutes. His heart was beating fast. He wasn't able to sleep until his anger had subsided.

Beside him, Kirsty entered REM sleep and began to dream. She had the dream about the gingerbread house again. She ran through the woods, saw the beautiful, tempting house and went inside. This time, the witch was absent, and Kirsty saw that the door handles were actually the most delicious-looking toffee apples. She took one and bit into it.

Like Snow White, a piece of the poisoned apple caught in her throat and she fell to the floor. As her eyes closed she saw a figure standing over her. The figure was wearing a black cloak and hood and she couldn't make out if they were male or female. All she could see was a pair of eyes, glowing in the shadow cast by the hood.

She woke up sweating, turned over and put her arm around Jamie. With her hand on his chest, she could feel the rapid, angry beat of his heart. Both of them lay awake for a long time, not speaking. They were both thinking about Lucy and Chris. Kirsty felt as if the poison from the dreamt-of apple had stayed in her body, and was seeping into her bloodstream. It was the last thing she thought of before she finally got back to sleep: herself poisoned, in a coma, lying beside Paul.

'Right, I'll pop up and feed that cat.' Jamie picked up Mary's keys.

'I'll come with you.'

'It'll only take one of us.'

'I know. But I want to have a look at Mary's flat. I haven't been in there yet, unlike you, you tart. Always visiting strange women's flats while your poor, long-suffering girlfriend sobs alone at home.'

'Yes, I suppose I could show you the spot where she jumped on me and forced me to shag her.'

'Oh yes. That would be a treat.'

They were both a little shaky after a night of bad dreams, but neither of them wanted to show it, over-compensating with humour. Jamie had half-expected to find a letter from the Newtons on the doormat, but so far there was nothing. He couldn't decide if he was relieved or disappointed.

They went up to Mary's flat hand-in-hand, noting the rain that pattered against the window in the stairwell. Jamie unlocked the door, pushing it open cautiously. They went inside.

'Nice place,' said Kirsty. She looked around, scanning the bookshelves, inspecting the Pre-Raphaelite prints on the walls. There were numerous bottles of oils and essences laid out on the table, and she picked up a few and sniffed them. Joss stick holders and incense burners lined the mantelpiece. An Indian throw hung on one wall. There were carved figurines from Africa and Asia all over the place. 'It's bigger than our flat, isn't it?'

'It's exactly the same.'

Kirsty returned to the bookshelves. 'Look at these. *Enchanted. A Practical Guide to Magick. The Wiccan Arts.* Loads of books about black magic. Hey, maybe Lucy was right about her.'

Jamie crouched beside her and looked at one of the books. 'These are about white magic,' he said. 'But look, here's a truly Satanic tome: *The Reader's Digest Guide to Alternative Medicine.* Now where's that cat?'

His question was answered immediately as Lennon came padding into the room.

'Hi cat,' said Kirsty.

They went into the kitchen, found the supply of cat food and Jamie forked some of the meat onto a plastic dish. Lennon ate away happily.

'So,' Jamie said. ' Have you had a good enough nose around?'

'Yes thanks.' She looked at the floor. 'Actually, while we're up here, I want to try something. I want to see how sound carries between these flats. We hardly ever hear Mary moving around, do we? You go downstairs into our flat and I'll run around a bit.'

'OK.'

He went downstairs and stood in the living room, knowing that Kirsty was standing right above him. It was silent in the flat, and he cocked an ear to the ceiling. He heard a light padding sound; he thought he could hear someone talking, but very faintly. He went back upstairs.

'So what could you hear?' Kirsty asked.

'Hardly anything. Very light footsteps, some muffled talking – but I had to really listen hard. What were you doing?'

'I was running up and down the room. I jumped a couple of times, like this.' She jumped and landed heavily. 'And I put the TV on and turned it up loud. Like this.' She flicked the TV on and boosted the volume. 'Are you saying you couldn't hear that?'

'Hardly.'

'It doesn't make sense. It can't be that the floorboards in our flat are extra thin. Lucy and Chris must have really sensitive hearing.'

'Yeah. Like dogs.'

Kirsty was right. It didn't make sense.

Eleven

Jamie couldn't stand the smell of hospitals. The cloying stink of disinfectant; the vapour trails of anguish and pain and disease. He was glad that Kirsty showered and changed when she got home from work – he would hate it if that smell clung to her all evening instead of the clean, warm natural smells of her body. He sometimes felt that he had a more finely-tuned sense of smell than most people – a sensitivity that made it impossible for him to stay in certain malodorous places. When he drove past a crematorium, he could smell ashes and fumes. Public toilets contained many horrors. The stink of body odour on the Tube made him want to be sick. But the worst smell of all was the smell of hospitals.

He sat beside Paul's bed, sucking a mint, exhaling in sharp breaths so its smell replaced that of the hospital. Walking up the corridor this afternoon he had seen a porter hurriedly pushing a trolley on which there lay a dead body, covered from head to toe with a green sheet. Now Jamie looked at Paul, his chest rising and falling, the steady pulse of his heartbeat amplified electronically by the machines that monitored his condition, and felt a rush of gratitude and relief: Paul was still alive, and whatever else happened, that was a blessing to cling to. Every morning, a nurse came to give Paul a wash and a shave.

Periodically, hospital staff trimmed his nails and cut his hair. In fact, Heather had asked if she could cut his hair herself and, having done so, she carried a lock with her in her bag. Jamie thought that was pretty morbid himself, but he understood Heather's motivation. Paul's body was still functioning – growing, aging, shedding, replenishing; all the things that bodies do. These things were a tangible reminder that Paul was still with them.

Jamie sat silently as usual. He had spoken to Dr Meer earlier, who said there had been no change in Paul's condition. Jamie wondered how far beneath the surface Paul was, if he was making any progress that they couldn't see. He wondered if, in his comatose state, Paul dreamed – and, if so, what he dreamed of. Women, probably. Megan Fox mud-wrestling with Rihanna.

He stood up. It was six o'clock – time to meet Kirsty and take her home. As he was about to leave the room he turned round and looked down at his friend. He could have sworn he had moved. He bent over him, holding his breath, searching for signs of movement or change. There were none.

'Must have imagined it,' he murmured to himself. He touched Paul's cheek. It was warm.

He walked back down the corridor and up a long flight of stairs. A pair of nurses passed him as he headed towards the children's ward. They recognised him, and smiled. After they'd passed by he heard them laugh, and he felt a stab of paranoia, convinced they were laughing at him. He hurried on, suddenly desperate to be out of here, away from the smell and the people and the bright, sterile lighting. He wanted to be at home.

But when he thought of home, he felt anxious too.

All day he had been haunted by a creeping sense of unease. Last night, they had written and delivered the letter to Lucy and Chris. Writing the letter had made him feel better, but after he'd got to work this morning he'd started to worry about what their response would be. Mike, the guy who sat opposite him at work, had asked him if he was alright, commenting that he seemed really spaced out, and Jamie had snapped at him, told him to mind his own business, feeling immediately remorseful. It was so rare for him to feel like this – he was usually so relaxed and easy-going. But he wanted today over with. Maybe tomorrow would be a better day.

'Hiya darling,' said Kirsty, when they met outside the main entrance. He was so pleased to see her he almost burst into tears.

'Are you alright? You look–'

He nodded quickly. 'I just want to get home.'

'OK.'

Kirsty took the wheel because Jamie didn't feel in the mood to tackle the traffic. He couldn't even stand listening to the radio. The news gave him a headache so he turned it off and they drove home in silence, Jamie resting his head against the window, gazing out at the city streets.

Litter twisted and turned as it danced along the pavement from the high street McDonalds. A group of boys stood on the corner outside the off-license, trying to persuade passers-by to go in to buy them some beer, hurling abuse after everyone who said no. A young Asian woman in a business suit stood at a bus stop, studying her reflection in the sheen of the glass that covered an advert for health insurance, reapplying her lipstick. A fat man stood close by with a Staffordshire bull terrier on a lead. The dog shivered as it pushed out a large turd, then the man produced a plastic bag and a scoop, cleaning up after his pet before hurrying away. Somewhere up ahead, a police car's siren wailed histrionically before stopping dead. This evening, the city seemed tawdry and sad. Jamie heard himself sigh. Kirsty touched his leg.

'Do you want to pick up a Chinese on the way home?'

'I'm not really hungry.'

'Suit yourself.'

He stretched out a hand and stroked her soft hair. 'I'm sorry, sweetheart. It's just, I don't know – I feel really down today.'

'Was it seeing Paul?'

'No, not really. In fact, seeing Paul made me feel slightly better, in a strange way. I guess I've been worrying about Lucy and Chris. I've got this horrible feeling that we're going to arrive home and find our windows smashed.'

'You are silly.'

'I know. But what if we don't get any response at all?'

'Oh I think we will.'

They pulled into Mount Pleasant Street and saw that the Newtons' car was parked in its customary position. Kirsty parked and they got out and went inside. Jamie checked the post. Among the junk mail was a handwritten envelope with no stamp. It was addressed to The Ground Floor Flat.

'This is it,' said Jamie, feeling his throat go dry.

Kirsty took it from him and carefully unsealed the envelope. She read the letter aloud:

HOW DARE YOU complain about the noise we made when we had our barbecue. Our friends were shocked and appalled that you have described them as having raucous laughter. I can't believe what hypocrites you are, especially as we have to endure the sound of your own shrieking and guffawing day and night. We can tell you that we will have our friends over whenever we like and will stay up as late as we like. YOU CANNOT tell us what we can and can't do. We believe in live and let live. Why don't you adopt the same philosophy?

Kirsty and Jamie stared at each other, dumbfounded.

"I'm absolutely...speechless,' said Jamie.

'*You cannot tell us what we can and cannot do.* Jesus wept. And this bit – *we believe in live and let live.*'

'Do you think they're being ironic?'

'No, I think they mean it.' She shook her head in disbelief.

Jamie read the letter through again, and as he did so he felt all the unhappiness and frustrations of the day stir up inside him, turning to anger, a rush of blood to his head that made his ears feel hot and his skull feel too tight around his brain. How dare they? How fucking dare they?

'I'm going down there.'

'Jamie...'

He ignored her and stormed out of the flat, out through the front door and down the steps. He banged on the Newtons' door, then banged again, harder.

'Come out here,' he shouted. 'I want to talk to you.'

Bang bang bang.

'Come on out!'

When there was no reply he ran back up the steps, brushing past Kirsty and marching through the flat into the bathroom. He unbolted the back door and went down the steps from the balcony into the garden.

The second his foot touched the grass at the bottom of the steps, Lucy came out of her own back door, waving her arms angrily.

'Get out of my garden.'

Jamie flapped the letter at her. 'I want an explanation of this. And I want you to erase the recordings you've made of us. Now.'

She shook her head. 'Get out or I'll call the police.'

'Go on then, and I'll tell them how you've been harassing us – recording us illegally. I'd like to see you explain that to them.'

She ignored him. 'Chris. Chris!' she called. 'Phone the police. Tell them we've got a trespasser.'

Jamie looked up at Kirsty, who was leaning over the balcony. He felt exasperated, unable to believe this was really happening. It was crazy. Completely stupid. He tried to see through the Newtons' open door, to see if Chris really was there. Half of him wanted Lucy to call the police. But really, he just wanted to get this whole, ridiculous mess sorted out.

He lowered his voice. 'Look, Lucy, can't we talk about this? We're supposed to be friends, aren't we? Let's sit down and talk about it.'

'No! I'm going to count to ten.'

'Let me speak to Chris.'

She smiled with one half of her mouth, a horrible, lopsided expression that made her look unhinged. 'Oh, you wouldn't want to talk to Chris right now. Let me tell you. You really wouldn't want to.'

'I bet he's not even in…'

'Lucy,' Kirsty called from above. 'Why are you being like this?'

Lucy's face had gone pink. Jamie thought she looked like she was about to burst something. 'How do you expect me to react when you write me threatening, insulting letters?'

'But it wasn't threatening. We were trying to make peace. And you wrote to us first.'

Lucy shook her head violently. 'No I didn't.'

'But Lucy, we've got the letter to prove it.'

Lucy threw her arms in the air and turned round, putting her hand on the door handle. In a calm, quiet voice, she said, 'I really am going to call the police now.' As she went inside, Lennon ran out of her flat and bounded up the garden. Jamie looked up at Kirsty as if to say, Did you see that?

Kirsty said, 'Jamie, come on, get back up here.'

He walked up the stairs slowly, defeated. The moment he got back inside and Kirsty shut the door, he started to shake. Kirsty put her arm around his shoulders, pulling his body against hers. 'I'll get you a drink.'

He sat on the sofa and Kirsty handed him a beer. He drank it without tasting it. All his life he had tried to avoid conflict – shying away from arguments, never going near a fight – and the scene with Lucy left him feeling shocked and numb. He could hardly believe it had happened to him. She had been so aggressive and irrational. When confronted with something as crazy as this, he didn't know how to react. It left him floundering.

'She's mental,' he said, looking up at Kirsty.

She sat beside him.

'Completely mental.'

Kirsty kissed him just above the cheekbone. 'I was kind of proud of you, though.'

'Why? What do you mean?'

'I don't know. Seeing you stand up for us. I know you want a quiet life, and I thought you'd always shy away from confrontation. It was actually quite nice to see you get passionate about something – to get angry.'

'I'm often passionate.'

She smiled. 'Yes, I know. But I don't mean in that way.' She paused and sipped her beer. 'But you're right – she's mental. Mad as a bloody hatter.'

'But what are we going to do?'

'I don't...'

The doorbell rang. They froze and looked at each other. 'Who is it?' Jamie whispered.

Kirsty stood up and crept to the front window, peering through the crack in the curtains. She turned and faced Jamie, her eyes wide. 'It's the police.'

'She really called them! I don't believe it.'

'But this is good, Jamie. It gives us the opportunity to tell them what's been going on.'

'You're right.'

Jamie went out into the hall and opened the front door. Two policemen stood there, one of them looking over his shoulder towards their car, which had already attracted the attention of several children, who crowded round it, peering in through the windows and – in the policeman's mind – threatening to remove the wheels and smash the headlights.

Jamie said, 'Can I help?'

The older policeman said, 'Can we come in, sir?'

Jamie shrugged. 'Sure.'

They followed him into the flat, the younger policeman seemingly reluctant to leave his car at the mercy of the local hooligans. Eventually, he managed to tear himself away, but it was obvious his mind wasn't going to be on the job.

'Would you like a cup of tea? Coffee?' Kirsty offered, as soon as the policemen were inside and Jamie had shut the door.

'That would be smashing,' said the older policeman, and his colleague nodded. 'Yeah, I'd like a tea, please.'

The older man turned to Jamie. 'I'm PC Dodds, this is PC Sutton. We've had a complaint.'

'We know what this is about,' Jamie said. 'And I can tell you right now, it's all a load of crap, whatever they've said about us.'

Sutton wandered across the room and looked at Jamie's computer, then moved over to the window and looked out in the direction of his car.

'What do you mean by that?' said Dodds, having to speak up above the roar of the boiling kettle.

'Well, tell me what Lucy and Chris said about us and I'll tell you what I mean.'

Sutton came back towards them. 'We've had a complaint that you were trespassing in your neighbours' garden.'

Jamie shook his head. 'I knew it.' He sighed. 'This whole thing is a total waste of your time. But I'll tell you the story from the beginning.'

He waited until the drinks were ready, then gestured for Dodds and Sutton to sit down.

'We moved in here in the summer.' He told them how they had befriended the Newtons, inviting them to dinner, chatting with them whenever they saw them, seemingly getting along fine. 'Then we went go-karting with them, and that's when everything went weird. Our friends Heather and Paul came along too, and Paul had an accident, suffered awful head injuries. He's in a coma right now.' He swallowed. 'The thing is, Chris was involved in the accident. He and Paul were racing, and, well, we don't blame Chris – it was an accident – but since then neither Chris nor Lucy have spoken to us. It's as if they're pissed off with us – as if we'd done something to one of their friends. We didn't really think much of it at first, though we were a bit annoyed that they made no effort to find out how Paul was. They didn't even send a card.'

'And then we received the first letter,' said Kirsty. 'I'll show it to you.'

While she dug out the letters from the desk, Jamie said, 'Basically, the Newtons are harassing us. For no reason. No reason that we can fathom anyway.'

Kirsty handed Dodds the first letter. He read it, then passed it to Sutton, who smirked as he read it. He looked at Kirsty and raised his eyebrows. Jamie could read the young policeman's mind. Noisy sex. He was wondering if it was true.

'We were really surprised by the letter. Firstly, we're not really noisy.' Jamie cleared his throat, suddenly feeling embarrassed. 'And secondly, we didn't understand why they couldn't come up here and talk to us. They didn't even refer to us by our names in the letter. We thought it was really odd.'

Dodds leaned forward, nodding sympathetically.

'And then we received the CD.'

'The CD? Of what?'

'Um...it was a recording of us having sex. They'd obviously set up a mike in their bedroom and recorded us. The noises on the CD are a bit muffled, but still quite loud. I can't believe that we sound so loud downstairs.'

'Have you still got the CD?' Sutton asked, looking at Kirsty.

'Yes, but...'

'We don't need to hear it,' said Dodds, giving his younger colleague a filthy look.

'We've got the CD,' said Jamie, 'and we know that Lucy and Chris must have the original file on their computer. We wrote to them, trying to be reasonable. This was after we'd been down there, trying to talk to them. But they wouldn't answer the door to us.'

'Did you keep a copy of your letter to them?'

'No. We had a rough draft but we threw it away. Shit, I wish we had kept a copy, but we thought our letter would resolve the situation.'

'What did your letter say?'

'Just that we thought we were friends and that we should be able to sort out any problems by talking about them. It was a very reasonable letter, except that we made the mistake of mentioning their barbecue. We were trying to make the point that when you live in a flat you have to be willing to put up with a small amount of noise – it's just the way it is. A little while ago they had a barbecue, which was quite noisy, and went on late, and we stressed in the letter that we didn't complain about their barbecue, so why should they complain about us? This is what we got back.'

He nodded to Kirsty who handed Dodds the second letter.

'We got this one this evening. I was so annoyed I went down to try to talk to them, but again they wouldn't answer the door. So I went down the back steps from our bathroom into their garden. I was just going to knock on the back door. I wanted to talk to them. That's all.'

'Lucy came out,' said Kirsty, 'shouting and making threats. She said she'd call the police, and after Jamie had tried to reason with her, he came back up the steps. That's the whole story. Jamie was not trespassing.'

Dodds stood up. 'OK. Well, obviously we'll have to speak to Mr and Mrs Newton, but as far as I'm concerned this trespassing thing isn't worth pursuing. I don't think going into your neighbour's garden to talk to them counts as the crime of the year. However, I should remind you that if someone asks you to leave their property, and you don't do so straight away, they have every right to call the police.'

'I understand that,' said Jamie. 'But what about Lucy and Chris's harassment of us? What can we do about that?'

Dodds shrugged. 'The only thing I can suggest is that you keep a log, a record, of what goes on. Keep any correspondence between you, including copies of anything you send to them. In fact, I'd strongly suggest that you stop writing to them – and that if you really do need to write to them you do it through a solicitor.'

'So you're not going to do anything?'

'What can we do?' said Sutton. 'They haven't done anything illegal. They haven't threatened violence, they haven't written anything obscene. They've just complained about the noise they say you make.'

'But what about the CD?' said Kirsty. 'Surely that's obscene.'

'I don't know,' smirked Sutton, 'I haven't heard it.'

Dodds said, 'It's perfectly legal to make a recording within the confines of your own home. People do it all the time if they're trying to make a case with the Environmental Health people against noisy neighbours.'

'But we're not noisy neighbours,' protested Kirsty. 'Neither of us have ever had problems with any other neighbours we've had.'

'I didn't say you were noisy. But the Newtons obviously think you are. It might be an idea to check with the council, see if your neighbours have complained about you to them. If they complain about you seriously, the council will send someone round to measure the amount of decibels coming from your flat.'

'I wish they would. It would make Lucy and Chris look bloody stupid.'

'Well, perhaps. But I think you should try to ignore them. Just get on with your lives. Keep any letters they send you, and let us know if they do make any threats, but otherwise try not to provoke them. I'm sure in time this will all blow over.'

Jamie saw the policemen out. Sutton looked profoundly relieved that their car was still in one piece.

'We're just going to call on Mr and Mrs Newton now,' said Dodds. 'We'll tell them we've had a word with you and that you won't go uninvited into their garden again, OK?'

'OK. Are you going to mention the letters and the CD?'

'Do you want me to?'

Jamie thought about it for a second. 'I think it would only antagonise them.'

'I agree.' Dodds paused and looked up at the house. 'Nice place you've got here. Must have set you back a bit.'

'It took us to the limit of what we could afford. But we love it. It's everything we want in a home. And we don't want it to be spoiled by a pair of nightmare neighbours.'

Dodds nodded. 'The way I see it, it's like a new cat moving in next to an established cat's territory. The established cat gets a bit fidgety, a bit jealous of its domain. But once it's shown the new cat where the boundaries lie, it settles down. That's what's happening here. Don't worry. In six months you'll all be right as rain. You'll probably be inviting them for dinner again.'

Jamie didn't think much of the policeman's cat metaphor. But he nodded and said, ' I don't know about inviting them to dinner. But I hope you're right. I really do.'

Twelve

The Tube train shuddered and groaned as it pulled out of the station. Kirsty had managed to grab the last seat in the carriage, beating a man with a combover to it by a whisker. Now he stood over her, hanging on to the overhead rail, the *tssk-tssk-tssk* that emanated from his headphones worming its way into her head. All around her people wore frowns, staring into their own personal spaces, wishing the journey away. A woman at one end of the carriage was eating a Big Mac, the gherkin and meat stink filling the train. There was a man with an acoustic guitar at the other end of the carriage, and Kirsty was worried that he would start playing at any moment, bashing out some tuneless rendition of a Beatles standard before lurching along the carriage with his hand out, demanding his reward.

God, she hated the Tube. If the man with the guitar did turn out to be a busker he wouldn't get anything out of her. She had already given away the last of her spare change to a woman sitting outside the station. Kirsty passed dozens of homeless people every day, and simply couldn't afford to hand money over very often, but this woman (this girl – she couldn't have been older than sixteen) had been holding a baby. The sight had chilled Kirsty, and she had reached into her bag and taken out her purse, emptying the coins into her palm and handing them to the girl. This certainly wasn't the first homeless girl with a baby she had come across, but it was the first since she had found out.

She rested her hands on her stomach, feeling the need to be protective, wishing she wasn't down here, in the unnatural heat, God-knows-how-many diseases drifting around. She should have got the bus, or taken a taxi. But there had been a part of her that had wanted to play the martyr, so that when she got home she could say to Jamie, 'I had to go on the Tube because of you.'

She wondered how he would react when she told him – not that she had been on the Tube, but that she was pregnant. OK, she didn't know for certain. She hadn't taken a test yet. But her period was four days late, which was unheard of for her, Miss Regular As Clockwork. And she had known anyway. She had felt it at the moment of conception, and she had a feeling Jamie had known too. She was sure he would be delighted – she knew he really wanted children – but was this the right time?

Yes. Yes it was. Despite everything that had been going on. Or maybe even because of it.

She had been thinking about telling him tonight. She knew he wouldn't be keeping track of her period (he was always surprised when it arrived – 'What, already? Surely it hasn't been a month?'), and he had been preoccupied lately anyway, so she knew she wouldn't be telling him something he already knew, even if he had felt the same sensation as her when it had happened. But she was pissed off with him now. He'd been supposed to pick her up from work, she had waited out the front of the hospital for half-an-hour and he hadn't turned up. She' gone back inside to ask if there had been any phone calls. There hadn't so, in a huff, she had stomped off towards the Tube station. He had forgotten about her. How could he?

To her horror, the man with the guitar pulled it to his stomach and began to play a tune. He did the first verse and chorus of 'She Loves You' then stopped and asked everyone in the carriage for cash. I should have been a fortune teller, Kirsty thought. She put her head down and made certain she didn't catch the busker's eye. Thankfully, the train pulled into a station before he reached her, and he got off.

She still couldn't believe Jamie had forgotten about her. It was very unlike him. What if he hadn't forgotten? What if something had happened to him? She hadn't been able to get hold of him on his mobile. She had a sudden image of him crashing the car, his head going through the windscreen, shards of glass spraying passers-by as Jamie bounced back in his seat, his lifeless body slumping. She quickly shook away the image. It was replaced by an image of him being attacked in the street, a mugger stabbing him in the chest and grabbing his wallet, Jamie falling to the pavement, soaked in his own blood, grabbing his chest as his life ebbed away.

What was wrong with her? Why did she have to think of such things? She felt beads of cool sweat stand out on her forehead. She looked at her watch. Ten more minutes before this awful journey ended – if they didn't get delayed, that was. She didn't feel angry with him any more. She just wanted to get home, to check that he was alright. There had to be a good explanation for his absence. She only hoped something hadn't happened with Lucy and Chris.

Since the night the police had been round, they hadn't spoken to the Newtons. Nor had they received any letters, or CDs, from them – not directly anyway. Instead, they had been flooded with hoaxes. Letters, parcels and phone calls. Even emails sent from an anonymous Hotmail account, although neither of them could work out how Lucy and Chris had found out their email addresses (which Jamie had now changed). Of course, none of the hoaxes carried their neighbours' names, but they knew who was responsible – just like they now knew who had been responsible for the first wave of hoaxes that had started almost as soon as they moved in.

There had been letters from credit card and insurance companies; circulars from Christian organisations; free samples of beauty products that Kirsty might have been pleased with if they hadn't been so obviously intended to offend: anti-wrinkle cream, hair dye to cover up those grey hairs, cream to rub into your cellulite, wax strips to remove unwanted facial hair. They had received more offers and parcels from websites and magazines, including subscriptions to the Shooting Times, and a porn magazine called Barely Legal, which was full of girls who looked underage but weren't really. They were sent several monstrosities from 'Collectables' companies, such as a porcelain clown that made Kirsty feel physically sick to look at, and a plate commemorating the Royal birth. All of this had to go back, which involved a phone call to the company and a trip to the post office, with a wait for the return label to arrive in between. It was inconvenient and stressful.

'Why don't we just dump them on Lucy and Chris's doorstep?' Jamie asked.

'Because then we'll get billed for them. And there's no way I want to be taken to court for not paying for DoDo the Ugly Clown or whatever he's called. Just enter it in the log. If we ever do end up in court, this will all be evidence.'

One thing they had done was ask the various mail order companies to send them scans of the original order forms. Several of the companies responded happily (they weren't happy that they had been hoaxed either) and when the forms arrived it gave Jamie and Kirsty the final piece of evidence they needed. Because all the forms were filled out in the same handwriting. And the handwriting matched that on the letters Lucy and Chris had sent them.

Jamie phoned the police station and asked for Constable Dodds. He told him about the handwriting.

'That's good to have, although it's not much use on its own. It's hardly the crime of the year.' Jamie realised this was one of Dodds' favourite phrases. 'Hold on to it and make sure you keep a record of everything, including conversations you have with the mail order companies. But I'd still advise you to hold fire for now. Sooner or later these people are going to get bored, I promise you.'

'What did they say when you went down there to see them?'

'To be honest, they didn't say very much. We told them we'd asked you not to enter their garden uninvited again, and they thanked us. That was pretty much it.'

'Were they both there? Lucy and Chris?'

'Yes. But she did all the talking.'

'I can believe that.'

When Kirsty and Jamie discussed the situation, which they did every evening, they found that without realising it they had begun to focus their anger and upset onto Lucy. She had become the arch villain, while Chris was just her sidekick, an acolyte who, despite being married to her, didn't share her insanity. It was always her writing on the application forms; it was her who stood in the garden and shouted at Jamie, while Chris hid inside. Jamie wondered if it would be worth trying to talk to Chris alone, to see if he could reason with him, man to man.

'No,' said Kirsty, when he suggested this. 'Stay away from them both. We might be wrong. Chris might be the driving force behind this. And the more I think about it, the more I blame him for what happened to Paul. If he hadn't taken us karting...'

That had been one of the most sickening pieces of mail they had received: an invitation to join the National Go-Karting Association. Jamie had marched down to the basement flat and rammed it through their letter box, fighting the temptation to put a brick through their window. The letter had made Kirsty cry, and only a great effort of willpower stopped her from going down and throwing that brick through their window herself.

She hated them. She had never hated anyone before, not like this anyway. She realised it was unhealthy, especially if she was pregnant. It would do her no good to fill her body with hateful poisons, to let malice and spite drip into her bloodstream. She had to stay calm, relax, chill.

And she had to get off this fucking Tube train.

Finally it halted at her stop, and she pushed her way through the hot, closely-crammed bodies onto the platform, where she gulped down air like she had just crossed the desert and the air was fresh water.

As she approached the flat, she saw Jamie's car. So he was home. She sighed with relief. She had almost begun to convince herself that something terrible had happened to him. Now, though, she wanted to know why he hadn't turned up at the hospital.

Walking up the path, she spotted Lennon, looking down at her from Mary's front window. A moment later, Mary appeared at the window. She waved and Kirsty waved back. Mary had bought them an expensive bottle of wine to say thank you to them for feeding Lennon while she was away. Kirsty was glad they had already drunk it, because if her suspicions were right, she wouldn't be able to drink for a while.

As soon as she got inside, Jamie hurried across the room and hugged her. 'Oh God, I'm so sorry,' he said. 'I was stuck in a meeting and my phone battery died and I couldn't find my charger. There's loads of shit going on at work – they're saying that this takeover might really be going ahead, and everyone was called into a big meeting that went on all afternoon. I couldn't get to a phone, and when I did finally escape I called the hospital and they told me you'd already left, so I came straight home.'

She kissed his cheek. 'It's OK, Jamie. Don't worry.'

'You're not angry?'

'Well, you will have to make it up to me.' She flopped down on the sofa.

He crouched in front of her and unlaced her shoes. 'A foot massage?'

'Mmm, that would be lovely. And a cup of tea.'

'Your wish is my command.'

She leaned back and closed her eyes as he rubbed her heels with his thumbs. It felt good. 'Any post?'

'The usual junk. A letter from Oxfam asking why you hadn't set up the direct debit you'd promised to after you told them you were going to sponsor a child.'

'Jesus.'

'And shortly before you got home, a taxi turned up and an extremely pissed-off driver told me he'd been sent here to take a couple to Battersea Dogs Home. When I told him we hadn't called him and that he'd been hoaxed he wasn't very happy, to say the least.'

'Have you written it all down?'

'Oh yes.'

Kirsty sighed. A broken promise to sponsor a poor child. This had gone beyond the realms of good taste long ago. She took deep breaths to keep her anger at bay, concentrating on the pleasant feelings in her feet as Jamie massaged them. She rested her hands on her stomach. Tomorrow she would go to the doctor, find out for certain. It was about time they had some good news.

Thirteen

Jamie twisted the wire and popped the cork, watched it bounce off the ceiling, stuck the foaming bottle-top in his mouth then poured himself a glass. He kissed Kirsty with champagne-flavoured lips. She held out her own glass.

'It's apple juice for you, I'm afraid.'

'Oh, it's so unfair. Nine months teetotal. I can't believe it.'

'Longer if you breastfeed.'

'God. Don't remind me.' But as she said it, she grinned. She hadn't stopped grinning since the test confirmed her instincts. Apart from five minutes on the way home, when she had sat on a wall on the edge of the park and pondered the enormous changes that were about to happen in their lives. She thought about money, work, sleep, her social life, her figure, and then she dismissed it all and the grin returned. This was what she wanted, more than anything else in the world. She was going to be a mother. What's more, she was going to a be a damn good mother. And she was with a man she loved, and she knew Jamie would make a fabulous dad. He had always talked about wanting a daughter, a little girl who would look up to him for love and protection, until she became a stroppy teenager, and if she was anything like Kirsty – who made her parents' lives a misery for about four years – she would be a nightmare. But that was a long way off. And anyway, Kirsty and Jamie were going to be friends with their kids. They would be proud to bring their friends home; they wouldn't have any secrets; they would talk openly about sex and drugs and all the other things that drove wedges between parents and children.

Kirsty smiled at her own naiveté. And then, sitting on the wall with football-playing boys looking on, she burst into tears. Big, fat, tears of happiness and relief. She could forget about Lucy and Chris now. She could forget about all the bad shit in her life (apart from Paul – she would never forget about Paul) because she had something wonderful to focus on.

'I guess a son would be cool, as well,' said Jamie now, guzzling champagne. 'We could play football, and computer games.'

'You can do that with a daughter too.'

'Yes. Actually, I don't care what we have. Hey, maybe it will be twins. One of each. That would be excellent.'

'Don't push it.'

Jamie kissed her again and ran his hand over her tummy. It was perfectly flat now, but soon it would start to bulge. He couldn't wait. There was something so sexy about pregnancy. Right now, he felt so proud of himself. OK, so any idiot could get a woman pregnant – and you only had to turn on the TV on any weekday morning to see exactly how many idiots did manage to make women pregnant – but it was a great feeling to know that he was capable of doing so too. He felt

immensely virile and potent. He was helping propagate the species –
he felt like beating his chest and making Tarzan noises. Right now he
felt like the luckiest man alive, and he wanted to celebrate.

'Let's have a bath,' he said. 'And then I'll take you out for a meal.'

They ran the bath and stripped off amid the swirling steam. 'I'm
sure your boobs have grown already,' Jamie said, as Kirsty settled into
the water.

She shook her head. 'You wish.'

'Well, they will grow won't they? God, there's so much I don't
know about pregnancy and babies. I'll have to look it up on the net.
Soon we probably won't be able to fit in the bath together.'

'No. I'm going to get really fat and stay fat and turn into one of
those earth mothers. In fact, we'll have to buy a new, extra large bath
because this one won't be big enough for me. I'll look like a Buddha,
with breasts like water melons.'

'Fantastic.'

They roared with laughter, and Jamie leaned forward quickly to kiss
Kirsty, sending a wave through the water which surged up and
splashed over the side of the bath.

'Oops.'

'Don't worry about it. Just kiss me.'

'So does being pregnant make you feel sexy?'

'Hmm. Although when I get bigger it'll be awkward.'

'We'll have to try out some new positions.'

163

'Hmm.'

He shifted forward and went up onto his knees. As he did this he slipped and banged his hip against the side of the bath.'

'Ah!'

Kirsty laughed. 'What a smooth operator.'

'Hey, you won't be able to criticise me in front of our child.'

'No. I shall always have to refer to you as My Hero.'

They laughed again, and immediately heard three loud bangs which echoed through the bathroom.

They stared at the floor.

'Oh my God, Lucy's got her broom out,' said Kirsty. Normally she would have got upset, but today she found it funny. It made her laugh even more loudly, provoking more banging.

'The witch is banging her broom,' said Jamie, making a v-sign and aiming it at the floor. 'She can't stand the sound of other people's happiness.'

'Miserable witch,' said Kirsty. Then she said it louder: 'Miserable witch.'

The bangs that followed made Jamie and Kirsty fall silent, staring at each other. BANG BANG BANG. It sounded as if the broom was going to come through the floorboards – and worse, the banging was accompanied by an ear-shredding scream.

'Oh my God.'

'She must have heard us.'

'I thought you meant her to.'

'Well…'

It didn't seem so funny any more. Jamie looked at the back door. He had a horrible image of Chris storming up the steps and smashing down the back door, which was only made of thin wood. The scream had made his blood run cold. Suddenly, he wanted to get out of the bath and get dressed.

He stood up and grabbed his towel. He looked at the carpet. There was a big wet patch around the edge of the bath. He imagined he could hear Lucy breathing beneath his feet. He knew she would be standing there, looking up at the ceiling, and, ridiculously, he felt vulnerable in his nudity. He dried himself vigorously and as soon as he was dry enough he pulled on his underwear.

Kirsty stood up. Water rolled down from beneath her breasts over her belly and dripped from her pubic hair. Jamie saw her touching her tummy and smiled. Why was he allowing himself to get so stressed out? He should calm down, chill out, enjoy this momentous day. There were more important things to think about than their neighbours.

'We're going to be alright, aren't we?' Kirsty said, still standing up in the bath, the water level descending slowly from her calves to her ankles, swirling down the plughole. Jamie imagined the water pouring through the ceiling onto Lucy's head, soaking her comically, and he smiled.

He bent and pressed his cheek against Kirsty's warm belly. 'Of course we are.'

The Cinnamon Tree was their favourite Indian restaurant. It was situated in a quiet backstreet, just a ten minute walk from the flat. It was a small restaurant which hadn't changed its decor since the early eighties, but the food was fantastic and cheap – or good value, as Kirsty preferred to put it.

It was a Wednesday, and the restaurant was only half full. Jamie and Kirsty took a table in the corner beside an enormous rubber plant. They ordered drinks – lager for Jamie, sparkling mineral water for Kirsty – and samosas for starters.

'I wonder if you'll develop any weird cravings later on,' Jamie said.

'Maybe. One woman at work had a craving for Cadbury's Creme Eggs. She ate about six or seven a day. She suffered terribly from morning sickness as well.'

'Hmm, I wonder if there was a connection.'

'I've read about women who have cravings for coal or wood. I'll probably just crave pizza and ice cream. And curries, of course.'

'And what kind of curry are you craving tonight?'

'Something mild I think. Vegetable korma with pilau rice.'

'Sounds good. I'll go for something a bit spicier.'

Their drinks arrived and Jamie drained a third of his pint in one go, gulping it down thirstily.

'Take it easy, Jamie.'

'Sorry.'

'You've been drinking an awful lot recently. You won't be able to carry on like that.'

'I know. We won't be able to afford it for one thing.'

'Are you worried about the cost of having this baby?'

He shrugged. 'I haven't had a chance to think about it yet. But no – I'm not too worried.'

'I'll have to go part-time, and nurseries around here are so expensive.'

'We'll be fine. There are people a lot worse off than us who get by.'

She touched his hand. 'I'm so glad you're so positive about this.'

'Why, did you think I'd be unhappy?'

'No. I knew you'd be pleased. It's just that with all that's been going on, I thought you might think the timing was bad.'

He placed both his hands over hers. 'Kirsty, we wanted this baby. That was understood from the moment you told me you'd stopped taking the pill. God, we could worry about the timing all our lives, and there'd always be something to make us want to wait. As far as I'm concerned, now is the perfect time. I don't want to sound like a drippy git, but I want us to be a family.'

She smiled. 'You do sound like a drippy git.'

'Ah well, sod it. Sometimes, a man's got to be drippy.'

The samosas came, along with a large pile of poppadoms, and they began to eat.

'This is gorgeous, isn't it Jamie?' There was no answer. 'Jamie?'

He was staring over her shoulder at the door, a samosa held in front of his open mouth.

'Jamie, what is it?'

He spoke quietly. 'Don't look over your shoulder, but guess who's just walked in.'

When somebody said, 'Don't look, but,' Kirsty was, without fail, compelled to look.

She wished she hadn't. 'Oh God. I don't believe it.'

Lucy and Chris came in through the front door and Chris spoke to the nearest waiter. They were directed to a table over the other side of the restaurant, close to the kitchens. They didn't look over at Jamie and Kirsty. Jamie thought they looked a little tense and on edge. Maybe they weren't used to eating out. Something about they way Chris studied the menu; the way that Lucy was ever-so-slightly overdressed for this modest backstreet Indian: it pointed to the fact that they weren't sure of the etiquette or the rules. They were more used to dining at home.

'Do you think they followed us?' Kirsty whispered, leaning across the table, not taking her eyes off her neighbours.

Jamie shook his head. 'No. It's got to be a coincidence. I mean, this is the local Indian, after all. Most people who live around here come to this place. Although they don't look like they've ever been here before.'

Chris was looking around, apparently studying the decor, and he looked straight over and caught Jamie's eye. Jamie immediately broke contact, fixing his vision on the tablecloth.

'They've seen us,' he said, and Kirsty looked over to find both Chris and Lucy gazing back at her.

'Shit. Did Chris look surprised to see you?'

'No. No, he didn't. Not at all.'

They let that fact sink in. Kirsty glanced over and saw that the waiter was standing by the Newtons' table, taking their order. Then Lucy stood up and followed the waiter out to the kitchens.

'What's she doing?'

'God knows.'

'Do you think she's friends with them?'

'Maybe she's an undercover health inspector.' He laughed. 'Actually, I expect she's asked if she can see the kitchen, so she can make sure everything's hygienic.'

'Can you do that?'

'Of course. Some people are really paranoid about that sort of thing.'

Kirsty sighed. 'We're supposed to be here to celebrate my pregnancy, and to get away from our neighbours, and here we are, looking at them, talking about them as always. You know how some people only have one topic of conversation – their children or their pets or their job – and everyone finds them really boring? Well, that's us – except we go on about our neighbours.'

'Do you want to go somewhere else?'

'No. Don't be silly. We've started eating now. And I'm not going to let them drive us away. No way.'

'That's the spirit.'

He reached across the table to squeeze her hand. She did have spirit. That was one of the things that had first attracted him to her. He had been out with weak girls before, girls who lacked that spark of defiance, that ironic glint in the eye that marked Kirsty out. He knew that Kirsty would never let anyone walk all over her. She wouldn't take anything lying down. She was strong – and right now he needed someone like that. Because there were moments when he felt like giving up, and in those moments he looked at his girlfriend and drew strength from her. He honestly didn't know what he would do without her.

'Kirsty,' he said, tentatively. 'Now that we're having this baby, do you think that, well, that we should get married?'

Her eyes widened. 'Is that a proposal?'

'I don't know. It's a question.' He paused, looking into her eyes, trying to gauge her reaction. 'It's just that, I don't know, maybe it would be the proper thing to do if we're going to have a child.'

'Proper?'

'Yes. Or is that horribly uncool of me?'

She laughed, then stopped and looked at him. He'd been drinking champagne and lager. He'd had an intensely emotional day. But the way he was looking at her…

'Are you serious? Absolutely? One hundred per cent?'

'One hundred per cent.'

'I don't know if it's the right reason to do it – because it's proper.'

'Kirsty, the reason I want to marry you is because I love you and I want to spend the rest of my life with you.' He shrugged. 'That's it.'

She took a bite of poppadum, swallowed it, took a sip of her drink. 'OK then.'

He looked into her eyes, trying to work out if she was being serious. 'Is that a yes?'

'It sure is.'

He got up, came round the table and hugged her, kissing her, tasting spices on her lips. What a day. He looked over at the Newtons – Lucy had come back from the kitchens, and she and Chris were sitting staring at each other, their lips not moving, no conversation between them – and he thought, Fuck them. Nobody can make me unhappy. Not now. Not tonight. He was drunk and sentimental. He thought: I'm having a child, I'm marrying the woman I want to be with forever. I've built my nest and nobody – nobody – is going to spoil it.

Just let them try.

'There are conditions, though,' Kirsty said, as he sat back down. 'I don't want a big ceremony. We'll do it at the registry office, just us and a couple of witnesses. I'm not interested in that big so-called fairytale thing and, anyway, everyone would think it was a shotgun wedding. I know our parents will be upset, but, well, to be honest I don't think they expect us to ever get married anyway. So they won't really be missing out.'

'Your dad will probably be pleased to save the money.'

'Perhaps. And, anyway, it's our day. I don't want every aunt and uncle and second cousin I've never met gawping at me as I stumble up the aisle with my bump.'

Their meal arrived. It smelled delicious. Jamie dipped naan bread into his curry and took a bite. It was so hot it made his nose run. That was a good sign. If an Indian didn't make his nose run it was too bland. When the waiter had brought the plates over, Jamie had asked for another pint of lager and a jug of water for Kirsty. They arrived now, and Jamie took a big gulp. He was so happy.

'Who will we have as our witnesses?' he asked through a mouthful of rice.

'Heather for one, I guess. We could have had Heather and Paul.'

'I know.' He tutted sadly.

'Even if he woke up tomorrow, we don't know what sort of state he'd be in. It might take him months or years to recover. He might never recover, Jamie. You have to accept that.'

172

'No. He will. I know he will. God, if he was here now he'd already be arranging a mental stag night for me, with strippers and handcuffs and lamp-posts and lethal quantities of alcohol. Instead, I'll probably be at home with a nice cup of cocoa.'

'Yes, and you won't be getting married with a hangover, looking and feeling like shit.'

They fell silent, each lost in thoughts of Paul, and continued eating.

'So who are we going to ask to be our witnesses?'

'We could always drag a couple of strangers off the street.'

Jamie had an idea. 'Hey, why don't we go to Gretna Green? That would be really cool. It would be a really funny thing to do, don't you think?'

Kirsty looked thoughtful.

'What do you reckon? Will Heather be upset if we don't ask her to be a witness?'

'To be honest, I don't know if she'd want to do it anyway. It might upset her too much. But yeah, Gretna Green's an excellent idea. Something to tell our kids about. And I've never been to Scotland before.'

'It's a beautiful place.'

They beamed at each other over the table.

'This is fantastic,' said Jamie.

'I know.'

'And you're pregnant.'

'You're right.'

'And we're going to get married.'

'Bloody hell.'

Jamie paid for the meal, leaving a big tip for the waiter, and they stood up. Jamie wobbled a little, the alcohol sloshing around inside him. He looked over at Lucy and Chris, who had just started their main course. They seemed to be concentrating hard on their food so they wouldn't have to look over at Jamie and Kirsty.

'Wait here,' Jamie said.

'What are you . . ?'

Jamie walked across the restaurant and stopped by Lucy and Chris's table. 'Good evening,' he said, looking from one of them to the other.

They didn't respond. They just stared at their plates and carried on eating.

'Enjoying your meal?' Jamie asked. 'The food's very good here, isn't it?'

Chris suddenly looked up and, to Jamie's surprise, he smiled. His mouth was full, making the smile look grotesque, his cheeks bulging. 'It's delicious,' he said, showing Jamie a mouthful of rice.

Feeling a bit sick, Jamie turned to Lucy. 'Are you enjoying it too, Lucy?'

She put her fork down and said, 'You're drunk. And you're embarrassing yourself.'

'Embarrassing myself? I don't think so. How could I embarrass myself in front of you two? After all, we share our most intimate moments with you. And I have every right to be drunk.' He held on to the back of Lucy's chair and leaned forward. 'We're having a baby.'

Lucy and Chris didn't react. Jamie interpreted this as a stunned silence.

'Yes. We're pregnant. And who knows – maybe you've got the moment of conception on your PC.'

The waiter appeared by Jamie's side. 'Is everything alright here?' he asked.

Jamie put his arm around the waiter's shoulder and breathed beer fumes all over him. 'Everything's fine, mate. In fact, everything's fantastic.' He released the squirming waiter, said, 'Bon appetit,' to Lucy and Chris and staggered across the restaurant to Kirsty, who looked more embarrassed than he'd ever seen her, her cheeks flushed pink.

'Come on,' she said sharply, pulling him out into the fresh air. She turned to look at him. 'What did you say to them?'

'I was just telling them that everything's fantastic.' He kissed her. 'Everything's fucking fantastic.'

Fourteen

Kirsty knelt by the toilet and threw up, one painful spasm followed by another. Finally, when she was certain she wasn't going to be sick any more, she pushed herself upright and pushed the handle to flush the remains of last night's curry away. She splashed cold water on her face and rinsed her mouth. Morning sickness already?

While she was cleaning her teeth, Jamie came rushing into the room, wearing nothing but his underwear. He threw himself onto the carpet by the toilet and vomited, making a terrible straining sound. When he had finished, he sat with his back against the bath. He was pale and clammy, strands of hair stuck to his forehead. His stomach hurt. He groaned.

'I feel like death warmed up. I don't think I can go into work.' He took several deep breaths. 'God, I'm hardly ever ill after drinking. I guess it must be because I mixed champagne and beer.'

Kirsty crouched beside him. 'I was sick too.'

'Were you? When?'

'Just now, before you came in and made throwing up seem like such a drama. I'm quiet when I throw up.'

'But you weren't drinking.'

'I know. And it seems a bit unlikely that my morning sickness would start the same morning you're sick. Unless you're going to be one of those blokes who has a phantom pregnancy. Please, Jamie, don't be one of those blokes.'

Jamie stood up and spat into the sink. He took a swig of mouthwash and swirled a mouthful of neon blue liquid around his tongue and teeth before gargling briefly and spitting the mouthwash out. That was a little better.

'Do you think it was the food?'

'I don't know.'

'We both had different main courses, but I suppose they could have shared some of the same ingredients. I wonder if Lucy and Chris are ill as well.'

'Why don't you go down and ask them?'

'Very funny.'

'After last night, I'm sure they'd be more delighted to see you than ever.'

Jamie groaned again, this time from the blurred memory of his behaviour. 'Was I really awful?'

'You were very embarrassing. Especially when you put your arm around the waiter's shoulder and called him mate.'

'Oh God. We can't ever go back there again.'

'I don't know if we'd want to if they've given us food poisoning.'

'Surely it's not really food poisoning.' He felt a rumble in his bowels and stopped talking. 'Oh shit, you'd better leave the room. Kirsty, I mean it.'

She left the room and Jamie pulled his boxer shorts down and sat on the toilet. It hurt. As he wiped himself, he heard the phone ring, then Kirsty's voice after she picked it up. She sounded shocked, and he heard her come to the bathroom door and open it just as he flushed the toilet.

'Who was that?' Jamie asked. More than anything else in the world right now, he wanted to go back to bed. Go back to bed and sleep all day.

Kirsty stared at him. 'It's about Paul,' she said.

They drove to the hospital as fast as they could, Jamie racking his brain for shortcuts, accelerating towards amber traffic lights, guiltily ignoring zebra crossings. The traffic was dense and the streets were full of pedestrians enjoying the bright autumn sunshine, soaking up a final dose of rays before winter darkened the skies. Jamie turned the radio on then quickly turned it off again. The chatter of the DJ was too much. The cars up ahead were too slow. At times like this, he wished he could fly.

'Take it easy,' Kirsty warned as he swung a hard left. 'I still feel like I'm going to be sick at any moment.'

He had forgotten the sickness himself, had rid his body of whatever it was that had upset it. And since he had heard about Paul he couldn't think about anything else. His thoughts would return to it later, but for now he only had one thing on his mind: getting to the hospital; getting to Paul.

'That was Paul's dad,' Kirsty had said, standing in the doorway of the bathroom. 'We've got to get to the hospital.'

Jamie's stomach had filled with ice water. In that instant he thought he had been wrong to believe that Paul would recover. But seeing the look of dismay on Jamie's face, Kirsty said, 'No, Jamie, it's good news. They think he might be coming out of his coma.'

They turned in towards the hospital car park. Some idiot in a blue BMW was blocking the entrance. Jamie thumped the horn, leant on it, gestured angrily at the other driver. After an agonising wait for the BMW to pull out of the way, with hostile looks exchanged between the two drivers, Jamie shot into the car park, straight into an empty space.

They ran into the hospital. Through reception – Kirsty waving quickly to the girl on the front desk – dodging a porter with a laden trolley, up the stairs, down another corridor to Paul's room. Puffing, they entered the room. Jamie had half-expected to see Paul sitting up in bed, drinking a cup of tea, saying, 'Where am I? What happened?', but he was still lying in the same position, the same bip-bip-bip providing the rhythm to this drama's soundtrack.

Paul's parents and Heather stood close to the bed, looking down at Paul, who was being examined by Doctor Meer. Heather turned round.

'He said my name,' she said.

Her cheeks were shiny and smeared with mascara where she had been crying. She was wearing her nurse's uniform. 'I was sitting here, talking to him, just talking away as usual, telling him about my day, when he suddenly spoke. He said my name!' She grabbed Kirsty's hands. She was shaking with excitement. 'He said "Heather". And at first I thought I'd imagined it, that it was wish-fulfillment, but then he said it again. So I rushed off and grabbed Doctor Meer.'

'And has he said anything else?' asked Jamie.

'No. But Doctor Meer says he's coming out of the deep coma. He says that Paul is now merely unconscious and that he could wake up any minute.'

'Or he could slip back,' said Paul's dad. Reacting to their shocked looks, he said, 'Somebody has to be cautious here. It might be a false–'

'I think he's waking up,' said Doctor Meer from his position beside Paul's pillow.

They stopped and stared. Paul looked like a man who's been out on the most incredible drinking binge of all time and had passed out… had been passed out for a long time. His skin was colourless, there was a trail of saliva emerging from the side of his mouth. But as they watched, his eyelids flickered and, a second later, opened. His mother gasped and they all inched closer to the bed, like pilgrims moving tentatively towards a miracle. Doctor Meer had to stretch out his arms to prevent them getting too close. Jamie's mouth went dry. Kirsty gripped his hand hard.

Paul focused his vision, looked at them, opened his mouth. He croaked and licked his lips.

'I feel…' he whispered.

They leaned closer.

'…like shit.'

Doctor Meer had sent them out of the room while he and another doctor conducted a number of tests on their newly-awakened patient. Jamie, Kirsty, Heather and Paul's parents walked towards the canteen in a daze. Heather and Paul's mother were both in tears. Jamie and Kirsty were silent. Paul's father kept rubbing his beard, dragging the palm of his hand across his face. None of them wanted to cheer or whoop or celebrate. They were all too worried that something might still go wrong – that Paul would not be the same as he was before the accident. Although nobody spoke them aloud, two words featured prominently in all their minds: brain damage.

He might have lost the use of his limbs. He might be suffering from amnesia. He might not be able to speak properly, although that didn't seem to be too much of a worry. Eventually, Paul's waking sentence would become a thing of legend among those who knew him. *I feel like shit*. It was so classic, so quintessentially Paul. Jamie knew that

Heather, though, would always remember that his first very word upon waking had actually been her name.

They bought tea and coffee and sat around a table in the centre of the canteen.

'I knew he'd wake up,' said Jamie. 'I always knew it. We just had to give him time.'

'It was our prayers that did it,' said Paul's mum. 'Our prayers and our faith.'

'It was time,' Jamie repeated softly.

'What did Doctor Meer say about keeping him in the hospital?' Paul's father asked Kirsty.

'He said that first of all there was no guarantee that Paul would stay awake. But if he does, they'll have to keep him in for a while for observation. His body's undergone a severe trauma. His muscles have been unused for so quite a while, so he's going to be ever so weak. He'll have to have a lot of physio. It won't be easy. Plus they have to check his brain, make sure there isn't any lasting damage. Even assuming he's all right, he'll probably be disorientated and confused. We can't expect him to be his normal self – not straight away, anyway.'

'He's back,' said Paul's mum. 'For now, that's all that matters.'

'I'm going to ask him to marry me,' said Heather.

All heads swivelled towards her.

'We could make it a double wedding,' said Jamie. Attention turned to him. 'Kirsty and I decided last night that we're going to get married. And we've got some other news.'

Kirsty shot him a look. Shit. He'd forgotten, in his excitement, that he was supposed to wait till she was twelve weeks. Before he could think of some other news to share – we're buying a new sofa, for example – Kirsty said, 'I'm pregnant.'

'Oh Kirsty!' Heather leaned across the table and kissed her. 'That's excellent news.'

'Congratulations,' said Paul's dad.

'It's been a somewhat overwhelming twenty-four hours,' said Jamie.

Kirsty stood up. 'I need to go to the loo.'

'I'll come with you,' said Heather.

'I wouldn't if I were you.'

Jamie said, 'Have you still got a bad stomach?'

'Yes.' To prove it, she hurried off.

'We had an Indian last night,' Jamie explained to the others, 'and we were both sick this morning.'

'Oh.' Nobody was very interested. Paul had woken up. That was all that mattered. The news about Kirsty's pregnancy was secondary right now. They were itching to get back to Paul's room. They needed to know how he was.

Kirsty came back looking pale, and a few minutes later a nurse appeared. 'Would you like to come back now?' she said.

'How is he?' asked Paul's mum.

The nurse smiled. 'Why don't you come and see for yourself?'

They filed back into the room. Doctor Meer was standing beside the bed, looking pleased, hands tucked into the pockets of his white coat. Paul was propped up with a pillow behind his back. He looked like the living dead, his eyes open but empty of feeling. Jamie wanted him to smile – wished his face would light up with that boyish grin – but he just looked at them, impassive. Heather, Kirsty and Paul's parents each went up to him and hugged him. He didn't reciprocate; his arms hung loosely by his side, his hands concealed beneath the sheets. When Heather pulled away Paul looked at her as if she was a stranger.

Amnesia, Jamie thought. He stepped forward, a cautious smile on his face. 'Alright, mate?' he said.

Paul nodded, still expressionless.

'You do remember who we all are, don't you?'

The others exchanged worried glances.

Paul looked at them all. After a long pause, during which Jamie noticed how silent it was in here without the constant bip-bip-bip of the heart monitor, he said, 'Of course I remember. Mum. Dad. Jamie. Kirsty. And Heather.' He pointed at the doctor. 'I don't think I've been introduced to this guy though.'

Doctor Meer stepped forward and told Paul his name.

'And you've been looking after me?'

'Not just Doctor Meer,' said Paul's mum. 'All the nurses here, and your dad and me, and Heather and Kirsty and Jamie. We've all sat with you, Paul, waiting for you to wake up.' Tears bubbled to the surface again, and she produced a damp tissue and blew her nose.

'So I suppose I owe you all my thanks.'

'You don't owe us anything, son,' said Paul's dad.

'We're just so pleased to have you back,' said Heather.

Paul brought his hands out from beneath the sheet and studied them. His voice was hoarse. 'I feel so weak. All my muscles – I feel like a newborn kitten. It feels horrible.'

'We're going to have to build you up again, Paul,' said Doctor Meer. 'We have a program of physical therapy already planned out for you. It's going to be hard work – but soon you'll be back to peak fitness.'

Paul rubbed his eyes. 'God, I had such dreams.' He looked up, cast his gaze over each of them in turn, finally settling on Jamie.

'I want to talk to Jamie,' he said.

'No, you need to rest,' said the doctor. 'Jamie can come back later.' He turned to the group. 'Paul's not ready to talk to all of you yet. He needs time to adjust to being back among...the living. I know you're all desperate to talk to Paul, but I have to put his well-being first.'

'I'll come back tomorrow,' Jamie said, as Doctor Meer ushered them out again.. As they left the room, Jamie looked back over his shoulder. Paul had already closed his eyes.

Over the next seventy-two hours, they were allowed in to see Paul one at a time. Jamie had to wait until Paul's parents and Heather had taken their turn. The waiting was agony, but made bearable by the fact that Paul was now conscious: that he was back among the living, as the doctor phrased it.

Jamie grabbed the plastic chair he had sat on so many times and pulled it close to the bed. Paul looked a little better now, the effects of the long sleep fading from his face. He was still on a drip, but that awful bip-bip-bip noise had gone. There were magazines piled up by the bed, which Paul hadn't touched.

'What happened?' Paul asked. 'Heather told me the details but I can't quite get my head round it. I want to hear it from you.'

'You don't remember it?'

'I remember the go-kart race. I know I won. But the last thing I recall is crossing the finishing line.'

'One of the other racers crashed into the back of your kart. I didn't see it, but we were told that Chris braked too quickly in front of the other racer, making him swerve into you.'

'That's what Heather said. Poor Chris. I bet he feels really guilty.'

'What? Why did you say poor Chris? He's not the one they carted off in an ambulance.'

'But to cause an accident like that, especially after we'd been getting on so well. He must have felt so…what's the word? Oh, my head feels fuzzy.' He concentrated. 'Remorseful.'

186

Jamie shook his head. 'He hasn't exactly shown it. Paul, you don't know what's been going on while you've been in here. Chris and Lucy have turned into the neighbours from hell. I've been trying not to think about it while you were in the coma, but it wouldn't surprise me if Chris had done it on purpose. They've been writing us letters, taping us having sex, joining us to endless clubs. You wouldn't believe what...'

Paul yawned, the high-pitched noise drowning Jamie out. He realised Paul hadn't been listening to a word he said. 'You'll have to tell me about it some other time. I'm too tired to concentrate.'

Jamie nodded. He didn't want to upset Paul or do anything to hinder his recovery. 'Do you want me to go already?'

'Not just yet.' He yawned again, and then a smile crept across his lips. 'I gather everyone was heartbroken and worried that I wouldn't come back.'

'You could say that.'

Paul's smile widened. 'That's good.'

Jamie was shocked. 'I don't think it's something to be pleased about. We've really suffered, Paul.'

'Oh come on, wouldn't you be pleased to hear that everyone was really worried about you? It's like going to your own funeral and seeing everyone crying over you and saying what a good bloke you were.'

Jamie shook his head. 'You're obviously not feeling yourself at the moment.'

187

Paul didn't say anything.

Jamie looked around the ward, at the flowers beside the bed, the MP3 player in the corner so Paul could be played his favourite music. 'The other day, you said something about having dreams.'

'Did I?'

'Yes. Before Doctor Meer asked us to leave.'

'Of course I've had dreams. I've been asleep for a long time.'

'What kind of dreams?'

Paul closed his eyes. 'I don't want to talk about it. Maybe I'll tell you later.'

'Were they bad dreams?'

'I said I don't want to talk about it.'

'OK.' He put his hand on Paul's shoulder. He was cold beneath his pyjamas. 'OK.'

Paul tried to smile. 'What have I missed while I've been away?'

'Oh, quite a bit. Kirsty's pregnant.'

He nodded. 'Yes, Heather told me. Congratulations.' There was little sincerity in his voice.

'And we're going to get married.'

Paul rolled his eyes.

Undeterred, Jamie said, 'Maybe it will be you and Heather next.'

'I don't think so somehow. God, I don't even know what she's been up to while I've been in here.'

Jamie exhaled. 'She's been absolutely grief-stricken. She's been coming here every day to sit by your bed. Every time I see her she ends up crying. For some bizarre reason – and don't ask me what it is – she loves you.'

'I suppose it's quite romantic, having a boyfriend in a coma. I bet it makes her feel really noble and worthy. It's a great way to get sympathy.'

'Paul! I can't believe you can think that.'

'Yeah, well. We'll see if she's still so keen now I'm back in the land of the living.'

All of a sudden, Jamie wanted to get out. He wanted to talk to Paul again after he'd had more time to adjust to what had happened to him. He knew this wasn't the real Paul talking. This was someone who'd just woken up after a long time in another place.

'I'd better go,' Jamie said. 'You need to rest.'

Paul nodded and Jamie stood up. He felt like he ought to be blissfully happy. His girlfriend was pregnant, he was getting married and now his best friend had come back from the dead. He ought to be ecstatic, but instead…

He shook away the feeling of foreboding and looked back at Paul, who was studying his hands again, flexing his fingers, casting shadows on the whitewashed walls.

'Welcome back,' he said, under his breath.

Fifteen

'So how was Paul?' Kirsty asked when Jamie got home. She had taken a couple of days off work; she still felt unwell, as if there was something poisonous still working its way out of her system. She was in bed reading a book about pregnancy, a glass of water beside her.

He shook his head. 'I don't want to talk about it. I've got a horrible headache.'

'Why don't you come to bed?'

'Good idea.'

He undressed and slid beneath the cool quilt, closing his eyes. It was early evening; the birdsong outside had ceased and shadows were beginning to darken the room.

Kirsty turned over to face the wall. She closed her eyes. She could still feel the rumblings deep down in her stomach. It was nothing to do with being pregnant. It was illness, impure and simple.

'It's so good to have Paul back, though, isn't it?' she murmured drowsily.

'Yes it is. But–' He realised that, within that second, she had fallen asleep.

When Jamie awoke, it was dark. He squinted at the bedside clock. It was nine. They'd been asleep for several hours. His mouth felt like something had died in it or like he'd been eating fur. He sat up and scratched his chest then crossed to the window, pulling back one edge of the curtain and peering out at the quiet night.

He sniffed. There was a strange smell in the air, faint but unpleasant. At first he thought it might be gas, but it was too pungent. In fact, it was making him feel sick so, despite the chill, he opened the window. It didn't help, so he pushed down the sash window, harder than he intended so it closed with a bang. In the bed, Kirsty groaned. 'What time is it?'

He crawled onto the bed and kissed her hot forehead. 'Just gone nine.'

'Bloody hell. We've missed the whole evening. Hey, what are you doing?'

'Lighting an incense stick. There's a horrible smell in the air.'

He found a packet of lavender joss sticks and lit one, waving it around like a Bonfire Night sparkler, trails of lavender smoke curling to the ceiling and cleansing the room.

Kirsty said, 'I couldn't smell anything.'

She got out of bed and stretched her arms above her head. Jamie moved towards her, putting one hand just above her hip, leaning into her.

'Ooh, your breath.' She waved him away.

'Thanks.' He put his arms around her and kissed her neck.

'You've got morning mouth, Jamie. Even though it is nine pm.'

'I'll clean my teeth.'

'Yes, do that. But I'm getting up now. I'm not in the mood for sex. My stomach still hurts a bit.'

'It's not because you're worried about making noise?'

She tutted. 'No. For God's sake, Jamie, I've just got a stomach ache.'

'Alright, there's no need to snap.'

He walked into the bathroom and cleaned his teeth. He felt guilty, but also concerned. Their sex life had dwindled since the Newtons had sent them the CD. Obviously, there was a lot more to their relationship than sex, but sex with Kirsty was still pretty much his favourite thing in the world and he hated the fact that it had been marred by the worry that they were being listened to every time they did it. They could pretend defiance, but when it came down to it, that knowledge meant they could no longer relax one hundred percent. Those bastards downstairs were clever – he had to give them that. He bet this was exactly the effect they had intended.

He splashed his face with icy water and told himself to snap out of it. What did it matter, anyway? Sex, or the lack of it, was the least of his concerns at the moment. His whole life was going to change. He leaned against the sink, water dripping from his face into the basin. He opened his eyes and caught sight of something running across the bathroom floor.

'I just saw a real fuck-off spider in the bathroom,' he said to Kirsty as they stood dressing in the bedroom.

'What? Where did it go?'

'Behind the toilet.'

'And you didn't try to catch it?'

'I wish I hadn't mentioned it now.'

Kirsty walked into the hall and peered into the bathroom without actually daring to go in there. Spiders terrified her and she hated herself for it: she didn't want to be a pathetic female stereotype; but then, surely everyone was entitled to have at least one irrational weakness? Arachnophobia ran in her family. Her mum, her grandmother, her dad: they were all hopeless when it came to small, eight-legged creatures. It was the way they moved…oh God it made her go all cold and shivery inside. And in her imagination, the spiders were always much bigger than they really were. Multiply their size by five, or ten, or more. An average household spider turned into a tarantula. A common or garden British spider became a bird-eating monstrosity; a funnel-web beast that lay in wait for her behind the toilet, all eyes and teeth and long furry legs.

'What did you mean when you said it was a fuck-off spider?'

'Nothing.'

'Was it really big?' she called out. 'Come on, you've got to tell me.'

Jamie was really regretting saying anything. 'No, not that big. It was barely bigger than a five pence piece.'

'You're just trying to make me feel better.' She went back into the bedroom and climbed on the bed. 'You'll have to catch it.'

'But it ran behind the toilet. It's probably disappeared beneath the floorboards by now. Kirsty, it was only a spider.'

She glared at him. 'You know how I feel about spiders. And I shouldn't be exposed to any stress in my condition.' She touched her stomach.

Jamie realised she had found a way of making him do anything she asked over the coming months. He sighed. He loved her but sometimes she drove him mad. Her terror of spiders was so irrational. She was about a thousand times bigger than a spider. If this was Australia and the spiders were poisonous he'd understand it. But these were British spiders. They were pathetic little things. Completely harmless.

He went back into the bathroom and got down on his hands and knees. He peered behind the toilet. There were some dust-smothered cobwebs, but no sign of the spider. It had been quite big – one of those brown spiders with furry legs that they sometimes found in the bath (with Kirsty having to disinfect it after Jamie had scooped the creature up and thrown it out the window) – but Jamie wished he hadn't described it as a 'fuck-off' spider. What with all the excitement and too much sleep, he hadn't been thinking straight. He wondered if he should pretend that he had found the spider and act out throwing it out the window. No, she would know he was lying, and that would only make things worse – especially if it reappeared later.

He went back into the bedroom and she looked up at him hopefully.

'Sorry, there's no sign of it. I'm sure it's long gone. Come on, let's put dinner…'

Kirsty let out a yelp and jumped backwards onto the bed. Jamie spun round. A brown spider was scuttling across the carpet towards him.

'Catch it!' Kirsty yelled.

He crouched and cupped his hand over it, then picked it up and took it over to the window. He could feel its feathery legs wriggling against his palm. With his free hand he opened the window – breathing in another lungful of that sickly sweet, foul smell – and tossed the spider down into the garden. He walked towards Kirsty.

She shrank away and pointed towards the bathroom. 'Go and wash your hands before you touch me.'

'It won't have given me any contagious diseases, Kirsty.'

'Just wash them. Please. I can't bear the thought that it's been on your skin.'

'OK, OK.'

He washed his hands halfheartedly, dried them, then walked back into the bedroom. His stomach growled. It was nine-thirty and he hadn't eaten all day.

'I'm going to put dinner on, OK? What do you want?'

'I don't mind.'

In the kitchen, he opened the fridge and stuck his head inside. Recently, they had been living on pre-prepared meals from Sainsbury's, with a side-serving of frozen chips or vegetables. Jamie pulled out a vegetable lasagne, shook some chips onto a baking tray and turned the oven on. Before closing the fridge he took out a beer and cracked it open. He went over and sat beside Kirsty in front of the TV.

'Was it the same spider?' Kirsty asked.

He had no idea. 'I think so.'

'You're not just saying that?'

'No. I'm sure it was.'

Thirty minutes later he crossed to the kitchen to check if the dinner was ready. Not quite. He took another beer out of the fridge.

'Are you having another drink?' said Kirsty disapprovingly.

'Well, I'm drinking for two now.'

She tutted.

'Actually, I'm celebrating – celebrating Paul's recovery.' He paused. 'Assuming he has recovered.'

'What makes you say that?'

'He just seemed a bit odd. Cold. He didn't seem particularly pleased to see me.'

'You can't expect him to be exactly as he was before the accident – not straight away. He's probably experiencing a form of shock. And having all these people expecting him to be just as he was before the accident – I expect he feels a bit confused and pressurised. Like you said earlier, it must be quite overwhelming.'

'I suppose so. I'll go and see him during the next few days.' He sipped his beer. 'I can entertain him with tales of all that's been going on here. Not that he was very interested when I tried to tell him today.'

'I bet he'll be really angry with Chris.'

'No, that's just it. He's not. He said he was sure it was an accident.'

'Really? Maybe the so-called accident's made him turn religious. Forgive those who trespass against you and all that. God, what if he had one of those near-death experiences, where he was floating towards the light and a voice was calling him? He might become a born again Christian.' She laughed at a sudden image of Paul standing in the street handing out religious pamphlets, trying to persuade lost souls to embrace their maker. 'Maybe he'll change his name to Lazarus.'

'You're dread...' He stopped dead.

'What is it?' She followed his gaze. 'Oh, shit!'

A small black shape crossed the threshold of the room and ran towards them on eight skinny legs. Kirsty jumped up onto the sofa, tucking her legs beneath her. 'It's come back.' In her eyes, the spider wasn't small or skinny. It was huge, with fat legs that drummed on the floorboards.

Jamie stood up. 'No, it's a different one. This one's stripy and has got shorter legs.'

She gasped. 'I don't want a fucking description of it. I want you to get rid of it. Quickly.'

He knelt down and reached out for the spider, which was heading straight towards him. He grabbed it and, as he stood up, he heard Kirsty cry out.

'It's alright, I've got it.'

'No – look – there's another one.'

A second spider scurried into the room, heading straight towards the sofa. Jamie could tell that the magnifying glass of Kirsty's arachnophobic vision made the spider swell to the size of a tarantula. 'I don't believe this,' Kirsty yelled, her voice cracking. 'What's going on?

Jamie ran over to the front window, opened it with one hand, threw the first spider out, then tried to catch the next one. It ran under the sofa. Kirsty jumped off and ran over to the other side of the room. She was breathing heavily, clutching her chest.

'It's alright,' said Jamie in a soft voice. 'It's only a little spider. It can't harm you.'

'Just catch it. Please. Oh my god…' She screamed and started jumping up and down.

Jamie turned towards the doorway, to the spot at which Kirsty was pointing. Another spider entered the room. Then another. And another, and another, and another. A whole family of spiders, all of them with fat brown legs – all of them enormous, poisonous, hungry, as far as the barefoot Kirsty was doubtless concerned – scuttling across the carpet towards her.

'Jamie!'

She screamed and threw herself back onto the sofa, eyes wide with phobic terror, clutching her feet to protect them from the wriggling legs that she was so scared of. She started to hyperventilate. Tears burned her eyes.

Jamie was frozen to the spot. He couldn't believe this. Where were they all coming from? There was no way he could catch them all, so he picked up his shoe and brought it down on the first spider.

'Kill them!' shouted Kirsty.

The body of the first spider was stuck to the sole of his shoe. He whacked the second spider, then a third.

Kirsty shrieked. She had never let Jamie kill a spider before. No matter how much she hated and feared them, she would never allow one to be harmed. Now she wanted to see them crushed. She wanted them all dead. 'Kill them!'

He killed them all, one by one, then sat back, panting, his heart thumping. He looked at the little wrecked bodies and immediately felt remorseful. They were only spiders, but they were so small and helpless. It was Kirsty's fault for getting so hysterical.

He turned towards her. 'Look what you made me do!'

'What?' She looked up at him. Her face was streaked with tears. He realised how petrified she had been, and now he felt remorse for shouting at her. He sat on the edge of the sofa and hugged her. She was shaking.

'Where did they all come from, Jamie?'

'I don't know, sweetheart. I really don't know.'

'They were coming straight for me. They wanted to get me.'

'Don't be silly.'

She wiped her eyes with a trembling hand. 'I bet it was them.'

'Who?'

'Them. Lucy and Chris. They sent them up here to get me.'

'How could they have?'

'Easily! They could have put them under the door, or I don't know, maybe they trained them.'

'What are you talking about?'

'You know what Lucy said about Mary being a witch. Well, maybe it's really Lucy who's the witch. She's evil enough. I bet they poisoned us last night. We saw her go into the kitchen in the restaurant. And then they made those spiders come up here to get me.'

'Kirsty, you should hear yourself. And how would they know you're scared of spiders?'

'They listen to us all the time. They've probably got it recorded.' Her voice dropped to a whisper. 'They're probably listening to us right now, gauging our reaction, laughing at us. Oh God.'

Jamie shushed her. 'Kirsty, this is crazy. Lucy and Chris are nasty, twisted people. We know that. But they're not witches. They're not able to command spiders and send them after people.'

Suddenly, the flat was filled with a deafening series of beeps.

'Shit! The dinner!' Jamie jumped up and ran towards the oven. Black tendrils of smoke emerged from the kitchen, setting off the smoke alarm which emitted a shrill, maddening beeping noise. He took the alarm down from its position on the wall, turned it off and then opened the oven door. A cloud rose up and made him cough. He pulled out the dinner. The chips looked like charcoal pencils; the lasagne was ruined.

Kirsty came over and looked at it. 'It's OK,' she said. 'I'm not hungry any more, anyway.'

Jamie opened the other front window to let out the smoke. Then he dug out the dustpan and brush and swept up the bodies of the dead spiders, throwing them out of the window. He deliberately let them fall onto the Newtons' doorstep. Hopefully Lucy was scared of spiders too.

After that, Kirsty made him check the bed, the bath, under the sofa and wherever else there was a nook or cranny that might possibly hold a spider. To his great relief, he didn't find any.

Kirsty didn't sleep that night. She lay awake, staring at the ceiling, imagining that giant spiders were in the bed, or were pattering across the bedroom carpet, coming towards her; coming to get her.

Sixteen

'So what are you going to do about it?'

'What?' Jamie was taken aback by the question.

Mike leaned forward across the desk, his face framed by two computer monitors. 'I said, What are you going to do about it?'

Jamie fell silent. He held a ballpoint pen between finger and thumb, tapped it on the edge of his keyboard, stared blindly at the screensaver on his monitor. All around him people tapped away at their keyboards, had important telephone conversations, wandered to and from the coffee machine. The server in the corner hummed noisily; the fax machine bleeped. But Jamie was oblivious to it all.

What was he going to do about it?

He had come into work this morning with the need to talk to someone, to pour it all out, to get it off his chest. He didn't expect catharsis, just some relief. Last night, at 3 a.m., Lucy and Chris had played extracts from *War of the Worlds* – the seventies 'rock opera' – not at full volume, but just loud enough for Jamie to hear it and for it to come seeping into his dreams. He had woken up and jumped out of bed in a state of shocked disbelief and stared at the floorboards. When he was eight or nine, his parents used to play this album late at night after he'd gone to bed. And as a little boy with a large imagination, he had lain awake, convinced that the Martians were coming for him. The album came with a booklet of paintings, in which men and women ran screaming through the Victorian streets, pursued by a Martian death machine; red alien liquid bubbled between once-glorious buildings; a priest held up a cross before an unimpressed Martian who fired off a death ray to obliterate him. All these images of horror and destruction floated before his eyes, along with a few original ones, conjured up by his pre-adolescent mind. In the end, after a week of nightmares, he reluctantly told his mum why he had been so tired and unhappy recently and, filled with remorse, she had binned the album, making him promise that he would tell her if anything scared him in the future. He shouldn't be ashamed, even if he was a big boy now.

Maybe I should phone her now, he thought. Tell her I'm afraid. Afraid because I don't know what I'm going to do about it.

How on earth had Lucy and Chris known? They had managed to pinpoint how the Newtons knew about Kirsty's arachnophobia – they'd mentioned it at the dinner party – but how did they know about Jamie's old fear? He racked his brains. Had he mentioned his fear of that music to them? No; no he hadn't. He'd never mentioned it to anyone. Not even Kirsty. In fact, he had practically forgotten that album existed. In the early nineties, someone had released a dance mix of the *War of the Worlds* music, and he found that it didn't scare him any more – not in the sweaty centre of a heaving, lively nightclub, anyway. But at three a.m., in the dark, the music coming up from beneath the floorboards brought back all those childhood terrors. He could almost see the alien tripods outside the window. He thought harder, tried to work it out – but there was no way they could have known about his fear. No way.

But he had to put a stop to it. Kirsty buried her head beneath the pillow while he dressed hurriedly, pulling on his jeans and a T-shirt without bothering with his underwear. He went outside and ran down the steps. It was freezing and, apart from the music coming from the basement flat, utterly silent.

He banged on the door and on the window pane. Unsurprisingly, there was no answer. He lifted the letterbox and shouted through it, 'I'm going to call the police.' But he knew he wouldn't. He would be too embarrassed. *The music scares me, officer.* How pathetic did he want to look? He went back upstairs and got back in bed, and at that very moment the music stopped. He lay absolutely still, dreading that it might start up again. Eventually, he tried to get back to sleep. But he was too angry; his heart was beating too fast. And it would be time to get up in a couple of hours anyway. So he got out of bed again and plugged the Playstation in. He played *Call of Duty*, imagining that every enemy soldier he mowed down was Lucy or Chris. Kirsty got up too and sat beside him, watching. She barely spoke.

Weeks had gone by since the spider incident. For the first week, Kirsty had made Jamie check the bed before he got in it; the bath before she would turn the taps on; the front room before she would enter it. She was convinced that it was going to happen again: another spider invasion. But when it didn't, she relaxed, and then crossed to a state beyond relaxed. She took on an air of calmness and serenity. She walked around with her hands on her belly a lot, even though she was far from showing. She bought parenthood magazines and looked up baby sites on the internet. She was imagining herself in a perfect future, a future in which she would have her child and everything would be alright. She seemed to forget all about the problems with Lucy and Chris. She stopped mentioning the spiders, although one evening a spider made an appearance on television and she shouted at Jamie to change the channel. Quickly. Quickly.

Now she sat beside Jamie and watched him exorcise his anger and frustration. At six thirty, as the sun struggled to lighten the sky, she went off to the bathroom to be sick. Morning sickness had arrived with a vengeance. And then they went to work.

Jamie drove her to the hospital – he drove her everywhere now, since she refused to go on the Tube or catch a bus, and he was glad to – and then he went to his own workplace. God, he was tired. He thought he might fall asleep at the wheel. He turned the radio up and let the DJ's relentless chatter keep him awake. At work, he took the lift to the floor where his office was located and went straight to the coffee machine. The pale brown drink that emerged from the machine didn't really taste like coffee, but it contained a trace of caffeine and he added a lot of sugar. As he carried the drink over to his desk a snatch of *War of the Worlds* entered his head and he shuddered.

'Are you alright, Jamie?' asked Mike, who sat at the opposite desk. Mike held the same position as Jamie – software installation engineer – and had joined E.T.N. a few months before. He was the same age as Jamie, with the same educational and occupational background, but he was more of a lad: a dedicated pleasure-seeker, firmly single, hanging out with a group of hard drinkers whose main interests were football and women – in that order. As far as Jamie was concerned, Mike was a good bloke to work with, but he wasn't a potential 'outside work' friend. They talked shop most of the time, but today, when Mike asked him if he was alright Jamie saw the opportunity to talk to somebody, no matter how unlikely his choice of confidante, and he grabbed it.

'So what are you going to do about it?'

That was the question.

'Why don't you move out?'

Jamie shook his head. 'No way. I refuse to let a pair of nutters like that drive me out of my home. I love that flat. I know we haven't been there very long, but it feels like the place I want to be. The place we want to be. All three of us.'

He and Kirsty had discussed this when the problems with Lucy and Chris started, and then again after the night of the spiders. Should they get away, try to find somewhere new? They both reacted with a firm No. This was their dream flat. Jamie remembered how happy they had been when they moved in just a few months before. It was the most fantastic place – it would be incredibly difficult to find anywhere as good in their price range. There was plenty of space for three, especially after Jamie had turned the spare room into a nursery (he already had grand plans about what he would do). Maybe in a few years, if they had a second child, they would need to find somewhere bigger, but that might also involve a move out of London.

'We can't let them win, Kirsty,' Jamie said. 'That's what they want, I bet. They want us to move out. God knows why – maybe they just don't like having people live above them. Or maybe it's us. Whatever the reason, I am not going to let a pair of psychos like that force me out of my home.'

'I'd feel exactly the same if I were you,' said Mike now. 'You've got to stand your ground. But I don't know how you've managed to keep your temper. If it was me I'd have been down there to sort them, taken some of the boys with me. I'd put a bomb through their letterbox.'

'I have been down there.'

'And what happened?'

'They won't talk to me. They never answer the door. And the time I went into their garden to talk to them they called the police.'

'Who were a dead loss, I expect.'

'Yes. They just told us to keep a record of what was going on.'

'Big deal.' Mike looked left and right to see if anyone was listening, then leaned forward. 'From what you say, these people need dealing with in a more direct manner. You can't be reasonable with people like them, Jamie. They don't speak the same language as the rest of us.'

'But they seemed so nice when we first met them.'

'Yeah. They were trying to get you to trust them. Or maybe they're less calculating than that. They might be schizophrenic. One minute nice and friendly, the next – ga-ga.' He twirled his finger beside his head and pulled a face.

Jamie laughed, despite himself.

'You must have the patience of a saint. God, people like them want putting down. I really can't believe that you're putting up with all their crap, especially with a pregnant girlfriend who's being scared out of her wits by them. I don't want to offend you, but you're not being much of a man, are you? A man's meant to protect his home – his cave. It's there, buried inside you, one of the most basic instincts a man can have. To look after his woman and child and their home.'

Jamie looked at Mike. It was easy for him to sit there casting judgement. To an outsider, the whole thing was black and white. But it was more complicated than it looked...wasn't it?

Jamie wondered. Maybe it wasn't so complicated at all. All he trying to do was build a home with his girlfriend – his future wife – and their unborn child. And the Newtons were, for whatever reason, trying to spoil it. Maybe it was a simple issue. Maybe Mike was right, even if he did term it in such an outmoded way. It was his duty to protect Kirsty and their nest. So far he had failed. Although Kirsty seemed calm now (too calm?) and happy about their forthcoming wedding, she had been through a lot recently, from the day of Paul's accident onwards. Jamie didn't buy into all that macho crap, but maybe, sometimes, there was a need to.

He looked up at Mike, who, apparently reading Jamie's mind, said, 'I know what I'd do.'

He slammed his fist into his palm.

Jamie left work early and headed straight to the hospital. He wanted to talk to Paul, to see what he thought. After his chat with Mike, his concentration had been shot: all he could of think of was Mike saying, 'What are you going to do about it?' and the way he had punched his palm. He wanted to ask Paul his opinion.

He found his friend sitting up in bed, flicking boredly through a copy of FHM. He put the magazine down when Jamie entered the room. He looked much better than he had the day he had woken up. A shade of colour had returned to his cheeks. Doctor Meer had told Jamie that Paul's recovery was the quickest and most complete he had ever seen. He was responding well to physiotherapy, he appeared to have suffered no memory loss and all his mental faculties were intact. It was all good news.

'All alone?' Jamie asked, pulling up a chair.

Paul frowned. 'Heather's just gone to the loo. She needed some tissues to dry her eyes.'

Jamie looked at him quizzically.

'We just split up. I told her I thought it was for the best.'

Jamie was shocked. 'Why?'

'She was getting on my nerves. She's here all the time, fussing and carrying on. God, the other day she even mentioned the possibility of us getting married. We were only together for a few days before my accident, for Christ's sake, and from what I remember it wasn't that great anyway. She's pretty crap in bed. Just lies there and expects you to do all the work, if you know what I mean.'

'But you seemed really happy together. That day at the go-kart track...'

'Did we? I don't remember.'

'And you'd fancied her for ages. You said she was really sexy and lovely and that you wouldn't stand a chance with someone like her.'

'Well, I changed my mind. She was getting on my tits, so I chucked her. She'll get over it.'

Jamie was speechless. He had never heard Paul talk like before. This wasn't the Paul he knew, the Paul who had never chucked anyone in his life. He remembered how Heather had flooded their flat with tears because she was so heartbroken by Paul's condition. When he awoke from the coma she was so happy. She had been round a few times since and all she talked about was Paul Paul Paul, but now in a happy way. She told Kirsty that she wanted a baby too, and that Paul would be a wonderful father. She told them how she had given Paul a blow job beneath the hospital sheets, when none of the doctors or other nurses were around. She went on about Paul so much that Jamie thought he might go mad if he heard the name once more. But now he could imagine how devastated she was going to be.

'Why are you acting so cold?' Jamie asked.

'Don't you start, Jamie. That's exactly what she said.'

'And don't you think that's because it's true? You were never like this before.'

'No, I was a poor sap who always let women walk all over me. I was a sad, desperate case. The kind of bloke that women want to be their best friend. I've had a lot of time to think since I've been in here, and I've decided I'm going to change. I'm going to do what I want, and I don't need some clingy slag holding me back.'

'Paul–'

'Paul Paul Paul! Why don't you all just fuck off and leave me alone.' His voice got louder. 'I'm pissed off with people treating me like a sick puppy.' He was practically shaking now. 'I'm going to get out of this bed and change my life. And if you don't like that, I don't want you in my new life.'

He picked up his magazine and hid his face behind it.

Jamie was so shocked he couldn't move. It took all his will power to uproot himself and walk out of the room. His legs were shaking; he felt like he'd been slapped hard around the face. Halfway down the corridor, he saw Heather come out of the toilets. He hurried over to her.

Her fringe was damp. Jamie guessed she had just splashed her face to wash away any sign that she had been crying. She looked forlorn, and when she looked at Jamie she almost burst into tears again.

'Did he tell you?' she asked.

He nodded. 'Come on, let's go and get a coffee.'

They went to the cafeteria and Jamie bought two coffees. Heather stared at the table, not wanting to catch anyone's eye or be seen by anyone she knew.

'Do you want me to fetch Kirsty?' he asked.

'No. She doesn't finish her shift for another hour.'

Jamie stirred brown sugar into his coffee. 'He told me to fuck off too.'

She looked up, surprised. 'But you're his best mate.'

'So I thought.'

'How long have you known him?'

He performed a quick mental calculation. 'Nearly ten years.'

'He's changed, hasn't he.'

Jamie nodded. 'I've never seen him like this before. I've never even seen him get angry before, not really.'

'It's the accident. It's done something to him.' She sniffed. 'Though Doctor Meer says he hasn't suffered any brain damage at all. He says he's responded to all their tests exactly as they'd hoped.'

'Their tests mean nothing. He's changed. We don't need tests to see that. We know him – we know what he was like before. He wasn't like this.'

Heather thumped the table. 'Shit. Why did we have to go to that bloody go-karting track that day? Why? If we hadn't gone, everything would be alright.'

Jamie said nothing. Heather started to cry, producing a damp hankie and pressing it against her eyes. Jamie knew why they had gone go-karting: because Chris had suggested it. Chris had taken them there, and then he had made that other driver crash into Paul. And now Paul had woken up, but he wasn't the same. He wasn't the old Paul they all loved. And it was all Chris's fault. He felt a current of hurt run through his veins; the sour taste of anger on his tongue. It was Chris's fault. Chris and Lucy. As Heather cried in front of him he thought of all the things they had done and the anger and hurt and hatred boiled and burned inside him.

They were trying to ruin his life.

They wanted to destroy everything he had.

They were threatening his sanity; upsetting his girlfriend; hurting his friends.

But what was he going to do about it?

Seventeen

They had to rush for the train in the end, despite their best efforts to get there in plenty of time. Kirsty had a last-minute packing crisis, ushering Jamie out of the bedroom while she packed her underwear.

'It's bad luck to see what knickers your wife will be wearing on your wedding day before the event.'

Jamie laughed. 'I thought it was bad luck to see the dress.'

'Yes, well, you've already seen that. But I have to keep some semblance of mystique.'

Jamie paced around while Kirsty rifled through her underwear drawer. Finally, she was ready; but the taxi turned up late; and then it got stuck in heavy traffic. It pulled up in front of Euston station with a mere five minutes to spare before the train was due to depart. They ran into the station, Jamie weighed down by the suitcase, lagging behind as Kirsty scanned the departures board.

'Platform three,' she shouted, sprinting off ahead, clutching the tickets which she showed to the ticket inspector at the head of the platform.

'My boyfriend's right behind me,' she said.

'He'd better get a move on.'

As she waited for Jamie to catch up, Kirsty realised that her conversation with the ticket inspector might be the last time she ever referred to Jamie as her boyfriend. By the end of tomorrow he would be her husband. It was a weird feeling, but also exciting. My husband. She smiled to herself at the thought of introducing him as such. Running off to Gretna Green to get married. What a cliché. But there was also something very cool about it. It was a funny thing to do. She knew the memory of it would always make her smile.

Of course, memory of your wedding, wherever it was, was meant to make you smile. But Kirsty had never been one of those girls who pined for a big white wedding. The idea of it – the fuss, the expense, all those eyes focused on you – was anathema to her. She told herself she would never get married. It was an outdated tradition, based on a sexist ritual of a father handing his daughter over to another man. When Jamie had suggested that they get married, her first reaction had been to baulk, but in the same split-second she had felt a rush of excitement at the idea, as long as Jamie agreed to certain conditions. And now here they were, on their way to Scotland to do what almost everybody does eventually. Kirsty was fully aware of the pattern she was conforming to: boyfriend, moving in together, marriage, baby, all in the right order, with a good career to boot. But at least they were doing it on their own terms, and at least she had got pregnant before they got married. She still had a streak of rebellion in her, even if it was only a small one.

They made it to their seats seconds before the train pulled away. Jamie hefted the suitcase onto the rack above and they sat back with a sigh.

'Made it.'

She kissed him and smiled. 'Husband.'

'Not yet.'

'Ah, but just twenty-four hours till the ball and chain goes round your ankle.'

'Can't wait.'

The train heaved its way out of the station, and they fell quiet for a while, watching some of the grimmer parts of north London roll by. Before long they had left the city altogether and were heading for Milton Keynes. Kirsty took a book out of her bag and Jamie went off up the aisle to buy coffee.

Kirsty settled back into her seat and smiled to herself. She opened her book and began to read.

Jamie queued at the buffet counter, swaying to keep his balance as the train rattled and vibrated. The man in front of him seemed to be on a mission to sample everything on the menu and was taking an age. Still, Jamie didn't mind. They had plenty of time to kill.

He had been looking forward to this trip. Not just because of what would happen at the end of it, but because for the first time in months he would have some 'dead' time. To him, that was one of the best things about going on a journey somewhere, being stuck on a plane or a train: you had five or six hours to spend in this unreal zone between points A and B; time in which to think or read or just stare at the scenery. The train would reach Carlisle in five hours time, which meant – with nothing to distract him – he had five hours to think, to mull over recent events, to try to get things straight in his mind.

Over the last few days, Kirsty's mood had improved amazingly, her cool serenity, which had taken the place of her edginess, had in turn been replaced by a perceptible happiness. Jamie was pleased but confused. She had Heather on the phone every evening, crying and cursing men, Paul in particular, wondering out loud what she had done wrong. Then there was Paul himself, who had announced that he didn't want any visitors apart from his parents, not until he was fully recovered, anyway. Kirsty had gone to see him at the end of a long shift, persuading her way past the nurse who acted as a kind of bouncer for Paul, but he had refused to speak to her, closing his eyes and pretending to be asleep. Jamie was furious when Kirsty told him, but she had simply shrugged and said, 'If it's what he wants.'

Then, of course, there was the continuing harassment from the Newtons. Lucy had written them another letter, saying that the sound of Kirsty thrashing the toilet brush round the pan on a Sunday afternoon, when they had been doing their weekly housework, had been intolerable. It was one of those letters that, at first, made Jamie laugh. But after reading it a couple of times it struck him how insane the writer must be, and he felt scared. Kirsty, however, had simply shrugged and said, 'I'll just have to thrash a bit more quietly, won't I?'

On Saturday, they took a trip to Covent Garden and bought their wedding outfits. Jamie bought a fabulous velvet suit and Kirsty spent a fortune they didn't really have on a beautiful dress from Whistles. Jamie put it on his credit card. He refused to worry about the expense – this was their wedding day, after all. When Kirsty came out of the changing room in the dress, Jamie felt like applauding. She was stunning. Kirsty looked at herself in the mirror and burst into tears.

Surely, Jamie thought, it couldn't be the wedding alone that was making Kirsty seem so happy, apparently oblivious to all the crap that was going on around them. Even the appearance of a spider in the bathroom the other day had not fazed her: she had calmly called for Jamie to get rid of it, whereas a few weeks ago she would have had a screaming fit. She was so calm that Jamie wondered briefly if she was on drugs. She was a nurse so it wouldn't be very hard for her to get hold of a bottle of tranquillizers. He quickly dismissed the idea, admonished himself for being stupid. Kirsty would never fill her body with drugs – she wouldn't risk harming the baby in any way.

'You seem to be handling all this much better than I am,' he said to her one night, sitting in front of the TV. 'A couple of weeks ago you were really stressed, but now you seem as if you're not worried about Lucy and Chris any more.'

She turned to him. 'It's not that I'm not worried, Jamie, but I'm trying to put things into perspective. I hate them. I'd be delighted if they moved out. I'd be pleased if they just stopped writing us such stupid letters. But it's not as if they've actually threatened us physically. In fact, I think they're staring to get bored. The hoaxes have dried up. We haven't seen them for weeks.'

'But their presence is always there.'

'I don't know. I've almost managed to put them from my mind.' She put her hands on his shoulders. 'Jamie, we've got so much to look forward to. We're going to be parents. That's a lot scarier than our neighbours, surely.'

He laughed.

She took his hand and rested it on her stomach. 'I simply want to think about the future, Jamie. And I don't have enough mental energy to waste my thoughts on Lucy and Chris.'

He nodded, but he couldn't quite tune in to her wavelength. He couldn't cast Lucy and Chris from his mind, no matter how hard he tried. And also, he wasn't sure how sincere Kirsty was being. It might just be that she was putting on a brave face, persuading herself that she needed to be happy. He was worried that her mood was a veneer, and that it could be torn away at any time.

He prayed that this wouldn't happen, because he needed her strength and optimism. He was doing enough worrying for both of them. Every night before he went to sleep he fell into a state of semiconscious worry, his mind focusing on one problem after another. He would worry about Paul, wondering why he was being such an arsehole, wondering if the doctors were wrong when they said he had suffered no mental damage. Then he would start worrying about something else. Work, money, how they would manage with one-and-a-half salaries when Kirsty had the baby and went part-time. He worried about how the baby would affect their relationship. He worried about how his parents would react when they discovered he and Kirsty had got married without telling or inviting them.

And most of all, he worried about Lucy and Chris. What would they do next? Would they play that awful music again? He felt as if there were two invisible trolls living underneath him – these malicious entities that he never saw, only heard or heard from. He wondered if they should move out, then reaffirmed his determination that they had to stay. At the end of his cycle of worries, he always fell asleep with two people on his mind: not Kirsty and their unborn child, as it should be, but Lucy and Chris.

What are you going to do about it?

The day after his big scene with Paul, he had been standing in the gents toilet at work, drying his hands. The door opened and Mike came in. He nodded hello to Jamie then stood at the urinal and unzipped. There was no-one else around.

Jamie finished blow-drying his hands and paused. He didn't want to go back to his desk. He had so much work to be getting on with. He had fallen seriously behind recently, putting all his hardest tasks to the bottom of the pile, even though he knew that was the last thing he should do. A software system he had installed at a school in Colindale was playing up and the headmaster had been on the phone urging him to sort it out. Jamie went down to the school and found that the printers only worked erratically, the internet connection was stupidly slow and the system kept crashing. He couldn't work out what was wrong with it but didn't want to admit as much, so he tinkered with it and went home. Now, the headmaster was on the phone every day, growing ever more irate. Jamie left his voicemail on and didn't return his calls. He knew it was only a matter of time before his manager got involved, but the whole thing made him feel sick with weariness. There were more important things going on than the headmaster's stupid computer system.

He leaned into the mirror and studied the bags beneath his eyes. God, he looked rough – rougher than a cat's tongue. He stuck out his own tongue. It was white and furry. Gross.

'You look terrible,' said Mike, turning around and zipping up his fly.

'Thanks.'

'What is it? More problems with your neighbours?'

'How did you guess.'

Mike shook his head slowly. 'I don't know how you put up with it, Jamie, I really don't.'

Jamie sighed and pushed himself up from the sink. 'Well what do you suggest I do?'

Mike put his hands up. 'Hey, don't get angry with me.'

'I'm sorry. I didn't mean to. I'm just so tired and it makes me irritable.'

'I understand.'

They were silent for a moment. Mike turned on the tap and rinsed his hands. He turned to look at Jamie and dropped his voice. 'Look, if you want to sort these two out, get them out of your hair, I might know a couple of people who could help you.'

Jamie stared at him, then laughed.

'No, don't laugh. I'm serious.'

'What do you mean by sorting them out?'

Mike shrugged. 'What do you think? Scare them a bit. Tell them to leave you alone.'

'I don't know.'

'These blokes I know would be happy to help. And it wouldn't cost you much. Actually, they owe me a favour so they might even do it for the price of a pint.'

Jamie shook his head. 'This is like some gangland film. I mean, are these people gangsters?'

Mike snorted. 'No. They'd love to be described as gangsters, but they're just a couple of hardmen.'

'It's crazy.'

'No, the people who live downstairs from you are crazy. And surely the most important thing is to protect yourself and your loved ones from crazy people like them.'

Jamie was silent for a moment. 'Why are you so keen to help? What's in it for you?'

Mike shrugged. 'You helped me out a lot when I first started here. You showed me the ropes. In fact, when I started I thought everyone here was a wanker. Except you. So this is my chance to return the favour.'

Jamie furrowed his brow. He remembered how when Mike had started it had been his job to desk-train him and show him around. He didn't remember being particularly kind to him – nothing out of the ordinary anyway. Still, that first impression must have stuck in Mike's head.

'So what do you think? Shall I give them a call?'

'I... No. No, it's not right. I'm not into violence. I find it abhorrent. The whole idea. Jesus.'

The door opened and a middle-aged man called Frank, who sat a few desks down from them, walked in. They said hello to him then Jamie went to leave. Before he did, Mike put his hand on his arm, the tips of his fingers digging like claws into the muscle.

'I think you're making a mistake,' he said.

Jamie shook his hand away. 'No. It's not right.'

'Well, if you change your mind.'

'I won't.'

Now, carrying his coffee through the train, back to where Kirsty sat with her book, he thought of the offer Mike had made and how tempted he had felt. He had been that close to saying yes. But he had done the right thing. At least he still had that: a sense of right and wrong. He still had some sense of morality.

The train rattled along, heading north, and as they moved further from London – away from the source of their troubles – Jamie relaxed. He felt the tension in his muscles ease; the pressure inside his skull subsided.

At Warrington Bank Quay a woman got on with a baby and took a seat adjacent to them. Halfway through the Lake District the baby started to cry, sonorous screams that seemed to make the train's windows vibrate. Up and down the carriage, people tutted, disturbed from their doze or just pleased to have something to tut about. To Jamie, the crying baby was far less irritating than the consistent stream of calls the man behind them had made on his mobile phone, all of which began with the words, 'I'm on the train.' Jamie glanced at Kirsty and saw that she was looking at the baby, a smile on her lips. Her hands went to her stomach – a now-habitual gesture – and the woman with the baby looked up and caught Kirsty's eye.

'You've got all this to come,' the woman said, above the baby's din.

Kirsty stroked the curve of her belly.

'Usually she's a little angel, but today I wish I'd left her at home with her father.'

The baby quietened suddenly, leaving a silence which Jamie felt the urge to fill.

'But you're happy?'

The woman looked surprised by the question. 'Happy? Oh of course, yes. She's the best thing that ever happened to me. However much they scream and misbehave, that fact never changes. This is what it's all about.'

When the woman got off at the next stop she wished Kirsty and Jamie luck.

'Not that you'll need it,' she said. 'You look like a lucky couple to me. Blessed.'

They changed at Carlisle then took another train to Gretna Green, where the station was merely a single platform situated between two fields.

The Bed and Breakfast where they were staying was five minutes walk away. They stepped down from the train and Jamie looked around. There was nobody around: nothing but fields and trees and open space. The air smelled so clean. Coming here had definitely been the right thing to do.

They were shown to their room by a white-haired man and as soon as the door was closed behind them they drew the curtains and took off their clothes. They were both aware that, for tonight, there was nobody around to listen to them; nobody to complain or bang on the ceiling. They lay down on the bed and looked into each other's eyes, and Jamie rolled onto his back so Kirsty could straddle him. She was already wet and it felt so good that he had to concentrate hard to stop himself from coming straight away. He propped himself up on his elbows and Kirsty leaned forward to kiss him, eyes closed, and rocked her pelvis back and forth, slowly, digging sharp fingernails into his back, drawing the focal point of sensation away from his cock. Her breathing quickened and he rocked with her, moving towards orgasm.

Losing himself in Kirsty now, Jamie was able to forget all about Lucy and Chris and all the other things that kept him awake at night. Here, in her arms, familiar flesh in a strange room, as light ebbed from the sky beyond the room, he felt free.

The wedding passed so quickly Jamie was surprised the photographs weren't blurred. They found a pair of old ladies in the newsagents across the road from the registry office who agreed to act as witnesses. Jamie guessed they were used to such requests. One of the ladies took a few photographs of them. One showed them outside the registry office, Jamie in his new suit, Kirsty in her lovely dress, his arm around her shoulders, the Gretna Green Fish and Chicken Bar behind them. They giggled all the way through the ceremony. It felt so absurd – but in a good way.

After the wedding, they went for a meal at a nearby pub. Everybody gave them knowing looks. They had decided to spend another night in Gretna before returning home, so they had the rest of the afternoon to fill. The sky was overcast and it wasn't very warm, but it was such a novelty to be out of the city, they wanted to make the most of it.

'Let's go for a walk,' Kirsty said. 'Enjoy the fresh air.'

They walked arm-in-arm through the village, cutting across an empty field and through a graffiti-strewn tunnel. They found a gift shop and Jamie bought Kirsty a small teddy bear. They stopped for tea, and whiled away the afternoon watching the tourists who, despite being just a few miles over the Scottish border, felt compelled to stock up on tartan and shortbread.

They took a few photographs as they wandered back to the B&B: Jamie in front of a 'Welcome to Scotland' sign; Kirsty beside a statue depicting an abstract couple making love.

'I can't believe I'm tramping around this village in the most expensive dress I've ever bought,' she said. 'I must look ridiculous.'

'You look fantastic.'

She really did.

'Let's get some pictures in here,' Kirsty said, as they passed a graveyard.

'Isn't it a bit gothic?'

'No. It'll look dramatic.'

They entered the little graveyard and looked at the stones, many of which were smothered in moss and unreadable. There were lots of graves gathered together in family groups.

'Do you think we'll be buried together?' Kirsty said.

'I want to be cremated.'

'And I'll scatter your ashes.'

'Hey, how do you know it won't be me scattering your ashes?'

She shrugged. 'Women always live longer.'

Jamie looked up at the church and saw a large crow land on the roof. It ruffled its feathers then settled, looking down at them. He pointed it out to Kirsty.

'Ugh.' She shivered. 'It reminds me of something Paul told me about. About the dreams he had when he was in his coma.'

'He told you about them?'

'I went to see Paul a couple of days before you and he had your big bust-up. Heather had told me she thought he was acting strangely and I wanted to check it out. He seemed fine to me that day – a little tired and subdued, but I thought, Well, he's just woken up from a coma. What can you expect? I thought Heather was over-reacting.'

The crow shifted and spread out its wings, but didn't take off.

'I asked him about the dreams. I wanted to know what they involved. He asked me if I was asking in a medical capacity. I told him I was asking as a friend.'

'And what did he say?'

'He said he could remember these horrible dreams. He dreamt that he was running down a hill, down towards a large town, and there were creatures flying above him: masses of them. A swarm, flying low, dive-bombing him as he ran, scraping the top of his head, getting caught up in his hair. He said they were large and black, like solid shadows, but he didn't know if they were birds or bats. He'd get to the bottom of the hill, the creatures swooping at him from all directions, and fall over onto his face. But at the point when he'd usually wake up, the dream would start again. Looping over and over.'

'Jesus. How awful.'

'I know.'

They were silent for a moment, looking up at the crow, which suddenly took off, its huge wings fanning the moisture-thick air, propelling it away over the graveyard.

'Are you still having those dreams about the gingerbread house?' Jamie asked.

'No. Not for a while. I haven't had any dreams for a while.'

They took their photographs, but the mention of Paul and his coma-dreams had spoiled the mood. Later, Jamie would study the pictures and see, behind Kirsty's smile, a hint of something else. It looked very much like fear.

'Shall we go back to the B&B?' Jamie asked, taking Kirsty's hand.

As they were leaving the graveyard, Kirsty paused to look at a final gravestone. There were two names on the stone. One was of a woman – Elizabeth Anne Robertson, born 1901, died 1924. So young, Kirsty thought. But beneath her name was another name – Jane Elizabeth Robertson. Born 1924. Died 1924. It took a moment for it to sink in. She was looking at the grave of a woman and her dead baby.

Beloved wife and daughter. The Lord took you together. May you both Rest in Peace.

Jamie pulled her away just as the sun retreated behind a cloud, casting a shadow over him and Kirsty and the grave; merging their shadows together while above them the crow circled before returning to the church roof. They could hear it caw as they pushed open the door of the B&B and retreated inside. In a single dark moment, their bubble of happiness had been burst.

Eighteen

'Somebody's been in here.'

As soon as Kirsty walked into the living room, just behind Jamie, she knew something was wrong. There were no immediate tangible signs, but she could feel it. The atmosphere in the room felt wrong. There had been a shift in the air, a strange shape imprinted on the molecules that hung around them and made up the fabric of the room. She could smell it, this unwelcome odour. She felt like an animal, its hackles rising as it caught the scent of a stranger, an invader, an enemy encroaching on its territory. She put down the fistful of post and walked very slowly into the room, looking around, scanning every surface for evidence that their possessions had been touched, moved or tampered with. She sniffed the air and turned round in a slow circle. She couldn't see anything obvious; there was nothing she could point to and say, Look, that's been moved – that wasn't there before, or Where's such-and-such – it should be there. But if there was such a thing as a sixth sense it was working now, telling her that someone had been in here. She felt cold. 'What are you doing?' Jamie asked nervously.

'Didn't you hear what I said? Somebody's been in here.'

'What?' He looked around, apparently checking for the same signs she had looked for. 'It all looks fine. Nothing's missing, is it?' His voice wavered; he didn't sound very sure of himself.

Kirsty shuddered. The idea of someone coming into the flat when they weren't there terrified her. Worse than being recorded. More awful than spiders. The only worse thing she could imagine was rape. This was the second worst violation.

Jamie continued to check around the room. He went into the bedrooms and bathroom, Kirsty clinging to his arm now, afraid that someone might leap out from behind a piece of furniture or appear in a doorway. They would be large and would almost certainly be holding a knife. They would tie Jamie up and make him watch as they raped and murdered her, also killing the unborn child in her womb. Then they would kill him. She gripped Jamie's arm tightly.

There was nobody there. There was no sign, in any of the rooms, that someone had been in there. The windows were shut and locked. The front door had been locked, as had the balcony door, which Jamie checked twice.

'I can feel it too,' he said. 'A lingering presence.'

Kirsty shivered. 'Jamie, you're scaring me.'

She was just beginning to recover from her moment of horror in the graveyard, and now this. The fact that that they could feel it but not see it made it even more scary. It was as if there was a ghost in the flat.

She had to sit down.

For the next ten minutes, Jamie combed the flat, opening cupboards, checking drawers, looking inside boxes, under the sofa. He studied the pictures on the wall, wondering aloud if the intruder might have moved one, accidentally brushing against it and tilting it. He took out photographs they had taken in the summer and held them up, comparing the room in the photographs to the room as it was now. Of course, they had moved things since the summer, added ornaments, shifted furniture, accumulated more junk. The photographs were no help.

'Maybe we're imagining it,' he said, finally sitting down beside Kirsty.

'But we can both feel.'

'That might be because we're putting ideas in each other's heads.'

She knew what he would do now – switch into reassuring mode.

'Look, we've both been pretty spooked since yesterday afternoon, and I know I was nervous about coming back. I've always been paranoid about burglary, plus I had this thought at the back of my mind that Lucy and Chris might do something while we were away. I suppose I brought my worries in with me and my imagination ran away with itself. But there's no evidence that anyone's been in here. The door was locked. The windows are shut tight.' He tried to smile. 'We must be wrong.'

'I guess so.'

It was growing dark outside, long shadows pointing towards the house as the sun went down. Kirsty yawned. 'I'm tired. That long journey's worn me out. I might go to bed for a while.'

'OK.'

She drew the curtains in the bedroom and slipped beneath the cool duvet. She lay there with her eyes wide open, shivering. She wanted Jamie to come to bed with her, to lay close behind her, keep her safe. But he didn't follow her into the room. She heard him moving around the living room, checking shelves and drawers, trying to prove to himself that his instincts were right, even though he wanted them to be wrong.

Night descended and Jamie went to bed. Kirsty had by now fallen asleep, and he kissed the back of her neck and put his arm around her, feeling the slight curve of her belly with his palm. He went to sleep in that position. Earlier, Kirsty had rung her parents and told them about the wedding. They had been not furious but disappointed, which was worse, and Jamie had listened to the brightness fade from Kirsty's voice as she'd tried to justify why they'd done it. The conversation had exhausted her.

Jamie was woken up by a creaking sound. He opened his eyes, a shot of adrenaline making him feel fully awake. The noise sounded close, almost as if it was coming from the next room. Jamie had a clear, horrible thought: What if there really had been someone in the flat – and what if they were still here?

No way, he told himself. We searched the whole flat and there was nobody in here.

But what if the intruder had been hiding somewhere they hadn't looked?

He felt a tremor of fear and sickness run through him. Beside him, Kirsty slept on, oblivious to the drama and tension that held Jamie in its grip. The sounds of footfall continued. Jamie checked the bedside clock. It was three a.m.

He slipped out of bed as quietly as he could and pulled on a pair of jeans and a T-shirt which lay on the floor beside the bed. He realised he wouldn't want to face an intruder barefoot – it would make him too vulnerable – so he groped around in the darkness until he found his trainers. He pulled them on and laced them up.

With his heartbeat booming in his ears, he gently pushed the bedroom door open, wincing and tensing his neck muscles as it squeaked – the squeak sounding as loud as an aeroplane taking off in the night-silence of the flat. He paused in the hallway beside the front door. The door's squeak had actually helped tear open the wall of silence and now the creaking didn't sound so loud. But it was still there. He could still hear it.

The fuse box was beside the front door and next to that was a heavy-duty rubber torch. Jamie kept it there in case of a power cut. He picked it up and felt reassured by its weight. He didn't plan to use it for casting light but as a weapon.

Holding the torch over his shoulder, ready to strike anyone who stood in his way, he shoved the living room door open and flicked the light switch. The room flooded with light and Jamie shut his eyes tight for a second then opened them, blobs of light appearing in his vision – but that was all. There was nobody in the room. It was as empty as he had left it when he went to bed.

'Jamie?'

He turned and saw Kirsty in the doorway, squinting against the light, her hair sticking up all over the place.

'What are you doing?'

He went over and put his arm around her. She felt cold.

'I heard a noise. I thought maybe someone was in the flat.'

'There's nobody here.'

'I know.'

'You must have imagined it. You probably dreamt it.' She yawned loudly. 'God, Jamie, I'm so tired. And you're going to have to get a grip of yourself. You're letting your mind play tricks on you, and it isn't good for either of us.'

He knew she was right – but he had heard the creaking so distinctly, even when he had got up and stood right outside the room. He knew he wouldn't be able to get back to sleep now. He would lie there for the rest of the night, trying to work out if he was losing his mind.

Kirsty went back to bed and Jamie went into the bathroom. He felt too lazy to stand up so he sat down and peed. Just as he finished he saw a fat spider scuttle across the carpet. He jumped up, grabbed it and threw it into the toilet, flushing it away. He quickly decided that he wouldn't tell Kirsty about it. He knew she would imagine it clinging to the pipes, resisting the flush, then crawling back up while she was sitting there.

Yes, best not to tell her.

Jamie woke up feeling relieved that he didn't have to go to work; pleased that he had booked an extra day's leave. He had, to his surprise, fallen asleep quite quickly after returning to bed, but only into a shallow sleep. He lay just beneath the surface of consciousness, jagged thoughts and dark music looping inside his head, preventing him from sinking into deeper sleep, where he wanted, and needed, to be.

As he lay in the light of morning, his eyes shut, trying to re-enter sleep, he felt Kirsty get out of bed and go into the bathroom. He heard the toilet flush, then the sound of her cleaning her teeth. He knew she had been sick, as she was most mornings. She came back to bed and went back to sleep.

Jamie left her in the bed. He needed to get out, to get some air to clear his head. His body felt like a boxer's the day after a big fight. He felt like somebody had squirted a tube of glue through his ear into his brain, and his thoughts were sticking, sluggish and clogged. He dressed and went out for a walk.

There was a small park nearby. He bought a newspaper and a coffee in a polystyrene cup and sat on a bench. He flicked through the newspaper, not really taking any of it in, and listened to the children in the distance, playing on the swings and slide, scaring themselves giddy on the roundabout. Mothers wandered by with pushchairs and prams. Jamie imagined himself and Kirsty coming to the park in a few years with their own child, sitting on a bench and watching him or her joining in with the other children. He wondered if he and Kirsty would hold hands as they sat watching. Would they still be in love? His own parents merely tolerated each other, staying together 'for the sake of the children'. Now those children had grown up and left home, they stayed together out of habit and fear. Whenever he spoke to his dad he complained about his mum; his mum did nothing but slag off his dad.

No, he and Kirsty would never be like that. They would be together forever. And stay happy. He stroked his wedding ring, rotating it on his finger. Kirsty might be up by now. He ought to be getting back.

Heading up the road towards the flat, he saw Chris and Lucy in their car.. He stopped dead and watched as they parked outside the flat and got out. Lucy was in her nursing uniform. Chris was wearing a smart suit. They loitered beside the car for a few moments, apparently in no hurry to go inside. Jamie saw Chris looking at his car and he had a sudden vision of Chris taking out his keys and scratching it, or bending down and slashing the tyres.

He felt a surge of anger – as if Chris had actually done it – and he broke into a run. Within a split second he stopped himself running, lurching to a halt before he had taken a full step. He felt foolish, his heart pounding, his cheeks full of colour. Had the Newtons seen him? No, he didn't think so. They were going inside now, Chris dragging his hand along the top of the wall. Lennon sat there and Lucy paused to stroke him, the cat pushing his head hard against Lucy's fingers.

The image had been so real. He had actually seen Chris scratch the car, slash the tyres. He had seen an evil grin on his face, a dark malevolent glint in his eyes. He shook his head to clear the mental imprint of the image and waited until he heard the Newtons close their front door before walking on.

Before going inside he checked his car. Not a mark on it and the tyres were fine. Shit, he was starting to get really paranoid. He needed to snap out of it. What he really wanted was a drink, but it was only eleven o'clock. He licked his lips, felt thirsty. He saw the picture again: Chris taking out his keys, smiling cruelly, etching a deep line in the paintwork from bonnet to boot. He would be able to have a drink at twelve. With lunch. That would be okay: socially acceptable. He licked his lips again.

'Are you up?' he called as he went inside.

'I'm in the bath.'

He went in and said hello. She looked tired, dark bags under her eyes, lines spreading out from the corners. Had they been there before? These signs of ageing only sprang to attention once in a while, like the horrible moments when he noticed that his hairline had retreated a little more, that the lines at the side of his mouth didn't disappear when he stopped smiling.

'What are you staring at?' she asked.

'Nothing.'

The lines actually made her look more attractive, he thought. When they had first got together she had been a girl. Now she was a woman. He had watched that transformation, had shared in it – had helped it happen, even. No-one else could say that. No-one else knew Kirsty like he did. They were a partnership, a team. All the moments of ecstasy and misery were moments they shared. One day they would be old, and he would be able to look at every line on Kirsty's face and see a story there, a moment from their life together. More than anything in the world, he wanted that. He wanted them to be together always.

'You were staring at me,' she said. 'What is it? What's wrong with me?'

He knelt beside the bath and submerged his hands beneath the warm, soapy water, stroking her belly.

'I was thinking how beautiful you are.'

'Yeah, right.'

There was a knock at the door.

'Oh no.'

'Don't answer it.'

'Why?'

'It might be them,' she said. 'Lucy and Chris. Complaining about the noise we're making.'

He blinked at her, surprised. What had happened to the optimistic Kirsty: the one who was trying to cast the Newtons from her mind? He said, 'We're not making any noise.'

'So? That won't stop them.'

Jamie stood up. 'I hope it is them. I really fucking hope it is.' He dried his hands, marching off towards the door, his courage and fury deserting him the second he opened it. He didn't know what he would do if it was Chris. He had a vision of himself pulling a gun out of his back pocket, blowing a hole in Chris's chest, laughing as he slumped to the floor, pumping more bullets into his slack body, pieces of bone and brain splattering against the clean white paintwork…

Jesus Christ, what was going on?

He opened the door. It was Brian.

'Hello, Jamie, I was – hey, are you alright?'

'What?'

'You look a bit…stressed.'

'No. I'm fine. I'm fine.' He blinked hard to clear the image of Chris's gunned-down body. 'How can I help you?'

'Well, it's my computer. The whole system seems to have gone kaput.'

'How do you mean?'

'It keeps crashing, and I can't open any of my files. I was wondering if you'd have a look at it for me.'

He really couldn't concentrate on what Brian was saying. He watched his mouth move, heard something about a computer, things going wrong.

He nodded. 'Sure. Wait there a second.'

He told Kirsty where he was going and followed his neighbour up the stairs. He hadn't seen or spoken to Brian for ages. Their paths seldom crossed.

Brian opened the door of his study and Jamie was once again struck by how spooky the room was, with its horror paraphernalia and dark walls. He sat down at the desk and switched the computer on.

'I'll leave you to it,' Brian said. 'Do you want a coffee?'

Jamie waited for the computer to boot up. There was no doubt about it – something had gone wrong. The hard drive whirred and made awful crunching noises as the system started up. Several worrying error messages flashed up before the desktop finally appeared. Jamie set about checking the system, trying to open Brian's Word files. As soon as he did this the system crashed and he had to reboot.

Brian came into the room with the coffee.

'Any joy?'

Jamie shook his head. 'It doesn't look good. What have you done to it?'

'Nothing. I haven't done anything different at all. I only use it for word-processing and the internet. I never fiddle around with it.'

'You'd better give me half-an-hour. I find it difficult to work with someone looking over my shoulder.'

Brian hesitated. 'I'm really worried. I've got my new book saved on there. It's almost finished.'

'You've got it all backed up though, of course?'

'Well…'

'Do you use Dropbox or anything?'

Brian looked blank. 'No. It's just saved on the hard drive.'

Jamie sighed. 'OK. I'll do what I can.'

Thirty minutes later Brian came back into the study, looking anxious. 'Have you found out what's wrong with it.'

Jamie swivelled round on the chair. 'You've got a virus. You probably got it from an email or downloading some dodgy program. It looks like the virus you've got is a brand new one. There might not even be an antidote for it yet. It's a bad one as well. It's running through your system eating the files on your hard disk. Have you got a virus checker on your system?'

'No.'

'OK. I've got the software downstairs. I can install it for you. First, let's try and find out where you caught it from.'

He doubled clicked on the email program, Outlook. The screen flickered and Jamie thought the system might crash again. Eventually, though, the inbox appeared, with a list of all the emails Brian had received.

Near the top of the screen, in the list of people who had sent emails to Brian, Jamie saw his own name.

'What the hell?'

'What's wrong?'

'There's an email here from me.'

'I know. You sent it to me on Saturday. What was it meant to be, by the way? I opened the attachment and it just brought up an empty Word document.'

Jamie stared at the screen, the mouse pointer hovering over his name. 'I couldn't have sent you an email on Saturday. I was in Scotland. I didn't send any emails over the weekend.'

'What?'

'I was in Scotland!'

'But that's definitely come from your email address?'

'Yes.'

Jamie knew he hadn't sent anything from his smartphone. *Somebody's been in the flat.*

With a trembling hand, he clicked on his name. There was no message, just a paper clip to say there was a file attached. He clicked the paper clip to bring up the name of the file. It was called Honeymoon.

He stood up and ran out of the room, down the stairs, into his own flat. He rushed over and turned the computer on.

'What's going on?' Kirsty asked.

He didn't reply. The PC was making the same grinding noises that Brian's computer had made. The desktop appeared and, one by one, Jamie tried to open his files. Nothing worked. He couldn't even open Outlook to check when emails had been sent from his account. After a few seconds, the computer crashed.

'Jesus Christ!'

'Jamie, what is it?'

'My PC – someone's put a virus on it.'

'What? How?'

He turned and faced her, his eyes wild. 'Someone has been in here. I was right. Someone's been in here and loaded a virus onto my computer and then sent emails to – God, to who knows how many people – and they're all going to think it was me!'

'Jamie, sit down. You're babbling.'

Brian appeared in the doorway. 'Jamie, what's happening?'

He looked up, panic bleaching his skin. 'I've been sabotaged. Somebody's been in here.'

Kirsty went over and closed the door, saying to Brian, 'You'd better call back later.'

'But my computer...'

'Later.'

She sat and held Jamie as he shook, his face buried against her chest. Eventually, he looked up and said, 'I've got some phone calls to make.'

It wasn't just that the computer was knackered. He had been violated, and his name was attached to the virus, which might have been sent to dozens, hundreds or thousands of people. God yes, he had been violated.

Somebody had been in the flat.

And he knew who.

Somebody had violated him.

Oh yes, he knew who it was.

But what are you going to do about it?

He stood up and looked at the monitor. As he stood there, a shaft of sunlight illuminated the screen. The dust on the screen twinkled and, horrified, Jamie saw a word etched in the dust, drawn with somebody's fingertip. A single word:

danger

He spent the rest of the afternoon on the phone to Norton Anti-Virus.. He had been right – the virus was brand new, so his own virus checker software, and the virus checkers of anyone else who might have downloaded it, wouldn't have detected the virus. He was going to have to rebuild his hard drive, and any work saved on the system was lost.

Still, that was the least of his worries.

He drove into work with dread in his heart. As soon as he walked into the office he knew his fears weren't unfounded. People looked at him then looked away quickly, their gazes burning his back as he walked to his desk. He sat down opposite Mike.

'I hate to say this, Jamie, but you're in deep shit. George Banks wants to see you.'

George Banks was the manager of Jamie's section. Jamie had never been called in to see him before. As he walked towards Mr Banks's office he felt like a Death Row prisoner walking towards the electric chair. His colleagues stared at him; he thought he could hear them whispering as he passed by.

He's going to get the sack. He's going to get the sack.

'Jamie.' George Banks leaned forward across the desk. He was in his late forties but, with his bald head and bloodshot eyes, looked older: a good advert, Jamie had thought before, for staying below managerial level. 'Do you know what I like to do on Saturday afternoons?'

Jamie shook his head.

'I like to play golf. Every weekend a couple of friends and I drive down into Kent and play a round. It's about the only relaxation I get these days.' He took a deep breath. 'This Saturday I only made it to the sixth hole when I got a phone call. I guess that'll teach me for taking my mobile onto the course, but the call told me my game was over. I had to come to the office. The entire computer system had gone down. Files were disappearing into a black hole. Thousands of pounds worth of damage was being done every minute. Do you know why?'

Jamie swallowed hard. 'The virus.'

'That's right. A virus that we traced back to an email sent by you and opened by one of your colleagues working overtime.'

'But I didn't send it.'

'What?' He spoke sharply.

'I wasn't anywhere near my computer on Saturday. I didn't send any emails that day. It was...'

'Jamie, we've ascertained that this virus wasn't even created until Saturday. I spoke to a chap at Norton this morning who told me that every reported case of this virus they've received came from the same source. An email titled Honeymoon. An email that came from your email address.'

'But...'

'Do you know how much damage this virus has done to us? How much it's cost? An amount not dissimilar to your annual salary. It would have been a lot worse if we hadn't noticed it so quickly.'

'It wasn't me! With respect, sir, I know how these things work. If I did, for whatever sick reason, want to send a virus to everyone in my address book, I sure as hell wouldn't be stupid enough to send it from my own email account!'

George Banks sighed and took off his glasses, rubbing his eyes. He appeared to slump in his seat. 'We're all under a lot of pressure here at the moment, Jamie, what with the takeover.'

'Is that definitely going ahead?'

'We think so. And our prospective new bosses certainly weren't too happy when they heard about this episode. We install software, for God's sake. If it got out that we had a deadly virus on our systems we'd lose all our customers overnight.'

George was clearly anxious about the takeover himself, like the rest of the staff. Nobody below management level even knew the identity of the company who were going to take over. People were worried about their jobs.

'Are you going to fire me?' Jamie said, his voice cracking a little. He pictured himself going home, having to tell Kirsty – his new wife, his pregnant wife – that he was unemployed. 'I swear, it was nothing to do with me.'

George Banks shook his head. 'I'm going to leave that decision to our new masters. I'm willing to accept that this was a mistake, that maybe you forwarded this virus by accident. Your record has been impeccable up to now. Everyone tells me what a good worker you are – how bright and reliable you've always been. I understand you've just got married and have a child on the way. Personally, I can't see what you could gain from sabotaging your own employer. But for God's sake, Jamie, you've got to be careful.'

'Yes sir.'

'Maybe you'd better take a few more days' leave. Some of your colleagues lost a lot of files and are – understandably or not – unhappy with you.'

'OK.'

Jamie stood up and George Banks opened the door. Before Jamie left the office, George said, 'It goes without saying that if I find out that you *did* do this on purpose, you'll be out of here so fast you'll catch fire.'

'Yes sir,' Jamie said bleakly. 'But I didn't.'

He walked through the office with his head down, ignoring the whispers and stares. He picked his bag up from his desk and walked towards the exit. Mike followed him to the lift.

'What happened?' he asked, eager for gossip.

'He told me to take a few days off.'

'He didn't sack you?'

'No.'

'Did you do it on purpose? Striking a blow for the workers and all that?'

Jamie hissed, 'Of course I didn't do it. But I know who did.'

'You do? Who?'

'My neighbours.'

Mike looked surprised. 'How could they have?'

The lift reached the ground floor. 'They broke into my flat and put the virus onto my PC then emailed it from there. Chris works in computing too so he'd know how to do it.'

'Fucking hell.' He shook his head. 'That's just…unbelievable.'

'Tell me about it.'

Jamie strode off, leaving Mike behind. For a second there, as the lift doors pinged open, he had been on the verge of asking Mike to contact his thug friends. Only a mixture of fear and willpower had stopped him from doing so.

He walked out to his car, taking his keys out of his pocket and rattling them in the palm of his hand. As he went to unlock the door he caught his breath. There was a long, deep scratch along the side of the car. He felt his heart fly up into his mouth. He rubbed his eyes, pinched the bridge of his nose. When he looked again the scratch had gone.

He had been so certain he had seen it. It had been there, right before his eyes, a thick silver line etched deep in the blue paintwork.

Jesus. The noises in the flat. And now this.

He drove home, convinced he was going mad.

Nineteen

'I asked for Dodds.'

'I'm afraid Constable Dodds is on leave, sir.'

'Well, what about Sutton then?'

'Who?'

'Constable Sutton. He was with Dodds when he came round. When I first explained to the police about all the fucking shit our neighbours have been putting us through.'

'There's no need to use that language, sir.'

'Why the fuck not?' Jamie clenched his fists, bit down on his bottom lip. 'I'm on the verge of going down there and…doing something.'

The young policeman put his hand on Jamie's shoulder. 'Sir, calm down.' He gestured towards the kitchen. 'Why don't you make a cup of tea?'

Jamie didn't want tea. He sighed and sat down on the sofa. The policeman pulled up a chair and sat in front of him.

'So you don't know PC Sutton?'

He shrugged. 'I haven't been in the Force long, sir. Sutton might have transferred to another station. It does happen.'

'But it was only a few weeks ago.' Jamie put his head in his hands. Right now he felt like he only had the most tenuous grip on reality. He imagined himself at the edge of a deep, deep pit, clinging on desperately, his knuckles white with the strain, his fingernails breaking as he clawed the earth, trying not to fall into the darkness.

'Well, I'm here now, sir. Why don't you tell me about it.'

'I don't want to have to explain the whole thing all over again. That's why I asked for Dodds or Sutton. They know what I'm going through. Why is Dodds on leave? Is he ill?'

The policeman – whose name Jamie had forgotten the moment it had been uttered – shifted in his seat. Jamie could tell he was growing impatient. 'Policemen are allowed leave too, Mr Knight.'

Jamie put his head in his hands. He simply didn't have the energy to tell the story all over again. He hardly had any energy at all. The only things that were keeping him going was his outrage and anger, twin engines of fury burning and smoking in his gut.

'Somebody broke in here while we were away at the weekend. They tampered with my computer, installing a virus on it. Then they emailed that virus to my workplace, my upstairs neighbour and God-knows-who-else. I'm waiting for my friends to start phoning me to tell me how much they hate me.'

The policeman took out a notepad and a pen. 'OK. Any signs of forced entry? Were any windows broken, doors kicked in, locks broken?'

'No.'

'Was anything taken?'

'No.'

'Any damage caused – apart from the computer virus?'

Jamie shook his head. 'No. God, I know this sounds ridiculous. But I also know that someone was in here. They wrote something on the computer screen. The word 'danger', drawn in the dust, mocking me.'

'Ah. Can I see it?'

'Of course.'

They stood up and both peered at the screen.

'I can't see anything, sir.'

The screen was shiny and clear. No dust. No words.

'I don't believe this, Kirsty must have cleaned it. Oh, that stupid…' He bit his tongue.

'Sir. You're shaking. Are you sure you don't want a cup of tea?'

'Will you shut up about tea!'

The policeman's mouth formed an O of surprise. Jamie saw his hand go beneath his jacket, ready in case Jamie got violent. How the hell had it got to this point, the point where he was yelling at a policeman? This was all wrong. He sat down again and the policeman relaxed.

'I'm sorry. I'm really sorry.' He lifted his head. 'I'm so stressed out by all this. I promise you, somebody was in here, and I know who it was. My downstairs neighbour, Chris Newton. He works with computers. He might know how to program a virus. If not, he'll certainly know someone who could.'

'What do you do for a living, Mr Knight.'

'Well, I work with computers too.'

'So you also know people who could create a virus?'

'Yes, but...' He trailed off.

'And would you know how to do it yourself?'

'I suppose so.'

The policeman tapped his notebook with his pencil. 'How did this person get into the flat? You say there was no sign of forced entry. I take it all the doors and windows were locked.'

'Of course they were. And I don't know how he could have got in. Maybe he's got a key. He's got a key for the outer door.' A thought sprung into his head. 'Maybe the previous occupants gave him a spare key in case they got locked out.'

'It's possible.'

'Yes. That explains it! That's why there's no sign of anyone breaking in.'

'Well, can you ask the previous occupants? Or give me their name and telephone number and I'll do it.'

'I don't know their telephone number. In fact, I wouldn't have the first idea about how to contact them. They were gone before we even looked at the flat. The sale was handled entirely by their solicitor and the estate agent.'

'You must know their name.'

'I can't remember it. It was a foreign-sounding name, I remember that.'

'Because if we can contact these people and they tell us that they did indeed give a key to your neighbours downstairs, that's evidence that they had the means to get in here.'

Jamie brightened at the sound of that word. Evidence. And then a chill went through him. If Lucy and Chris did have a key, who knows how many times they had been in the flat?

'I'll find the house buying documents. Wait there.'

He ran into the spare room, where all their documents and old bills were kept in a battered bureau that had been in the family for years. When the baby was born it would have to go to make room for the cot. It was a hideous thing anyway.

Jamie pulled out a fat foolscap document wallet and carried it into the living room, where the policeman was examining the DVD collection.

'Here it is. Ms L Pica. But the only address given for her is this one. Hmm, the flat was only in her name. No mention of her boyfriend.'

'That's not unusual.'

'I guess not.'

The policeman made a note of the name. 'OK. We'll see what we can do. But any help you can give us will speed things up. To be honest, at the moment we have absolutely no evidence that a crime even took place.'

'But I was away when the emails were sent. I have proof of that.'

'Is it not possible to program a computer so it will send an email at a future date? And besides, don't you have a smartphone?'

Jamie paused. 'Yes....'

'Well, there you go. Frankly, sir, at the moment, as far as the law is concerned, you're wasting everybody's time.'

As soon as the policeman – whose name, Jamie found out, was Lockwood – had gone, Jamie phoned the solicitor who had handled the sale for Miss Pica. He was put on hold for five minutes before finally getting through to him.

'I'm afraid Ms Pica left explicit instructions that her new address should not be passed on to anyone.'

'But it's important. I have to talk to her.' He started to explain about the break-in and what the policeman had said, but the solicitor interrupted.

'Whatever story you have to tell – and I imagine it's a very long story – it won't change the fact that I cannot give you the address.'

He hung up.

'Bastard,' Jamie shouted. Then he had a thought: Surely Ms Pica and her boyfriend must have left a forwarding address with one of the neighbours just in case any mail turned up here for them? That was what Jamie had done at his last address, just in case anything turned up after the Royal Mail stopped redirecting their post. Who was the most likely candidate? Maybe Brian and Linda, though he didn't really want to talk to Brian at the moment. He would try Mary first.

On his way up the stairs, he remembered what Lucy and Chris had said about the previous owners of the flat. They said they were noisy and difficult to get on with. Not so much hypocrisy as a malicious lie. He could imagine Lucy at work, telling her colleagues how awful it was having to live below Jamie and Kirsty: They put us through such hell; I can't sleep; I'm sure they do it to spite me. And her colleagues saying, Poor you, poor Lucy.

What were the odds that the Newtons had put the previous occupants of the flat through exactly the same kind of hell they were now inflicting on Jamie and Kirsty? They probably had awful stories to tell about Lucy and Chris. I bet that's why they moved out, he thought. They couldn't stand it any more. They gave in.

His heartbeat accelerated. They would be able to back him and Kirsty up. Then the police would have to listen. If Ms Pica and her partner got on so badly with the Newtons, it was unlikely that they would have entrusted them with a key. That was bad news, because it left the question of how Chris had got in unanswered. But it would still be worth talking to them. At the moment, Jamie felt like hardly anyone believed him when he told them about the Newtons. It seemed too far-fetched to be true. But if someone else told the same story, not only would other people have to listen, but Jamie would no longer feel paranoid that he was dreaming all this up.

He knocked on Mary's door and paced around in the hallway waiting for her to appear. But there was no answer. He knocked again but to no avail. He decided to go up and try Brian and Linda.

Linda opened the door. In her forties, she was still an attractive woman, with pale red hair and bright blue eyes, a striking combination. She conformed to Jamie's stereotypical idea that male writers always attract good-looking women, beauty drawn to intellect. He couldn't imagine her behind the counter of Boots. It was a fact that clashed with the other things he knew about her – which wasn't much, admittedly. Of all the people in the block of flats, she was the one he had had least contact with.

'Brian's in his study,' she said. 'Come in.'

'Is he angry with me?'

'What for? The computer?' She smiled. 'He hates computers anyway. Blames them for most of the ills in society. I think he was actually quite pleased when it all went wrong. It proved to him that he was right after all.' She called out: 'Brian, Jamie's here.'

Brian came out of his study, wearing a par of reading glasses that made him look about ten years older than he was. 'Hi Jamie. Got the day off work?'

'The whole week, actually.'

'Very nice.'

'Hmm. How's the computer?'

Brian laughed. 'Dead.'

'Oh.'

'Hey, don't worry about it. I was thinking of getting rid of the bloody thing anyway.'

'What about your book? Wasn't it all lost?'

'No, I had it all printed out so it's just a matter of retyping it. In fact, doing that has allowed me to make a lot of improvements, so really you did me a favour.'

'Oh. Good. Perhaps you should invest in an external hard drive, so you'll have everything backed up in future.' Jamie was relieved. He had been worried that not only would the downstairs neighbours hate him, but the ones upstairs would begin to as well.

'How's Kirsty?' Linda asked. 'You both must be very excited. The patter of tiny feet and all that. If you ever want a babysitter, just give me a shout.'

Jamie wanted to ask Linda why she didn't have any children of her own. She was obviously keen on babies, from the way her eyes lit up when she talked about them. And Brian was a kids' author. It was another fact that didn't fit. The most obvious answer was that they were unable to have children – for biological reasons – and he didn't want to bring up such a sensitive subject.

'Has Kirsty got the week off too?' Brian asked.

'No. She's at work. I get more leave than her.'

'Lucky you.'

Jamie was silent for a moment. Then he said, 'The reason I came up – apart from to see if your computer was alright – was to ask if you have a forwarding address or telephone number for the couple that used to live in our flat.'

Linda shook her head. 'Letitia and David? No, we don't.'

'I seem to recall they moved out in a real hurry. We didn't know about it until after they'd gone.' Brian removed his reading glasses. 'Mary was closer to them than us. She might have an address for them.'

'She's not in.'

'I just heard her front door close,' said Brian.

'Really?'

Jamie thanked them and went back down the stairs. This time, Mary answered her door straight away.

'Jamie! Hi!'

Despite her enthusiastic greeting, she looked like she had a cold. Ginger obviously hadn't worked for her. He knew he ought to enquire after her health, but he wanted to get straight to the point and ask her his all-important question.

'Come in,' she said, before he could open his mouth. 'I was just making a tea. Do you drink herbal tea?'

He was going to be asking a favour. It would only be polite to say yes, even though he thought herbal tea was revolting. 'Yes, that would be lovely.'

He followed her into the flat, looking around for Lennon. 'Is Lennon here?' he asked.

'No. He's out and about somewhere.' She took two floral-patterned mugs down from the cupboard.

She chattered away about the cat while she made the tea. Camomile. Jamie tried not to grimace when she handed it to him.

'You know the people who used to live in our flat?'

'Letitia and David?'

'Yes. I don't suppose you have a forwarding address for them? Or a telephone number? It's just that some mail has come for them and it looks quite important.'

Mary looked at him as if she were trying to see inside his mind, to ascertain if he was telling the truth. He blinked innocently.

'Yes, I have got their address,' she said. 'Postal address, not an email unfortunately.'

His heart leapt.

'I was forwarding their mail to them. I'll forward the mail you've got as well, if you want.'

'No! I mean, no, it's OK. I'll do it.'

She studied him for a long moment, then said, 'Alright.'

She picked up her address book – decorated with a picture of a fat white cat – and copied the address onto a piece of card. She handed it to Jamie.

'Scotland?'

'Yes. Quite a remote village, as far as I'm aware. They told me they wanted to get as far away from London and people as possible.'

That sounded very much like evidence to Jamie. Wanting to get away from people. Isn't that exactly what you'd want to do if you'd had a bad experience with your neighbours? He sometimes fantasised about it: living in the remote countryside, among sheep and chickens, no people nearby to cause you grief. Except he was determined not to be driven out of his home. He was not a quitter.

'Thank you for this,' he said, holding up the scrap of card.

Before he left, Mary gently caught hold of his arm. She looked into his eyes. 'You're not in any kind of trouble are you, Jamie?'

'No. What makes you ask that?'

'You just seem a bit stressed out.'

'No. Everything's fine. Just got married. Baby on the way. We couldn't be happier.'

She clearly didn't believe him, but she didn't push it. Instead she said, 'If you ever need any help, Jamie, you know where I am.' She squeezed his arm.

He hurried down the stairs.

He dialled directory enquiries and tried to get a telephone number for the address Mary had given him. The operator told him the number was ex-directory. He wasn't exactly surprised. He Googled Letitia Pica too, but despite it being an unusual name, nothing showed up.

Okay. If he couldn't call or email them he would have to write them a letter. He found some writing paper – the same paper they had used to write to Lucy and Chris – and sat on the sofa with a cushion on his lap.

Dear Letitia and David

Firstly, let me introduce myself. My name is Jamie Knight. My wife, Kirsty, and I bought your flat from you earlier this year. I will not beat around the bush. We have been having a few problems with Lucy and Chris downstairs and I wanted to ask you if you had had similar experiences.

I also need to know if you ever gave them a key to the flat…

He let it all flow out. By the time he had finished, the letter was nine pages long. He read over it, corrected a few spelling mistakes, and then folded it and put it in an envelope before he changed his mind. He didn't have any stamps, so he needed to go to the post office.

Leaving the flat, he froze. Lucy was standing in the entrance hall, looking through the post.

He took a few steps towards her. 'What are you doing?'

She ignored him.

'I said, what are you doing?'

She rolled her eyes, huffed, then turned and looked at him. 'I was checking the post. Seeing if there was anything interesting.' She looked back down at the shelf of mail, where a number old letters for previous occupants and junk mail lay. 'For us, I mean.'

'If anything comes for you, I'll bring it down.'

Lucy turned fully towards him, folded her arms and looked him up and down. 'Would you really?'

Talking to her made him feel sick. 'Yes, I would.'

'How's Kirsty?'

'What?'

'It must be weird, having something living inside you.' She looked up at a cobweb on the ceiling and said faintly, 'I would hate it.'

'I can't picture you as a mother.'

She stared at him. Her expression was blank, her eyes unfocused. It would have been less creepy if she'd given him daggers, or sneered at him. Instead, she broke into a smile.

'I have to go,' she said brightly. 'We're expecting company.'

He exhaled.

As she stepped through the front door she paused. 'Be careful, Jamie,' she said. And then she was gone.

Twenty

Kirsty and Heather sat in the staff canteen. Heather was going on and on about how Paul had ruined her life.

Kirsty was sympathetic, but she was also tired of hearing about it. Firstly, it wasn't as if Heather was the first person in the history of the universe to get chucked. It happened every single frigging day, but Heather was acting as if life had conjured up a cruel punishment for her alone; something unique. All that had happened was that Paul had decided that he didn't want to be with Heather any more. He had been through a trauma. He clearly had things to work out and work through, and Heather was in the way. End of story.

Secondly, Kirsty had problems of her own. The dreams had returned – the terrible dreams of delight turning to horror inside the gingerbread house. To make things worse, details from Paul's coma dream had seeped into her dream, so the roof of the house was battered by flying beasts, creatures with sharp talons and a rank smell, creatures that – she knew without a doubt – wanted her dead.

Waking up offered little respite. Jamie was in a world of his own, paranoid and jittery, convinced he was going to lose his job and all his friends because of this business with the computer virus. He had stayed awake all night, making these bizarre grumbling noises. She didn't think he was aware he was doing it. He had looked really shocked when she had taken a blanket with her into the living room and curled up on the sofa.

She was sick of it all. She wanted out.

Their dream home had turned out to be, well, a nightmare. They were living above a pair of psychopaths. That was the only word for them. Sending spiders in to terrify her; taping her in her most private moments; robbing her of the ability to relax. That was one of the worst things. She had a really stressful job – ten times as stressful as Jamie's job, dealing as she did with mortality and sickness every day – and she needed a sanctuary. Somewhere to switch off, chill out, recover from the stresses of the day. But no – she was forced to tiptoe around her own flat, and if she forgot about the Newtons for a second, Jamie would say something to remind her. Before they went to Gretna, she had been coping. The thrill of finding out she was pregnant and the thought of being a mother had made her feel calm and happy. She had managed to switch off; she had made a conscious effort to leave the worrying to Jamie. She couldn't afford to worry. She had another life inside her. Anxiety and stress were bad for the baby. That was common sense.

That had all changed in Gretna. As soon as she saw that grave she knew she had been kidding herself. And when they got home and found that word written on the computer screen – proving that someone had been in the flat – that was the last straw.

She wanted to leave the flat. Because now, not only did she feel stressed in there, she felt unsafe as well. Her own flat was the gingerbread house in her dream. Her subconscious had been warning her for months, telling her to get out. In retrospect, she had thought there was something not right about Lucy the first time she met her. Something about Lucy had made her bristle, although she hadn't admitted it at the time. Kirsty thought Lucy was dangerous – more so than Chris – and she didn't want her child anywhere near her.

It was no place to bring up a child – in an atmosphere like that. Children needed space, somewhere to run and play. They couldn't spend their lives on tiptoe. All that 'children should be seen and not heard' crap had gone out of the window years ago. And it wasn't just that. If anyone she had ever met was capable of violence – including violence against children – it was Lucy. She wouldn't say this to anyone, because they would think she was mad, but living above Lucy felt like living next door to a child molester.

Her mind was made up on the train home from Scotland. They were going to have to move.

But Jamie refused to even think about leaving the flat. 'If we do,' he said, 'we'll be giving in to them. It's what they want. We can't quit.' Or, 'Once they get used to us living here they'll probably stop harassing us.' Or, 'We can't afford to move anywhere else.'

Well, that last excuse was bullshit. They could sell the flat and get a similar one somewhere else. Or they could sell the flat and buy a house outside London. They could find new jobs, make new friends. It wouldn't be that difficult. That part of Jamie's argument was easy to shoot down.

She knew Jamie didn't really believe that the Newtons would get bored or accustomed to them and leave them alone. She had once tried to persuade herself of that, but now she knew she had been foolish, naive. And Jamie knew as well as her that things would only get worse.

So that left the real reason he didn't want to move. Typical male shit. He didn't want to be seen to give in, to quit, to wave the flag of surrender. As if leaving would make him less macho somehow. At first she had actually agreed with this point of view. She didn't believe in being pushed around. She didn't want to give Lucy and Chris the satisfaction of knowing they had won. But now things were different. They had the baby to think about. Kirsty had seen an image of death, heard the portentous caw of the crow.

They were going to move out. And if Jamie didn't want to go with her she would go alone.

Twenty-one

On his way home from posting the letter, Jamie saw Paul – just Paul's head at first, then neck, shoulders, torso – coming up the steps from Chris and Lucy's flat.

Jamie stopped in his tracks. He blinked hard, not quite believing what he was seeing. He felt like a husband who had just found his wife in bed with another man. Shocked. Betrayed.

He hurried up the path. Paul turned and saw him, a smile spreading across his face.

Jamie marched right up to him. 'What the hell are you doing?'

'What?'

'Where have you been?'

'I was just coming to see you.'

'But you've been down there. You've been to see Lucy and Chris!' As he spoke, he realised how indignant he sounded – how hurt. Well, good. Let Paul know how he felt. He was sick and tired of bottling everything up.

'Jamie, you're acting like a dick. I've just been to see Chris to talk about what happened at karting track.'

Jamie's eyes widened. 'And now you're going to go to the police?'

'What are you talking about, Jamie? Why the hell would I be going to the police?'

'Because – because Chris tried to kill you. He put you in that coma.'

Paul laughed. 'Oh Jamie, you should hear yourself. It was an accident. I can see that, and I was the one who was in a coma. Why can't you see it?'

'Because I know Chris. And because I was there.'

'You didn't see the accident though. You were in the cafe. Chris and I were having a race. We allowed things to get out of hand. We were being stupid, getting over competitive. Chris was pissed off that I beat him, of course, and he braked the second he crossed the line, causing the driver behind him to swerve into me. Chris shouldn't have braked so suddenly – he knows that. But Jamie, you have to believe me – it was an accident.' He clapped his hand on Jamie's shoulder. 'An accident. That's it.'

Jamie opened his mouth to speak, to protest, but seeing Paul staring at him, a broad smile on his face, he fell silent. He felt so confused. He hadn't seen Paul since that day in the hospital when Paul had been so nasty to him. His friend had been so cold that day, but now, with that smile on his face and that light in his eye, he seemed like the old Paul. A voice in Jamie's head was screaming that Paul was wrong – that it hadn't been an accident – but he was so pleased to see Paul smiling again, up and about and acting like himself again, that he didn't argue.

273

'Are you feeling better?' Jamie asked. His voice was hushed and he became aware that he was holding his breath.

Paul nodded, his hand still on Jamie's shoulder. 'I feel great, actually. Better than ever. I feel, y'know, reborn, clean. I've had loads of time to get my head together and, God, I'm really sorry I was such a bastard in the hospital. I felt trapped and I was finding it difficult to cope. The frustration of lying there, unable to get out because my muscles were too weak – it was unbearable. And the constant stream of sympathy. It was too much. Everybody treated me as if I was some kind of crippled Lazarus. How was I supposed to react?'

'Well, you reacted like a complete bastard.'

They both laughed.

Paul pulled a face. 'I guess I had a bit of brain damage.'

'What? Impossible! There's nothing there to damage.'

They laughed more, still standing there at the top of the Newtons' steps. Paul looked serious for a second. 'I do feel different though, Jamie. And, well, there's something I've decided to do. Something I need to talk to you about. I was going to call on you after I'd been to see Chris. In fact – just in case you feel second-best and get all sensitive – I did call on you first but you were out.'

'OK. Let's go inside.'

As Jamie took his keys out of his pocket, he heard the door slam at the bottom of the steps. He jumped, then went rigid. Footfall sounded on the steps and, before he could react, Chris appeared.

'Alright mate,' Paul said to Chris.

Chris smiled at him, 'Haven't you cleared off yet?' Then he turned to Jamie. 'Hello Jamie.'

Jamie's heart was beating so fast and loud it almost drowned out Chris's voice. It was the first time Chris had spoken to him for a long time. He expected to feel hatred. He had fantasised about hurting this man, about doing him damage. But instead of hatred or anger, he felt fear, and confusion. Most of all, confusion.

'Hi,' he managed to croak.

'You alright?' He was talking to him as if nothing bad had ever passed between them. As if there had been no letters or CDs; no threats; no virus. As if they were simply neighbours who exchanged a friendly hello whenever their paths crossed.

'I'm–' Jamie broke off, unable to speak.

'You don't look too good, mate,' Chris said, and he stretched out his hand to touch Jamie's arm.

Jamie leapt backwards as if a bullet had torn into him. Chris and Paul both looked shocked. Jamie instantly felt ridiculous, foolish. He tried to compose himself. He stood up straight, coughed, ran a hand through his hair.

'I'm fine,' he said.

Chris gave him a strange look – the kind of look you might give to a patient in a mental hospital; a potentially dangerous patient who you didn't want to upset. 'Good. That's good.' He turned to Paul. 'Anyway,

I must get on. Got that business meeting to attend. Good luck and all that.'

'Thanks.'

They shook hands, then Chris walked off and got into his car.

Paul turned back to Jamie, who was shaking as if he'd been in a car crash. 'Wow, you really don't like him, do you? I don't understand what your problem is. He's a good bloke.'

Jamie was speechless.

'Come on,' Paul said, 'let's go in.'

It felt colder in the flat than it did outside. Jamie cranked up the heating. He could feel goosepimples beneath the sleeves of his shirt, the hairs on his arms bristling.

'Do you want a cup of–' He changed his mind halfway through the sentence. 'Do you want a beer?'

'I'd love one.'

He took a couple of tins of lager out of the fridge and tossed one to Paul. Jamie cracked the ringpull and took a slow, greedy sip. God, he had needed that, although he was still cold and shaky. Maybe he should open that bottle of whiskey. Firewater – that's what he needed. He could almost taste it, could feel it scorching his throat, burning his chest, seeping into his bloodstream and washing away the pain. He licked his lips.

'You were so lucky finding this place,' said Paul, interrupting Jamie's train of thought. 'I think that every time I come round.'

'You haven't been round here for quite some time.'

'I know. But I expect it seems longer to you than it does to me. The weeks I was in a coma, while you were living your lives, passed like that.' He clicked his fingers. 'From the moment of the accident to the moment I woke up. My body was ageing but I lost a chunk of my life. Hey, I'm not explaining myself very well, am I?'

'No, I do understand what you mean. But did it really pass in a flash? You told Kirsty you had bad dreams.'

Paul stared into his beer; Jamie thought he saw him shudder. 'Yeah, but I only remembered that afterwards. It wasn't as if I was aware of being in a coma.'

'You didn't find yourself floating close to the ceiling, looking down at your body?'

Paul laughed quietly. 'No, and I didn't find myself in any long tunnels either, floating towards a bright white light.'

'No voices calling you back? Paul, Paul, come back – your time is not up.'

'Afraid not.'

Jamie had pulled up a chair and was sitting close to Paul. He studied him closely. He looked so much better. Healthier than ever before, in fact. Almost glowing.

'So you feel better now?'

'God yes. I feel great. Fantastic.' He rubbed his palms together vigorously. 'I feel so full of energy, you know? I wake up in the morning and instead of groaning and pulling the quilt up over my head, I get up immediately. And you'll never guess what I do then. I go out for a run.'

Jamie almost choked on his beer. 'You? Running?'

'I know. It doesn't seem natural, does it? But I was such a slob before. My body was starting to atrophy. So was my brain. All I thought about was sex and food and drink and having a laugh. Obviously, those things are still important' – he laughed – 'but – I don't know – I just feel that there's got to be more. Maybe this happened to me for a reason. Like I was given a message.'

'Oh shit– you've gone and discovered God.'

They cracked up. Paul leant forward, rocking with laughter. Jamie laughed so hard that tears rolled down his cheeks. It felt so good to laugh, to laugh so hard that your stomach hurt and your ribs ached. Like a release of pressure, a slap to the system. They laughed and laughed.

Eventually, Paul recovered enough to say, 'No, not God. But, please. Let me be serious for a minute.'

They quietened. Jamie drained the remains of his beer.

'I've decided to go away,' Paul said. 'I'm going travelling.'

Jamie absorbed this.

'I'm going to start by catching a ferry across to France, then make my way from there. Head south to Spain, maybe spend some time down there, find some work, whatever. Then I'm going to go east through Europe into Asia. India, Thailand, China, Japan. Wherever the wind carries me, basically. I'll work out my route as I go.' He leaned forward, so his face was just a few inches away from Jamie's. 'I don't want to spend the rest of my life stuck here, in this city. There's so much to see out there. I want to fly. I want to gather stories. When I die and the whole of my life flashes before my eyes, I want the flashes to contain beauty and excitement; gold temples; blue seas; women with black hair and deep chocolate eyes.'

Jamie still didn't speak.

'This is the conclusion I came to lying in that hospital bed. I almost died, Jamie, and if I had – if I had died – what images would have flashed before my eyes then? My average childhood. Entering the father and son talent contest at Butlins and coming fifth out of seven. That time I walked four miles to Gemma Baker's house to give her a valentine card and the look of horror on her face. Falling asleep at the back of the lecture hall at university. Snogging Wonderwoman at your party. What a life, eh? There's got to be more.'

Jamie looked up. 'So is that what you think of my life? That's it's dull. That I'll have nothing to remember on my death bed? Thanks a lot.'

'No, no – of course I don't think that. You've got Kirsty. A woman who really loves you and who you love back. You've got this fantastic flat. You're going to have a baby. Those are the really important things, Jamie. You've got your nest here. You're a lucky man. But I've never found anyone that I've wanted to settle with and grow old beside.'

'What about Heather? She was crazy about you. For some unfathomable reason.'

He sighed. 'I really like Heather. She's gorgeous and she's really sweet. But it's not enough. I wouldn't want to marry her or have a kid with her. I don't meant to be horrible, but that's the way it is. And to make things even worse, our relationship could never be a normal one. A couple of days after we started going out, I fell into a coma. She then went into this long period of mourning, followed by delight when I woke up. She'd already imagined a past and a future for us while I was oblivious to my own existence, let alone hers. How could I live up to her fantasy version of Paul? I couldn't.'

Jamie stood up. 'Do you want another beer?'

'I'd love one.'

Jamie went over to the fridge, fetched two more tins of beer and returned to his spot beside Paul. He still felt cold. Even colder now, in fact. He so wanted to feel happy for Paul, to feel glad that he was going to go off and do something he really wanted to do. But all he could think was that he was losing his best friend. Again. Only a minute ago they had been laughing together like they always used to.

Now Paul was going away. Jamie knew he was being selfish and immature, but he couldn't help it. Right now, he needed all the friends he could get.

Paul was about to start talking again when they heard the front door open, rattling a little where it had begun to stick again, the hinges squeaking shrilly. Kirsty came into the room, dropping her bag at her feet. She had taken a taxi from the hospital.

'Oh.' She was surprised but pleased. 'Hi, Paul.'

'Alright, Kirsty?'

'Are you boys having a party?'

'Just a little one.'

She studied them. 'So have you two kissed and made up?'

Jamie looked away while Paul smiled and said, 'Yes. We have. Isn't that right, Jamie?'

He nodded. 'Yes. That's right.'

'Good. I'm glad to hear it. It didn't seem right, you two not talking.' She looked at Jamie as if to say, See, I told you he'd get better; that he just needed time.

'Paul was telling me that he's going away.'

'What do you mean?'

Paul stood up and went over to her. 'I'm going travelling.'

'Wow. That's great. How exciting! When are you going?'

'The day after tomorrow.'

Jamie was shocked. 'That soon?''Well, yeah. There's no time to waste.'

'And the physio says you're fit enough?' Kirsty asked.

'Says I'm as fit as I'll ever be. Apparently, my recovery has been quite astonishing. And that's a direct quote.'

'Well. That's fantastic. Have you told Heather?'

'No.Why should I?'

'Because she's still...' Kirsty rubbed her tailbone and sighed. 'You know you've really hurt her, don't you?'

'Yes, but I was just explaining to Jamie–' He ran briefly through his reasons for breaking up with Heather again.

'I do understand,' Kirsty said when he had finished. 'I'd probably have done the same in your shoes. It's just a shame that you're going to leave the rest of us to clear up the mess.'

'I know, Kirsty. But what else can I do? I mean, I could have tried to give it another go. I could have strung her along for a while. Maybe I could have gone away with the promise that I'd write every week and that eventually I'd return to her arms.'

'She'd probably have wanted to go with you.'

'Exactly. And I need to do this on my own. Singular.' He smiled and touched her stomach lightly. 'Whereas you are about to become plural.'

'Well, in six months.'

'What does it feel like, having another life inside you?'

'It feels like the best thing ever.'

'What, better than having Jamie inside you?'

She slapped him playfully. 'You're so rude! But it's nice to have the old Paul back. Not that miserable git we had to put up with in the hospital.'

'Anyone would be miserable in your hospital.'

'Up yours.'

Jamie came over and put his arm around Kirsty's shoulders. He knew this would be the last occasion he saw Paul for a long time. But what Paul had said was true: he had Kirsty and they were going to have a child. He was going to be so busy when the baby was born he probably wouldn't notice that Paul wasn't around.

Probably.

They both hugged Paul goodbye at the front door. Jamie kept a wary eye out for Chris, but his car was still absent from its spot, and there was no sign of Lucy either. It was chilly outside; the pigeons on the rooftops opposite huddled together for warmth, puffing up their feathers.

'We can email each other wherever I am and I'll no doubt put loads of pics on Facebook, just to make you sick with jealousy.'

The mention of emails made Jamie feel slightly ill. It made him think about work. And Chris. Their intruder.

'You take good care of her, Jamie. You really are a lucky man, you know. Even if you don't feel like it all the time.'

Jamie nodded.

'Right. I'm going to go before I get all soppy and start blubbing. That wouldn't be a pretty sight.'

'No.'

They hugged again. Kirsty had tears in her eyes. Jamie felt a hard knot in his throat and tried to swallow it.

'Take care,' he said.

'And you.'

They watched Paul walk off down the hill, then went back inside. Jamie looked around the flat. It seemed a little emptier, even though Paul had only been here an hour. Maybe it was that his life felt a little emptier.

Kirsty said, 'I'm going to bed.'

'But it's only six o'clock.'

'I know. But I'm so tired. I feel sick, I've got a headache and my back hurts.'

'Do you want me to give you a massage?'

'That would be lovely.'

She sat on the edge of the bed with Jamie kneeling behind her. She kept her bra on and Jamie had a pang for the days when she would undress completely and lie on her front. He squirted massage oil into his palms, rubbing his slippery hands together to warm them. He pushed his hands over her shoulder blades, moving his thumbs in small circles to penetrate the tense muscle tissue.

'Hmm, that feels nice.'

'Good.' He concentrated on the massage for a few minutes. After a while, he said, 'Do you want to know what Paul did before he came round here?'

'Mmm. What?'

'He went to see Lucy and Chris.'

She turned her head. 'You're joking.'

'I wish I was.'

'What the hell did he do that for?'

'He still seems to think they're alright. He even tried to persuade me of the fact.'

'Did you tell him about all the things they've done?'

'I've told him before. But he still thinks Chris is a really good bloke. And guess what? While I was outside, talking to Paul, Chris came out and said hello to me.'

Kirsty turned around so Jamie had to stop massaging her. 'What did you say to him?'

'I didn't really say anything. I was so shocked I nearly fell over.'

'You should have told him to get lost.'

'I couldn't. Not with Paul there, and them being all matey.'

She exhaled. 'Maybe it's a good job Paul is going away.'

'I don't know. Maybe if Paul was acting as a sort of go-between, we could become friends with Chris and Lucy again.'

'What?'

'I don't know. It's just…maybe Paul's right. Maybe Chris is an alright bloke. Sometimes, Kirsty, sometimes I feel like all this is going on inside my head. That I've imagined half of it. What if we were being really noisy and they were within their rights to complain? Surely the spiders were just spiders, like everyone gets. And maybe I did send that virus, by accident.'

'No!' She rolled over, sat up, and grabbed his arms. 'What about the recording they made of us making love? Did they have the right to do that? And all the junk mail and hoaxes. That was all in our imagination, was it? The rats left outside the front door – I bet that was them. And what about the word written in the dust on your computer screen?'

Jamie rubbed his oily hands together. 'I meant to ask you about that. Why did you wipe it off? I wanted to show it to that policeman, and it had gone. I looked really stupid.'

'But I didn't wipe it off.'

'Are you sure?'

He breathed in sharply. 'Maybe I imagined it, then. Maybe it was a hallucination.'

'But I saw it too.'

'Maybe we both imagined it.'

'Jamie, you're mad.'

'That's what I'm afraid of.'

She slapped his face. The crack of her palm against his cheek resounded through the bedroom, bouncing off the walls, echoing in the stunned silence.

He stared at her.

'Jamie, I'm sorry.' She wrapped her arms around him, pulled his face into the space where her neck and shoulder met. 'You mustn't say things like that, OK? It isn't in your imagination. It's them. Lucy and Chris. They're doing it all. And that's why we need to get away from here. I've decided, Jamie, we should move.'

He struggled out of her grasp.

'No! We're not moving.'

'But Jamie, we can't bring a child up here. Not with those people downstairs.'

'No. I won't give in.' He jumped off the bed and began to stamp on the floor. He shouted, 'I won't give in! I won't give in!' And the tears came, flooding out of him, pouring forth, months of pent-up frustration. It had been a day for catharsis. The laughter earlier. Now the tears. He shuddered as he sobbed, and Kirsty held him, stroking his hair as he drenched her with his tears.

'I won't give in,' he whispered.

She held him, and he could feel her chin on his shoulder. 'OK, for your sake, I'll give it one more chance.'

Twenty-two

Several weeks later, Kirsty stood naked in front of the mirror, examining herself. For years, she had wanted a flat stomach – achieving it by spending countless hours doing sit-ups – and now that flat 'ideal' had gone, replaced by a slight curve: the gentlest of contours, but a contour nonetheless. And she didn't care. In fact, she felt wonderful. Her hair was shiny, her breasts had swollen and her nipples had darkened. She was amazed by them, thought she looked like a Page Three girl. Jamie was amazed by them too, predictably. She had always thought it was a cliché, that pregnant women glowed. But she felt it, in her skin, deep in her flesh. Apart from the occasional bout of sickness, she loved being pregnant. I'm radiant, she thought, giggling to herself.

Jamie came into the room and stood behind her, put his arms round her, resting his hands on her belly.

'You're beautiful,' he said.

They kissed gently, moving towards the bed. Jamie sat down on the edge and Kirsty leant towards him, her tongue touching his, her fingers unbuttoning his shirt. Some women craved bizarre combinations of food when they were pregnant. Right now, she craved this. She threw Jamie's shirt aside and he lifted himself up so she could pull down his jeans and boxers. She curled her fingers around his penis, making his breathing become deeper.

'Lie back,' she said.

He pushed himself backwards onto the bed and lay down. She leant over him, her soft hair tickling the skin of his chest and stomach. She took the tip of his penis between her lips, ran her tongue over the head. He said her name. She removed it from her mouth and moved up to kiss him on the lips, so he could taste himself. They kissed deeply. He tried to pull her down, but she put her hands on his chest and held him there, flat on the bed.

She positioned herself over him and took his penis in her hand, holding it so she could lower herself onto it, slowly, so it sank into her millimetre by millimetre, until he was fully inside her.

'Kirsty.'

She moved so, so slowly, her eyes closed. He gently stroked her belly, her large breasts, feeling the novel weight of them in his hands. She licked the tip of her middle finger and put her hand down behind her, between his thighs, sliding the tip of her finger into his anus.

'Oh Christ.'

He tried to wriggle, but she pushed down on his chest with her free hand, pinning him down. She stretched out her finger and slid it in as far as she could reach.

'Kirsty.'

He came, shouting as he did so.

She withdrew her finger, leaned forward, kissed him and rolled onto her back. He went to kiss her lips again but she pushed his head down over her belly and towards her thighs, down between her legs.

'My turn,' she said.

Jamie drove to work. The first day back after his enforced holiday, he had been terrified. Firstly, he was afraid that they would have decided to sack him after all and, secondly, if they didn't do that, he was afraid that his colleagues would hate him. He had almost been sick in the lift up to his floor. But the moment he had stepped out of the lift he had seen Mike, who had come straight over to talk to him.

'Welcome back,' he said.

'Thanks. Has my desk been cleared while I was away?'

'Eh? No, of course not. You don't think they'd sack you over that, do you?'

'I was worried they might.'

Chris rolled his eyes. 'Listen, the management have got more important things to worry about than you and your virus. Have you heard?'

'What?'

'The takeover's definitely going ahead.'

They walked over to their desks and sat down. All around them, people were chatting, gossiping, an electric current of nervous excitement buzzing around the office. Nobody paid any heed to Jamie. He relaxed, felt the knot in his shoulders untwist itself.

'Has it been officially confirmed?'

'Not exactly. We had a memo to say that the rumours were correct, that the company was on the verge of accepting an offer from another company, but that we shouldn't panic, blah blah blah.'

'Panic about what?'

Mike gave him a funny look. 'What do you reckon? Our jobs. That's been the number one topic of conversation this last fortnight. Will there be redundancies? Who's for the chop? Lots of worried faces around – especially among the management. The word is that we plebs are pretty safe, but the middle managers are going to be – what's the word? – culled.'

'Ouch.'

'Yeah. Ouch, indeed.'

'And do we know who's taking over?'

Mike shook his head. 'Not officially. But I reckon it's going to be Software Logistics.'

'That Croydon firm? Really?'

'I'd put money on it.'

Jamie switched his terminal on. To be honest, he didn't care who his boss was, as long as they paid his wages and didn't interfere too much or try to change things for the sake of it. And he was so relieved that he wasn't a pariah among his colleagues. Now he just wanted to get down to work. Lose himself in it for a while.

At lunchtime, Mike said, 'So how are things at home? Have you had any more grief from those neighbours of yours?'

Jamie paused. 'Well, it's strange. We haven't. I saw Chris – that's the bloke downstairs – and he said hello to me. He was quite civil, actually. I was a bit freaked out.'

'I bet.'

'But since then, we've heard nothing from them. No letters, no hoaxes, no banging on the ceiling. Nothing weird has happened at all.'

Jamie thought back to that day, the day they had said goodbye to Paul. After that day he had felt wrecked, emotionally drained by all the tears and laughter. But he also felt a little better. Their sex life had reignited, although at first he had been worried about harming the baby (Kirsty had to assure him that it would be OK). Even though, unable to help themselves, they had been quite noisy they hadn't received any complaints. Jamie had even done a bit of DIY, putting some shelves up in the spare room, which was going to be the nursery. He was sure Lucy and Chris would write to them about the hammer blows, or even his footsteps as he walked around stripping and painting the walls, but no. Not a peep from them.

'Well, maybe they've given up,' Mike said. 'You never know.'

Jamie smiled. It would be so wonderful if they had given up. Or maybe – just maybe – they felt remorseful about what they had done.

Wouldn't that be fantastic?

A month had now gone by. Thirty one days without a threat or a complaint. There hadn't even been any spiders in the flat, although, Jamie thought, that was probably because of the cold weather. As each day went by, he felt himself relax more and more, massaged by this new trouble-free life. He worked on the nursery in the evenings, painting the walls a neutral, sunny yellow. Kirsty spent a lot of time curled up on the sofa, reading; sometimes novels, sometimes books about pregnancy and motherhood. The results of her scan had been good, and she carried the photograph around in her bag, showing it to anyone who was interested. As Jamie painted away in the nursery, and Kirsty brought him a beer, he thought, God, my life is so run of the mill. But he didn't care. He was pleased.

Paul had emailed them, telling them that he was in Ibiza, working in a restaurant, having a fantastic time and sleeping with another traveller, an American girl called Sam. Jamie wasn't envious at all. This – right here – was the life he wanted. He still felt tense at times – still worried about the neighbours, still trod quietly – but it was nothing compared to how he had felt a few weeks ago. He knew he had been heading towards a breakdown. He felt like he'd had a lucky escape.

Kirsty hadn't mentioned moving out again, either. Jamie got the feeling she had adopted a policy of 'wait and see'. He knew she didn't entirely trust this current state of peace, but as the days passed, and the baby inside her grew, and the Newtons' campaign of terror failed to start up again, she relaxed too. She was four months gone now, almost halfway. They bought a cot and a couple of mobiles to hang up in the child's room. When he had finished working in there, they went through lists of names together.

Heather came round some evenings. At first she had been maudlin and lovelorn, but now she seemed to be recovering. She insisted that she hadn't slept with Paul on his last night, although both Jamie and Kirsty were sure she was lying. She insisted on reading Paul's emails and got a bit upset when she read he was seeing someone else – but not too upset.

Christmas wasn't a million miles away. Their first Christmas in the flat; their last Christmas when it would be just the two of them. They decided that they wouldn't see anybody on Christmas day – no family squabbles, no arguments about Kirsty's vegetarianism, which happened every year when the turkey was carved, as predictable and boring as the Queen's Speech. No, this year, they would buy each other loads of presents, eat a ton of chocolate and spend the day in bed. Total bliss.

Three weeks became four. Still no threats or complaints. Jamie allowed himself to breathe a huge, huge sigh of relief. It seemed that the worst was over.

It was a mild Sunday; a warm island in the arctic sea of winter. Jamie got up, got dressed and went out to buy a paper. When he opened the front door he saw Chris coming up the steps.

He didn't know what to do. Although it was true they hadn't had any trouble from the Newtons lately, they hadn't spoken to them either. A ceasefire existed between them, but not friendship. At that moment, Jamie remembered the letter he had sent to the previous occupants of the flat. He hadn't received a reply. In a way, he was glad. He wanted to forget all the shit that had happened.

Both men paused.

'Alright,' said Chris.

'Hi,' said Jamie.

'Lovely day, isn't it?'

'Gorgeous.'

They fell silent. Jamie felt uncomfortable. He wanted to go, but he didn't want to appear rude. With surprise, he realised he was afraid of upsetting Chris.

Chris broke the silence. 'Have you heard from Paul?'

'I've had some emails. He's in Ibiza, having a great time by the sound of it.'

'That's good.'

More silence.

Chris again: 'I've noticed that your front door's started sticking again. And making this bloody awful squeaking sound.'

'Yeah, I know.'

'Want me to take a look at it for you?'

Jamie felt a shiver of deja vu. Of course, it wasn't really deja vu. He could remember Chris making the same offer months ago. Maybe it was just a case of history repeating itself. Maybe this was their opportunity to start over, to become friends again – without allowing things to go wrong this time.

'That would be great.'

'OK. I'll take a look this afternoon.'

'Cool.'

Jamie turned away, nodding to himself ever so slightly. Yes, this was their chance to reforge their friendship. They could put everything behind them. OK, he wouldn't ever be able to forgive Chris and Lucy for some of the things they had done – and he still thought there must be something wrong with them to have done it in the first place. But surely this was better than being at war? They could co-exist, side by side. They wouldn't be bosom buddies. But they could be good neighbours. It would make life a lot easier.

As he turned to walk down the hill he smiled.

Later, Jamie sat reading the paper, the radio on quietly in the background. He heard a noise at the front door and looked out of the window. It was Chris, kneeling by the door with his toolkit. He looked up and waved at Jamie. Jamie waved back.

About an hour later he heard the front door shut, then Chris's footsteps going down to the basement. Jamie got up and went out into the hall. He tried the door. It didn't stick or squeak any more.

'He's fixed it,' he said to Kirsty.

'Good. You were never going to get round to it.'

'Yeah, well, I wasn't actually that bothered by it.'

'Chris obviously was. Or maybe he was just bored.'

'Maybe…no, it's stupid.'

'What? Tell me.'

'I just thought maybe he did it to try to make us happy. To try and make amends.'

'Hmm. Who knows.' She went into the kitchen and opened the fridge. 'We've got nothing in.'

'We've got that pie.'

'Yuk.'

'What do you want to do, then? Go out for dinner?'

She kissed him. 'What a nice offer!'

He rolled his eyes. 'I've been conned.'

She headed into the bedroom to change, putting a long, loose-fitting dress on. She looked lovely. Watching her touch up her makeup in the mirror, Jamie felt a rush of love that made his heart beat faster and compelled him to cross the room and hug her, burying his face in her hair and inhaling her. What would he do without her? He couldn't contemplate it. She was both his compass and his map, and he would be lost on his own. Lost in the darkness.

'Jamie, careful.'

She gently pushed him away, wincing.

'You'll hurt me or the baby if you squeeze me like that. You don't know your own strength sometimes.'

'I'm sorry.'

She kissed him. 'It's OK. Just be careful.'

They finished dressing and Jamie picked up his keys. They left a light on but drew the curtains. It was only seven but it was pitch-black outside. They headed out towards the front door.

Jamie patted his pockets. 'Shit, I haven't got my wallet.'

Kirsty tutted. 'Better go and get it then – I don't want to end up doing the washing up. Give me the key and I'll go and get in the car.'

He handed her the key and went back into the flat to find his wallet.

Kirsty opened the front door – hey, no squeak! Chris must have oiled it well – and was hit by a blast of icy air. No cloud cover, she decided, remembering an ancient geography lesson. She stepped down from the doorstep onto the path, and her foot made contact with something slippery.

The world dropped away.

Afterwards, she couldn't remember if she had screamed or not. She must have, the way Jamie came running. She remembered that he had yelled her name. His voice was strangely high-pitched; he sounded like a woman.

Kiirrst...

Her right foot touched the path, but it was like an ice rink. That was her first thought: ice. Like the air. Like the weather. But it wasn't ice. It was oil. A patch of oil left behind by Chris; a patch of the same oil that made the door sound so nicely squeak-free.

...tiiieee.

Her right foot slipped away from her, and to stop herself doing the splits she instinctively pulled her left leg forward. As she did this, she twisted – twisted right round so she was facing the door. And as she twisted she pitched forward, her hands trying to grab the doorframe – but she had her bag in one hand and the keys in the other. She twisted, pitched forward and fell.

Smack.

Her belly hit the concrete step.

Jamie sat outside the operating theatre, Heather beside him, holding his hand. Heather was wearing her nurse's uniform. She was still meant to be working.

Jamie couldn't stop shaking.

He had come running out of the flat, shouting her name. He had seen it happen: seen it even though he was inside the flat; her scream conjuring up a clear image. The slip, spin, smack. Her hands were full of objects and no use in stopping her from falling, or lessening the impact as she hit the concrete. Hard.

She had looked up at him, her eyes watery with pain. 'My...'

He expected her to say 'stomach'.

She said, 'My baby.'

The wait for the ambulance. The ride across town, sirens cutting through the night. Onto a trolley, down the corridor.

He couldn't stop shaking.

'She's going to be alright,' Heather said. 'I can feel it. She's going to be alright. She's going to be–'

'Mr Knight?'

The doctor came out of the room. He was frowning. Did that mean bad news? Not necessarily. Doctors always frown when they come out of the operating theatre. He had seen it on TV. The doctor sat down beside him, cleared his throat.

Jamie didn't speak. He couldn't. He heard Heather say, 'How is she?'

Everything went out of focus. The doctor's voice slowed down, like a stretched tape. The lights in the corridor were so bright. He tuned back in.

'Kirsty's going to be fine,' the doctor said. 'But I'm afraid–'

The voice warped. Jamie heard fragments of words that he would piece together later into some semblance of sense.

'…the baby…trauma to the abdomen…placenta detached…sorry Mr Knight…'

Everything went black.

Twenty-three

Jamie stood outside and looked at the front door. The patch of oil had gone. There was no longer any trace of the mark Kirsty had made when she skidded and fell. He pulled the door to and fro. No squeak. He looked down the steps towards the Newtons' flat. The curtains were drawn, a chink of light visible between them. He wondered what they were doing right now. Watching TV? Sitting side by side, reading? Or making plans, plotting, deciding their next move?

He picked up a large stone and weighed it in his hand, turned it over in his palm. He felt dizzy. He swayed and had to catch hold of the door to stay upright. He dropped the stone and it thudded harmlessly on the path.

The police had turned up at the hospital. Again, they were policemen he hadn't seen before. Why was there no continuity? He wished there was someone who knew the story, who would believe him when he said that his downstairs neighbours wanted to destroy his life. Whenever he tried to tell the tale he saw the listener's eyes glaze over; saw their mouth set in a sympathetic but disbelieving half-smile. Here was a man whose wife had just had a miscarriage, understandably angry and upset, ranting away in a hospital corridor, trying to pin the blame on someone, on the man who had kindly fixed their front door but had unfortunately – and accidentally – left some oil behind on the path.

'I understand, sir,' said the policeman. 'You're upset...'

'Of course I'm fucking upset!' Jamie shouted. People further up the corridor looked, attracted to the drama. A man shouting at a policeman. 'That bastard has murdered my fucking baby! My wife had to deliver the baby – it was a girl. A little girl.'

Jamie collapsed onto a seat, covering his face with his hands, crying. Heather put her arm around him. The policeman shook his head. Sympathetic. But disbelieving.

Jamie came home on his own that night. Although Kirsty's life was not in any danger, she was being kept in. Jamie went and sat beside her before he left. He kissed her cheek, which was wet with tears. She wouldn't open her eyes.

The doctors had talked to them about what had to happen next. Jamie listened to it all in a daze. There was no need to register the birth, but the hospital offered a simple funeral service if they wanted one. Kirsty had nodded yes, tears running down her cheeks, her whole body shuddering with grief. The service was going to take place in a couple of days.

Jamie walked up the front path. There was the skid mark in the oil. And it had rained a little while he was at the hospital. There were colours in the oil. A bright rainbow. He sat down on the wall and stared at it, at all the pretty colours. The childhood mantra ran through his brain: Richard of York gave battle in vain. Red orange yellow green blue indigo violet. Battle in vain.

In vain.

(What are you going to do about it?)

The next evening, after a whole day at the hospital, he came home and found that the oil was gone. After hefting the stone, considering what damage he might be able to do with it, he went inside, into his empty flat. He got into bed and stared at the ceiling. There was a terrible sound in his head, like a radio that wasn't tuned in properly. A hissing sound with a hint of voices and music behind the white noise. He strained, trying to hear what the voices were saying, but he couldn't make it out. Maybe they weren't human voices he was hearing at all. It sounded more like the chatter of monkeys or birds. He was about to fall asleep when he heard the music start. The music from *War of the Worlds*. At first he thought that too was in his head, breaking through the wall of static, but no: it was definitely coming from downstairs.

He got out of bed and got dressed. He went outside and spent the night in his car.

'Come on, sweetheart.'

He opened Kirsty's door and offered her his hand.

'I'm not an invalid,' she said.

'I know. I was just–'

'Yes yes. I know.'

As they walked up the path she kept to the left, warily eyeing the patch where she had slipped. They got inside and Jamie offered her a cup of tea. She looked at the door of the nursery. It was firmly closed.

'I'm going to bed.'

'I'll come with you.'

'Whatever.'

Jamie lay beside her, listening to her crying. He felt so useless and helpless. His emotions swung between grief, hatred, misery, guilt and anger. His whole body felt weak, atrophied. His heart was dead. The funeral service had been the worst experience of his life. Kirsty sobbed throughout. Jamie had stood there feeling sick, useless, wishing he had a shell he could withdraw into. Their daughter, who now had a name: Lily. Jamie tried not to think of her as a living baby, a toddler, a little girl. He tried not to think about her wearing dresses with ribbons, sitting on his lap, laughing, cuddling him and calling him daddy.

He couldn't bear the painful feelings of love so he smothered them with hatred.

He couldn't believe he had been so fucking stupid. Why had he trusted Chris? What had made him believe that they could be friends, or even just friendly? Chris and Lucy were sick, warped, evil. Words ran through his head – words he'd heard in films and read in newspapers to describe psychopaths and criminals; serial killers; Third World tyrants; people who tortured animals; fascists; rapists; teenagers who walked into schools with guns and mowed down their classmates and teachers.

Words like that were bandied around so frequently, they had almost lost their meaning. Now he understood the impact that evil can have on ordinary lives. There was no point trying to figure out why. (Did they have unfortunate childhoods? Had something happened in their past to make them like this? Was it inherent in their nature?) It wasn't a question of why. It was a question of what:

What are you going to do about it?

He lay awake all night. By the time the sun had risen he had made up his mind.

Mike was standing by the photocopier talking to a blonde girl called Karen. Jamie went straight up to him and said, 'I want your friends to help me.'

Karen gave them both a strange look. She remembered suddenly what had happened to Jamie's wife – the sad news was all round the office – and she quickly made her excuses and left them alone.

Mike took Jamie by the elbow and turned him towards the wall so their voices wouldn't carry.

'What?'

Jamie looked him in the eye. 'You know what I'm talking about. I need your friends to help me sort out my neighbours. I want them hurt. Badly. I want them scared. So scared that they'll move out.'

'Jamie, are you sure?'

'Yes. I'm certain.' He leaned forward until his nose almost touched his colleague's. His voice dropped to a whisper. 'They killed my baby.'

Mike pulled back. 'I thought it was just a fall, an accident?'

Jamie shook his head vigorously. His eyes were wide, unblinking. 'I want you to help me.'

Mike studied him. 'OK. If it's what you really want. I have to say, I don't blame you. If it wasn't an accident. I'll give my friends a call this evening and make sure they're up for it.'

'Tell them I'll pay them.'

Mike put his hand on Jamie's arm. He spoke quietly. 'Look, I told you, they owe me a favour. I'll give them a call later, then, if they're able to do it, you can give me all the details when I next see you. I'll need the address, descriptions, plus details of what you want done to them.'

'I want them hurt.'

'Yes, yes – but they might be able to tailor it to your requirements, if you see what I mean.'

Jamie nodded. 'That would be good.'

Mike smiled. 'Now, if I were you I'd go and get a cup of tea. Or go home. You look wrecked, mate.'

Jamie nodded again. 'Yes, home. Good idea.' He turned and walked away.

As Jamie stepped into the lift there was an announcement over the tannoy system. 'Can all members of staff report to the board room on Floor C for an important meeting. I repeat, can all members of staff …' Jamie stopped listening. The lift reached the ground floor and he walked out to his car. He was going to go home to his wife.

He got back to the flat and said Kirsty's name as he opened the front door. He noticed that the door to the nursery was still closed. He wondered if she had been in there. He couldn't bear to. He didn't want to see the cot and the mobiles and the piles of tiny clothes. People always said that you couldn't miss what you'd never had. What crap that was. What bullshit.

Kirsty was in the living room, ironing her nurse's uniform. The TV was on. Some abysmal American talk show. Two women were arguing over an astonishingly ugly man whose face appeared to be sprouting sharp pieces of metal. Jamie turned the volume down.

'What are you doing?' he said.

'Ironing my uniform.'

'I can see that. But why are you doing it?'

'Because I'm going into work tomorrow.'

'Kirsty, it's too soon. You should rest. Isn't that what the doctors told you to do?'

She stopped moving. Jamie could see how stiff her shoulders were. She was tensed up like she was afraid the world intended to hurt her. A single tear rolled down her face and landed on the blouse she was ironing.

'I can't stay at home. If I stay at home I'll have nothing to distract me. And I'll know that they are close by.' Her voice dropped to a whisper. 'Listening to me.' She looked up. 'I have to get out of here, Jamie. We're going to put this place on the market. You can go into town tomorrow and do it, OK? We have to get out. I don't want to live above them any more.'

'But...'

'No protests, please. I'm too tired to argue.'

'OK. But shit, Kirsty, your uniform!'

She had been holding the iron down on it while they were talking, and now it had started to smoke. She pulled the iron away and a cloud of pale smoke rose upwards, making her cough.

'Oh fuck.'

She picked up the blouse and studied it. There was a brown scorch mark where she had burnt it. She held it against her face and began to cry. Jamie came around to her side of the ironing board, unplugged the iron and put his arms around her. They sat on the sofa and cried together for the first time since the accident. They sat there until it grew dark outside.

Jamie stood up and fetched a bottle of wine from the fridge. They both needed alcohol, to numb the pain, if only for one evening. Kirsty sat with her head on Jamie's shoulder, her feet curled under her. She kept touching her belly, as if she was testing to see if it was really true, if it had really happened.

'You will go to the estate agent tomorrow, won't you?' she said.

'Yes.'

'There's no point trying to fight them, Jamie, you do know that, don't you? We've already lost. And I just want to get away, start again somewhere else. We'll buy a house, somewhere quiet. Outside London. You can commute. I'll get a transfer. We'll be OK.'

He nodded and kissed her forehead.

'I take it the police weren't interested,' she said. There was so much weariness in her voice. Jamie wondered if she had taken anything: sleeping pills, tranquillizers, downers. He wouldn't be surprised if she had.

'They weren't interested at all. "Just an accident, sir." That was their line.'

'That's what I thought they'd say.'

They were quiet for a while. The TV was still flickering away silently. There was some kids' programme on now: humanoid puppets in primary colours, dancing around. Jamie found them quite creepy with their mock-human gestures and huge, unblinking eyes. He looked away.

They finished the wine and Kirsty said that she was going to take a bath. Jamie ran it for her, adding loads of bath oil and lighting scented candles around the perimeter of the bath.

'Can you leave me alone?' Kirsty said as she stepped into the warm water.

'Really?'

'I'm not going to drown myself, Jamie. I just want to lie here in peace for a while.'

'Okay.'

He went back into the living room and put the ironing board away. The wine was all gone so he opened a can of beer. He thought about what he and Mike had discussed earlier. He felt a shudder of revulsion, a spasm of nausea in his gut. He hated violence, had always abhorred it. But it had to be done. They deserved it. They needed to be punished.

It was important that Kirsty didn't find out. She hated them too, but he knew she wouldn't approve. To her, escape was the only solution. But why should they be the ones to flee in terror? Let's drive Lucy and Chris out. Watch them run.

He listened to her splashing in the bath. He loved her so much, but there were things she didn't understand: things like masculine pride. There were times when it had to be right to fight. Kirsty had said they had lost already, but he wouldn't – couldn't – accept that. They hadn't lost. Shit, they hadn't even started fighting back yet. And no, this battle would not be in vain.

He sat down with his beer. As he lifted the can to his mouth he noticed his hand was trembling. He gripped his wrist with his free hand. He reminded himself that he was a man, that he had to be calm. It didn't help.

He called in sick the next day and drove Kirsty to work. They had both slept deeply, helped by the alcohol, although that hadn't kept the bad dreams at bay. Jamie woke up and realised he'd had Paul's coma dream: the birds (he was sure they were birds, not bats) swooping down at him, chasing him, terrifying him. How could a dream be passed from person to person? It made him feel like his grip on reality was even more tenuous than he feared.

'Are you sure you want to do this?' he said.

Kirsty nodded. 'I'm certain.'

'Alright.'

He kissed her cheek and she got out of the car. She waved and then vanished into the hospital. He had told her he would go straight to the estate agents, and that was what he planned to do. He didn't want to lie to her, so he drove across the city and parked outside the estate agents where they had first seen the flat advertised. He remembered that day so clearly. The estate agent had told them what a fantastic property this flat was, that it had just come onto the market, that it was sure to be snapped up really quickly.

'The seller said she hoped it would go to a young couple,' the agent said. 'It's a perfect first home. A great place to build a little nest.'

He sat in the car and looked at the pictures of houses and flats in the estate agent's window. He wondered if the estate agent had been telling the truth when he said that the seller hoped a young couple would buy the flat. It didn't really make sense. If Letitia and David had suffered at the hands of Lucy and Chris, why would they want another young couple to undergo the same fate? Maybe Lucy and Chris hadn't driven them out like he suspected. Or, most likely, it had just been the estate agent spinning them a line, a bit of spiel, like estate agents do. He considered going inside to ask. But what was the point? He doubted if they would remember, or tell the truth. And it wasn't important anyway. The matter was in hand.

He drove away, back to the flat. He was sure Kirsty would understand eventually. Once Lucy and Chris had been dealt with, there would be no need to move out. They could build their little nest in the flat after all. They could still win.

Later that afternoon, he went to pick Kirsty up from work. She wasn't waiting outside, so he parked the car and went in. He checked the children's ward but he couldn't see her. He spotted Heather over the far side of the ward and went over to her.

'Hi Heather.'

'Oh, hi Jamie.'

He hated the way she looked so sorry for him, like he was some pathetic loser. When would people realise, he was going to win? He would show them. He wasn't weak. He would show them all.

'Where's Kirsty?' he asked.

'She finished about fifteen minutes ago. I thought she'd be waiting outside.'

'She's not.'

Heather's eyes widened. 'Oh God, do you think she's alright? You don't think she'd do anything stupid, do you?'

He felt a fluttering in his stomach. That was exactly what he'd thought last night when she said she wanted to be left alone in the bathroom. That she would try to harm herself.

'Come on, follow me.' Heather led him towards the doctor's offices. She knocked and entered. 'Have you seen Kirsty Knight?'

Nobody had.

'Jamie, I'm sure she's OK.'

'So why did you ask me if I thought she'd do something stupid?'

'I don't know. I was just...' She broke off. 'Come on, she's probably in the canteen.'

They set off at a jog towards the staff canteen. It was half-empty. Jamie scanned the room quickly. She wasn't there. He could feel the cold tentacles of dread spreading out, flexing themselves inside him. He could picture her in some store cupboard somewhere, half empty jars of pills lying beside her body. Or her body in a shower, wrists slashed, blood running into the drain. He pinched himself, twisting the skin on his arm until it bruised, trying to expel the visions.

Heather grabbed his arm. 'Come on. I've got an idea where she might be.'

He followed her again: down the stairs, along a corridor, up another long corridor. It was so bright, so stainless. But the smell of death was less noticeable down here; it was replaced by a different scent. In the distance he could hear a baby crying. He suddenly realised where they were heading.

The maternity ward.

They found Kirsty standing against the glass, looking at the babies in the premature baby unit. There were six or seven babies in incubators; a couple of nurses moving among them. Kirsty leant against the glass, gazing in.

'They're so tiny,' she said. 'Look at them. That one over there was two months premature.'

Jamie put his arms around her and slowly led her away. Heather placed a hand on her back.

'I was so worried,' he said softly. 'We were scared.'

She broke away from him. 'Scared of what? That I'd kill myself. Or, hey, maybe you thought I'd try to snatch a baby?'

'No, Kirsty.'

'Leave me alone!'

She ran down the corridor. Jamie chased after her, their footsteps echoing through the sterile spaces. He caught her at the bottom of the stairs and wrapped his arms around her, holding her tightly until she stopped struggling and went limp in his arms.

Heather caught up. 'Is she alright?' she asked.

Jamie nodded. 'I'll take her home.'

He led her out to the car. People gave them strange looks. He could read their minds. How disgusting – that nurse was clearly drunk. And what was wrong with the fellow who was holding her up?

Why was he crying?

Twenty-four

Jamie awoke with a start. He had been dreaming again: dreaming this time that there was a baby crying in the flat. It had been so real he could still hear it.

'Jamie.' Kirsty woke up and gripped his arm.

He blinked in the darkness. The loud, shrill cries of a hungry, attention-seeking baby were still audible. But why? Why could he still hear it?

Kirsty sat upright. Her breathing was heavy and quick. She threw the quilt aside and jumped out of bed, flicking the light on, looking around the room wildly. She ran out of the bedroom and into the nursery. Jamie got out of bed and followed her. It was freezing in the flat but he barely noticed. He could still hear the baby. What the hell was going on?

Kirsty was standing in the nursery (spare bedroom, spare bedroom – that's all it is, Jamie reminded himself, until he could persuade Kirsty to try again) staring into the empty cot. Above the cot, a mobile rotated. Farmyard animals – a pig, a chicken, a cow – spun slowly left then right, then left again. The room was lit by moonlight, and the animals cast lifesized shadows on the walls. Jamie switched on the light.

Kirsty turned to look at him. 'Jamie, can you hear it too?'

'Yes.'

She clamped her hands over her ears. 'I thought it was in my head. But you can hear it too? You promise?'

' I promise. Come on, let's get out of here.' He took her hand and led her back to the bedroom.

The baby's cries were so clear. Short bursts of treble-heavy crying, followed by long wails that seemed to get louder and louder before suddenly falling silent. For ten seconds, the crying stopped altogether, and Jamie and Kirsty stood in their bedroom, clutching each other, just the sound of their chests beating in the darkness. Then it started again, even louder than before.

Kirsty fell onto her hands and knees. 'It's coming from downstairs.'

Jamie had known that already. Had known the moment this started.

'They've got a baby down there,' Kirsty said in a hushed tone, her eyes wide. 'Jamie, they've got a baby – Lucy and Chris – they've got a baby.'

Jamie knelt beside her, leant forward and put his ear to the floor. He tried to think: how long was it since he had seen Lucy? Had she had a bump? Could she have been pregnant?

No – it didn't make sense.

'It's a recording,' he said. 'That's what it is. It's a fucking recording.'

'No!' Even now, after all this time, Kirsty acted as if she was shocked by the lengths Lucy and Chris would go to. She pummelled the carpet with her fists, weak blows which would have been barely audible downstairs, especially over the cries of the baby. She punched and punched, until she collapsed on her front and lay still.

The recording stopped. Halfway through a cry of distress, the baby was hushed. Jamie pressed his ear to the floor again. His whole body was tense, like a spring, waiting for the crying to begin again.

He didn't know how long he knelt in that position for. Eventually, he became aware of a pain in his neck – a muscular spasm – and he sat up and rubbed it, tried to ease the ache. Kirsty was still lying on the carpet, her face turned away from him. He stroked her hair, pressed his face against the back of her head, whispered in her ear, 'It's alright.'

She didn't move. He leant over so he could see her face. She was just lying there, staring into space, unblinking. She looked lifeless, like a mannequin. It scared him.

'Kirsty.' He touched her cheek. 'Kirsty, talk to me.'

For a horrible, irrational moment, he thought she was dead – for the second time in twenty-four hours. But then she stirred. She blinked and looked up at him. But she still she didn't speak.

'Come on,' he said. 'Let's get you back into bed. Come on, sweetheart.'

She allowed herself to be helped up. He walked her over to the bed and she crawled beneath the covers, burying her head beneath the quilt. He got in behind her and lay with his arm over her, holding her hand. They lay like that all night, neither of them falling fully into sleep. At one point Jamie heard a bird cry outside, and he felt Kirsty flinch. He shushed her and kissed her. The pain and hatred swelled up in him.

They got up as soon as it was light. Kirsty had a bath and Jamie made breakfast. They sat on the sofa and ate, although neither of them had an appetite. Upstairs, Mary had her radio on, and every so often a muffled snatch of recognisable music would break through. The volume must have been up loud.

'How long do you think it will be before we can move out?' Kirsty asked. 'What did the estate agent say?'

'He said he was sure he could get a quick sale.' He felt sick. He hated lying to her, even when it was necessary. Actually, he only lied to her when it was necessary.

'Good. Because I don't care about the price. I just want to get out.'

'They'll have to come round to do a valuation.'

'When?'

'I don't know He said it could take a week – or two.'

'Jamie, that's not good enough. I'll call them today, tell them they've got to make it sooner.'

He felt a flutter of panic in his gut. 'No – I'll do it. Don't you worry.'

'Don't forget.'

He put down his coffee before she could see his hand was shaking.

'Are you going in to work today?' she asked.

'Yes. I think I'd better. Just to show my face. What about you?'

'I'm not staying here on my own in the flat. Not with them downstairs.'

'Well, I could call in sick again and stay at home with you.'

'No. No, it's better if we both go to work. We can't hide away. We have to get on with our lives, Jamie.' She shook her head. 'God, I feel so pitiful. I hadn't even had the baby. Every day I see people whose children are ill. Some of them are dying; some of them do die. Those people have given birth; they've seen their children grow, seen them speak and walk.'

'But you've had a miscarriage. That's like...' He couldn't say it.

'It's not exactly the same, Jamie. My whole life with this baby was imagined. It was something in the future. A promise – a promise that has been broken.' She looked up at him. 'We can have another baby, can't we? Can't we? And this time we'll be somewhere safe.'

She pressed her face against his shoulder.

'Yes. We will.'

I'm going to make this place safe, he thought. And then we'll try again.

He drove Kirsty to the hospital, then on to work. His knuckles were white where he gripped the steering wheel so tightly. He had the radio up loud. The people outside the car – walking along the streets, coming out of shops, getting off buses – seemed like phantoms, blurs of pink and brown, colours running into one another, like rain on a chalk pavement drawing. The music was loud but he couldn't hear the tune; the lyrics were a babble. It was just noise.

He strode into the building, into the lift, up to the fourth floor. He looked at himself in the lift's mirror. His face was the colour of undercooked fish; his hair was sticking up in tufts; his tie was crooked, his shirt only half tucked in. He ran a hand through his hair, tried to straighten his tie. It was a half-hearted attempt, and a second later the lift chimed to announce its arrival at his floor. He stood there for a second, looking out. Everyone seemed very busy, moving around in fast-motion, industrious worker bees droning among the humming computers. Above the hum, Jamie could hear the cries of the baby from last night, a sound buried at the back of his brain, pulsing beneath the surface of his skull. How could they have done it? How could anyone be that sick, that cruel? He felt anger boil up inside him again. He breathed deeply.

There was Mike, sitting at his desk, sorting through his in-tray. Jamie strode over to him.

'Mike.'

He looked up. 'Jamie, hi. I didn't think you'd be in today. Are you alright?'

'I'm fine.'

Mike didn't let him speak. 'It's all been going on around here. The takeover's been finalised. It's happened already. The new manager's been brought in and George Banks has been given the push, with a nice pay-off I expect. After all that rumour and build-up, it practically happened overnight, like some sort of military coup. Still, they say we won't be affected much.'

Jamie had lost the thread of his thoughts. He opened his mouth to speak but his brain couldn't formulate a sentence.

Mike continued: 'Hey you know I thought it would be Software Logistics who took over? I was wrong. It's actually Scion.'

'Mike, have you...' he stopped, suddenly realising what Mike had said. He stared at him. 'Did you say Scion?'

'Yes. Apparently they're a really good firm to–'

'Scion?'

'Christ, Jamie, that's what I said. Hey look there's our new manager now.'

He nodded towards the far side of the room and Jamie turned and followed his gaze. He watched Chris come out of the manager's office and look around, a proprietary smile on his face.

Jamie's knees buckled. He sat down.

Oh. Jesus.

Almost before he had touched the seat, he was up again. He grabbed Mike's upper arm. 'I need to talk to you. I need to talk to you now.'

'Alright. Calm down, Jamie. I'll go into the gents, you follow. OK? Count to ten before you follow. I don't want people to think we're going in together.'

Jamie watched Mike push open the door of the gents. He was trembling. He couldn't bear to look back over at Chris, though he knew Chris was looking at him: he could feel his stare drilling into him. He started to count to ten, but got lost around six. He hurried over to the gents, aware of Chris's gaze following him. It felt like a laser, burning the back of his head. He could almost smell the smoke and the singed hair.

Mike was standing by the washbasins, inspecting his hair in the mirror.

'Jamie, you look like you've seen a ghost, mate.'

Jamie didn't speak.

'It's OK. I've checked the cubicles, there's no-one in there. We're alright to talk. I know what you want to talk to me about. I haven't been able to get hold of my mates, though I left a message saying I had a job for them. I'll try again tonight.'

'That's him.'

'Who? What are you talking about?'

'The new manager. It's him. Chris Newton. My neighbour.'

'Chris?' His jaw dropped. 'You're joking.'

'No. He works for Scion. I bet – he must be behind the whole takeover.'

'Jesus.'

Mike walked over and put his hand on Jamie's shoulder. 'In that case, I'm going to have to call my friends off.'

'What? You can't.'

'I can. And I'm going to have to. For Christ's sake, Jamie, I can't be involved now. He's my boss. I mean – yeah, the bloke sounds like a psycho – but I can't afford to lose my job. I can't risk it.'

'But you have to.'

'No I don't.'

'Please.'

'Jamie, I'm sorry, alright? But it's out of the question.'

He made to leave the room but Jamie stepped in front of him. Mike tried to dodge round him but Jamie grabbed his sleeve.

'Jamie, leave it. I cannot get involved. That is it. My final answer.'

'Mike, please.'

'If you don't take your hands off me I'm going to have to hit you.'

Jamie let go. 'Let me contact them myself.'

'What?'

'Your friends. Give me their number and I'll contact them myself. They don't have to know it's got anything to do with you. I'll tell them I heard about them through someone else. I'll make something up. You hadn't already given them my name, or Chris's or Lucy's, so just give me the number and I'll sort it all out. Nobody will even know you were involved.'

Mike exhaled through his nose.

'Please.'

'Oh, for fuck's sake. OK. But if you mention my name to them you'll be their next victim.'

'Alright. I promise I won't mention you.'

Mike pulled a scrap of paper and a pen out of his trouser pocket. He scribbled a number down. 'The name to ask for is Charlie. Alright?'

'Right.'

Mike left the room, having instructed Jamie to wait another ten seconds before leaving the gents. Jamie looked at the number in his hand. He put it safely in his wallet, then pushed open the door and looked left and right. There was no sign of Chris. As he walked towards the lift he took a last look around. He knew he would never be coming back to this place again. How could he, with Chris working here – as his boss, no less? He now understood why Chris had sent the virus, in Jamie's name, to his workplace: so he would have an excuse to sack him after he became the manager. God, he was clever. But fuck him. Jamie wouldn't give him the satisfaction.

He had never realised Chris was so high up at Scion. He thought he was just a lowly wage-slave like himself. But he was obviously powerful enough to engineer the takeover of a smaller company and move himself in as manager. Jamie felt quite sick with the shock of it: the lengths the man would go to to destroy him.

What had he ever done to him?

OK, when they had moved in they had thrown a party, but they had invited all their neighbours so it wasn't their fault Chris and Lucy had chosen not to come. And when they apologised afterwards they were told by Lucy that Chris had slept right through it! The very first lie she had told them.

What else had they done? Had sex – but no more noisily or frequently than any other couple their age. Played music – but certainly not at excessive volumes. How could any of that lead Chris and Lucy to do such terrible things? Especially when sound hardly carried between the flats.

The truth was, they had done practically nothing to provoke them, but they had still invoked their wrath. Jamie had lain awake at night thinking about it, and it all came back to one simple fact: Lucy and Chris were evil. They enjoyed causing misery; they revelled in other people's pain. And they were prepared to put themselves to great trouble and effort to cause that pain. If it wasn't happening to him, Jamie wouldn't believe it possible. But it was true. It was really happening – and it was happening to him and Kirsty. Life wasn't meant to be like that. It wasn't fucking fair.

All this, caused by two apparently normal people. They weren't monsters. They weren't vampires or demons or phantoms. They were just people. Actually, Jamie thought, that made sense. There was Brian upstairs writing his horror stories for kids: supernatural tales in which werewolves and witches terrorised children. He shouldn't be writing about monsters or magic, though, not if he wanted to teach children a lesson about life. He should be writing about people like Lucy and Chris.

He climbed into his car and sat back. He fished out his wallet and looked at the phone number again. What was the name? Charlie. He didn't yet know what story he would make up to explain how he had got the number, but he would think of something.

He put his wallet away and drove home.

He spent the afternoon sitting outside a small cafe on the high street. Driving away from the office, he had been overcome by an overwhelming urge for a cigarette. He hadn't had one since he was at college. He hated smoking. The smell and the taste of it made him feel sick. But here, now, he felt the most awful craving: his bloodstream calling out for nicotine. His fingers and lips needed something to keep themselves occupied, and nothing else would do.

He watched himself unwrap the white and gold cigarette packet he'd just bought in a newsagents with a sense of horrified, guilty wonder.

He sucked smoke into his lungs. He coughed. The old woman at the next table smiled. He took another deep drag and a moment later felt the rush of nicotine, making him dizzy. He drank his coffee and smoked the cigarette, then another. He felt sick, but he also felt calmer.

The afternoon went by quickly. He went inside, ate lunch, drank three more cups of coffee, ate a Danish pastry, then came outside and smoked more cigarettes. He watched people go into the cafe then come out again. He was aware that the waitresses were talking about him, wondering what he was doing, but they were happy enough to take his money. Eventually, at half-four, he paid, leaving a £10 tip on the table and walked off into the late afternoon light. He drove to St Thomas's to pick Kirsty up.

'Have you been smoking?' Kirsty asked, sniffing the air as she got into the car beside him.

'No. I was talking to Mike at work, outside the office, and he was smoking.' He sniffed his own sleeve. 'I didn't realise how badly it would cling to my clothes.'

'You stink. I'll have to wash everything you're wearing when we get home.'

'Sorry.'

The rest of the journey passed in silence. When they got home, Jamie undressed and put his clothes in the washing machine. It was so cold in the flat. He wrapped up in a thick jumper with two T-shirts underneath.

'Cup of tea?'

'Hmm.' Kirsty was sorting through the desk, examining paperwork. She wore a puzzled expression. 'Jamie, which estate agent did you register us with?'

He felt his blood go chilly. 'The same one we bought it from. Anderson and Son.'

She stood up and waved a letter at him. It bore Anderson and Son's letterhead. It was the letter the estate agent had sent them to confirm the acceptance of their offer on the flat. Jamie had once suggested framing it, but they never got round to it.

'So how come when I called them today to ask them if they could hurry up the valuation, they didn't know what I was talking about?'

He swallowed. 'Did you call the right branch?'

'I called the branch that we bought it from. And they called both their other offices. They had no record that you'd been in to put the flat on the market.'

'They're so incompetent.'

'Don't lie to me!' She threw the letter to the floor. 'I know you haven't put the flat on the market. So don't make things worse for yourself by trying to lie.'

'Kirsty, I'm–'

She folded her arms. 'You're an idiot, Jamie. A fucking idiot.'

She marched out of the room into the bedroom. Jamie followed her, feeling as if all the blood had drained out of him. I'm bloodless, he thought. A husk. Kirsty stood on a chair and took the suitcase down from the top of the wardrobe. She threw it on the bed and unzipped it.

'What are you doing?'

'I'm going, Jamie.' She opened the top drawer of her chest of drawers and pulled out a handful of knickers and socks, tights and lacy things that she rarely wore. Jamie stood helplessly by the bed, watching her.

She turned to him. 'I can't live here anymore, Jamie. I know you think it's giving in. I'm not stupid. I know you haven't put the flat up for sale because you see it as quitting. And – I don't know – maybe it is. Maybe I'm a coward. But you have to understand, if I stay here one more day I'm going to go mad. I keep bursting into tears at work – and not just because of the baby. I dread coming home. I actually feel afraid to come into my own flat – and shouldn't your home be your sanctuary? We've lost that.'

She opened the wardrobe and removed shirts and dresses, putting some back but placing the others in the suitcase, very calm and methodical. Jamie sat on the bed beside the suitcase. A husk.

'It makes me feel so sad doing this,' she said, speaking evenly but wiping away a tear that had fallen onto her cheek. 'We were going to be so happy here, weren't we? It was our little paradise. We were going to be a family here.' She smiled. 'Whatever's happened since, we'll always have those early weeks. It was really good then.'

'Don't go,' Jamie croaked. 'It can be good again.'

She lay her palm against his cheek. Her hand was warm. She looked down at him and her face was so full of sadness he wanted to die.

'It can't,' she whispered. 'Not here.' She held her hand against his cheek for a few more moments, then resumed her packing.

'Are you going to come with me?'

He didn't answer.

'I'm going to go to my parents'. I've already ordered a taxi to take me to the station. I want you to come too.'

He put his face in his hands. He so wanted to go with her. He knew what she said was right, that it was the most sensible thing to do. But he couldn't. He couldn't give in and let Lucy and Chris get away with it. He had to stay – at least until after they had been dealt with. And then Kirsty would come back. Yes, that's what would happen. He would punish Lucy and Chris – drive them away! – and then Kirsty would come back to him and they would reclaim their paradise. Yes.

'I can't.'

She looked away, squeezing her eyes shut to hold back the tears, and carried on with her packing.

A car horn sounded in the street outside. It was Kirsty's taxi. Jamie felt a shiver of panic. He could still change his mind.

'Will you carry my case out for me?'

'Of course.'

He carried the case outside. The taxi driver tried to take it from him but he kept hold of it, putting it into the back of the cab himself. Kirsty opened the door of the taxi and got in.

'Come with me, Jamie,' she pleaded.

He couldn't look at her. 'I can't. I have to stay and fight.'

'You're being an idiot.'

'I'll call you,' Jamie said. 'I love you.'

She didn't reply.

The taxi driver looked back at Kirsty. 'Where to, my love?'

'Charing Cross.'

She closed the door of the taxi and looked away. Jamie watched the cab disappear into the night, its engine still audible after it had vanished from sight. He stood on that spot for a long time before turning round and going back into the flat.

Alone.

Twenty-five

Jamie picked up the piece of paper, studied the phone number, lifted his phone. His finger hovered over the first digit: 0.

He dialled the number.

He spent the morning working out. The weights and rowing machine that he had bought during the summer had sat in the corner for a while now, untouched, gathering a gossamer skin of dust. He ran his index finger along the barbell, licked the dust from his finger. He lay on his back and lifted the weights above his chest. Up, then down. Up, then down. It hurt but he kept going until his muscles felt like they would combust.

He stood up and lifted the weights above his head. He gripped a smaller dumbbell in each hand and pulled them in towards his body – in, out, in, out. He sat on the rowing machine and rowed, back and forth, back and forth. This was how he filled the days, with monotonous exercises that didn't require thought and at the same time obliterated thought. All he could think about was the pain in his arms and legs and chest; the ache in his back and shoulders. When he was straining to lift a barbell above his head for the fortieth time he didn't think about Kirsty. He thought about the strain on his body; the bead of sweat that trickled down his forehead and hung above his eye, threatening to fall.

He wasn't trying to make himself strong. He wasn't preparing himself for a fight. He was just trying to stop himself thinking. Because thinking hurt too much.

Up, down. In, out. Back, forth. Push-ups, sit-ups, squat thrusts. Crunching his stomach muscles. Forth, back. Out, in. Down, up.

And repeat.

Sometimes he would drop a weight by accident, or fall onto the floor himself, and as the bang reverberated through the flat he would tense, hurting himself as he pulled his muscles inwards, trying to shrink, an animal instinct to hide taking over. He would crouch there in fear, waiting for the banging to start, or a knock at the door. Sometimes the banging came, the sound of a broom knocking against the ceiling, going on for perhaps ten minutes without pause. Sometimes nothing happened and, eventually, after sitting rock-still for five minutes, he would relax and wait for his muscles to stop cramping At such times, he always needed a cigarette. He lit up, inhaled, exhaled, flicked ash into an overflowing ashtray, a graveyard of cigarettes that he never emptied, filling the flat with a charred nicotine stink.

Up down in out back forth.

Every day.

It was a mobile number. He wouldn't have expected anything else. He imagined a bear-like man at the other end, cradling a tiny mobile phone in his huge paw. They would listen to him and laugh and put the phone down. But he wouldn't give up. He knew he could persuade them to do it.

He held the receiver in one hand and a cigarette in the other. He dialled the number that Mike had given him and listened to it ring and ring. He expected it to cut to a voicemail message at any moment, but it kept ringing. He was about to put the phone down and try again – thinking there must be some technical problem at the other end – when the ringing ceased.

'Hello?'

Jamie took a deep breath, and couldn't think of what to say.

'Hello?' the man repeated, confused and a little irritated.

Jamie sensed that the man was about to cut him off. He panicked. 'I need you to help me.'

'This isn't the Samaritans.'

'No.' Jamie spoke quickly. 'I know who you are. You're Charlie. I need you to help me deal with someone.'

There was a long pause at the other end. Jamie could hear the sound of machinery in the background; drills and JCBs, men talking, cars rushing by. Jamie thought he had been cut off, but then the man said, 'Who is this? How did you get this number?'

'A friend gave it to me.'

'What friend?'

'I can't tell you.'

He heard the man suck in air through his teeth. 'Put the phone down and I'll call you back.'

'But–'

The line went dead. Jamie waited. Five minutes passed – five long, long minutes of dread – before the phone rang. Jamie grabbed it, almost hitting himself in the face with it.

'What do you mean "deal with"?' the man asked. The background noise had gone. Jamie guessed the man had gone inside somewhere. He imagined him sitting in a car, or a portakabin in a scrap yard. His head was full of movie images: the safe world of movie violence, vicarious thrills for those who lived far from danger. Jamie felt himself to be part of that world now. It was more terrifying than he had ever suspected.

'I want somebody hurt. Scared.'

A low chuckle. 'That's all?'

Jamie realised he was asking if he wanted someone killed. 'God, no. I mean yes. I mean hurt, but not killed. Frightened off.'

'What's your name?'

Jamie hesitated.

'If you don't tell me your name you can fuck off right now.'

Jamie paused. 'It's James.'

There was silence at the other end. He realised that the man had put his hand over the mouthpiece and was talking to someone else. Mike's other friend. He wondered if either of them was actually called Charlie. He doubted it. He strained to hear what they were saying, but couldn't make out anything but the low drone of voices.

'Give me the details.'

Jamie took a deep breath. 'OK. It's my neighbours. There are two of them. They've made my life hell and I want them scared off. I want them to know that I'm not going to put up with it any more.'

'So we're talking about a warning?'

'Yes. A warning.'

He heard the man say something to his friend but, again, couldn't make it out. 'What the fuck makes you think we'd do something like that? Who told you?'

Jamie had known all along that they wouldn't do it without knowing who had put him onto them. As far as they knew, he could be a policeman. He could be anyone. And he hadn't been able to come up with a plausible story. Sorry Mike, he said in his mind, and then he told them.

'Really?'

They conferred again. Jamie wished he hadn't had to tell them Mike's name, but what choice did he have? He knew Mike had left them a message saying he had a job for them. His only worry was that Mike would have contacted them again and told them that if someone called them asking them to deal with his neighbours, they should tell that someone to fuck off. But he was willing to gamble that Mike would have left it alone, not wanting to get involved any more than he already was. Maybe he thought that Jamie would chicken out; that he wouldn't have the guts to go through with it. He was wrong.

He waited for the man to return to the phone. After a long wait, the man said 'OK. Here's what happens. I'm going to call you back later this afternoon and we'll exchange details. You tell me the names and the address. I'll tell you where to leave the money.'

'The money.'

The man chuckled. 'You didn't think was a free service, did you, James?'

'No, of course. How much?'

'Ten grand.'

Jamie caught his breath. £10,000. He did a quick calculation in his head. There was just over £10,000 in his and Kirsty's savings account – money they had been saving for a long time; money that was not supposed to be touched. Half it was Kirsty's, and they both needed to sign the form to withdraw the money. That was easy enough – he had forged Kirsty's signature many times, when paying bills, etc. But what about Kirsty? Wouldn't he be stealing from her?

You're doing this for her, a voice inside his head whispered. You're doing it for both of you, to make your home safe again. Once this is over, Kirsty will come back and everything will be fine. You'll be able to try for another baby. Everything will be fine. Kirsty will understand.

He didn't even think about how skint he would be if he gave them that money. He had already given up his job. Yesterday, he had received a call from personnel, asking him why he hadn't been in. Was he still ill? 'No,' he had told them. 'I'm not coming back. I quit.'

£10,000.

'OK,' he said.

The line went dead.

He waited all afternoon for the man to call back. He worked out, pumping weights, rowing back and forth, back and forth. When he dropped the barbell on the floor – causing a great crash – he didn't care. He felt powerful, energy flowing through him, direct current making his bones strong, his mind sharp. Fucking hell yes, they were going to pay. Oh fucking hell yes.

Kirsty would come back.

Everything would be OK.

Life would be sweet again.

The man rang back at five o'clock. Again, there was no background noise. The man spoke quietly. 'Right. Do you know where Mile End stadium is? Good.' The man proceeded to give Jamie instructions of where to meet them. 'We won't pick up the money ourselves. Our courier will use a code word to prove who they are.'

Jamie almost laughed, giddy with a mad kind of euphoria. This was like the movies.

'The code word is neighbour.'

'Good choice.'

The man spoke in a low tone, shot through with menace: 'This isn't a game, James. If you think that, we can call it off right now.'

Jamie felt another surge of panic: 'No, no, I don't think it's a game. It's the most serious thing I've–'

The man cut him dead. 'Yeah, yeah. Save it.'

'It will take me a couple of days to get the money. It's in a savings account.'

'Yeah, whatever. We'll make it Wednesday then. Thirteen-hundred hours.'

'Fine.'

Halfway through the word, the man terminated the call.

He drove to the local branch of their bank and picked up the form he needed to fill out in order to withdraw the money. He took the form back to the car and signed his own signature on the left and Kirsty's on the right. His hand trembled as he did so, and the 't' in Kirsty's 'Knight' wobbled a little. He remembered watching Kirsty practising her new signature when they got married. 'Kirsty Knight. KK. Thank God my middle name's not Katherine or Kate – I could never marry you. Or I'd have to keep my old surname.'

'You could keep it anyway,' he had said.

'No.' She kissed him. 'I like the idea of us having the same name. It will be easier for our child, as well.'

Jamie's eyes misted over and guilt stabbed him in the gut. Get a grip, he whispered to himself. Be a man.

He filled in the amount that he wanted to withdraw – £10,000, everything they had – then took the form back to the bank.

'This will be available in 48 hours,' said the clerk.

He nodded.

Two days passed. The two slowest days of his life. Minutes felt like weeks; hours like months. He tried to occupy himself. He smoked, he played computer games, he even tried to masturbate, but he felt no desire, had no feeling down there, as if all the nerve endings had shrivelled and died. He exercised endlessly. He drank coffee. He tried to eat but he wasn't hungry. He felt too sick; there was no saliva in his mouth. He paced up and down.

He checked his emails. There was a message from Paul. He was still in Ibiza, but he had dumped the American and moved on to a local girl. She was beautiful, he said. He might stay in Ibiza for a while longer. He said he hoped everything was OK with him and Kirsty, that he was looking forward to seeing the baby when he got back and that he gladly offered his services as a godfather. He ended the message by saying, If you see Chris and Lucy, say hi to them from me.

Jamie turned the computer off without replying to the message. He unplugged it from the wall.

'You are so wrong about them, Paul,' he said to himself. 'How could you be so wrong?' It actually scared him – that his best friend didn't believe what he said about Lucy and Chris. Nobody ever believed him – not Paul, not the police. In fact, the only person who had believed him was Mike: who he had just betrayed.

It was such a mess.

But it would all be sorted out soon.

He picked up the money – 500 £20 notes, bundled together with elastic bands. Somehow he had expected £10,000 to look a lot more substantial. He held the money in his hands and thought about what he could do with it. He could go on a long holiday; maybe go to see Paul in Ibiza, live out there for while. He could live on the money for a few months, pay the bills. He could put it towards moving.

But no, this money was meant for one thing only.

He drove to the East End, parked in a side street off Mile End Road and walked down the road towards the stadium. The sky was slate grey and drizzling rain soaked his face and hair and clothes. He had the money in a carrier bag in his inside coat pocket. His hands were so cold he couldn't feel his fingers. He shoved them into his pockets, but it didn't help much.

He passed a group of teenagers in designer sports wear. One of the boys bumped into him, and he grabbed at the money, paranoid that he was going to be mugged. A look of fear passed across the boy's face. Jamie was confused. Why did the boy look frightened? He stopped and looked at himself in the side mirror of a parked car. His eyes looked wild; he was gaunt, his cheeks hollow, his lips bruised where he kept biting them. No wonder the teenager had looked so afraid. He must have thought Jamie was a lunatic, or a junkie. Somebody unstable and dangerous: a volcano ready to blow.

Minutes later, he found himself standing on the spot that the man had specified, behind the stadium. There was nobody around; the rain made sure of that. He looked at his watch. Ten to one. He had time for a cigarette.

As he crushed the cigarette out under his boot, he spotted a small girl of about seven or eight coming towards him from the direction of the main road. She was walking straight towards him. But where the hell was the courier? He didn't want to be pestered by a little kid.

The girl walked right up to him. 'Neighbour,' she said. She was tiny, her face pinched and waxen like she'd never really breathed fresh air, like a miniature OAP.

He looked at her, surprised. She held out her hand. 'Come on,' she said. 'I haven't got all day.'

Jamie reached into his pocket and pulled out the carrier bag containing the bundle of money. All his savings. All his and Kirsty's savings. He had a sudden glimpse of the absurdity of what he was doing: handing all this money over to a little girl to pass on to two men he had never even met, one of whom might or might not be called Charlie. But what choice did he have? He had to deal with Lucy and Chris. He gritted his teeth in determination. He would not let them win. And this was the only way. The only way.

He gave the girl the money. She ran off, swinging the bag as she went.

Jamie tried to follow her. He wanted to catch sight of the men who would be doing his dirty work, but the girl was too quick. She darted off between two parked cars and ran across the road. A bus went by, obscuring her from view, and when the bus had passed by she had vanished.

Shit.

Oh well, it didn't matter anyway. In fact, it was probably better that he didn't know who they were. He didn't want to know. As long as they did what he paid them for – that was all that mattered.

He walked back to his car, smoking another cigarette as he went. He had arranged for the men to visit Lucy and Chris on Friday evening. He knew they never went out on Fridays. They hardly ever went out, full stop. There had been that time that he and Kirsty had seen them at the restaurant when, he was convinced, Lucy had somehow tampered with their food while he was in the kitchen.

Otherwise, they seemed to stay in every night. Boring, stay-at-home psychopaths. It was almost funny.

Back at the flat, he checked the answerphone, hoping that Kirsty might have called. She had called just once since leaving, to let him know that she was at her parents and that she was safe. It was a tense, brief phone call. He could hear her parents talking in the background, speaking loudly, saying things about him. He didn't know if Kirsty would tell them the whole story – he doubted it, as she wouldn't want her parents to become involved – but no doubt they would blame Jamie for her miscarriage. They had never got on with him. Going away to Gretna Green to get married had been the final nail in the coffin of their relationship.

He sat on the sofa and thought about what he had done; the wheels he had set in motion. Had he done the right thing? He couldn't think straight. His head was too full of images of pain and violence; pain and regret; pain and sorrow. Yes, it had to be the right thing to do. Kirsty would be so pleased to hear about it. Her face would light up with joy as he told her the good news: that the Newtons weren't going to bother them any more. She would run back to him, throw her arms around him, cover him with kisses. He couldn't wait.

Yes, it was the right thing to do. And anyway, the wheels were in motion now. It was too late to change things.

Twenty-six

He waited for Friday with a boulder of dread and excitement in his stomach. The men whose names he did not know were due to turn up at eight. He would see their car pull up out the front; he would watch as they went down the steps to the basement flat; he would listen as they knocked at the door; he would hear what happened next.

He thought about going out to the pub. He wasn't sure he wanted to hear the violence. He wondered if there would be screams, shouts for mercy. He didn't know if he would be able to stomach it. Maybe it would be best to go and hide somewhere for a few hours, try to forget it was happening, and then when he came back it would be all over.

But no: he had to know it had happened. He needed confirmation. His plan was to turn up the stereo as soon as the men arrived; turn it up loud to drown out the sounds from below. He didn't even know if there would be noises. Maybe the men worked in silence – pointing guns, whispering threats and promises. He had no idea how they worked. The thing was, he couldn't imagine either Lucy or Chris giving in easily. They were fighters, that was certain. They would no doubt try to stand up to the men. That would be their mistake.

After the visit, and confirmation from them that the visit was a success (and he hoped to see a FOR SALE board appear outside the basement flat very soon), he would wait until morning and then call Kirsty to tell her the good news. He couldn't wait. In just 48 hours, this would all be over.

His appetite had come back. In fact, he was ravenous, as if all the days of abstinence were catching up with him, and his brain had suddenly discovered that his stomach was empty, apart from that boulder of dread. He drove to the supermarket and used his cash card to withdraw money from the hole in the wall. He saw his balance on screen and gulped. E.T.N. hadn't paid him for his final month: his penalty for not giving notice before he left. Chris had probably been involved in that decision. He had just enough to stock up on food. Still, that was OK. Kirsty would be back soon. She was on extended sick leave now, as she had explained when she phoned him, but she was still being paid. And when she came back he would feel well enough to go out and find another job. It wouldn't be too hard for someone with his skills and experience.

He pushed the trolley round the supermarket, buying all the things he liked but that Kirsty disapproved of: Pot Noodles, TV dinners, packet pasta that just required milk and water to spring magically into edible form. He bought a carton of 200 cigarettes and a large bottle of vodka. He handed over £100 and got 73 pence change. He had just enough petrol in the tank of his car to get home. He was now officially broke.

For dinner he heated up a foil carton of macaroni cheese and washed it down with a glass of neat vodka. He ate crisps and watched television. He didn't pay much attention to what was on. His mind was elsewhere.

His mind was on Friday.

On Friday morning he went out into the hall to check the post – nothing for him – and bumped into Mary.

'Hello,' she said, looking him up and down in a way that made him realise he still looked a mess. 'I haven't seen you for a while.'

'No. I've…been busy.'

'I haven't seen Kirsty either. How is she?'

'She's gone away. On holiday. With her friend Heather.'

'And left you all on your own.'

He forced a smile. 'Yes. But I don't mind.'

'I suppose she wanted a last holiday before the baby comes along.'

'Yes. That's right.'

'Where's she gone? Anywhere nice?'

'Ibiza.' It was the first place that popped into his head.

'Really? Not partying too hard, I hope.'

He couldn't cope with any more of her questions. He couldn't cope, either, with the intense way in which she was looking at him. He had the feeling that she didn't believe a word he had said. 'I've got to get back inside,' he said. 'I've left the hob on.'

She nodded. 'OK. I won't keep you.'

He moved to walk by her and she said, 'Jamie.'

He turned to go back inside.

'If you need to talk to anyone, you can always talk to me.'

He shook his head vehemently. 'No, I'm fine. I don't know why you think I'm not.' He went inside and shut the door firmly behind him.

He leaned against the door, breathing heavily, and listened to Mary go up the stairs. He heard her door shut and thought he heard her call Lennon. He looked at his watch. It was only ten-thirty in the morning. He had a whole day to kill. He couldn't stay in all day, waiting for the men to turn up. He would go insane. But he had no money and no petrol in the car. It was raining outside. There was no-one he could go and see. He hadn't contacted any of his friends for months. The only person he could think of was Heather, but she would probably be at work.

He scanned the bookshelves looking for a book he hadn't read before. He saw Brian's book – the one that had scared Kirsty. He certainly didn't want to read anything scary. There was nothing here that he wanted to read. He checked the spines of his DVDs. There was nothing he wanted to watch either. The thought of playing a video game bored him. He felt so tense, like a polar bear going mental in its enclosure at the zoo. He had to get out. He put on the coat and went walking in the rain.

He walked all day, walked until his feet throbbed, his clothes were soaked through and even his underwear was wet. He walked along the canal, passing by people in raincoats with miserable, drenched dogs. He wandered through the deserted park, watched the ducks and swans glide across the pond. He walked and walked until it was getting dark, and then he headed home.

He hung his wet clothes on the radiator and got in the bath. He sat in the bath with the scissors and cut most of his hair off, so there were just a few clumps left, sticking up in ugly clumps on top of his head. He shaved, nicking himself a few times but ignoring the pain and the blood that dripped into the water, where hair and stubble floated among the foam. He got out, smothered himself in talcum powder and pulled on a set of clean, dry clothes.

He waited.

At half-seven he found himself standing before the window, looking out at the dark road. He had been working out, and his muscles ached pleasantly. He ran his hand over his scalp, thinking how strange his hair felt. He wondered if Kirsty would like it when she saw him.

The minutes trickled by. Seven thirty-four. Seven forty-one. He made himself a coffee and scrolled through iTunes again, trying to decide what to play when the men arrived.

Seven forty-eight. Seven fifty-four.

He waited.

Eight o'clock arrived and there was no sign of them. He wasn't worried. In fact, he had expected them to be a little late.

By half-eight, he began to wonder if they had got stuck in traffic.

By nine – when half his fingernails were gone, chewed up and spat out – he felt thoroughly sick and a cold, clammy sheen of sweat covered his body. Should he phone them? He didn't want to piss them off. They had probably just been delayed somewhere. Maybe they had another job to do.

By half-nine, he had started to wonder if they had definitely agreed on eight o'clock. Had they actually said ten? The man had spoken in twenty-four hour clock, and Jamie was sure he'd said twenty-hundred, but maybe he'd said twenty-two hundred. Yes, that must be it. He relaxed a little. But only a little.

He realised he was standing in the dark, and had been for several hours. He wished he'd gone out after all. Except he didn't have any money, and he would have got home expecting the job to be done…and what if it hadn't?

What if they weren't coming?

He sat down. It was now ten-thirty. He knew, with sudden and sickening conviction, that he had been conned, taken for a ride. They should have been here two-and-a-half hours ago. He bent over and his stomach spasmed. He ran to the toilet and threw up. He had been fucked over. For £10,000.

The realisation of what he had done made him start to shake. He had given away all of his and Kirsty's money – his and Kirsty's – to a pair of men whose names he didn't even know. He started to laugh. He fell onto his knees, his laughter growing louder and louder. He clutched his stomach, trying to hold in the pain. Oh Jamie oh Jamie…you stupid fucking idiotic moron…

Eventually, the hysteria subsided. He lay perfectly still in the dark. He tried to think. What could he do?

He heard a car door close outside. They were here. At last. Oh thank God.

He leapt to his feet and ran to the front window. It wasn't the men. It was Brian and Linda, coming home. He sobbed, bit his tongue, fell to his knees.

He crawled across the floor and grabbed the phone. He dialled the men's number. The line was dead.

£10,000.

Kirsty had gone and he had stayed behind because he had planned to get some men to scare off Lucy and Chris. The men had taken his money and not done the job. Kirsty was going to be so angry that he had taken the money that he couldn't even go after her now.

He was stuck.

He was fucked.

He lay on the sofa all night, the heating turned up as high as it would go, listening to noises in the street. He still thought they might come; they might turn up in the middle of the night, which, he persuaded himself, would surely make their actions more effective.

Jamie woke up shortly after the sun had risen. The flat was like a furnace and his clothes stank of stale sweat. He would take them off and put them in the washing machine with all the other unwashed clothes; clothes that reeked of cigarettes and sour, unhealthy perspiration. It was half-eight. He tried to remember when he had last looked at his watch during the night. About three, he thought. Maybe they had come after that, stealing in during the early hours of the morning, getting Lucy and Chris out of bed. But a few minutes later, any last hopes he might have had were dashed. He saw Lucy and Chris come up from their flat and walk down the front path to their car. They looked animated and happy: as happy as he had ever seen them.

He was so tired. He wanted to lie down and sleep forever.

He tried the nameless men's number once more. The mobile was still switched off. He doubted if they would ever switch it on again. They had probably bought a new phone out of the £10,000 he had given them.

He pulled the curtains and undressed. He got into bed and tried to sleep.

He barely noticed Sunday morning or afternoon. Then, on Sunday evening, he heard sirens outside. The noise frightened him. He had a horrible fear – a feeling that had been with him all day – that the men had tried to do the job but had got the wrong address. What if that siren was an ambulance, carting away some other poor souls, people who had suffered because of him, because of mistaken identity?

There was a knock at the door. Jamie froze. What if it was the men? Or the police come to arrest him? He imagined "Charlie" being arrested on the way to the job – pulled up by traffic police who ran a check on the vehicle and realised it was stolen (Jamie's imagination had gone into overdrive) and giving the police Jamie's name. Maybe the police had been watching the two men, listening in on their calls. Maybe they knew all about it.

He looked out of the front window. There was a fire engine out there, several fire fighters standing beside it.

Jamie went out to the front door. The fireman in charge looked him up and down.

'Where's the fire?' he said.

Jamie said, 'There isn't one. I think you've been hoaxed.'

The fireman's eyes flickered with anger. 'What did you say?'

'Someone's hoaxed you. It's happened before. There's no fire.'

'It had better not have been you, pal.' He sounded incredulous. Another fire fighter came over, who Jamie recognised from the night of the party.

The second fireman said, 'I thought I knew this address. You've done this before, haven't you? What the hell's wrong with you? I told you before, it's an offence to hoax the emergency services.'

'It wasn't me,' Jamie said weakly. He had an inkling of what he must look like to them. He expected he made them feel sick.

The first fireman said, 'Then who was it?'

Jamie shook his head sadly and closed the door. He went back inside, ignoring the furious knocks. Eventually he heard them go away, not wanting to waste any more time on this loser. For the rest of the day he waited for the police to come, to arrest him for hoaxing the fire brigade. For once, he was pleased that the police round this part of the city never seemed to do anything.

On Monday morning he called his old office and asked to speak to Mike.

The woman who answered the phone asked who it was. He heard her say something – to Mike, he assumed – then she said, 'He doesn't want to talk to you.'

Jamie shouted, 'I have to talk to him. Get me him now!'

The woman gasped, then there was the sound of murmuring, and Mike came on the line. 'Fuck off, James, I don't want to talk to you.'

'They've stolen my money.'

'You deserved it, you twat. And how dare you drop me in it.'

'Mike, you've got to help me.'

'Go fuck yourself.'

He slammed the phone down, leaving Jamie with the taste of bile in his mouth. That bastard. That fucking...

Who was he trying to kid? He did deserve it. He had broken his promise, he had behaved like a moron. He didn't blame Mike for not talking to him.

He had to face it: he was never going to see that money again.

He stood up and looked out at the street. He had lost all his money, his job, his best friend, his wife and his baby. All that remained in his possession was this flat. It was the only thing he had left to cling on to. If he moved out of the flat he would have lost absolutely everything. He felt like he'd been playing that board game, Risk, in which each player starts off with a group of countries and has to guard their own countries while trying to take over other people's. The winner was the one who took over the world, capturing all his opponent's territories. Jamie had started the game with Kirsty, Paul, his money and his job; he had acquired the flat and was soon going to have a baby. Now almost everything he had started with, and everything he had acquired, had been lost to his opponents downstairs. All apart from one last territory: his flat.

He was not going to relinquish it. He would guard it with his life. No matter what Lucy or Chris did, no matter what attacks they tried, no matter how the dice fell, he was staying here. He would work out some way of paying the mortgage. He was not moving.

He was not going to lose.

Twenty-seven

The letter arrived on a Tuesday morning.

The night before, he had eaten the last of the food he had bought on his final trip to the supermarket, and had lain awake half the night wondering what he was going to do. The quickest solution was to sell something. He didn't want to sell any of his possessions, but the most obvious thing was his Playstation 3 and accompanying collection of games. He still had the games console's original box, so he packed it up and put it by the door, along with a bag of games.

He walked down the hill with the box held out in front of him. There was no petrol left in his car, but luckily there was a shop nearby that bought second hand goods like computer games and videos.

The man in the shop offered him £50 for the lot. Jamie haggled and ended up with £65. On the way home he stopped at the local Co-Op and bought enough groceries to last a few days. He also bought more cigarettes and another bottle of vodka; the other one was long gone.

When he got home the post had been. There was a single letter lying on the doormat. He picked it up and studied it: it was for him, with a handwritten name and address.

He almost dropped it on the pile of letters that had accumulated over the last few weeks, post comprised of two distinct groups. Firstly, there were the bills and reminders, letters informing him of all the direct debits that had failed: the mortgage, the house insurance, the council tax, the phone bill.

Secondly, there was the junk mail. Lucy and Chris had started that campaign again. Letters from the Samaritans asked him if he was feeling lonely, depressed, suicidal? Worst of all were the letters from charities who raised money for parents who had lost babies; envelopes that bore statistics about Sudden Infant Death Syndrome; letters asking him to make a contribution towards research. Then there were the letters from pro-life groups, whose envelopes always bore pictures of foetuses; letters that spelled out exactly how developed an embryo or foetus was at four weeks, six weeks, eight weeks, twelve.

Jamie threw both types of letter onto a pile and refused to look at them. The thing with the junk mail was that he knew this was mild for Lucy and Chris. It was as if they weren't really trying very hard. He knew that sooner or later they would try something bigger. He didn't want to think about what that might be – but whatever it was, he was staying put.

He carried the handwritten letter in and sat down with it on the sofa.. He thought at first that it might be from Kirsty – who he still hadn't spoken to – but a second glance told him that although it was similar to her writing, this hadn't come from her. He lit a cigarette then tore the letter open.

It was from Letitia, the previous occupant of the flat. His heartbeat lost its steady rhythm for a moment. He had practically forgotten he had written to her, back when he was trying to find out whether she had lent the Newtons a key to the flat. He started to read:

Dear Jamie

Firstly, please accept my apologies that it has taken me so long to reply to your letter. At first, I thought the letter had been sent to the wrong person, because it was addressed to L Pica. My name is Matthews – it always has been, and David's surname is Robson. Pica is the name of the woman we sold the flat to and, I assume, who you bought the flat from. I guess you never met Ms Pica – we never did either. It seems she bought the flat from us and then sold it on to you very quickly. I don't know how much you paid for the flat, but she bought it from us very cheaply so I guess she made a tidy profit. Anyway, that isn't important.

The other reason for my delay in replying is that your letter upset me a great deal. I had hoped to forget the names of Lucy and Chris Newton. I wish now that I hadn't left a forwarding address with Mary. I had intended to sever all links with that flat. Before we left I scrubbed every inch of it. I wanted to wipe it completely from my memory.

Although that has been impossible.

Since we moved out in May, I have had the same dream every night. I am running through the woods when I spy the most wonderful looking gingerbread house, like in Hansel and Gretel. I go inside, and there is the witch. Lucy Newton, with that bastard husband of hers by her side. Chris Newton. That fucker.

Excuse me. But I cannot write their names without shaking. Yes, many of the things they have done to you, they did to us as well. The hoax letters, the banging on the ceiling, the constant complaints about noise, even though we are both very quiet people. In fact, since living in that flat, I have developed an extreme aversion to noise. Several therapists have tried to cure me, but the only cure is peace and quiet. That is why it is so wonderful living here. We live in a small stone farmhouse on the edge of a very quiet village. Our nearest neighbour is a mile away. It is bliss.

I suppose I should start from the beginning, although I am afraid it upsets me too much to write about this at great length. I will try my best, though.

Jamie finished his first cigarette and lit another. He read on, enrapt.

We moved into the flat in April last year, thirteen months before we moved out. The flat seemed perfect. No, the flat was perfect: it was the neighbours who made it less so. The space, the light, the warmth. It seemed like the ideal place to start out. We were so full of optimism.

362

Well, you say the very same thing in your letter. We thought it was paradise. We were under the impression that we were lucky.

When we moved in we saw that the flat downstairs was empty but had a Sold board up. A week later, Chris and Lucy moved in. The next day, they came up to introduce themselves. They said they had moved to this part of London from Ealing; they said they had left because they had had a run-in with a previous neighbour. I sympathised. Hah! I wonder now who that poor sod might have been and what kind of state they're in now. Whatever, it seems that Lucy and Chris had grown tired of their old haunting ground and decided to try somewhere new. Fresh blood, as it were.

Sorry if I sound cynical and angry. Writing this is bringing it all back. David just told me to throw this letter away, to forget about it, but I feel we owe you something. We should have left a warning. Although I bet you wouldn't have believed us. You saw the flat and fell in love with it like we did. Who would heed a warning about such a lovely place?

Anyway: At first, the Newtons were friendly – just like they were with you – coming to dinner, meeting our friends. We went to the pub with them once or twice. We lent them books and DVDs. I thought it would be a long, mutually-rewarding friendship.

Then one day, we went swimming: not just the four of us, but also two of our friends, Angela and Steve. We went to the beach at Camber Sands. Chris brought a dinghy and we took it in turns to go out in it. It was great fun. It was a hot, sunny day, and after going out on the dinghy, we lay on the sand, sunbathing, chatting, basically having a really nice time. Then Chris said that he wanted to go out in the dinghy again, and he asked if any of us wanted to come along. Most of us were too hot and settled where we were. Lucy hadn't been out anyway, as she said she couldn't swim. Chris made a point of asking Angela and Steve if they wanted to go out. Steve said no, so Chris turned to Angela, really badgering her until she said yes.

I ought to point out that Angela was my best friend, and had been for many years, since we were at school in fact. I knew Angela didn't feel very confident in the water – she wasn't a strong swimmer – but I also knew that she fancied Chris a bit (God knows why – he makes my flesh creep – and no, Angela wasn't going out with Steve, in case you're wondering). I thought it was peculiar that Lucy didn't seem to mind the way Chris was flirting with Angela and trying to get her to go out on the dinghy. Lucy had always struck me as the jealous type. She hated Mary – called her a witch – and I thought it was because she thought Mary fancied Chris (again: uugh). But today, she seemed oblivious to Chris and Angela's behaviour, and when Angela gave in and said she would go out on the dinghy, Lucy didn't bat an eyelid.

I think you can probably guess what happened next, Jamie. We were lying on the beach, not paying much attention to the dinghy, which was by now a speck in the distance. Chris had gone a long way out. Afterwards, the lifeguards told me that they had been a little worried, and were keeping an eye on the dinghy.

Which was why they reacted so quickly when it capsized. I remember seeing two of the lifeguards run past us and into the water. I looked up and tried to focus on the dinghy. The sun was so high in the sky I couldn't really see.

The four of us stood up and ran down to the water's edge, where a small crowd had gathered, watching the lifeguards. I could see the dinghy in the distance, bobbing around. There was no-one in it.

Lucy let out this strange sound, which I thought was a yelp of distress. I think now it was actually excitement. We waited on the edge of the beach, the sea lapping at out feet, helpless, waiting to see what the lifeguards would do.

They eventually towed the dinghy in to shore. An ambulance was on its way. I ran over to the dinghy. Chris was sitting up, rubbing his face with his hands. One of the lifeguards was giving Angela the kiss of life. He kept blowing into her mouth then thumping her chest, then trying again. Eventually, another lifeguard touched him on the arm and told him it was no good. It was too late.

Chris's story was that Angela had lunged at him, trying to kiss him. Appalled by the idea of being unfaithful, he had backed away quickly, capsizing the dinghy. Angela fell in and when she didn't emerge, Chris dived in trying to save her. It was deep and the current was strong. It was too late. The lifeguards said that when they got there Chris was

diving under and under, trying to find Angela, but without success. The
lifeguards dove deep, found her and pulled her out. But she was
already dead.

We came home in a state of shock. At the time, I believed Chris's
story. I went into a period of mourning for my best friend. I didn't see
Chris or Lucy for a while. The next time we had contact with them was
when the hoaxes and threats started.

You see, that's what they do. They hurt – or kill – someone you care
for in order to make you weak. And then they move in for the kill. Your
friend was lucky that he didn't die. I imagine Chris and Lucy were
rather upset by that. But you were still worried about him, and
therefore you weren't at full strength. You were still vulnerable enough
for them to attack you.

Over the next year they waged a campaign of hatred against us.
The letters and hoaxes I could put up with (in fact, as with yourselves,
the hoaxes had begun before that trip to the beach – taxis turning up
all hours of the day, which led to us being blacklisted by a lot of firms,
and endless parcels). It was the other stuff that eventually drove us out.

They played recordings. Every night, almost all night long, they
played these awful recordings of people whispering or screaming,
talking or shouting. God, I can hear them now. On and on and on they
went, getting inside your head until you thought the voices were
actually <u>originating</u> inside your head. You could never quite make out
what the voices were saying. Sometimes you could make out a line of

dialogue, but because the volume was just too low, you started to make things up yourself. I thought I could hear Angela talking to me, asking me to help her, telling me she was still under the sea, drowning. Sometimes the voices sounded foreign, or they would let out ear-piercing screams in the dead of night. It was indescribably awful. Chris and Lucy had devised a way of torturing us, and it worked. In the end, we had to wear headphones in bed and listen to music. By then, though, it was too late. The damage had been done.

I went to the police and showed them the letters. I told them about the recordings. I asked them to come round in the night to listen to what we had to endure, but they never did. They thought I was making it up – especially when I accused Chris of murdering my friend. I saw bulbs light up above their heads. This mad woman – who spoke in a whisper – was upset with her neighbour because he had been involved in an accident with her best friend, and she blamed him. It was an easy conclusion to reach.

Jamie paused. Why were the police so useless? When he had complained about the Newtons, shouldn't the police have looked them up in their records and seen that other people had complained before? Dodds had seemed sympathetic, but he hadn't done his work properly, had he? It was a joke.

He read on.

Eventually, after months of torment, I couldn't bear it any more. I was having violent dreams in which I attempted to kill Lucy and Chris and always failed. My psychiatrist told me I should move. I think one of the worst things was knowing that Chris was free, even though I was sure he was a murderer. I saw him nearly every day. He was a constant reminder of my loss.

I guess I have gone on at length, after all. I suppose I should be feeling some sort of catharsis now, but I don't. In fact, I feel worse.

I really wish I could help you in some way, but I'm simply not strong enough to come down there. You could show this letter to the police to back up your story, but I don't want to talk to them again about it. All I want is to forget.

In answer to your question – no, we didn't ever give a key to the flat to Lucy and Chris. I thank God we didn't.

Please don't write back to me. Like I said, I want to forget. It's going to take a long time, but I hope I might get there in the end. We both, however, wish you luck. My advice is to get out, go far away. But if you find a way of making Lucy and Chris pay for what they've done, I'll be cheering you all the way – even if I do have to remain invisible in the background.

With very best wishes

Letitia and David

Jamie put the letter down. Thoughts refused to knit together properly in his head. Somehow, though, he knew, all this could have been avoided. If only.

It was too late for if only.

Suddenly, he had to get out of the flat. The rooms felt haunted. He put his coat on and ran out into the hallway. He collided with Mary and knocked her backwards, almost forcing her to lose her balance.

'Jamie, mind where you're… Hey, are you alright?'

He couldn't speak. He just stood there, staring at her, mute.

'Jamie, what's happened? What's wrong?'

He still couldn't speak or move. He seemed to have gone into some sort of catatonic state.

'Jamie? Wake up?'

He blinked at her, and she slowly came into focus. 'Mary,' he whispered.

'Come on,' she said, 'let's get you back in your flat.'

'No! I don't want to.'

'Why? What's wrong?'

He shook his head.

'OK, come on. Let's get you upstairs.'

She led him up the stairs. He was in a trance, and the next thing he knew he was sitting on Mary's sofa, beside Lennon, who was purring steadily. Mary bent over him and offered him a mug of hot, steaming liquid. Jamie sniffed it. Some kind of herbal tea. Ugh.

'What's the matter, Jamie?' she said.

'It's…everything.'

'Has something happened to Kirsty?'

He shook his head. 'She's gone. She left me.'

She nodded. He guessed she had probably figured that out already. After all, Kirsty hadn't been around for a while.

'Do you want to talk about it?' she said.

He sipped the tea. He was beginning to feel a little calmer, but his mind was still racing, remembering what he had read in Letitia's letter. 'You remember I asked you for the address of Letitia and David? I received a letter from them today.'

Mary shook her head. 'I don't understand. What's that got to do with Kirsty?'

'No. It's not Kirsty – it's Lucy and Chris.'

'What about them?'

He sighed. And then he told Mary everything, right from the beginning: from the first hoax, when the fire brigade turned up at his party, through the dead rats ('I'm embarrassed to admit that I suspected Lennon at first,' he said) and the letters and Paul's supposed accident and the spiders and Kirsty's miscarriage, all the way through to the second incident with the fire brigade. The only bit he left out was the part about the men he had given the money to. He was too ashamed to tell her about that.

After he had finished telling her she was silent for a while. Eventually she said, 'My God, Jamie. I had no idea. I knew you were having some sort of problems, but I thought maybe it was just the worry of starting a family. I've never liked Lucy and Chris. I always thought there was something a bit nasty about them, but I really didn't think–' She shrugged. 'Well, who would? It's not the kind of thing that's supposed to happen in real life, is it?'

'I know.'

'Poor Kirsty. Poor you.'

'And Letitia and David too. The letter I got from them today explained that they'd been through pretty much the same as us.'

'I always thought something had happened to them. They were so happy when they moved in. I remember Letitia coming up here and telling me how excited they were to have found the flat. I knew about Letitia's friend dying, and I thought that was what made them want to move away. I feel so stupid. Maybe if I'd known, I could have helped.'

At that moment, Lennon walked into the room, sparking a memory in Jamie's head. 'You know when Lennon went missing and you were really worried about him? I saw him with Lucy. In fact, I'm sure she was keeping him in their flat.'

Mary's mouth dropped open.

'I expect she knew how worried you'd be and got a kick out of it.'

On cue, the cat jumped onto Mary's lap and she wrapped her arms around him.

'Perhaps you could help me now,' Jamie said.

'Of course. Anything.'

He put down his drink. He had only drunk half of it. 'I need to get into the Newtons' flat. I've been to the police about Lucy and Chris and they think I'm inventing it all. The same happened to Letitia and David. If I can get into the basement flat I might be able to find some evidence. A key to my flat, for example, to prove that Chris could have got into my flat to plant that virus. Or a diary. That would be good. There has to be something in there that will incriminate them, especially if I put it together with Letitia's letter and remind the police that Chris has been involved in two accidents: three if you include Kirsty's miscarriage.'

'Isn't that enough? Surely if you remind the police about Letitia's friend...'

'No, because there's no evidence. It would never stand up in court. It wouldn't even get to court. I need something more. I'm certain that if I get into their flat I'll find it.'

Mary nodded. 'So what can I do?'

'I need them out of the way for an hour or so. Maybe you could ask them to dinner or something.'

'But, Jamie, they don't like me.'

'I know. Lucy says you're a witch.'

Mary raised an eyebrow. 'Does she indeed. I wish I was. I'd turn her into a mouse and let Lennon play with her.'

372

Jamie laughed.

Mary said, 'I've got an idea. Stay here. I'll be back in a minute.'

She left Jamie on his own and left the flat. She was gone for over half an hour, leaving him twiddling his thumbs, wishing he had his cigarettes with him. He chewed his fingernails, trying to work out another way to get into the flat if Mary couldn't help him. What was she doing? He had a sudden horrible feeling that she had gone to tell Lucy and Chris what he planned to do; that she was colluding with them. A minute later she came back, and he realised he was being paranoid and ridiculous. She had Brian with her.

Jamie stood up and Brian said, 'Mary's just explained everything to me. I just feel sorry that I didn't know about it before.'

Jamie shrugged. 'It doesn't matter.'

'You should have told us, Jamie. We might have been able to help.'

'I didn't know you well enough, and anyway, nobody I told ever believed me. Apart from a friend at work.' Yes, and his attempts to help had ended disastrously.

Brian nodded. 'We're here to help you now. We don't want people like that living in these flats. It makes me feel ill. I quite understand your need to gather evidence, so' – he looked at the ceiling – 'as much as it will pain me to have those people eating from our plates and drinking from our cups, Linda and I will invite them to dinner. We've always got on alright with them. Obviously, we're lucky that we don't live in the flat directly above them.'

Jamie took hold of Brian's hand and shook it. 'Thank you so much.'

Mary said, 'How will you get into the flat?'

'I don't know. I can't break in because I don't want them to know I've been in there.'

'I think we can help on that score too,' Brian said. 'An elderly couple used to live in the basement flat.'

'Mr and Mrs Chambers,' said Mary.

'Yes, and Linda and I were very good friends with them. It was very sad: Mr Chambers died and Mrs Chambers ended up in a home. Anyway, they were quite forgetful – a bit of a scatty old couple, actually. They locked themselves out a couple of times. In the end, they gave me a key in case they did it again. I've still got it. I know I should have given it back when they moved out, but I forgot. Luckily.'

'Problem solved,' said Mary.

'Assuming the Newtons accept our dinner invitation.'

Jamie waited while Brian went upstairs and looked for the key. A few minutes later he returned and handed it to Jamie. 'I just hope they haven't changed the locks. If you go back to your flat now, I'll call you and let you know if they've accepted the invitation.'

'OK.'

Before he left, Mary hugged him. 'We'll sort this out for you, Jamie. Don't you worry.'

Later that evening, the phone rang. It was Brian.

'It's all set,' he said. 'They were delighted to accept. I told them we'd planned a dinner party, even bought all the ingredients, and then our friends had dropped out. They didn't seem to mind that they were last minute replacements.'

'So when is it?'

'Tomorrow night. Seven-thirty.'

Twenty-eight

They had worked out a series of signs. When Lucy and Chris arrived at the top flat, Linda would stamp twice on the kitchen floor. Hearing this, Mary would then ring Jamie, letting the phone ring twice before hanging up. That was his cue.

He sat beside the phone, every muscle in his body tense.

The phone rang. Once, twice. Went dead.

He picked up the key that Brian had given him. His arms felt weak. But there was no way he was going to back out. This had to be done. Chris was a murderer; Lucy his accomplice. Jamie was the only person who could do something about it. He wasn't really thinking about justice, or the greater good. He wasn't even thinking about revenge. He merely wanted his life back.

He had decided to wait five minutes before going downstairs. He could imagine Lucy and Chris getting up there then realising they had forgotten something: a bottle of red wine perhaps.. He'd be in the flat and they would come down and find him. He shuddered at the thought.

He watched the clock for five minutes, counting every second, part of him hoping Lucy or Chris *would* come down the stairs so he wouldn't have to go through with this. He forced himself to get a grip.

The five minutes were up. He walked out into the hallway, closing the flat door quietly behind him. He opened the front door, gripping the basement flat key firmly in his sweaty palm. It was dark. He had thought about this: it would be OK to turn the lights on in the flat. Lucy and Chris were well out of the way. Unless they leaned out of Brian and Linda's front window and peered down, they would never see that their lights were on.

He went down the steps to the basement. Now was the first moment of truth. Had they changed the locks since they had moved in? At first he thought the key wasn't going to fit, but it was because his hand was trembling. It slid into the lock, he turned it and the door opened.

He stepped inside.

He stood in the hallway, thinking that they must surely be able to hear his heart beating from the top flat. There was a strange smell in the air; a smell that had once wafted up to his and Kirsty's nostrils. He still couldn't identify it, but it made him feel ill.

The layout of the flat was the same as those above it: living room and kitchen at the front; bedrooms and bathroom at the back. He opened the door to what he knew must be the main bedroom and squinted into the semi-darkness. This bedroom had patio doors which led into the garden. There was something odd about the room. The curtains were open and the moon shone in, creating a little light. It took him a second, while his eyes adjusted, to realise that the room contained only a single bed.

He must have got it wrong -this must be the spare room. And yet when he opened the other bedroom door he saw that this bedroom too only had a single bed in it. Hanging above the bed were pictures of Chris: huge, blown-up pictures. There were tins of men's deodorant on the bedside table. Mansize tissues; computer magazines. It was clearly Chris's bedroom.

He closed the door and looked back into the other bedroom. The walls were blank, painted magnolia, no pictures or posters. There were women's perfumes, make-up on a dressing table, a hi-fi with large speakers. Lucy's care assistant uniform hung on the front of the wardrobe.

Separate rooms.

He could imagine Lucy lying alone in this bedroom with her phone, recording him and Kirsty making love. Did she get a thrill out of it? Maybe she masturbated while she did it. Was Chris in the room too? Did they play the recordings back for their own private titillation? He felt angry, all of a sudden.

He pulled the door to, a little too firmly. The door banged and he froze, his heart booming. He flicked the light on in the living room, still terrified that Lucy or Chris would appear at any moment and ask him what the fuck he was doing. It was so strange seeing the place where his tormentors lived. He had begun to imagine them as trolls that lived under a bridge. He thought they would live in some squalid cavern, pages of newspapers stuck all over the walls like the rooms of serial killers in movies. Instead, the room looked perfectly normal with its sofa, armchairs, coffee table and rug – but look closer and there was something 'off' about the room. There were no personal touches, no ornaments on the mantelpiece, no books anywhere. There was no mess, no photos of family, nothing that indicated that real people lived here. It was like being in some future museum where a typical early 21st century living room had been reconstructed, but they'd left out all the personal touches, the things that would make it real. There were no wedding photos anywhere either, Jamie noticed, no photos of Lucy and Chris together at all, just a number of pictures of them both on their own. What with the separate bedrooms, it made Jamie wonder if the Newtons' marriage was a sham. It made a sick kind of sense. Two psychopaths getting together, getting married and living together, but only because they realised they could work better as a team. They were two people who were incapable of love, hugely egotistical – as the pictures of Chris in his bedroom testified – and narcissistic. He shuddered. This place gave him the creeps.

Jamie noticed another strange thing: there were two televisions. One looked like a normal TV – almost the same as Jamie's, in fact, with a DVD player underneath it – but the other was in one of those old-fashioned wooden television cabinets, with the doors closed. He could see flickering light around the edges of these closed cabinet doors. Weird. He opened the doors of the cabinet.

It wasn't an ordinary television. The picture was in black and white, grainy and unclear. The present date and time were displayed in the bottom left hand corner of the screen. Jamie realised he was looking at a CCTV monitor which was displaying a live picture of somebody's living room.

His living room.

He stepped back. 'Fuck,' he said aloud. That was his sofa, his bookcase, his armchair. There was the picture Kirsty had brought with her from the house she shared with the other nurses: the picture of the mermaid on a rock.

He bent double. He felt as if someone had punched him in the kidneys. Lucy and Chris had not only been listening to them. They been watching them. There had to be a tiny camera hidden somewhere in the flat, somewhere opposite the sofa. He tried to picture it, but couldn't work out where it could be hidden. But he would look for it later. He would find the fucking thing and tear it out of the wall and stamp on it, grind it into the floorboards.

Jesus Christ. How long had this been going on for?

He noticed something else. The CCTV monitor was resting on top of a hard drive. It wasn't recording now, but...

Oh fuck.

He looked around, frenziedly scouring the shelves of the bookcase which housed mostly DVDs with handwritten titles on the spines: J&K 1: PARTY; J&K 2: DECORATING; all the way up to 12: J ALONE.

He pulled the DVD labelled J&K 11 from the shelf and inserted it into the player attached to the ordinary TV. He pressed 'play' and after a few seconds an image appeared. It was him and Kirsty standing in the living room. Kirsty doing the ironing. The video was silent, but Jamie could remember what they had been talking about. He watched their lips move. He watched them move over onto the sofa. They were talking about the baby; the miscarriage. Kirsty started to cry and Jamie held her, crying too.

He pressed stop. Hatred and anger flowed through him, replacing the sadness. He clenched his fists and stood up. He wanted to smash everything in the room; he wanted to destroy this place, the home of the those fuckers, those...

He told himself to calm down. He took more deep breaths.

Then he noticed a DVD labelled J&K 8: AWAY. He slotted it into the DVD player and pressed play. Again, it was the interior of their living room, empty. Nothing happened for the first couple of minutes and Jamie almost switched it off, but something told him to wait – and at the two minute mark someone entered the room. Chris. Jamie's mouth went dry. He watched Chris walk over to the hidden camera and peer into it.

Staring straight at the lens, Chris smiled coldly, then licked his lips.

Lucy followed Chris into the room, looking around, before settling down on the sofa. Chris was out of shot now – this must have been when he installed the virus on Jamie's PC – and all Jamie could see was Lucy sitting immobile on the sofa, staring impassively at the camera. Then, still looking into the lens, she leaned back and pulled her skirt up around her hips. She had no underwear on and Jamie watched stunned as she began to touch herself, her head thrown back as she masturbated for a couple of minutes until she came, her mouth opening wide for a moment before closing, her expression one of release rather than ecstasy. Then she pulled her skirt back down over her knees and sat still again, her hands crossed modestly in her lap.

Jamie pressed stop, terrified of what he might see next.

He tried to think straight. How had they got in to the flat? They must have a key.

He needed to find it. He was sure he had enough evidence now to go to the police with, but if he could find the key he would feel safer. He wouldn't be afraid they would come in and murder him in his bed while he slept. Because surely that was next? They had killed his unborn daughter, driven out Kirsty. He knew Chris had killed before. Jamie was certain he was next on the list, and his experiences with the police so far told him they wouldn't be quick to act.

He dropped the DVD on the floor and moved over to the desk. He pulled open the top drawer and began to rifle through it. Electricity bills, bank statements, Council Tax bills. Nothing useful. He opened another drawer. There were photos of Chris, standing on a sandy beach, pointing out to sea and smiling. There was a newspaper cutting: MAN IN COMA AFTER KARTING ACCIDENT.

He pulled open the door beneath the drawer and groped inside. There was a carrier bag at the back of the compartment. It was full of glasses: around twenty pairs of spectacles, most of them old - fashioned, with brown frames. Jamie furrowed his brow and emptied the bag, tipping the glasses all over the floor, revealing a couple of what he quickly realised were hearing aids, and a single USB stick. Not knowing what to make of all this, he slipped the USB stick in his pocket and moved on.

He dug deeper in the cupboard, finding a manila folder. Inside it was a marriage certificate. He almost threw it aside, but a word caught his eye:

Pica.

His heartbeat skipped.

The two names on the certificate were Christopher Robert Newton and Lucy Marie Pica.

He tore through the rest of the desk until he found a letter with the estate agent's heading: Anderson and Son. He read the letter in stunned horror. It confirmed the sale of the ground floor flat, 143 Mount Pleasant Street to Jamie Knight and Kirsty Phillips from Ms Lucy Pica. He dug deeper. There was another letter, dated May, confirming the sale of the flat from Letitia Matthews and David Robson to Lucy Pica.

Lucy had bought the flat in her maiden name from Letitia and David and then sold it on to Jamie and Kirsty, making a healthy profit – and getting two new people to torment into the bargain. And as the sellers of the flat, they would have the keys and plenty of time to install surveillance equipment so they could watch and listen to their victims' suffering to make their pleasure even greater. The recordings of them having sex weren't made through the ceiling as they'd suspected: as well as the camera in the living room there was probably a microphone somewhere in their bedroom, hidden beneath something, which would account for the muffled sound on the recordings. The keys also gave them the chance to walk into the flat at any time that Jamie and Kirsty weren't at home.

Jamie threw all the papers to the floor. A wave of anger crashed over him, blinding him. He stood in the centre of the room. The walls spinning around and around, getting faster, everything going white, blurred; going red, crimson, the colour of blood.

He roared. The cry ripped something in his throat, made the room shake around him. He pulled the CCTV monitor out of its cabinet and threw it against the wall. All his working out had made him strong. The monitor hit the wall with a deafening crunch; shards of glass flew across the room. Jamie roared again.

There was only one way to deal with this.

He stomped across the room into the kitchen, throwing open the cupboards beneath the sink. He pulled out bottles of cleaner, bleach, rubber gloves, throwing them behind him. Then he saw what he had hoped to find: a large bottle of white spirit, almost full and extremely flammable. He unscrewed the top and went back into the living room.

He splashed the white spirit around, up the walls, over the furniture. He carried it into the bedrooms and splashed some on the beds. He threw some against the poster of Chris. He trailed the stinking liquid from the bedrooms back into the living room.

He took his matches out of his pocket, then pulled out his cigarettes. He threw the empty white spirit bottle onto the carpet in front of him and wiped his hands on his trousers. He lit a cigarette, inhaled, and stood there, motionless, for a moment. He would be burning all the evidence, erasing any proof of what Chris and Lucy had done. He had one moment to change his mind.

He threw the lit cigarette across the room.

It hit a patch of spirit and immediately blue flames flickered to life, racing across the carpet, growing as they spread, orange replacing the blue, smoke quickly filling the room. The flames caught the end of the curtains, ran up the sofa. The crackle and roar grew louder and louder. Fire danced on every surface, and started heading towards Jamie, who had backed up to the threshold of the room. He stood in the doorway for a second, entranced by the flames, and then turned to get out.

It was at that moment that Chris ran into the flat and crashed into him.

Jamie went flying into the living room. Above the roar of the flames he could hear Chris bellowing a stream of expletives. He looked around wildly, taking in what was happening to his flat, his hands on his head, his mouth open. Jamie was surrounded by smoke. He coughed harshly; his eyes started to blur and run with tears. He knew it was only a matter of minutes before the fire consumed the whole room. He tried to get to his feet and Chris kicked him in the chest.

'You fucker!' Chris screamed. He kicked Jamie again, his boot connecting with the side of his head. He reached down and pulled him up. God, he was so strong. He threw Jamie against the wall, punched him in the stomach, then the face. Jamie felt something crack; his cheekbone. Chris punched him again and blood spurted from his nose. He just managed to stay upright. There was so much smoke; he couldn't breathe. He felt his knees sag and thought he was going to fall.

But then he remembered what he had discovered in the flat. The CCTV. The letters from the estate agent. Another wave of anger gave him strength, made him cry out, hurting his throat. He threw himself at his neighbour, his hands reaching out and grabbing Chris round the throat, pushing him against the door frame. Chris tried to hit Jamie's arms to break his grip, but Jamie was possessed, overwhelmed and empowered by anger, by all that had happened to him since he had met this man. He squeezed harder, digging his thumbs into Chris's windpipe. Chris hit his arms again, hit them harder. He managed to knock Jamie's arms away and fell sideways into the living room. He held his own throat, making a horrible choking sound.

Jamie could hardly see. The whole of the living room was on fire. Thick black smoke obscured everything. Jamie staggered down the hall, pulled open the front door and fell onto his knees on the doorstep.

He sucked in air, trying to replace the smoke that filled his lungs. Beside him, the front windows of the flat smashed, blown out by the heat. Glass covered him, sticking in his hair. Smoke billowed out into the darkness.

He pushed himself up and went to stagger away. Then he remembered Chris. He was still inside, in the living room. He hated him – hated him so much – but, despite everything, he couldn't just leave him to die.

He pulled off his shirt and screwed it up into a bundle, pressing it against his face. He went back into the flat. He could hear Chris calling out, his voice weak.

'Help.'

Jamie moved towards the sound, but another blast of heat threw him backwards. A patch of ceiling collapsed in front of him, plaster and wood falling on top of him, knocking him to the floor. He was blinded, but he managed to roll over and crawl, back towards the front door. He couldn't hear Chris calling out any more. The whole living room was gone; an inferno.

Jamie threw himself over the threshold, ran up the steps, collapsed on his knees on the front path. He felt someone grab hold of him. It was Brian. He tried to say something but all he could do was cough.

Brian pulled him away from the flat. Mary and Linda were standing on the pavement, staring at him. Mary was holding Lennon, who was wriggling, trying to get away. Brian was shouting at Jamie. 'Where's Chris? Where is he?'

He still couldn't speak.

He looked up, and there was Lucy. She wasn't screaming, or crying, or trying to get into the flat. She was simply staring; watching the smoke pour out of her flat, rising up towards the night sky. She watched the flames spread upwards until they could be seen behind the windows of the ground floor flat. Jamie followed her gaze. There it went. Their dream home. Up in smoke.

He lay on the pavement and laughed, coughed, laughed again. He could smell something pleasant. He realised it was the smell of singed hair. His eyebrows had been burnt off, as had most of his hair.

He heard the wail of sirens in the distance.

Epilogue

Jamie sat down on the bed and looked around at his new room. The walls were plain white, except for a couple of posters: an aerial view of London and a picture of an urban fox, the kind that had caused a tabloid panic recently when a baby was dragged from its bed. The posters had belonged to the previous occupant of the room, and he had been told he could take them down if he wanted to, but he quite liked them. He wasn't scared of foxes.

The furniture in the room was basic: a single wardrobe, a bedside cabinet, a small chest of drawers. The mattress creaked beneath him. The room smelled stale, of dust and disinfectant, but he had opened the little window to let in some air. The room was fine, he told himself. It was a good place to get his life back on track.

He had been waiting a while for this room, slowly inching his way towards the top of the allocation list after a long time moving between B&Bs and a spell on the streets. There were dark holes in his memory, holes burnt into his brain by alcohol. But now he was on the wagon. That was part of the deal when they offered him a room in this hostel. He would stop drinking. He was even going to quit smoking.

He looked around again. Yes, it was fine. This would be a good base for his relaunch into society.

He went downstairs and saw Carol, one of the women who ran the hostel.

'Hi Jamie. What do you think?'

'Of the room? I like it.'

'Good, good.' She smiled. 'We've got another couple of people moving in today. One will be moving in to the room next to yours.'

He nodded. 'I'm going to go out for a walk. Check out my surroundings.'

'Sure.'

He went out and walked into the wind. It was cold and he was relieved that he wasn't still out on the streets. He saw a man sitting in the doorway of an abandoned shop. The man nodded at him, recognising a fellow spirit; another person who had fallen on hard times. But Jamie was on his way up. He felt a stab of guilt, knowing that soon he would again be part of the world that walked past the homeless without a glance. He told himself he would never forget what it was like to have nothing, but secretly hoped he would forget.

He walked down to the river and found an empty bench, then sat looking at the choppy water. He didn't want to cross the river; he didn't like crossing to the north of the Thames any more. That way lay the past, and a flat that had been gutted by fire. Two flats. The Newtons', and his and Kirsty's.

It had been in all the papers. There was a delay in the fire brigade coming to Mount Pleasant Street because the address was on a blacklist of hoaxers. Even though it had been Brian who called 999, the address had triggered an alert. A few minutes passed as the firemen checked that this wasn't another hoax. Five vital minutes. An anonymous fire fighter was quoted as saying that if it wasn't for that five minute delay, they might have arrived in time to save Chris. As it was, they were only able to stop the fire spreading further than the ground floor flat, saving Mary's flat.

After he was well enough to leave hospital, Jamie was arrested and charged with murder. He was refused bail and spent months in prison awaiting trial. He pleaded not guilty, on the grounds that he had been driven to his actions by his neighbours. The trial became known as the 'Magpies' trial, after Jamie's lawyer described Chris and Lucy as a pair of magpies, birds renowned for destroying the nests of other birds. This phrase caught the imagination of the press and the jury, who were also impressed by the evidence given by Letitia and David, who were persuaded to travel down from their Scottish retreat and speak up on Jamie's behalf. Kirsty gave evidence too. And in the burnt-out remains of the flat, the police forensics team found a tiny charred spy camera concealed in the picture rail. They also found a microphone, hidden beneath the carpet in the bedroom.

Jamie was found not guilty and released.

He looked at the water now. After the trial, he had come down to the river and thought about ending it. He had nothing left. Among the papers that perished in the fire was a letter from the house insurance company telling him his last direct debit had failed. When the flat burnt down, it was uninsured. He had stood beside the river and wondered what it would feel like to throw himself in, for the waters to close over him – but he couldn't do it.

He was glad he hadn't. Because after a long time on the edge, he was finally regaining control of his life. He had been given a second chance and he wasn't going to waste it.

For a long time, he had wrestled with his conscience. Because although he had pleaded not guilty, he felt guilty. With the evidence he had found in the flat, he could have gone to the police and shown them that Lucy and Chris had been making their lives a living hell. But because he had lost it at that moment, a man had died. He was responsible for the death of another human being, even if it was Chris, one of the two people he hated more than anyone else in the world. He wondered what had happened to the other one: Lucy. She had sat on her own during the trial, staring at Jamie, making him feel cold and vulnerable. Jamie's lawyer had urged Jamie to ask the police to prosecute Lucy for harassment. Jamie said no. He just wanted to forget about it. He imagined she was living with someone else now, in a flat somewhere, making somebody else's life miserable.

Last week, he had been sitting in a small cafe in Brixton when Heather walked in. She did a double take, then came over and sat down.

'Wow,' she said. 'Your eyebrows.'

'I know. Apparently, they'll never grow back.'

'God.'

She bought him a coffee and they talked. Jamie told her what he had been doing since the trial. She tutted a lot and looked sympathetic. She was now working at a hospital nearby. It was no fun working at St Thomas's since Kirsty left.

'Have you heard from her at all?' she asked.

'No. The last time I saw her was at the trial. I tried to talk to her afterwards but she hurried off with her mum and dad.' He paused. 'Are you in touch with her?'

Heather nodded. 'Yes, although I don't see her very often. She lives in Reading now.'

'Is she married?'

'No, but she has got a new boyfriend. Andrew. I feel awkward telling you.'

'It's OK. I didn't expect her to spend the rest of her life on her own.'

'I know – but they've got a little girl as well. Six months old. Her name's Isabel.'

Jamie stirred his coffee slowly. He smiled. 'That's good. I'm pleased.' But he felt a hard lump in his throat and he was unable to speak again for a few minutes.

'Have you heard from Paul?' he asked.

She laughed. 'That bastard. I can't believe how cut up I was over him.'

'You were a nightmare.'

'God, don't remind me. But I've got a new boyfriend now, and he's twice the man Paul was. Or is. I haven't heard from him at all.'

'He must still be out there, wandering the world.'

Heather looked out at the rain. 'Yeah, and I bet he's somewhere a lot sunnier than this. I'll never understand why he became so friendly with Lucy and Chris. Did you ever contact him, tell him what they did?'

'No.' Thinking about Paul was painful. Something had happened to him when he'd had his accident, something that still didn't make sense. If Jamie had been a religious or superstitious person he might believe that something supernatural had happened to Paul while he was in that coma, that he had lost part of his soul. But there had to be a rational explanation for it. Had the accident done something to the wiring inside Paul's brain? Maybe it had made his brain more like Lucy and Chris's: the mind of a psychopath, self-centred, cold, acting without conscience. If that was the case, then Paul would have had more in common with his new friends than he did with Jamie and Kirsty.

He kissed Heather goodbye and she gave him her number, told him to call. On the way back to his digs, he screwed it up and threw it in a bin. Heather was a link to the past. If he was going to make a fresh start, all such links had to be severed.

Now, he stood up and decided to head back to his room. Tomorrow, he would go to the job club, get his CV updated, check out the job sites. He had a lot of experience, even if his knowledge of computers was no longer completely up to date. It wasn't going to be easy finding a new job, but he knew he could do it. And once he had one he could rent a flat. Sooner or later he would meet someone new. Maybe they would buy somewhere together.

A house, this time. A detached house.

He reached the hostel and went inside. Carol was in the hallway, talking to someone on the phone. She gestured for Jamie to wait. While he waited he looked around. Yes, this was a nice place. He was going to like it here. He knew they would support him, look after him while he regained his balance. He felt a rush of optimism. He would never be able to sort himself out if he was still in a B&B. God, if this place hadn't taken him in, he might have ended up on the streets again, begging, drinking, starving. Dying. But here he was. He felt like giving Carol a kiss. He had been saved.

She put the phone down and said, 'Your new neighbour's moved in, in room D. I thought you might want to say hello, introduce yourself.'

'Good idea.'

He climbed the stairs and knocked on the door of Room D. From within, a woman said, 'It's open.'

Jamie wondered what she would be like. Maybe they could be friends. A small voice in his head wondered if they could be something more. He hadn't been with a woman for a long time. Smiling to himself, he pushed open the door. A blonde-haired woman was facing the window, looking out at the city beyond. She was very tall.

It was Lucy. She had found him. His heart yo-yoed into his stomach.

But when the woman turned around he saw, with a whoosh of relief, that it wasn't her.

'Are you alright?' she said. 'You look like you've seen a ghost.'

He muttered something and backed out of the room, going into his own. Great, now she thought he was a weirdo. He decided to distract himself by unpacking his backpack, pulling his clothes out and folding them up, putting them in piles. He didn't have many. He took out the framed photo of himself and Kirsty that had survived the fire. As he lifted the backpack towards the top of the wardrobe, it tipped upside down and something fell out.

He crouched and picked it up. A USB stick. Where had that come from?

Curious, he took it with him and went downstairs, where Carol was watching TV.

'Is there a computer here that I could use.'

She smiled sympathetically. 'I'm sorry, we don't have a public computer.' But seeing his disappointed expression, she said, 'But you can borrow my laptop for a few minutes if it's important.'

'Yes, thank you.'

He took the laptop upstairs and sat down on the bed, inserting the USB stick into the slot. There was one folder on the device, named

'Lucy - Collection'. He opened it. There were eighteen image files. Jamie clicked on the first, which was entitled 'Jane'.

It was a scan of a death notice from a newspaper.

Jane Wilkins (nee Fry) peacefully in her sleep, aged 83, at Orchard House. Beloved mother of Simon and Margaret, grandmother to...

He clicked on the next file. Again it was a death notice, this time for a man.

Cedric John Jenkins, aged 85, died peacefully at Orchard House. Will be much missed...

He clicked through the others, faster and faster. Not all of the death notices mentioned Orchard House, but most of them did. Orchard House was the nursing home that Lucy worked at. And he remembered now where the USB stick had come from. It had been in the carrier bag he'd found in the Newtons' desk, the bag full of spectacles and hearing aids.

A chill ran through Jamie's entire body.

They were souvenirs.

The treasures of an angel of death.

Hand shaking, he ejected the USB stick and slipped it into his pocket. He took the laptop downstairs and gave it back to Carol.

'Find what you were looking for?' she asked.

'More than I bargained for, actually. Is there a police station near here?'

She gave him directions, and he thanked her and set off. The bag of glasses had been destroyed in the fire, and the pictures on the USB stick were not evidence, on their own, of any wrong-doing. To Jamie, they told a story of murder, of a serial killer preying on the elderly people she was supposed to be caring for. How did she do it? A pillow over the face? An 'accidental' wrong dosage? Perhaps the scanned death notices were more innocent; maybe Lucy simply liked to keep a record of the deaths of people in her care. That would be sick, but not criminal.

He walked along the road towards the police station. A fantasy ran through his head: the police taking him seriously as he explained what he'd found; the launch of an investigation into the deaths; the eventual conclusion that Lucy had murdered all of those old people. Then came her arrest, the tabloid headlines, the scathing words of the judge and finally, imprisonment.

Jamie smiled to himself as he pictured Lucy in a cell.

He hoped she'd have nice neighbours.

ACKNOWLEDGMENTS

Thanks to:

Sara Baugh, who not only makes it possible for me to pursue my
dreams but is also an insightful and honest reader;
Louise Voss, for pointing out all the bits that could be better;
Jennifer Vince, who yet again created a great cover;
Sarah Ann Loreth, for giving me permission to use her wonderful
photograph;
Sam Copeland, for being a great agent.

This book was inspired by real experiences. Although my own real-life
magpies weren't as evil as the ones in this novel, I would like to thank
them for giving me the idea – you know who you are.

ABOUT THE AUTHOR

Mark Edwards is the co-author, with Louise Voss, of All Fall Down, Killing Cupid and Catch Your Death, which was the first novel by 100% 'indie' authors to hit No.1 on Amazon UK.

He lives in Wolverhampton, UK, with his young family.

Contact Mark

Twitter: @mredwards

Facebook: www.facebook.com/vossandedwards

Web: www.vossandedwards.com and www.indieiq.com

KILLING CUPID

Louise Voss and Mark Edwards

"Astonishingly good" –Peter James

"Vivid and unsettling" –Elizabeth Haynes

A gripping stalker thriller with a unique twist.

Alex Parkinson is obsessed with his writing tutor, Siobhan. He will do anything to be with her. He stalks her on Facebook and finds out where she lives, buys her presents using her own credit card and sends her messages telling her what he wants to do to her. He breaks into her house and hides in her wardrobe, reads her diary and listens to her while she takes a bath… Soon, he believes, she will realise they are meant to be together. But when a 'love rival' comes on to the scene, Alex has to take drastic action. Soon, a young woman lies dead on the concrete after tumbling from the roof of her house. Now there is no-one standing in the way of him and his unwitting true love…

Buy from Amazon.co.uk

Buy from Amazon.com

CATCH YOUR DEATH

Louise Voss and Mark Edwards

"A fast-paced conspiracy thriller that stays suspenseful and unsettling to the very last page." –Emlyn Rees

"'A genuinely tense medical thriller, with Crichton-esque pacing and tension. Masterfully done." –Matt Haig

Imagine if Dan Brown and Michael Crichton sat down together to write a fast-paced medical conspiracy thriller set in the English countryside, featuring evil scientists, stone-cold killers, a deadly virus and a beautiful but vulnerable Harvard professor.

That's CATCH YOUR DEATH, the new novel from Louise Voss and Mark Edwards, a No.1 bestseller on Kindle and No.1 thriller on iTunes.

Esteemed virologist Kate Maddox thought she was escaping to a new life. But before she can face the future she must deal with the ghosts of the past.

Buy from Amazon.co.uk

Buy from Amazon.com

ALL FALL DOWN

Louise Voss and Mark Edwards

"This book got my heart thumping, my mind racing, and put me in a state where I was totally oblivious to the outside world" –Kim the Bookworm

Two years on from uncovering a terrifying conspiracy of rogue scientists, all Kate Maddox wants is to lead a normal life with her partner Paul and son Jack. But then a face from the past turns up, bringing chilling news.

A devastating new strain of the virus that killed Kate's parents is loose in L.A. – and when a bomb rips through a hotel killing many top scientists, it becomes clear someone will do anything to stop a cure being found.

While Paul goes on the hunt for answers, Kate finds herself in a secret laboratory in the heart of California, desperately seeking a way to stop the contagion. But time is running out and soon it will be too late to save their loved ones, themselves, and the world…

Buy on Amazon.co.uk

Buy on Amazon.com

Printed in Great Britain
by Amazon.co.uk, Ltd.,
Marston Gate.